The Scene of Foreplay

performance works

SERIES EDITORS
Patrick Anderson and Nicholas Ridout

This series publishes books in theater and performance studies, focused in particular on the material conditions in which performance acts are staged, and to which performance itself might contribute. We define "performance" in the broadest sense, including traditional theatrical productions and performance art, but also cultural ritual, political demonstration, social practice, and other forms of interpersonal, social, and political interaction which may fruitfully be understood in terms of performance.

The Scene of Foreplay

Theater, Labor, and Leisure in 1960s New York

✦

Giulia Palladini

NORTHWESTERN UNIVERSITY PRESS
EVANSTON, ILLINOIS

Northwestern University Press
www.nupress.northwestern.edu

Printed in the United States of America

10 9 8 7 6 5 4 3 2 1

Library of Congress Cataloging-in-Publication Data

Names: Palladini, Giulia, author.
Title: The scene of foreplay : theater, labor, and leisure in 1960s New York / Giulia Palladini.
Description: Evanston, Illinois : Northwestern University Press, 2017. | Series: Performance works | Includes bibliographical references and index.
Identifiers: LCCN 2017003472 | ISBN 9780810135239 (cloth : alk. paper) | ISBN 9780810135222 (pbk. : alk. paper) | ISBN 9780810135246 (e-book)
Subjects: LCSH: Performing arts—New York (State)—New York—History—20th century. | Performing arts—Economic aspects—New York (State)—New York. | Off Off-Broadway theater. | Experimental theater—New York (State)—New York—History—20th century. | New York (N.Y.)—Social life and customs—20th century.
Classification: LCC PN2277.N5 .P255 2017 | DDC 792.09747109046—dc23
LC record available at https://lccn.loc.gov/2017003472

CONTENTS

ACKNOWLEDGMENTS

This book has been deferring its accomplishment for quite some time. As a foreplay of sort, the pleasure of doing research, thinking, and writing this book has accompanied me over the last seven years, along with a certain resistance, on my part and on the part of the material itself, to reach its final form. This labor of love would not have been possible without the invaluable support I had from a number of individuals, and circumstances, which have sustained the pleasure of this work even when I was so sick of it that I was no longer able to perceive it.

The initial research behind this project began during my Ph.D. research, which the University of Pisa supported with a scholarship: I am grateful to my supervisor, Maria Ines Aliverti, and to the Dipartimento di Storia delle Arti. During this period in Italy and afterwards, I also enjoyed conversation with a number of scholars who, in different ways, have contributed to the development of my research: among them, Valentina Valentini, Fabio Cleto, Marco Pustianaz, and Federico Pagello.

I am also grateful to have spent one year as a visiting scholar in the Department of Performance Studies at New York University (NYU). This was made possible by the invitation of Richard Schechner, and I am thankful for his support and hospitality. At NYU I also benefited enormously from the encounter with a number of people who have contributed in many ways to the development of this project: among them Tavia Nyong'o, Mark Sussman, Joe E. Jeffreys, and José Esteban Muñoz. A number of people who, at the time, were studying for the M.A. in Performance Studies at NYU have been in friendly conversation with me during this period: among them, Marcos Steuernagel, Angela Marino Segura, Serap Erincin, Jimena Ortuzar, and Stefanos Tsigrimanis.

A number of artists have talked to me, opened their houses and archives, and allowed me to feel in a cross-temporal proximity with the 1960s scene I was writing about. First among them is Ellen Stewart, the encounter with whom, in 2004, has been the sparkle of so many things and who has supported me immensely throughout these years in many of our encounters in Italy and in the United States. In New York I was fortunate to meet John Vaccaro (with whom I had unforgettable walks, and numerous lunches in his favorite Italian restaurants), Ruby Lynn Reyner (whose stories and strength I treasure), Penny Arcade (who supported my research with great generosity), and several others who, in different ways or in shorter encounters, have contributed to enrich the landscape of my study. I am also grateful to Joseph

Preston, Jackie Curtis's cousin and the affectionate keeper of his estate, and to Craig Highberger, who have shared with me their collections of Curtis's pictures and memorabilia, as well as to Elspeth Leacock, who has showed me the footage of Curtis's first wedding. I am grateful to Ozzie Rodriguez and Rachel Mattson, from the La MaMa Archive, and to Marvin Taylor and Sophie Glidden-Lyon of the Downtown Collection at the Fales Library, who have helped in my work with the materials of these collections over time. I am grateful to Charles Silver of the MoMA Film Study Center, who helped me in my study of Andy Warhol's *Screen Tests* Collection, and to Jonas Mekas, for having welcomed me in the Anthology Film Archives and for having shared with me his memories. I also wish to thank dearly all the copyright holders of the pictures included in this book, and especially Marianne Barcellona for the generous work she did on the images.

Over the last seven years I have also enjoyed a range of opportunities to present part of this work, in progress, at conferences such as Performance Studies international (PSi) in Copenhagen (2008), "Le Arti performative e le nuove generazioni di studiosi: Prospettive e campi di ricerca" at the Università La Sapienza in Rome (2010), and the American Society for Theatre Research in Montreal (2011).

I have also presented my theoretical work on the notion of foreplay, which developed in parallel and also independently from this book, in a number of invited lectures, which have contributed to making me see more clearly my hypothesis: among them, the lecture "On Foreplay: Amateur Labor, Theatre, and the Pleasure of Idleness" at the University of Roehampton, London, United Kingdom (2012), the lecture 'Foreplay in Many Axioms," in the symposium "The Art of Being Many: Towards a Theory and Practice of Gathering" at Kampnagel, Hamburg, Germany (2014), and "La Labor del juego previo: Sobre la materialidad y la desobediencia del placer," at the Universidad de las Artes in Guayaquil, Ecuador (2015). I am grateful to the organizers of these events (Joe Kelleher, Martin Jörg Schäfer, and Bertha Diaz, respectively) for conversations that these occasions afforded. I am also grateful to Rolf and Heidi Aberhalden of Mapa Teatro, for inviting me to share my work in the platform *Experimenta/sur* in Bogotà, which was an incredible source of inspiration for my thought: the conversations I had in this context resonate in various ways throughout these pages.

Parts or earlier versions of material appearing in this book were included in the essays "Queer Kinship in the New York Underground: On the Life and Legend of Jackie Curtis," *Contemporary Theatre Review* 21, no. 2 (2011): 126–53, and "Towards an Idle Theatre: The Politics and Poetics of Foreplay," *The Drama Review* 56, no. 4 (T216) (2012): 97–105, copyright © 2012 New York University and Massachusetts Institute of Technology. I am grateful for the feedback I received from the editors in those contexts.

At Northwestern University Press, this book has found a wonderful home: I am grateful to Mike Levine, Gianna Mosser, Maggie Grossman, Anne

Gendler, and all the other members of the editorial team who have supported this project throughout, and to the series editors Patrick Anderson and Nick Ridout, who have provided me with very insightful feedback on my project. I am also thankful to anonymous readers for the press for their brilliant comments and suggestions, from which the book has greatly benefited.

During the writing of this book, my parents Silvana and Massimo, my family, and my friends have been a constant source of inspiration, rescue, and encouragement, especially in the many moments when the project felt "unfinishable." I am grateful to all of them, and in particular to Azzurra Ricci, Laura Di Giuseppe, and Chiara Novelli, who have offered me concrete support and constant solidarity. I have been writing this book in several cities over these years, and I wish to thank all the people who have shared their homes with me during this time, contributing to my quiet and focus in the making of this project in New York and Berlin: among them, Eveleena Dann and Kirk Bradley Peterkin, Ivy Risser, Harold Dean James, Paul and Jen Nikkel, and Anita Whilem.

Other friends and colleagues have been crucial to this project: without Joe Kelleher and Nick Ridout, this book would simply not have taken shape. They both, at different times, read numerous drafts of this work, talked to me about it, helped me craft the language in which I wrote it, and always made me feel that it was important that I bring this work to completion. Their friendship, insights, and intellectual generosity have mattered enormously to me, and I am immensely grateful to them both.

Last but not least, I wish to thank Boyan Manchev for the intellectual complicity and persistence of these years together.

The Scene of Foreplay

INTRODUCTION

> In place of a hermeneutics we need an erotics of art.
>
> —Susan Sontag, "Against Interpretation"

> Being sexual people is our gift to the theater.
>
> —Jill Dolan, "Building a Theatrical Vernacular"

The changing room of a theater, in downtown New York. An actress is getting into costume, preparing the elaborate appearance of her character on stage. She has finished arranging her hair, her dress, her earrings, rings, and bracelets. She continues putting on her makeup until her mouth disappears under the lipstick, until her eyes become small cracks under the glitter.

A fun house in Coney Island. A woman stands on a subway vent, at the end of her payday, letting the breeze blow up her skirt and enjoying the scene of her own pleasure. Nearby in the same amusement park, a naked, muscular boy is staring at his image reflected in the mirror maze.

A loft in Soho, in the middle of the night. Androgynous, flamboyant creatures slowly build a heap of junk as a theatrical architecture, in front of spectators who are sleeping, or rolling a joint, or taking part in the performance.

An Off-Off Broadway theater, close to Times Square. A parade of "freaks" dressed in bright colors spread red glitter and carnival sounds all around, offering a range of attractions on the eroticized space of a stage, looking like a sideshow.

A stage lit with a blue light, in a café-theater on Lafayette Street. A woman with fuchsia hair and a pink dress is speaking and gesticulating, while throwing around her white sheets of paper she takes from a bookstand.

A rooftop in the East Village. A man in a bridal dress is holding a carton of milk and hugging two friends, one of whom is dressed in the costume of a priest.

An apartment on the top of a red building, on East 4th Street. A woman is telling the story of a pushcart, which she built one day in order for her friends to be able to work in the theater.

A gray wall, in a former factory space, in midtown Manhattan. A portrait of a pale woman staring at a camera without blinking for almost three minutes, before involuntarily shedding a tear, in front of unknown spectators.

These are all scenes of foreplay, and they are part of a bigger "scene" of foreplay which this book stages and discusses. They are both lived and theatrical events, and they inhabit a common scene: the scene of their proximity to one another in the history of 1960s New York, and the scene of thinking in which my argument recollects them today, in and beyond that very history. These scenes are also short preludes to chapters to come: later on, you will reencounter these scenes in their historical context, attached to the names of authors, plays, or places. You will discover that the first is the background story (or at least, the way I imagine it) of a picture by Francesco Scavullo portraying Ruby Lynn Reyner, the second comes from a play by Tom Eyen, the third from Jack Smith's legendary midnight performances, the fourth from the Play-House of the Ridiculous's *Heaven Grand in Amber Orbit*, the fifth from Penny Arcade's last show *Longing Lasts Longer*, the sixth from Jackie Curtis's first wedding performance, the seventh from Ellen Stewart's foundation of La MaMa, and the last one from one of Andy Warhol's *Screen Tests*.

But first and foremost, I propose to regard these scenes as snapshots of a distinctive movement of theater pleasure projecting itself toward a future, like foreplay.

Borrowing the expression from sexual terminology, I propose foreplay as a theoretical description of a particular mode of performance production, existing outside of predetermined structures of recognition in terms of professionalism, artistic achievement, and a logic of eventfulness. Such production consists of artistic labor not inscribed in its enactment, in a predetermined order of value, and yet it cannot be considered as existing purely outside of a trajectory toward evaluation in dominant capitalist regimes: these performances exist outside of a market rationale, only insofar as they are *not yet* recognized as valuable in any profitable system of performing arts.

I use the term "foreplay" to account for performances sustained by a labor of pleasure on the part of performers and spectators, and which exceed the frame of a singular event; performances not organized according to a climax, but which develop in an extended interval of leisurely enjoyment, and within a complex economy of attention and distraction.

Foreplay is a way of thinking about playful activities that are both implicated in, but yet somehow also avoid, the teleology of productive labor. Foreplay defines a quality of activity which anticipates and postpones a productive outcome, but is not a form of preparation, nor a training toward a future craft. It names an accidental prelude to an unforeseeable future, a form conjuring a potential value realization that might, however, never take place in actuality, or if it does, not as intended or expected.

In the *Oxford English Dictionary*, the word "foreplay" features as an entry under the suffix "fore," and it is defined as "stimulation or love-play preceding sexual intercourse."[1] According to the *Merriam-Webster Dictionary*, foreplay is also any "action or behavior that precedes an event":[2] the nature of the event whose advent foreplay announces and prepares is not specified. By its own definition, foreplay appears as a slippery territory of crescendo that cannot claim the status of an arrival. Foreplay is not its own stable signifier: its function is ascribed retrospectively, a future occurrence is entrusted to open the time proper to the activity itself. The concept, therefore, inhabits a paradox: the "event" that might possibly bestow its ontological status is precisely what would put an end to foreplay as such. The emphasis on the event as the finality of foreplay is evident when considering the linguistic equivalent of this word in other European languages, such as Italian or French: the sexual activities preceding intercourse are here referred to as *preliminari*, or *préliminaires*, explicitly pointing to a merely teleological aspect of sexual intercourse: an outcome, understood as actualized pleasure. *Preliminari* conjures the achievement of a goal: each gesture would entail the expectation of a linguistic object supposed to complete the finality of *pleasure as an event.*

The word "foreplay," however, retains a longing towards the future—kept in the suffix "fore," which gives the additional sense of "before."[3] But the activity made explicit by the suffix—to play—doesn't imply a teleological form. For however much expectation the "fore" creates, the word "play" reshuffles finality backwards in a semantic and temporal imprecision. In a sense, this suggests that the supposedly final event extends beyond its own singularity. In the expression "foreplay," that is, we can glimpse the idea of the deferral, rather than the accomplishment, of pleasure. While pointing towards a future play, foreplay names a loitering in a longing for a play that was *before*, the previous times in which desire took place, even without reaching a climax.

By liberating and insisting on this other sense, I appropriate the paradox haunting the ontological status of foreplay as a parasitical entity, as well as its intrinsic potentiality as an alternative technology of pleasure and theater labor, operating from within a system which supposedly validates such labor and incorporates such pleasure.

What Is the Scene of Foreplay?

This book, and the idea of foreplay which stands at its core, took shape as the unlikely encounter between two lines of inquiry which have punctuated my work over the last seven years, proceeding simultaneously and progressively interlocking in these pages. For the sake of clarity, I will introduce the first line as a historical investigation into performance history, and the second as a theoretical inquiry into modes of performance labor in contemporary capitalism.

The historical inquiry is a research into the performance history of 1960s New York, based on field and archival work in New York public, private, and oral archives between 2007 and 2014, conducted forty years or so after such events had taken place. My focus, in this research, soon became a particular aspect of this history: the pleasure offered by theater-making among a small group of people active in the downtown art scene, for whom this practice was not a job, but functioned as a key element in a system of recognition in which those people lived, and during this living played, with a view to entertainment. The spotlight of my investigation turned in particular on a series of figures operating in this context, such as Ellen Stewart, John Vaccaro, Ruby Lynn Reyner, Jackie Curtis, Andy Warhol, Tom Eyen, Jack Smith, and Penny Arcade. These figures, however, stand out in my inquiry not primarily because of their work as "authors," but for their contribution to making the scene more broadly: through their performing, their taking care of securing places and conditions for performance, their documenting through pictures and stories, their constructed public personas. Around these figures, many others give added depth to a scene which, in my study, started extending over time beyond the 1960s, in the echoes coming from the past of New York performance history, since the end of the nineteenth century, and in those reaching the present.

From the landscape of the future, this scene appeared to have the quality of a love adventure. Pleasure motivated these artists' mode of being together and working in performance, and it gave shape to a distinctive quality of theater. It was a theater made and witnessed by amateurs who were occupied with this practice in a space of common free time, clearly identifiable neither as a time of leisure nor as a time of work. It was a theater moved by a longing toward certain gestures, certain images, certain songs—and by a desire to inhabit and reproduce them, in a mode of enjoyment shared between artists and spectators. In this theater, artists learned to perform by being spectators. First, they had been spectators of old Hollywood movies, which they had watched in movie theaters as children and adolescents, and later on television. Second, they were spectators of each other's performances, on small stages and in everyday life.

Learning, in this case, was something radically different from a training course. It was neither conceived nor organized as an educational process. The theater produced in this love adventure had a childish quality to it. It existed beyond the temporality of adult productivity, although it still participated in its economic structure. It was made with no expertise, no training, no seriousness, and was witnessed in distraction, while drinking or taking drugs. In short, borrowing Bertolt Brecht's beautiful expression, it was a theater that took up its "lodging in the realm of the merely enjoyable."[4]

This theater would happen in places where artists and spectators engaged in relations exceeding the single occasion, and the task-oriented horizon of work productivity. These places did not preexist the entertainment they gave lodging to, but were rather informed by it; they shared its temporality and its human temperature. They were places often not entitled to occupy a legitimate position in the city, and in which theater production was not regulated by work hours or wages. They were places where people would loiter and do things together: take pictures, gossip,[5] play with shared visual obsessions, have sex, make theater. They constituted a landscape in which time was not oriented toward an outcome in terms of artistic purposes, but pivoted on itself, in the multifaceted experience of a night (or an afternoon, an evening, an early morning, a weekend) of entertainment.

This "social space"[6] (I echo, here, Henri Lefebvre's sense of the term, referring to a space containing specific relations of production and reproduction) was that of a shared and polymorphous play, which was neither identified, sold, nor organized as work. However, relations of production, reproduction, and consumption were elaborated, and passed on in the places that composed this scene: places like the Caffe Cino, the Café La MaMa/La MaMa E.T.C., the restaurant Max's Kansas City, the Chelsea Hotel; as well as many apartments used as performance spaces, such as Diane di Prima's, Tom O'Horgan's, Billy Name's, Johnny Dodd's, and most of all Jack Smith's, who made his living space the perpetual deposit of his life-performance. This social space was characterized by a distinctive temporality. People attended these spaces both before the beginning and after the end of showtime, in the proliferation of an expanded performance. Spectators featured first of all as guests, secondly as potential performers. There, performances persisted in time through memories, conversations, references, and memorabilia.

The context, events, and documents I have considered during my investigation have been addressed before me in a number of studies. A brief tour through such scholarship should touch at least Stefan Brecht's illuminating notes on "queer theatre,"[7] written in the course of the 1970s while the author was taking an active part in the experiments in art and social life of the New York downtown scene. Brecht's writing can be itself considered a form of *foreplay*: his texts offer a precise and passionate account of performances often received by the theater critic in a state of leisure, rather than of concentrated work. This is evident in the form he chooses for these texts, and in their rhythm, attuned with the author's affective proximity to these experiments. For example, as I shall discuss in chapter 1, Brecht describes Jack Smith's slow and phantasmagoric midnight performances while accounting for his own distinctive mode of spectatorship: witnessing the performance would encompass also a short nap, or smoking pot with the performers and the distracted, scarce, and yet engaged audience of friends and strangers alike. In a sense, playing with the famous definition proposed by the theater critic's own father, Bertolt Brecht, Stefan Brecht was a particular kind of "smoking spectator" for the 1960s queer theater scene: a man at leisure, sharing the scene of idleness of the particular theater labor he was observing, but capable at the same time of documenting the critical and political insights which such theater suggested.

Sally Banes's book *Greenwich Village 1963: Avant-Garde Performance and the Effervescent Body*[8] offered another significant contribution, portraying the art scene of downtown New York with accuracy, critical acumen, and a passionate historiographical take. Written thirty years after 1963, Banes's analysis recognizes in the downtown scene of that period important patterns of social and artistic cooperation. She suggested, for example, that the structures of solidarity and collaboration, as well as the bonds of friendship, love, and mutual support among artists active in these contexts, can usefully be read in terms of kinship, and that this aspect also appeared distinctively in artistic work. Her account also theorized the particular presentation and representation of the body on the stage of such artistic and social scenes[9] the body not disciplined according to codes of morality, gender, and decency, and experimented with in different forms in artistic work produced in the 1960s New York scene, was an "effervescent body," a body open to the world, to other bodies, to its own horizon of transformation. Along the lines of Banes's intuitions, my analysis explores the implications of such practical and queer kinship in art and social life, interrogating it especially as a distinctive structure of production and reproduction. Likewise, my study addresses the grotesque, monstrous body first sketched out by Banes in light of a set of references from a specific spectacular tradition, that of vaudeville and the freak show, suggesting that this tradition, which so powerfully resurfaces in the 1960s scene, is a distinctive *genealogy of leisure*, rather than of theater work, for the 1960s scene.

Other books published in the last decade have cast light on specific moments, artists, and poetics within the 1960s New York scene. In particular, the work of Stephen Bottoms and David Crespy[10] has advanced historiographical knowledge on the Off-Off Broadway theater circuit, highlighting the particularities of theater developed in this context in comparison with other contemporary trends in experimental theater. Bottoms's work has also recuperated to the domain of theater the term "underground," with its own long cultural history and intimate connections with film culture, and addressed the aesthetic particularities of the theater work developed in what he identifies as the four houses of the Off-Off Broadway—the Caffe Cino, La MaMa, the Judson Memorial Church, and the Theatre Genesis—and by their associated theater groups and artists. He rightly claims critical attention for some unrecognized theatrical innovations of Off-Off Broadway theater, such as a new style of playwriting, including the experimentation with distinctive dramatic forms (like the one-act play) and styles of performance (such as the solo performance). Along the lines of Bottoms's exhaustive survey, I also found it important to consider the distinctive forms of theater work produced in the underground scene; but I am more interested in their meaning as units of theatrical labor than in their position as aesthetic accomplishments in theater history. Likewise, as I shall discuss at greater length later on, while I find it interesting to recoup the word "underground" for discussing this particular theater history, I also address the transhistorical tension between the "underground" and the process of valorization intrinsic in its historiographical and economic posthumous valorization.

The study of the 1960s Off-Off Broadway and underground scenes has also been enriched by monographic studies such as Cindy Rosenthal's on Ellen Stewart and La MaMa, or Dominic Johnson's on Jack Smith,[11] both combining attentive historiographical research and a strong interpretative stance. Rosenthal positions Ellen Stewart and La MaMa in the context of the New York avant-garde theater tradition; Johnson contextualizes Smith's performance work not only in the history and theory of visual arts and film, but also in relation to queer theory. Johnson's work and perspective are in dialogue, as much as my book, with a specific strand of scholarship in queer and performance studies: a number of works which have explored the proximity of the 1960s performance with Andy Warhol's Factory in light of the "queer time and space" (borrowing Judith Halberstam's expression)[12] that different artistic experiments commonly inhabited. The number of connections between artists active in this context, and the theoretical implications of the bonds of friendship, queer love, and collaboration among them, have been significantly explored, for example, by Jennifer Doyle, José Muñoz, Douglas Crimp, Gavin Butt, and Marc Siegel.[13] In this scholarly context, Warhol's work has been read as an important site where forms of solidarity, sexual generosity, and cooperation were experimented with and displayed. For example, Doyle and Siegel have emphasized that Warhol's film work, and the artistic and social context it portrayed, queered standard notions of hierarchy, authorship, and collective work.[14] Along the same lines, José Muñoz reads Warhol's work alongside other pieces from the 1960s pre-Stonewall gay culture in New York which prefigure (echoing Ernst Bloch's theory) a glimpse of a futurity where freedom, as well as relations of production and reproduction in sex and in work, could be imagined differently by those whose lives remain constrained by the current political and normative agenda. In his discussion of the utopian dimension of queer art and social life, Muñoz suggests that the relation between bodies and the sensible experience of their "touching"—in time and over time, in ephemeral form—which was distinctive of this artistic and social tempo might well be understood in terms of a utopian drive working at the level of potentiality, even if it does not take place as possibility.

This diverse landscape of scholarship constitutes a multifaceted history of the 1960s scene, which I have encountered first through the mirror of this collective narrative, then again in its bodily survival in oral and material archives. In my survey, I have worked with sources from the La MaMa Archive, the Downtown Collection at the Fales Library, the Lincoln Center Library for Performing Arts, the Celeste Bartos Film Center at the Museum of Modern Art (MoMA), as well as from several private archives, such as the Jackie Curtis Estate held by Curtis's cousin Joe Preston, and Ruby Lynn Reyner's private collection. In New York, I also encountered some of the people who had inhabited this scene back then or contributed to its documentation, such as Ellen Stewart, Tom O' Horgan, Michael Arian, Agosto Machado, Jonas Mekas, Ruby Lynn Reyner, John Vaccaro, Penny Arcade, and Elspeth Leacock. Most of these encounters took place in leisure circumstances: over dinner, during a walk, in the context of everyday interactions. The particular approach I chose to use, in order to account for such historiographical research on a leisure time long gone, anticipates a concept of Gertrude Stein's to which I will return in the course of the book: the practice of "listening and talking" as a specific form of engaged access to oral history. Throughout the book, I deliberately chose to base my argument not on interviews conducted by way of conventional fieldwork, but to consider those interviews instead as part of an extended practice of "leisure conversations."

From the Landscape of the Future

Eventually, my own investigation became less an account of what happened *back then* than an inquiry into the potentiality and ambiguity of the pleasure I recognized as a key affect in the mode of performance production of such a scene. To echo Michel Foucault's description of his approach in the *History of Sexuality*, although this book is certainly a study of history, it is, however, not the work of a historian.[15] The set of materials I have gathered during my research became the basis for a theoretical inquiry looking out into the past, and into the future: an inquiry which recognized in such shared habits of "performing labor" during free time patterns common to other amateur, gratuitous performances realized at the margins, or as antechambers, of the show business industry long before the 1960s, such as in the amateur nights of late nineteenth-century vaudeville, or long after this decade. Borrowing the terminology of Walter Benjamin, the gratuitous labor I investigated in the 1960s started to appear in my constellation as the incarnation of both previous and subsequent patterns of unrecognized labor and amateur performance. The figures and circumstances I considered became pointers for an inquiry into pleasure, temporality, and theater labor under capitalism: the capitalism which, actually and symbolically, regulated artistic and knowledge production in the 1960s, as it still does today.

As I anticipated, in fact, a second line of inquiry kept me busy during the time I have been composing this book. It is a line of inquiry formulated precisely from the landscape of the future, from which I am speaking. This is a future in which pleasure has continued to function as an invaluable engine of artistic production, and free time has increasingly turned into a time of unregulated, unpaid, and gratuitous work for potential workers. The questions I started to confront, as I was making my way into the complex nexus between labor and leisure in the theater production of 1960s New York, soon started exceeding my historical object and interrogating the present, summoning me up as an author, as a producer of knowledge, as well as a witness of developments in artistic production today. They became questions about the place of pleasure and of gratuitous labor in contemporary capitalism, a context which I experience, as someone working in the cultural field, as characterized by two basic predicaments. On the one hand, artistic labor is hardly recognized as such in the moment of its enactment, but is projected toward the horizon of its potential realization in terms of value, for example, through applications for funding for each project, or in terms of career, too often suspended before starting, toward a series of opportunities of supplementary professional training, in the forms of stages or workshops, which often function as hidden forms of voluntary labor. On the other hand, love's labor—labor done during free time, for the sake of pleasure, and without wages, perhaps as preparation—functions as an invaluable deposit of labor power, available for exploitation or self-exploitation especially when conditions of production are precarious. Both these predicaments mark a condition of "eternal preliminarity," entailing for an artist the demand to inhabit a temporary space in which production supposedly incubates for an indeterminate period of time, before it can be actualized. Furthermore, especially in the case of artistic production, this condition is also imbued with an ambiguity which seems almost intrinsic to the praxis of art-making: the long-lasting cliché according to which artistic work functions according to logics other than those of "production," and intrinsically requires a self-investment of gratuitous (because invaluable) creativity.

This condition of "eternal preliminarity" bears striking resemblances with the interval of gratuitous creativity experienced by young artists operating in the 1960s Off-Off Broadway scene. There too, access to paid employment on the professional stage was difficult, and at the beginning of their careers artists were in a condition of "amateurism," projected toward a potential development into a career. There too, experiments made without an immediate return in terms of wages or recognition could be considered as antechambers of productivity. In fact, some of the artists who started in the "small time" of Off-Off Broadway later made successful careers in mainstream theater or film. Or, alternatively, the memory of their work acquired value in historiography and cultural history. Furthermore, the process of belated recognition of performances presented for the first time in amateur contexts is a constant in the history of New York performing arts: from the small stages of the late nineteenth century Bowery theaters, featuring opportunities to make a break in the vaudeville for dilettantes, but where likewise major stars of New York theater had their debut; to the dichotomy Broadway/Bowery, first, and then Broadway/Off-Broadway, and the internal dynamic according to which shows presented with low budgets downtown would be later produced professionally uptown for Broadway audiences. The 1960s New York scene, in this sense, is no exception: the pleasurable activity of theater making, punctuating the young practitioners' free time, can be considered a prelude to a value yet to come. What I call "love labor," in the 1960s scene as much as in contemporary forms of "preliminarity," is not a leisure activity or an after-work diversion, already granted a place in the time regime of capitalist leisure. It is a particular kind of amateur activity, a practice taking place in after-work hours simply because it is not itself a sufficient source of livelihood, and in which artists are busy during free time because unpaid labor does not count as one's business if unremunerated, no matter how busy one may be with it.

The blurring of boundaries between leisure and labor, in contemporary neoliberal capitalism, has been welcomed by some as an achievement for creative workers. For example, Richard Florida has described with enthusiasm the new economic model based on this transformation in what he calls the "creative economy,"[16] where a class of young professionals work in art, fashion, music, design, and other creative sectors, inhabiting a social time beyond traditional demarcations between "leisure" and "work," and free time functions as a territory of investment for the human capital of the future professionals. According to Florida, this makes these self-exploited free time workers "valuable" in the capitalist economy, and also contributes to the transformation of urban spaces, becoming the agents of gentrification and the posthumous valorization of marginal parts of the city. In this "leisure class," self-promotion is reinforced by the production of recognizable images, and forms of subjectivities "on sale" in the expanded scene of social labor.

In the collective imagery, Warhol and his Factory have become the paradigm for a certain kind of image economy which became predominant in what we could imagine Florida's "creative class" to be. Elisabeth Currid's book *The Warhol Economy*[17] affirms this explicitly, proposing Warhol's Factory—hub of the encounter between Pop and underground, art and fashion, money and unemployment—as the site where it became increasingly apparent that "creativity was very marketable,"[18] and that nightlife was an "institution by which cultural forms were performed and evaluated."[19] Besides the tremendous influence of Warhol's engagement with photography, fashion, portraiture and self-portraiture, style, and narcissism on today's youth and media culture,[20] the structural similarity between the amateur artistic labor of 1960s New York, captured by Warhol's camera, and today's creative economy deserves more attentive consideration. This similarity, in fact, speaks of the valorization of amateur labor and gratuitous creativity as self-investment, which neoliberal capitalism proposes as its paradigmatic feature and which, likewise, was a crucial dynamic of the 1960s New York scene.

The ways in which "new style capitalism" has cannibalized "modes of existence" and "subjective forces" first experimented as artistic, political, and social movements in the 1960s and the 1970s has been described by Suely

Rolnik as a form of "pimping."[21] According to Rolnik, the 1960s movements have recuperated to the sphere of production and reproduction a creative force which subverted "a disciplinary Fordist regime that reached its height in the 'American way of life' triumphant in the postwar period."[22] Social and political movements, such as feminism, gay and lesbian movements, as well as queer and experimental art, have collectively challenged the Fordist regime of "products" and emphasized, instead, the processuality of work and the potentiality of imagination, as well as positing the body—its vulnerability, its sensible matter—at the center of such work understood as a process. This liberated creative potential ended up modeling, paradoxically, the "flexible and processual subjectivity" which neoliberalism requires: "this kind of pimping of the creative force," Rolnik suggests, "is what has been transforming the planet into a gigantic marketplace, expanding at an exponential rate, either by including its inhabitants as hyperactive zombies or by excluding them as human trash."[23]

The flirtation between Warhol's imagery and mode of production with Florida's "creative class" has been bothering me throughout the writing of this book, as much as the argument which, overall, Florida makes about workers in the creative industry in which I myself, as a cultural producer, also operate. It made me uncomfortable to think about the life of an artist, a producer, whose temporality is completely exploitable as "potential labor," in which images and behaviors offer themselves to posterity in delayed commodified form even if they were not produced during work time. It made me uneasy to consider that we work all the time, even when dancing, or having drinks with our friends, in nightlife, and that our participation in social movements or artistic scenes[24] will later become the grammar of trends, objects of institutional valorization, and ultimately, after finding a place in a specific market of attention, become capital later on. As Paolo Virno put it, writing about the subsumption of human labor in capitalist production: "Nobody is as poor as those who see their own relation to the presence of others, that is to say, their own communicative faculty, their own possession of a language, reduced to wage labor."[25] In this case, in the creative class modeled and demanded by neoliberal capitalism, the blurring between free time and work corresponds to a condition in which communicative faculty, creativity, and amateur labor are not even reduced to wage labor, but to *a potential horizon of value.*

A New Vocabulary

The unease that such associations created in my inquiry fostered in me the need to understand this dynamics of valorization, along with the pleasure at stake in the mode of labor I was confronting, both in the present of my work as an author and in the materials of my historical research. It also encouraged me to clarify for myself what was at stake in my interest in the interval of potentiality of the 1960s scene. Why was I fascinated by its history, and despite all odds, why I could still see in this specific past and forms of production an emancipatory potential?

The idea of foreplay is the epistemological model I elaborated to explore this potential, to do justice to both the 1960s scene's projection toward the future of capital realization, and to its loitering in a space of pleasure, in the idle rehearsing of its own futurity in a temporality of enjoyment. This potential is certainly akin to the longing for otherwordliness that Muñoz glimpsed in the queer aesthetics of the 1960s and which he saw propelling "us onwards, beyond romances of the negative and the toiling in the present,"[26] rejecting "the here and now" by exceeding the "straight time"[27] of capitalism. Such potential has to do, as well, with the "experimental force of creation" which, as Rolnik emphasizes, in the 1960s has "shattered the 'bourgeois' lifestyle at its politics of desire,"[28] affirming new forms of being together and working within and beyond artistic production, which reclaimed sensual pleasure as a crucial site of subjectivation. But first and foremost, the emancipatory potential I saw in this artistic moment had to do with the position of "eternal preliminarity" it has occupied.

Even as they were the preparatory stage for a value to come, the amateur experiments in art and social life performed in the 1960s enacted a playful subversion of the modes of production, reproduction, and consumption of professional theater. The performance circumstances I observed spoke to me about an unproductive laboring, organized through times of fragmentation and endurance, and which did not inscribe itself in a progressive course of evaluation. On the contrary, such laboring was a loitering in the pleasure of theater-making as a "doing," inhabiting what for me appeared as a semiautonomous habitat of production. The emancipatory potential I glimpsed was that pleasure might function as a force of renewal and reproduction as much as an engine of production.

Hence, I set myself to construct a new vocabulary to write this book, to build a different argument to that which predicated the 1960s gratuitous economy of the "underground" as always already a prelude to the neoliberal creative economy, and to use different conceptual tools for addressing the object of my inquiry. I set myself to investigate the epistemological status of the "preliminarity" common to both the 1960s amateur labor and to contemporary forms of precarious labor, predicated today upon the fragmentation of production characteristic of the "project logic."[29] In this task, I found strong support in theoretical investigations of the complex overlapping between free time and work in artistic production under capitalism.[30] This concern has been central especially to a line of political philosophy indebted, in one way or another, to Marxist theory. Or rather, in such a (diverse, multifaceted, nonorthodox) Marxist tradition I found a discursive habitat offering specific insights to my argument, which led me also to consider Marx's own theory of value and to interrogate it in specific relation to the domain of the production of the performing arts.

First and foremost, I found invaluable insights in Walter Benjamin's work, and in particular in his magnificent (and unfinished) *Arcades Project*, a materialist inquiry, as well as a poetic phantasmagoria, on a specific era of capitalism, the nineteenth century. Paramount in this inquiry appears the figure of the flaneur, which Benjamin reads in a constellation with other figures, such as the prostitute, the sandwich man, the unemployed, or the street musicians:[31] all figures standing in a position of perpetual "potentiality" of work. The flaneur, an early incarnation of the cultural self-entrepreneur, is not only someone working during free time, offering her own labor power on display as in the shopping windows of nineteenth-century Paris, but is also a prototype for the ambiguous position of the artist in relation to the structural demands of the market, involving especially matters of temporality. Benjamin's work was crucial for me as a methodology, but also as a pointer to forms of amateur labor which the 1960s had "inherited" from an obliterated past: the leisure phantasmagoria of turn-of-the-century vaudeville culture, whose fragmented tempo of performance and whose icons so often resurface in performance and film works from 1960s New York, not only as images, but more substantially as rhythms and forms of performance.

I found another important reference in the strand of autonomist Marxism developed since the 1970s, for example by André Gorz, Antonio Negri, or Paolo Virno, and in the definition of "immaterial labor" elaborated in this context. Understood as a result of structural changes in the system of relations of capitalist production, especially evident in post-Fordism, immaterial labor involves a series of activities not immediately recognized as work, but identifiable rather as forms of communication, relations, and affective and bodily engagements contributing to economic production but not directly identifiable with a wage-labor system of evaluation. Crucial nodes of the debate on immaterial labor also involve demands placed upon the immaterial worker in terms of skills not directly derived from a standard professional training, and the flexibility of time invested in the labor process.[32] Paolo Virno's work on the figure of the "virtuoso"—someone whose labors have no end product and coincide with the process of production, as well as depending on a public sphere in order to be enacted—is especially relevant for discussing performance work.[33] The virtuoso, in Virno's analysis, appears as the emblematic figure of immaterial labor, insofar as her own bios—psychophysical faculties, communicative capacity, and so on—is put to work, at least in potentiality.

Reflecting on the perfomer's virtuosity was important for me not only to describe patterns of production and reproduction of the 1960s artistic scene from the future in which such immaterial labor has been subsumed, already, as capital. It was also useful to understand distinctive features of this labor in relation to the reflection on "professional work" developed in the discursive environment of the 1960s experimental theater,[34] and especially by theater groups like Richard Schechner's Performance Group and Joe Chaikin's Open Theatre, as well as Jerzy Grotowski's Theatre Laboratory. This constellation of work and practice placed great emphasis on the singularity of performance as "event," and on the potential of theater as praxis radically different from production, although deeply rooted in an ethics and a horizon of work. A crucial role in this reflection, systematized especially by the writing of Richard Schechner, was played by education: in the 1960s, both the actors' training, as well as the process of rehearsal and preparation of a public performance, were put under scrutiny by practitioners and theorists alike. In contradistinction to this discursive environment, what I call the scene or foreplay took place outside of a horizon of work altogether, normatively understood in terms of *professional activity* and *craft*. Exploring this difference allowed me to address two orders of value, beyond the monetary one, which became predominant in the 1960s theater scene: the idea of work as a process, deeply embedded in the redefinition of the place of education in theater-making, and the nonrepeatability, singularity, and climax-like temporality of performance understood as actualized event.

In my research on the 1960s, I confronted not only the immaterial labor of performance, but also a great deal of material labor, which enabled the artistic scene to endure. Namely, I encountered the traces of bodily engagement with building and sustaining living environments, organizing structures of solidarity and kinship-like relations, and the reproduction of such relations in artistic work. In my effort to reconceptualize what counted as "labor" and "production," I found crucial insights in feminist critique, and in particular in pivotal works such as those of Silvia Federici, Maria Rosa Dalla Costa, or Marilyn Waring,[35] which have challenged the traditional consideration of the labor of reproduction in social, political, and economic terms, emphasizing the necessity to extend the idea of production to non-monetized activities, such as housework, which have been traditionally relegated to the private sphere of domesticity and to the nebulous terrain of women's "free time." Such scholarship was crucial to account for the affective labor supporting the material subsistence and endurance of a social or physical environment (for instance, a small theatre), encompassing not only practical tasks—that is, providing basic means for living and working—but also affective ones—that is, inventing structures of intimacy for living and remembering. Furthermore, feminist scholarship has also contributed to recuperate and remobilize Marx's theory of value in directions which turned out to be especially useful for my work.[36] In particular the work of Miranda Joseph has opened for me invaluable insights for thinking about the relations of production and reproduction in theater, and the supplementarity which the notion of community has had in the development of neoliberal capitalism.[37] In line with her analysis of the labor of consumption, I too started considering the "work of the audience; their productive consumption of the [performance] work, their act of witness"[38] as participating in the production of exchange value under any circumstance, especially if we understand exchange value as a distinctive discursive articulation, contributing to define—beyond direct monetary trade—the ontological status and social identity of the theater labor witnessed by spectators. This understanding will have specific theoretical consequences for my reading of the mode of spectatorship entailed in the amateur performance-making of the 1960s artists, as well as for reflecting on the economy of attention which functioned in this context as a secondary (or preliminary) market of potentiality.

Foreplay: Between Production and Consumption

The notion of theater "production" I ended up employing throughout the book encompasses all stages of circulation and exchange, and hence includes consumption as a fundamental stage, insofar as it actualizes as "product" that which in earlier stages of the process existed only *in potentia*. As Karl Marx made clear, in all processes of production consumption retrospectively grants an ontological status to the product itself—or more precisely, it brings to completion what the product of labor aspired to be in the very first place:

> A railway on which no trains run, hence which is not used up, not consumed, is a railway only *dunamei* [potentially], and not in reality. . . . Consumption produces production in a double way, (1) because a product becomes a real product only by being consumed . . . thus the product, unlike any mere natural object, proves itself to be, *becomes*, a product only through consumption (2) because consumption creates the need for new production, that is creates the ideal, internally impelled cause for production, which is its presupposition.[39]

The notion of foreplay names that "intermediary movement" that "takes place between production and consumption at the same time"[40] which Marx explores in detail especially in his *Grundrisse: Foundations of the Critique of Political Economy* (itself a prelude to what is considered Marx's major work, *Capital*). There, Marx emphasizes that as much as production leads to consumption providing its object, consumption constitutes the "determining purpose of production,"[41] offering *an active subject of desire* for the object brought about by production. While production as an act is posited at the origin of the whole process, "it is only consumption that consummates the process of production," creating first (before production) a conceptual predisposition to produce and then completing "the product as a product by destroying it, by consuming its independent concrete form."[42]

Furthermore, production also induces its own mode of consumption: it produces not only objects, but also subjects, its own consumers. Interestingly, Marx stresses this point by offering an example pertaining explicitly to the field of art: "an *objet d'art* creates a public that has artistic taste and is able to enjoy beauty—and the same can be said of any other product."[43] The same principle applies if we observe the process the other way around. According to Marx, consumption not only turns a product into a product, but also a producer into a producer: "by its need for repetition consumption leads to the perfection of abilities evolved during the first process of production and converts them into skills."[44] According to Marx's scheme, then, the audience's urge to consume is also crucial to the professionalization of a given artistic praxis (the conversion of abilities into skills, evolved during the productive process), which also involves training for productive work, learning and acquiring the know-how of production. The artist's mastery, therefore, is itself a product of the specific consumption that artistic production induces, and it develops in strict relation to the horizon of consumption.

In Marx's formulation, however, the horizon of consumption is not only that of an audience, but it is always already embedded in the act of production itself: the producer is the first consumer of her own act. That is, in order to develop her abilities, the producer also expends them, dissipating them "just as in natural procreation vital energy is consumed."[45] This passage speaks directly to the domain of theater production, as it postulates the simultaneity of production and consumption in the time of the event. At the same time it directly evokes sexual activity, positing it as a distinctive form of production. Significantly, Marx speaks of an objet d'art rather than of an "art work"—emphasizing the outcome of artistic practice rather than the work process of art-making. Likewise, he evokes sexual activity not as a process, but only in view of its supposed outcome, which is considered equivalent to a product. In this passage, sex is posited as something exclusively functional to procreation. The logic supporting this equivalence, with its emphasis on "expenditure of vital energy," explicitly follows the ejaculatory scheme that, as Michel Foucault has carefully reconstructed, has accompanied the reflection and policing of sexuality since ancient times, involving not only the question of procreation, but also that of pleasure.

According to such a scheme, sexuality is traditionally attuned with economy as it secures, by means of heterosexual intercourse, the reproduction of the labor force. But it also bears crucial relations with economy in terms of body politics: the body, in fact, is first and foremost a unit which "produces and consumes,"[46] and in the sexual act—at least conceived as an expenditure of vital energy—this process is exemplified.[47] In the "androcentric model of sexuality"[48] orgasm features as the equivalent of a product, regardless of its productivity in terms of procreation. On these premises, female orgasm has been long considered an anatomic anomaly, first of all since it is unnecessary for and hence independent from procreation (it has no connection with fertility), and secondly because it follows a temporal logic which is extraneous to the androcentric model: the means of production of female orgasm are in fact different from those which lead to male orgasm.

As Rachel Maines explains in her study of hysteria and female orgasm, both medical and cultural history have considered the capacity to reach orgasm in women (especially by means of penetration) in terms of "ability," in a logic very like the one positing genital sex as the "real thing,"[49] whereas a whole other range of sexual activities have long been considered as merely supplementary. One of the reasons why female orgasm has been long regarded and treated as a problem is its structural failure to meet the androcentric logic of pleasure, according to which orgasm marks a point of no return in the sexual act: thus the capacity to reach multiple orgasms during sex is itself a powerful threat to the idea of ejaculation as the ultimate goal of coitus.

Freud had a hard time in coming to terms with the systematization of his theory in relation to the dynamic of fore-pleasure: a pleasure not oriented toward discharge, but rather pivoting on itself. His psychoanalytic approach regards sexuality as a developmental praxis, positing a sequence which, if completed, even recapitulates as "normal" supposed "aberrations," that is, all sexual gestures not directly aimed at the fulfillment of heterosexual genitality, which he assumes as the "normal sexual aim." In *Three Essays on the Theory of Sexuality*[50] Freud systematizes the same sequential narrative regarding both the course of life—the supposedly progressive stages of human sexuality, from childhood to adulthood—and intercourse, from foreplay to orgasm, reached by means of genital sex. In this context, he could read what he called "sexual aberrations" (such as homosexuality, fetishism, scopophilia and exhibitionism, sadism and masochism) not as aberrations proper, because he thought they participated in a developmental sequence, as childhood experiments preliminary to the proper "sexual aim." Accordingly, lingering on sexual behaviors deviating from genital finality is read by Freud as a failure to meet an adult organization of the sexual components; hence, as Leo Bersani put it,[51] "the perversion of adults therefore becomes intelligible as the sickness of uncompleted narratives."[52] Furthermore, Freud conceived an equivalent developmental sequence for the sexual act itself: whereas a certain amount of "touching and looking" is indispensable to the achievement of the "sexual aim," the fondness for looking and touching becomes for Freud a perversion if not aimed at preparing a subsequent act, the reaching of ultimate pleasure—ultimate in the sense of maximum achievement, as climax, and as a closing point of no return.

Bersani, however, explains that in addressing the relation between sexual excitement and satisfaction, Freud himself spotted a failure in his own systematization of sexuality. "In spite of himself," Freud ends up delineating infantile sexuality and adult sexuality as "*two distinct ontologies of sexuality itself*,"[53] rather than—as his hypothesis otherwise suggests—two consequential stages of sexuality. In fact, Freud distinguishes between fore-pleasure (arising from the stimulation of erotogenic zones) and end-pleasure (related to the discharge of sexual substances), but in this scheme end-pleasure would consist primarily of the complete extinction of pleasure itself, with the orgasm. Not surprisingly, Freud tends to figure sexual excitement as something like an itch, to be scratched in order to be eliminated. In this scenario, sex is not only posited as a productive activity, but the production is itself presumed to be of a particular kind. The production of the itch inaugurates a process culminating in the disappearance of the itch itself, in the moment in which the itch is completely "consumed." However,

> in sex preceding discharge the analogy [with the itch] no longer holds. We scratch, after all, in order to remove an itch, but—to hold one more moment to the analogy—now we are confronted with an itch that seeks nothing more than its own prolongation, even its own intensification. If, Freud writes, you touch the skin of an unexcited woman's breast, the contact will produce a pleasurable feeling that "arouses a sexual excitation that demands an increase of pleasure."[54]

It seems to me that what is at stake, in the different ontologies of sexuality figured in Freud's argument "in spite of himself" (rather: in Bersani's reformulation of Freud's aporia), is a question of value. Whereas in genital sexuality orgasm is posited as the measurement of realized value for pleasure, in the "immature" sexuality that lingers in fore-pleasure there is no measure of value other than the endurance of enjoyment. Likewise, there is no mastery of the means for reaching that value, nor a defined sequence for love labor. The latter produces values that fall outside any value judgment, reversing the logic of development which Freud proposes as inherent to sexuality: in the labor of love pleasure becomes an engine for continuation and renewal, rather than a goal.

Looking back at Marx's schema, and "correcting" the androcentric model which he assumes in his comparison between the consumption and expenditure of vital energy, interesting points seem to emerge. If consumption completes production by providing "an active subject of desire" and "leads to the perfection of abilities evolved during the first process of production," converting them into skills, it is possible to question what kinds of skills are produced in a process not regulated by a sequential logic, according to which the actualization of production ratifies what is recognized as appropriate preparation. The intermediary movement between production and consumption embodied by foreplay can be considered as an interval of experimentation with forms of production not deemed as proper, but which generate values and skills that fall outside a progressive course of evaluation.

Using the notion of foreplay as a theoretical tool to discuss performance-making, I read amateur theater production throughout this book precisely in the light of an ontological status wholly distinct from what is conceived as professional work, and hence as a praxis that has a duration and deploys procedures that are not necessarily oriented toward a "proper" development. My argument therefore repudiates the negative ontology of amateur labor: what it is not, or not yet. Accordingly, it does not address it as a surrogate activity—that is, an imperfect copy of a work praxis which otherwise and elsewhere exists in its full development. Countering the orgasmic logic postulating desire as a labor reaching its point of exhaustion and vanishing, the idea of foreplay accounts for a longing for theater which exceeds the logic of an itch, to be scratched and extinguished in the time and space of an event. It points to a desire which overstays, queering the singularity of performance as event, multiplying its focuses toward a possibility of theater pleasure in a multiplicity of temporal articulations.

My argument also points to a distinctive relation between performance-making and spectatorship, between production and consumption: it is a relation in which these two domains play with their identity, staging consumers as producers and producers as their own consumers. The mode of production I call foreplay is figured as a counterforce within productive economy, as a prelude where value is not yet conferred upon labor. I observe this force in relation to its potential valorization, not only in terms of productive value (career achievement, posthumous recognition in performance history) but also in an alternative economy enacted in the present.

Scenes of Foreplay: Summary of Chapters

The four chapters composing this volume focus on examples of this alternative economy, and various politics of performance labor, such as the production of scenes of familiar recognition, or experiments with temporalities of performance subverting a regulated order of work productivity. In this different economy, I propose that valorization does not coincide only with professional achievement, but offers a horizon capable of opening a temporary space in which performance labor is prolonged as a "doing," rather than a development toward accomplishment in professional terms; it is prolonged as a labor that is happening, to say it with Rebecca Schneider's terminology, "in the meantime."[55] The 1960s artists' continuing engagement in theater both as a form of work and as their *pastime* does not follow a progressive course from one state (supposedly "free," independent, and autonomous) to another (its "incorporation"). It seems to inhabit both states at the same time, while slowly proceeding from one to the other. In this book, the playful persistence of foreplay in such meantime affirms that there is indeed no outside of exchange value in performance, but there is still the possibility of pleasure—and more precisely, of labor as pleasure.

The first chapter explores the theater work of Tom Eyen, the Play-House of the Ridiculous, and Jack Smith as forms of stylized amateurism, and the particular temporality at stake in these performance as a form of *show-idleness*.

In contradistinction with this context, I discuss the 1960s conceptual reframing of performance-making as a craft, as well as its reformulation in terms of "process" rather than of "product," as it emerges in the writing and theater practice of Richard Schechner and of Jerzy Grotowski; artists operating outside of the mainstream circuits who challenged the system of performance work in structural and technical terms (with alternative strategies of artistic training and education, countering conditions of work and recruitment in professional entertainment through the form of the collective and the workshop). Poles apart from this discursive context, in the scene of foreplay performance-making did not involve an attempt to reformulate or reorganize theater work, or its technique. Theater was, in a sense, a labor of idleness, a notion I posit, drawing from Benjamin's work, as something altogether different from both leisure and sheer inactivity. The comparison between different modes of organization of labor and temporality, in the 1960s theater practice, offers a chance to discuss more broadly the complex and interlocking discursive relations governing production and reproduction in theater, which—just as in sexual relations—have a direct relation with an economy of pleasure, alternatively considered as something to repress, abstracting it as "work," or to figure as a service, which can either be sold or supposedly donated, as in sacrifice.

In the second chapter, I read the non-teleological mode of performance emerging from 1960s scene of foreplay in a line of discontinuous genealogy with other instances of amateur entertainment, which had been part of the New York scene and its imagery since the turn of the twentieth century, and which were produced in leisure circumstances, but which also participated in processes of subsequent valorization in show business. I suggest that the temporality of performance discussed in this book called upon a mode of spectatorship reemerging from an obliterated past: a way of attending theater that disavowed an appointment in time, that took place amid other activities such as drinking, chatting, and meeting friends. It was a mode of attending theater which had survived, since the nineteenth century, not so much by means of a linear tradition of theater work, but rather by means of nightlife sociability. Focusing on the performance *Heaven Grand in Amber Orbit* by the Play-House of the Ridiculous, I discuss the return of previous practices of performance that once glimmered in the city landscape and then moved into the mainstream entertainment industry, and which by the 1960s had started to fade from public visibility. Among them were the leisure nonproductiveness of the "amateur hour" on the nineteenth-century Bowery, the distracted mode of participation of nightlife sociability in vaudeville spectatorship, and Coney Island amusements, such as freak shows and sideshow: all these were examples in which private enjoyment and public spectacle were negotiated and intertwined through performance practices taking place in a suspended space between leisure and work. At the end of the chapter, I follow up the analysis of *Heaven Grand in Amber Orbit* by discussing a film starring one of the actresses involved in the Play-House of the Ridiculous, Ruby Lynn Reyner: *Heaven Wants Out*, shot in 1970 by Reyner and director Robert Feinberg, and released in 2009.

The third chapter addresses the alternative modes of production and reproduction elaborated in the scene of foreplay focusing on Jackie Curtis and Ellen Stewart, along with the artistic and social community that not only received, but contributed to articulate the performative invention of their two personas. I observe in particular the forms of memorability which Curtis and Stewart elaborated in the display of their life-performance. These include, for Curtis, the eight weddings he performed from 1969 to 1984 all around New York City, and the complex gender-bending identity mixed up with personal obsessions, social habits, and the participation in a peculiar social intimacy which Curtis displayed throughout his life, nourishing and shaping his performance project. For Stewart, it concerns her performance of "motherhood" as a specific engine of reproduction in the foundation and renewal of the legendary history of La MaMa, which Stewart reproduced through a politics of "insistence." In both cases, these performative modes of work and existence did not advocate an openly oppositional strategy for alternative relations (as in the agenda of many political movements in the 1960s), and they reveal a deep interconnection with the codes and figures of mainstream and normative culture. However, precisely by playing off the codes of mainstream culture and normative organization of social relations these performances enact their "disidentification."[56] Interweaving the notion of queer kinship alongside the idea of the 1960s scene as a small-scale star system, I read Jackie Curtis's and Ellen Stewart's persona-building processes as embedded in the production of "memorable scenes," which were both a way of suturing kinship-like relations and asserting a public personality, projected toward a utopian future of (imagined, fantasized, or actual) success.

The last chapter engages Andy Warhol's work, focusing in particular on the series of *Screen Tests*, shot between 1964 and 1966, film portraits presented as non-teleological testing for a film project "yet to come." Andy Warhol's *Screen Tests* borrow the structural format of the audition—a core unit of the professional entertainment industry—withdrawing it from finality by removing the horizon of a forthcoming film in view of which the subject's skills are assessed and selected. Detaching the audition from its structural function, in the *Screen Tests* Warhol turns the recorded exposure of the labor of appearance into a portrait in which no skills can be recognized as proper, and unexpected skills can prove to be effective for attracting the audience's attention. The screen test can be considered a distinct form of foreplay: an interval of potentiality of performance, hoping to realize itself in the future. Addressing the mode of production and consumption of the *Screen Tests* collection, I read Warhol's performative portrait gallery as an archive of the particular theatrical imagination of the 1960s scene of foreplay as well as an example of camp production. At the end of the chapter, I discuss the circumstance in which I, as a researcher, have encountered the *Screen Tests* collection and paid homage, on my turn, to the poser's long-lasting labor of idleness.

The book also encompasses two interludes, which at different points integrate the narrative proposed throughout the chapters. Both interludes are written, returning to the wording previously adopted, from the landscape of the future: they look into the history of "what came after" the scene of foreplay, and account in different ways for echoes of this time reaching the present, as well as focusing on different orders of value for the labor of pleasure enacted in the 1960s scene. The first interlude, which follows and builds upon this introduction, confronts the process of retrospective valorization of performance labor inherent not only in the careers of artists active in the 1960s scene, but also entailing the afterlife of their work and narratives. Looking at the growing value that the 1960s scene has acquired both in scholarly work and contemporary art, I suggest that this valorization somehow reiterates the dynamic of posthumous recognition I address in the book through the notion of foreplay. The second interlude, positioned in the middle of the book and functioning as a bridge between chapter 2 and chapter 3, is devoted to the work of Penny Arcade, and casts the spotlight on the "radical value of pleasure" which the artist powerfully affirms in her work to this day, and which I read as a form of legacy and a mode of renewal of the scene of foreplay, in which Arcade has taken an active part since the 1960s.

Interlude I

✦

Paying Homage to the "Underground"

Foreplay and What Came After

> We demonstrated nightly that theatre was affordable for anyone who had a light, a floor, a fantasy, and someone willing to embody it. . . . There began to be mini-mentions, in corners of papers, about a "theatre movement" downtown. Someone kiddingly called us Off-Off Broadway. We called us "underground" or "café theatre."[1]

From early in my investigation, I referred habitually to the object of my study as the "1960s New York underground scene," adopting a term—"underground"—long understood as the signifier of a set of artistic practices taking place outside of mainstream cultural circuits. As Juan A. Suárez has pointed out, especially in the American context the notion of underground brings forth a broad set of resonances related to "the evolution of the American intelligentsia in the postwar decades,"[2] and at the beginning of the 1960s it was already an expression with strong connotations. Its widespread use can be traced back at least to the 1950s Beat culture (featuring Jack Kerouac's *The Subterraneans* as one of the most prominent examples), and already in that context "implicit in the term is a certain glamorization of marginality, a desire to thrive outside (or underneath) the mainstream that seemed inherent to earlier waves of radical culture."[3] Furthermore, the term "underground" was part of a vocabulary already employed in 1960s New York: notably, this term was launched by Jonas Mekas in 1962 in the pages of *Film Culture* and the *Village Voice* with reference to the film work of a group of New York directors which Mekas considered the core of a new movement in American cinema.[4] According to Mekas, the use of the expression "underground" originated from a speech delivered by Marcel Duchamp at the Philadelphia Museum of Art in 1961, where Duchamp suggested that "the only solution for the artist of tomorrow is to go underground."[5]

Furthermore, most of the directors included in Mekas's "underground" shared an appreciation for and affective attachment to old-fashioned

Hollywood movies, including not only mainstream productions but also low-budget films realized between the early 1930s and the 1950s. As Suárez suggests, it seems not by chance, then, that the term "underground" had already been employed in the late 1950s in a famous essay by Manny Farber, precisely in relation to a certain typology of films produced in Hollywood between the 1930s and the late 1950s: low-budget movies such as those of Raoul Walsh, Howard Hawks, or William Wellman, which had inhabited the Hollywood industry performing a subversive cultural role from the inside.[6]

The term "underground" has been recouped more recently in theater studies by Stephen Bottoms, who devoted his *Playing Underground: A Critical History of the 1960s Off-Off Broadway Movement* to an investigation of the New York downtown theater scene, proposing an account which, while adopting a different approach, touches in many points the context of my inquiry. In Bottoms's work, the term "underground" is employed with the explicit intent to "draw a distinction . . . between the 'avant-garde' (at least as familiarly constituted) and the 'underground,' " based on the acknowledgment of a "relative disregard of 'agendas' whether political or aesthetic"[7] as a crucial and defining feature of the "underground" approach to art-making. According to Bottoms, whereas avant-garde artistic research often existed in an ambivalent relation of dependency with the establishment, the scene he defines as the "1960s New York underground" was "fundamentally nonbourgeois," insofar as it "comprised artists of all social backgrounds and classes";[8] furthermore, it entailed a broader freedom in experimenting with procedures and styles not embedded in a preestablished agenda, and hence allowed a "more genuinely antiestablishment dynamic."[9]

I remember a conversation with Ellen Stewart which took place at the beginning of my research, in 2006, in which I said that I was working on a mapping of "the 1960s New York underground scene." Stewart interrupted me quite abruptly, in the vehement tone that she used to have when she was disappointed by something. "First of all, then, you need to stop using this word 'underground,' darling. We never meant to be *underground*. We never thought of ourselves as underground. From the beginning, we were always struggling in fact to go *over-ground!*" At the time, I didn't take Ellen Stewart's protest seriously. I had already learned how resistant she could be to any attempt to deal with the history of her theater. I tried to never use this word again in her presence, but kept considering my research in these terms long after this conversation, during the course of my investigation in the following years.

Stewart's vehement remark, however, stayed with me longer than I expected. Without my permission to do so, this remark did its own work inside my thought, and many years after that conversation it finally came back to me. That is, not in its intended meaning—not as a command "not to" use a certain terminology. But rather, as an insight into the hypothesis that I had developed over the years while observing the traces of the scene I had been researching and considering, in line with the historiographical articulation briefly outlined—in terms of the "1960s underground." Her remark touches upon an aspect of the 1960s New York scene that troubles the narrative according to which its artistic experiments were located outside of the mainstream, in a supposedly free, antiestablishment domain of the "underground." Or more precisely: such a narrative still stands, as long as one avoids considering how the events that happened back then were profoundly interlocked with their own future, as a foreplay of pleasure loitering toward its potential actualization, and already participating in a circulation of sorts. Far from seeking to undermine the subversive "aura" of La MaMa's early years, which Stewart had carefully taken care of (and built upon) throughout the last four decades, her comment meant exactly what it said: a great part of what came to be known as "the underground" never intended to be any such thing. It was rather a concrete longing toward a "work" which might one day be done as a job, produced, and consumed, that is, in a "proper" theater. It was the shelter for a labor of desire projected toward a possible accomplishment, in terms of both recognition and the consequent achievement of the status of "production." Rather than simply emphasizing a question of intentionality, the attempt to go over-ground also meant that if the structure of the theater and film establishments were challenged by the artistic praxis of the underground scene (organized according to a completely different economic logic than that governing mainstream show business), the establishment was not generally contested as a structure; it stood rather as a horizon which could be reached, one day.

I am not interested so much in Stewart's comment as a basis for proposing a taxonomic discussion on terminology: that is, for questioning whether it is correct to employ the category of "underground." Rather, I am interested in picking up this comment for the unexpected way in which it intercepted the thinking process which led to the composition of this book. The fact that this labor of desire happened outside the establishment, for most of the artists involved in the so-called 1960s underground, seems to have been almost an accident on the way to the mature development of a career in American show business. This did not happen for everyone, but many of those who made their debut in the small time of the 1960s New York underground subsequently made their way, and in some cases with a very successful career, into the mainstream: notable examples are Sam Shepard, Tom Eyen, Bernadette Peters, Lanford Wilson, and Tom O'Horgan.

I remember how surprised I used to be, when I started my fieldwork in New York, to hear many of the people I interviewed—including Ellen Stewart—proudly announcing to me that the musical *Hair*, symbol of the Age of Aquarius at the peak of its market value, opened on Broadway in 1968, and was directed by Tom O'Horgan, written by James Rado and Gerome Ragni, and was conceived in the Off-Off spaces of La MaMa and Caffe Cino. Almost as if there were no contradiction whatsoever in this commercial success (and the commodified spectacle of "the 1960s" it proposed) and the theatrical experiments which were developed for free in small theaters far from Broadway in the course of the 1960s. Likewise, in talking with Tom O'Horgan I realized how in his recollection the passage from directing queer pieces like Rochelle Owen's *Futz* (pivoting around a zoophilic love story between a farmer and his pig) in tiny spaces like La MaMa or Caffe Cino to colossal "counterculture" musicals on Broadway[10] was free of any fear that he might be considered to have somehow "sold out." Indeed, he recalled with the same sweetness and generosity of detail the beauty of having friends performing on an improvised stage in his loft on West 3rd Street (later used as one of the sets of Warhol's *Chelsea Girls*) and the opening of *Hair* on Broadway.[11]

Clearly, the only person embarrassed by this narrative and the sort of continuity it entailed was me, who had approached this study imaginatively locating it in a space radically different from the mainstream, as a political, aesthetic, and cultural choice. It would have been hypocritical on O'Horgan's part to behave otherwise, looking back at that 1968 success; that is, to pretend to be ashamed for having gained the success which many of the artists involved in the scene where O'Horgan was operating were longing for.

As a matter of fact, many artists with whom I have talked in the course of the following years, or whose accounts I have come across,[12] happen to mention—more or less with nonchalance—the names of people somehow involved in the Off-Off Broadway scene back then, who later became stars in some mainstream context: for instance Robert De Niro (who starred in Jackie Curtis's *Glamour, Glory and Gold* at La MaMa in 1965); Bette Midler (who made her debut in Tom Eyen's *Miss Nefertiti Regrets*), or Jim Wise who wrote the music for the show *Dames at Sea*, which had its debut at the Caffe Cino in 1966, marking the longest-running show in the Cino history, and which afterwards became an international hit.

Taken together, these references participate in an interesting narrative: one in which what happened afterwards, in the life of individual artists or works, retrospectively casts a spotlight on certain presences, certain events, rather than others. For most of the people who were actively engaged in the underground scene of the 1960s, however, these references to mainstream outcomes are little more than a quirk. More established, in the collective imagery and traditional narratives, as well as in the historiographical accounts of that period such as Bottoms's, is the image of 1960s New York as a moment of outcast experimentation, which precisely by virtue of its independence from mainstream demands enabled a particular kind of artistic work to develop as such, and to end up radically influencing the history of performing arts and of American culture in general. In this prevalent narrative there recur, for instance, definitions of that momentum in terms of "the birth of," alternately associated with a diverse range of domains: from performance art to gay theater.[13]

Whether we consider this narrative in terms of those who "made it" into American show business or in terms of those artists or events who strongly influenced a future legacy for art and performance history, 1960s New York is recurrently portrayed as a huge incubator of what "came after." The story of "what came after," however, is complicated and continuously shifting too. Just like all the stories collectively lived and elaborated, it is impossible to consider outside of its very narratability: the always renewed possibility of having individual identities and destinies, as much as events, entering into relation and continuity, in one or many conflicting pictures. This narratability, throughout this book, interests me almost as much as the "faithful" history of what happened then.

Already in 1966 Michael Smith, a careful observer and involved participant in the growth of Off-Off Broadway and its story, wrote in the introduction of *Eight Plays from Off-Off Broadway*:

> Off-Off Broadway started, actually, as a way-station on the road to success. But disenchantment with conventional definitions of success is now widespread, and Off-Off Broadway increasingly is seen as an alternative to the established theatre rather than a way into it. Increasingly those who work Off-Off Broadway have learned to value the freedom it offers and discovered that work done there can be more rewarding despite its smaller scale, and sometimes superior in quality; and they began to relinquish their dreams.[14]

As Smith suggests, the alternative provided by the way station of Off-Off Broadway in 1966 still provided a space which unexpectedly offered a creative autonomy that encouraged people to over-stay there, rather than rushing out of it as soon as possible. And this over-staying, this loitering in a time/space which was supposed to be temporary is perhaps the topic of this book. But along with that, I am also interested in the inherent coming overground of the underground.

Already in 1966 and thanks also to publications like the collection *Eight Plays from Off-Off Broadway*, which followed Smith's weekly reviews in the *Village Voice* (since 1965 organized in the column "Theatre Journal") and the inclusion of Off-Off Broadway shows in the Obie Awards assigned by the *Voice*, the spotlight had started to turn toward the downtown scene, and the effects of this attention—first in terms of recognition, then in economic terms—started to be tangible. As Bottoms shows in a section of his book entitled "Changing Times, 1966–1973," the mid-1960s moment is marked by a series of events which transformed the configuration of the downtown scene, beyond its mere recognition in mainstream circles (which, however, occurred precisely around that time: the first articles devoted to the scene appearing in the *New York Times* are dated 1965). Crucially, in 1965 the Showcase and Workshop Code was issued, establishing that union members could work without pay only for short-run productions with no admission fee, not advertised to the general public and in front of a maximum of a hundred spectators. From this moment on, every time a union-affiliated actor (presumably a young actor with little chance of continuous employment on Broadway) wanted to take part in Off-Off Broadway productions, permission had to be asked of the union. This new regulation was also accompanied by a strong policing of some distinctive features of Off-Off Broadway, such as the habit of collecting voluntary contributions from the audience by passing a hat around the room, the contents of which at the end of the show was shared among the participants or reinvested in further productions. At the same period the first round of grants sponsored by the federal government reached the downtown scene, received for instance by St. Mark's Church or the Judson Memorial Church, and the first funds from private corporations, such as the Ford and Rockefeller Foundations, were received, for instance by La MaMa, enabling Stewart to occupy the building where the theater is today.

The story of the mid-1960s as "the beginning of the end" is also a common topos in the mythology of the 1960s underground. Scholarly surveys devoted to this history, such as those of Bottoms and Crespy, have advanced hypotheses on the facts, causes, and consequences of the mid-1960s transformation in the configuration of this scene. Artists themselves, in the last forty years, have made public their memories in numerous autobiographies and collective volumes, composed of archival materials and retrospective narratives of "what happened back then," and actively participating in the history which was being written by scholars and offering to share their personal memories with those who—born many years after the curtain had closed on this scene—have worked to systematize its chronology and line of historiographic development. These accounts offer a multifaceted picture which, just like Stewart's comment on my use of the term "underground," interests me not in terms of factual truth, but as echoes which this scene has kept engendering to this day.

There are those who, like the playwright Robert Patrick and director Marshall Mason, have referred to Michael Smith as one of the engines of the transformation which brought the small time of the underground into a system of recognition in which people started to work in a different modality. Having allowed the Off-Off Broadway theater to reach visibility and promoting it as something "worth attention" and awards, Smith would contribute to taming the undisciplined spirit of the early days and project it toward a different order of value from that experienced "in" the scene. Interestingly enough, however, Mason's memoir in the collected volume *Return to the Caffe Cino* starts with a tale about his own arrival in New York with the intention "to conquer Broadway."[15] Apparently, then, Mason's remark on the role of Smith's reviews in the "beginning of the end" is not intended as a defense of Cino's marginality against the lures of success. Rather, it appears as a melancholic trace of ineluctability, almost as if Smith, even beyond his own intentions, found himself playing this part in a play which somehow had always already been written.

In different tones and context, another personality accused of having participated in the transformation which led the underground into an establishment of sorts is Jonas Mekas, who was not only Michael Smith's colleague at the *Village Voice* (where he wrote, from 1958, a weekly column called "Movie Journal"), but was also the editor of the journal *Film Culture*, and most importantly, the founder of the Film-Makers' Cooperative. Mekas was famously attacked, with rage and creative genius, by Jack Smith who, since the mid-1960s, started referring to him in his personal bestiary by several degrading nicknames, such as "Uncle Fishook," "Uncle Roachcrust," "Uncle Pawnshop," and, significantly, "Lucky Landlord."[16] In Smith's view, Mekas had taken advantage of the succès de scandale of Smith's movie *Flaming Creatures*[17] in order to advance the social position and visibility of his cooperative—which in the late 1960s finally consolidated its position, accompanied by the establishment of the Anthology Film Archive.[18]

More substantially, in Smith's phantasmagoria Mekas came to epitomize the cancer of property and ownership, which not only suffused the logic of capitalism that governed every aspect of American life, but also haunted the so-called avant-garde. First of all, property meant in this context the right to establish a frame in which recognizable products such as "artworks" existed and circulated, understood as finite units of labor, and around which—as secondary yet crucial feature—discourses could be established deeming the products to be worthy or not. In an explicit response to the supposed exploitation by Mekas of his first movie, Smith refused to ever complete another movie: even *Normal Love*, currently projected and circulated as a finite work, was in fact never considered as such by Smith.[19] Also in this case, as Mekas pointed out in our conversation on the subject, Jack Smith's *J'accuse* seems to have found in Mekas the embodiment of a destiny which he was committed to counter, rather than an actual enemy;[20] a destiny in which the unfinishability of work could and would constantly exceed a system of recognition in terms of "market value."

Similar to Mekas's predicament is Ellen Stewart's, who, for instance, appears in Robert Patrick's novel *Temple Slave* (a peculiar sort of fictionalized memoir, written thirty years after the closure of the place Patrick considers his first theatrical home, the Caffe Cino, and which appears in Patrick's book in the "drag name" of Espresso Buono) as a character named first "the Manager" of the Drama Loft—the pseudonym chosen for La MaMa in Patrick's novel—and later on, as the 1960s advance in the narrative, as "the Owner." In the novel, which draws a line of development through Patrick's "theatrical apprenticeship" as a playwright and offers a portrait of Off-Off Broadway in its early days, Patrick depicts the Manager as a cunning self-promoter who made and consolidated her position by quickly learning to "package" the plays which had come out of a specific social context into forms more suitable for mainstream productions in order to better publicize them outside the Off-Off Broadway circuit. Especially in the last chapters of the novel, the Manager, who has now become the Owner, is increasingly characterized as someone who took advantage of all the opportunities opened up by the advent of private funding in order to secure stability for her theater in the mid-1960s, privileging less risky plays and emphasizing the intercultural dimension as a brand identity, since that seemed a likely way to access funding and achieve visibility. The dichotomy established by Patrick's narrative is between the Owner and Joe Buono (pseudonym of Joe Cino), who clearly stands out—not only in Patrick's novel, but in the collective imagination and legendary narrative of the underground—as the symbol of an era, whose decline seems to be fatally crystallized in his suicidal gesture, theatrically staged in the Caffe Cino in 1967. On other occasions, Patrick himself has had words of admiration for Stewart, and crucially, he has always made a point of clarifying that *Temple Slave* is entirely fictional: nevertheless, the Owner's portrayal in the novel seems to be following the same narrative to futurity as that presented in the many episodes and recollections in the oral history which makes up the great part of the historiographical survey of the 1960s scene.

Interestingly, whether or not we decide to read the character of "the Owner" as a fictional persona of Stewart, the main critique that Patrick seems to make of the Owner throughout his novel is that she behaved as a "producer" before any means of production were available and any show had even been conceived as a "product." Here too the question at stake seems not to be about working inside or outside the mainstream, but rather about working in a certain way, independent of the logic required by mainstream production. *Temple Slave* also features the following passage, describing a conversation between Patrick and a young actor working Off-Off Broadway, who—Patrick had just learned—came from a very wealthy family:

> "Look" I said. He looked. "Have you been disinherited for acting or something?"
>
> He started shaking his head negatively and continued to do so until he started nodding positively after I asked "Then do you have money of your own?"
>
> "From Grandma," he explained.
>
> I reached up delicately and stopped his head. "Then why don't you just buy yourself a Broadway starring role?" I asked.
>
> That was a very hard one for Rod. He started to gesture with that hand that held the coffee. . . . "I want to be respected and judged on my own merits. I don't want to be like one of those who buys himself a career. I want them to want me."

"Rod, who, for Christ's sake? Who is there in that wonderworld uptown whose opinion you respect so much that you'd wait to be validated by them? Hell, we all pay for our own shows down here. You can do that anywhere. Why wait?"[21]

Patrick's suggestion might sound provocative, but it grasps a tension that seems inherent in the theatrical activities of the Off-Off Broadway scene. That is, it emphasizes an aspect which this book, in a way, tries to address: in the 1960s New York scene not only were shows realized for free (i.e., neither playwrights nor actors nor directors were paid for their work) but it was actually *paid for* by those who were engaged in it. That is, not only by "entrepreneurs" like Ellen Stewart or Joe Cino, who provided basic material conditions for the shows, but also by artists who would offer their labor without any prospect of a wage. Hence, we might say that they *invested* their free time in an activity that they loved, but which also, at the same time, might potentially lead to a paid career.

The potential of the Off-Off Broadway scene as a showcase for artists whose work could be seen and lead to "real jobs" elsewhere, in fact, soon enough became evident. In his novel, Patrick himself suggests that this dynamic progressively brought the core group of artists who had initiated the scene to be increasingly less involved in its activities once their work had started to be produced Off-Broadway or on Broadway. To put it another way, and outside of any moral judgment, artists had less and less free time to invest in their potentiality and pleasure of performing for free. In this respect, it is significant that the continuation of La MaMa's activities coincided with the introduction of a different economic logic in its management. Not only was Stewart an active promoter of plays first presented at her theater in other contexts (through such initiatives as *Six from La MaMa*, or the organization of the first European tour of two troupes presenting plays from La MaMa in 1965),[22] but since the permanent workshop of La MaMa Troupe led by Tom O'Horgan was established, supported by a grant imposing upon the theater precise regulations, the economic scenario in which La MaMa operated was radically different from that of the early 1960s. As Bottoms summarizes:

> The Rockefeller Foundation stipulated that their other 50,000 should go toward maintaining Tom O'Horgan's La Mama Troupe for the next two years, with each actor being paid $50 per week for six months out of the year. This offer sets an important precedent for the right to be paid not only for rehearsals and performances but for sustained periods of research and experiment. Once again, though, Equity intervened, declaring that if the Troupe's actors were to be paid, then any Equity actor working at La Mama would also have to be paid at the same rate. Stewart refused to comply. . . . but Equity declared that from now all actors working in La Mama "showcases"

> must be paid a minimum of 55 per week for performances. Failure to comply would mean permanent blacklisting. Stewart reluctantly consented to the ultimatum, thereby necessitating her continuing search for further grant funding, and conceding a major step in the direction of La Mama's "professionalization."[23]

It is interesting that La MaMa's professionalization is marked not only by its consenting to accept such a new economic logic, but by the simultaneous generation of a need to seek out new funding, hence binding itself to precisely the economic logic of neoliberalism which I have previously discussed.

Leaving aside individual recollections or personal resentment, it is evident that Stewart and Mekas are among those people who not only survived the 1960s, but established their position on an international and local level thanks to the role they had played as promoters of a community of artists, intercepting a creative momentum which later became something for which they both could claim credit, and on the basis of which they were able to establish long-term projects, in both cases physically embodied by the acquisition of real estate. On the other hand, it is undeniable that both Stewart and Mekas, who could certainly not foresee back then the result of their actions in the long run, had been since the early 1960s among those who took direct responsibility for the scene in question, not only—as the mythological narrative would have it—running actual risks (such as being arrested, as they both were, for promoting controversial works or allowing theater activities in unlicensed spaces), but also taking care to establish conditions of reproduction (looking for spaces, signing contracts for renting them, organizing screenings and performances, battling with the city authorities, and collecting archival materials of the scene) that enabled this scene to endure. They devoted a substantial amount of affective labor in order to invent techniques of renewal for the artistic scene in which they participated.

This desire to make this scene last, on Stewart's and Mekas's part, can also be recognized in other terms. Both La MaMa and the Anthology Film Archive host important archival collections and have put the transmission of the memory of the 1960s (and what came after) at the core of their missions. Indeed, having worked in both collections in the course of this research, I acknowledge how valuable it is, for a latecomer spectator like me, who encounters this scene forty years too late to take part in it, to access the visual, textual, and film materials these collection hold. As valuable as the collection of Caffe Cino Papers, kept today in the archives of the Billy Rose Theater Collection of the Lincoln Center/New York Public Library for Performing Arts, which also features a collection of James Gossage's photographs documenting visually the Off-Off Broadway scene from 1965 to 1975. As valuable as the massive quantity of folders and remains conserved in the Downtown Collection (including more recently also the John Vaccaro Papers) located in the Fales Library inside the Bobst Library of New York

University, encompassing a great number of remains and private archives documenting New York downtown art from the late 1960s to today, which the Fales Library (hosting the Downtown Collection) was able to purchase, often at quite substantial prices, directly from artists, heirs, and the like. The Bobst Library itself was part of the broader colonization of downtown Manhattan by New York University, a private institution which contributed substantially to a refashioning of the area surrounding Washington Square in term of both economic investment and modes of living. It was through my readings of editions of the *Village Voice* from the 1950s that I learned about the thousands of polemics defending Washington Square Park against Robert Moses's systematic program for the development of New York.[24] The *Village Voice*—one of the newspapers which, at the time, backed neighborhood committees and activists such as Jane Jacobs in their struggle against this program—is now kept in microform format in a library, the Bobst, whose construction those activists had struggled to prevent, and which now stands overlooking Washington Square Park.

"Valuable" is precisely what these collections have turned out to be in the course of the years, as the narrative of the 1960s underground has consolidated itself in cultural history as a landmark of New York art, finally becoming an attractive subject for big institutions, which increasingly, in recent years, have welcomed exhibition projects, conferences, and events related to artists active in the New York underground scene.[25] This wave of interest on the part of museums and institutions such as New York's PS1, Lincoln Center, or London's ICA has been accompanied and fostered by important scholarly work done on the subject in the last years. The projects proposed in these institutions are remarkable initiatives, both in terms of curatorial work and the careful effort put in by curators and surviving protagonists of that scene. Also remarkable is that, besides those artists who (like Magie Dominic, Robert Patrick, Ellen Stewart, or Penny Arcade) have been directly involved in the archiving and promotion of the 1960s legacy throughout this period, these projects also involved artists who had completely withdrawn from the art world. Emblematic in this respect is the "comeback" of performer Rene Rivera aka Mario Montez, who was invited to Berlin for the event *Live Film! Jack Smith! Five Flaming Days in a Rented World* after having been tracked down by the filmmaker Mary Jordan during her research for the documentary *Jack Smith and The Destruction of Atlantis* (2009), and subsequently involved by Marc Siegel in a series of conversations.[26]

Jordan's documentary participates in the blossoming of documentary works realized in recent years on related subjects, among which are projects that bring together valuable collections of memories in the form of archival materials or interviews.[27] Last but not least, the widespread, mainstream interest in the New York underground was also catalyzed by Andy Warhol's presence in or proximity to this scene. Embodying a supreme ambiguity in relation to the so-called establishment, Warhol occupies a central position in the narrative of the underground, not least because of his collaborations with many other artists, from Jack Smith to Ronald Tavel, Mario Montez, Mary Woronov, Beverly Grant, and many others. Crucially, in some versions of the story of mid-1960s decline, the fatal embrace with Pop—physically embodied by the space of Andy Warhol's Factory—is also seen to have contributed to the transformation of the underground scene. In many accounts (such as Patrick's *Temple Slave*) the increased use of hard drugs in the Caffe Cino is attributed to the presence of the "Factory crowd," famous for its excessive lifestyle and which since 1964 had started to participate more frequently in the performance culture of downtown Manhattan. Secondly, the proximity of Warhol to the world of fashion, publicity, New York pop society, and capital certainly played a role in the exposure of this scene to other logics of profit.

From the landscape of the future—a future in which my project also participates—the *over-ground* position reached by the so-called 1960s underground is impressive. Its projection toward a future inhabits both the economic value of the "works" realized by those who made a career in established show business (including not only those who had mainstream success, but also all those who did make a living out of their artistic work, making theater as a remunerative activity) and the affect sustaining the projects *paying homage* to the memory or the legacy of particular artists or places from that time. The attempt I have undertaken, in my study, is to explore the tension intrinsic in such a projection, accounting for both the ambiguity of foreplay as a prelude to "what came after" and for the labor which made this scene endure, before and beyond its subsequent valorization. It is an attempt to regard the particular tempo of this scene as a movement of pleasure, which continues writing marginal notes to this "development," reactivating desire in forms which are posthumous to any accomplishment, and which exceed both the archive and the historiographical data.

Chapter 1

✦

There Is No Idleness Like Show-Idleness

On Preliminaries, Amateurism, and Work in the 1960s

> We all loved Joe, and, mostly and intermittently, each other. No one questioned the validity of what we were doing: Theatre. We workshopped nothing.
>
> —Phoebe Wray on the Caffe Cino

> I do no more care to be called an artist, except by my friends and by the people who love me, than I would care to be called a lover, publicly.
>
> —Stan Brakhage, "In Defense of Amateur"

Once Upon a Time in Coney Island

There is a woman who every payday, after finishing work, takes a train to Coney Island, reaches the amusement park, and positions herself on a breeze-hole, in the fun-wax house. She wears a skirt, which fans out around her legs as it is blown by the air coming from below. Her name is Hanna, and she devotes her leisure time to the breeze-hole, partly playing for herself the famous skirt-blowing scene from Billy Wilder's film *The Seven Year Itch*, partly just enjoying the feeling of the breeze on her naked legs. This is her *pastime*.

Not far from her, in the fun house, there is a young, muscular boy whose name is Arizona. He also goes to Coney Island in his spare time. His pastime is positioning himself in front of the mirror maze and seeing his own image reproduced time and again on the mirroring walls as a narcissistic hallucination. Hanna and Arizona are alone, alongside each other, in their solitary pastimes, although accidentally exposed to each other's sight—to someone else's amusement. They occupy a precarious space in the funhouse, which is conceived as a place to walk through, and in which, in fact, they loiter and overstay, with no purpose other than their own enjoyment, the physical pleasure of the activity itself, along with the pleasure of imagining their own picture in the scene they set up for themselves. During these moments of pleasure, they are spectators and actors of each other's phantasmagorias. They are producers and consumers of their own performance labor.

The enjoyment of their pastimes somehow defines this space as temporarily theirs, even though there is no thought of property in this inhabiting: they own no space in the amusement park other than the time of their childish enjoyment. It is an enjoyment which, however, might well be considered a spectacle, from the outside. Not surprisingly, at the end of the day the voice of the barker, advertising the many attractions of the amusement park for a paying audience, announces among its attractions Hannah's and Arizona's pastimes:

> VOICE OF THE BARKER: See "How Rome Burned While Nero Played," see "Lovely Marie Antoinette at the Guillotine," see "Why Hanna's Skirt Won't Stay Down" . . . And see our new attraction, "Smiley, The Smiling Narcissistic Wonder, Trapped in the Mirror Maze."[1]

We are in 1965. The scene I have just described is the one around which pivots the play *Why Hanna's Skirt Won't Stay Down*, written and directed by Tom Eyen at La MaMa Experimental Theatre Club,[2] and constituting to this day one of the plays most affectionately attached to the history of La MaMa, as well as to the legendary narrative of the Off-Off Broadway scene. Eyen's characters, performing for themselves and for others, along with the specific temporality of their scenes, offer an interesting allegory of the mode of performance I call *foreplay*: a playful praxis sustained by the pleasure of being enacted, rather than by an outside evaluation in professional or economic terms. (See figure 1.)

The two characters of Eyen's play perform their scenes without wages: they are neither employed as attractions in the amusement park, nor do they behave as workers in show business. Their scenes are performed in the characters' spare time as part and parcel of a private pleasure of attending the amusement park, a space which—or so we may guess—they accessed by purchasing a ticket. Rather than work (the day job that presumably secures the income Hanna and Arizona spend in their leisure time), their labor of desire is self-accomplishing in its promise of entertainment, and is self-consummating. They do not play *for* someone, although they might happen to be seen by someone while they are playing. Hanna and Arizona are each other's spectator: each of the two leisurely performers sees and recognizes the other's presence and theatrical attitude, and on this basis, in Eyen's play, a queer intimacy develops between them, which allows the narrative of the play to be enacted. In cinematographic fashion, Eyen constructs the dialogue between the two characters as the frame to a sequence of flashbacks on Hanna's and Arizona's life stories, during which each of them takes the other's lines and plays characters in the other's life story, returning to their own character afterwards, to be each other's spectator in the present. As Michael Feingold remarks, "Eyen's characters are stuck in time—in their past, in their futurelessness, in their involvement with each other—but Time itself is fluid, so that neither Eyen nor his audience are trapped with them."[3]

Hanna's and Arizona's performances, however, might also be seen by the visitors to the amusement park, as becomes clear when the barker announces their scenes as part of the amusement on offer, at the end of the play. Crucially, their performances take place without a horizon of reception granted in advance, outside of the expectation of their performance *being an event*. By virtue of their being exposed, their performances may be recognized as "entertainment." Hence their behavior may enter a system of evaluation in which it is detached from everyday life and perceived, instead, as something worthy of attention, or else—employing an expression especially suited to the history of Coney Island—as an attraction.

In the last scene of the play, after the two characters realize that they are in the process of being incorporated into the spectacle of Coney Island, Hanna says to Arizona:

> Look, sonny, you're new here so I'll give you a few complimentary tips of advice. When the gate out there opens and those stupid people pay their greasy dimes, they want what they're told they'd see. Thy want you to smile. They want Hanna's skirt up at all times. They want Rome to burn. They don't want to know why; they don't give a damn about your confused childhood. They won't even notice that Hanna's skirt is nothing but shreds now. They want their illusions. So be a good kid and you'll go far. They might even send you to the big time—the London, Paris houses. I hear they get as much as fifty cents admission over there. And all you have to do is keep your mouth shut and smile.[4]

While she delivers this speech, however, Hanna starts "freezing slowly"[5] and Arizona, while trying to resist incorporation into the barker's carousel, starts freezing too, until they are both left, at the end of the play, as "frozen, wax figures, human impostors,"[6] with the barker sweeping the floor around them, cleaning the dust encrusted on their long-exposed bodies. In a sense, the end of Eyen's play suggests a bitter ending to Hanna and Arizona's fantasy of leisure and pleasure, as if the destiny of incorporation offered in fact no possibility of escape: as if there were a progressive course according to which, in the end, work and pleasure have to counter each other in order for the performer to survive.

However, looking closely at Eyen's script, we might imagine another reading. We may notice that the author indicates, as the time setting of the play, "Five minutes to seven. Yesterday, today, but hopefully not tomorrow."[7] According to the play's stage directions, Hanna's and Arizona's acts are already advertised on large posters which are meant to be part of the scene from the beginning: hence, their incorporation might already have taken place, before they start telling us their stories of pleasure, before they start enjoying their love's labor for the time being. Their incorporation might happen again, today, Eyen suggests, "but hopefully not tomorrow." Most of the stage directions of Eyen's plays are characterized by camp irony of this sort which functions in a sense as a utopian drive (echoing José Muñoz's use of the term "utopian")[8] hinting at a tactical escape from the logic of *incorporation as attraction*. That is: the scenes of pleasure that we witness at the beginning of the play appear as pure free time, although they are in fact co-opted by the economic dynamic regulating spectacle in the amusement park, where everything is potentially an attraction, as long as a paying audience considers it such.

However, from within the productive economy in which, more or less voluntarily, they are exploited, Hanna and Arizona are also able to write their own narrative, to broaden the space-time of their pleasure. Not by chance, the two tell their stories "as if" they were not working as frozen figures, and while enjoying their performances they also experiment with an intimacy exceeding the value of their act as attraction. Such intimacy, it seems, constitutes the base for the daily renewal of their encounter in the play.

Although Hanna and Arizona are two fictional characters, I am interested in the image of their pastimes as an insight into the social and artistic context in which this show took place in 1965 New York—a context in which leisurely performances such as those of Hanna and Arizona inhabited a state of "preliminarity." The theater production of Off-Off Broadway can be considered a (however accidental) preliminary phase of a career, and of a posthumous course of valorization. The ambivalent position of Hanna's and Arizona's pastimes in the Coney Island fun house points to this scenario, but it also adds to the picture two more crucial features, which will be the focus of this chapter.

The first feature is the fact that—as for Hanna and Arizona—performance labor developed in places like the Caffe Cino or Café La MaMa mostly outside of any course of training or education, and it also happened outside of a horizon of work, not only in terms of wages but also in terms of any ethics and organization of time and space according to the development of a craft. Hanna and Arizona's self-learned performance numbers, their capacity to transform their private pleasure in an activity of public interest, is not a "work" in any sense of the word. Hanna and Arizona stand for a performance praxis developed almost accidentally, in accordance with leisure rather than with work rhythms. Their performance-making is not a professional performance work, but amateur labor.

The second feature is the fact that performances are not "events." As in Hanna and Arizona's case, the pleasure of performing does not depend on the encounter with spectators as a measure of achievement. Their performances do not crystallize in a single encounter, and are not so much centered in "presence" as in memory and potentiality: the memory of previous times in which the two of them lingered in their performances of pleasure, and the future in which they might do so again. Their pleasure of performing loiters in the extended time of their leisure, continuously deferring the moment in which it could be actualized (and appropriated and marketed) as an event worth attending.

Curiously, the narrative of *Why Hanna's Skirt Won't Stay Down* seems to presage the trajectory of Tom Eyen's own career. While participating in the downtown artistic scene (he was especially active at Caffe Cino and La MaMa),[9] in the 1960s Eyen made his living working as a sketch-writer for the revue Upstairs at the Downstairs, located in midtown on West 56th Street. In 1970, with the show *The Dirtiest Show in Town* (with parodic reference not only to air pollution but also to the pollution of American politics, as well as to the contemporary theater's triggering of audiences with ad hoc sexual provocations)[10] Eyen's work moved Off Broadway, to the Astor Place Theatre, where it received great public acclaim, and later transferred to London's West End. The same year Eyen's company received an $8,000 grant from the Guggenheim. It was only in 1981, however, that Eyen became a mainstream star of American theater, with the musical *Dreamgirls* (written in collaboration with the lyricist Henry Krieger), which was produced on Broadway and won six Tony Awards, one of which—Best Book—was specifically Eyen's. In the twenty years before *Dreamgirls* Eyen did a great deal of work, often not recognized as such. As Richard Eyen recalls, in a recent text about the beginning of his brother's career collected in *Return to Caffe Cino*, the budget of an early Eyen production could be a mere fifteen dollars.[12] Clearly, a great amount of love's labor supported Eyen's experimental theater activity downtown, which may well be the prime reason for the deferral of Eyen's entrance into Broadway's realm. In other words, instead of making his way into mainstream theatre by crafting his abilities as sketch-writer to comply with the standards of Broadway entertainment, to a certain extent Eyen allowed himself to linger in the interim space of Off-Off Broadway—a space which was itself embedded in theater production while also, in a sense, challenging its logic.

In the pages that follow I argue that the interval of amateurism, a sort of overstaying on the way to a professional career, which characterizes the engagement with theater in the 1960s Off-Off Broadway scene of artists like Tom Eyen, overturned (or at least played with overturning) the logic of capitalist temporality and professionalism. I shall suggest that a playful subversion of theater temporality was key to experiments of the time with a kind of performance work nourished by pleasure rather than achievement. This made it possible for events to endure beyond the actualization of amateur labor as professional success, or even as artistic event, although such actualization always and already haunts any experiment done for free.

The Scene of Foreplay as "Stylized Amateurism"

Looking at photos and video recordings from Tom Eyen's 1960s shows such as *Why Hanna's Skirt Won't Stay Down*, or *Miss Nefertiti Regrets,* kept today in the La MaMa Archive, the most immediate reference that comes to mind is neither to the aesthetics of the best-known 1960s experimental theater, nor to traditional drama: it is to the artificiality, imprecision, lack of theatre technique, and cheap scenic devices of amateur theater. Likewise, many reviews of the Play-House of the Ridiculous (including very enthusiastic ones) refer to "high-school pageantry," "amateur theatricals," and "fraternity skits,"[13] commenting repeatedly on the Play-House of the Ridiculous's bad acting, dilettantism, lack of technique, juvenile playfulness, and its approach to performance-making as an unseasoned "put-on."[14] The same could be said for the 1960s "home movies" of Andy Warhol and Jack Smith (and for the performance work of the latter) featuring not only almost exclusively amateur performers but also an explicit aura of dilettantism, amounting to a seeming lack of seriousness and expertise, or craftsmanship and preparation.[15]

Furthermore, the films of Warhol and Smith were themselves inscribed in a tradition of New York self-produced, self-organized independent filmmaking (including, among others, Robert Frank, Marie Menken, Stan Brakhage, Jonas Mekas, and Maya Deren) that since the late 1950s had explicitly invoked amateurism as a distinctive trait of its film praxis. In a famous 1959 essay, significantly entitled "Amateurs Versus Professionals," Maya Deren had defined how the concept of amateur was understood in this artistic context:

> The very classification "amateur" has an apologetic ring. But that very word—from the Latin "amateur"—"lover"—means one who does something for the love of the thing rather than for economic reasons or necessity.[16]

In 1971 Stan Brakhage wrote illuminating notes in defense of amateurism, reviewing in the light of this notion his fifteen-years-long career in film and staking out with pride the disparagement that had been cast upon activities done during leisure rather than as work by the "professional." The latter is described with contempt by Brakhage as

> always much admired in the public life of any time. He is the Don Juan whose techniques (of sex or whatever), whose conquests in terms of number, speed, duration or mathematical whatever, whose stance of perfection (whatever can be intellectually measured to determine a competitional winner) does dazzle any man at any time he relates to the mass of people. . . . He may even come to be Don Juan himself, forever in the "hell" of admiration of other people's public life.[17]

Advocating for the praxis of filmmaking a direct relation with the domain of love, understood as sensual pleasure and private enjoyment but also as a distinctive inexpertise in artistic practice, Brakhage proposes the amateur as the figure not deemed to live in the "admiration of other people's public life," and hence self-entitled to a different, private habitat of measurement for his love work. According to Brakhage, amateur labor is a "more real and thus honorable activity than work which is performed for some gain other than the work itself gives."[18] Even when working in collaboration with others, "the true amateur is always working alone, gauging his own success according to his care for the work rather than according to the accomplishments or recognitions of others. Why then," asks Brakhage, "have critics, teachers and other guardians of the public life come to use the term derogatorily?"[19] The answer offered by the filmmaker has again to do with the fact that the amateur elaborates a private gauge for the value of her amateur labor, whereas the professional is deemed to fulfill the demands of the public and, more importantly, the goals she herself has set up for her professional achievements, in relation to the public needs. Brakhage suggests that the figure of the amateur is culturally constructed and stigmatized with shame

> because an amateur is one who really lives his life—not one who simply "performs his duty"—and as such he experiences his work while he's working—rather than going to school to learn his work so he can spend the rest of the life doing it dutifully; and the amateur, thus, is forever learning and growing thru his work into all his living "clumsiness" of continual discovery that is beautiful to see, if you have lived it and can see it, as to watch young lovers in the "clumsiness" of their lack of knowing and the joy of their continual discovery of each other, if you have ever loved and can appreciate young lovers without jealousy.[20]

Brakhage's description of the "clumsiness" of the amateur implicitly evokes the modality of love and work I call foreplay: the nearing and tarrying of a theater with no intention of development, enjoying its own continuation, regardless of its posthumous valorization (although very much concerned with its own memorability). The particular quality of amateurism described by Brakhage seems kindred to the shows put on with little or no training, but more importantly with no other gain than the leisure of work itself, in the 1960s and 1970s New York underground. In these performances likewise the clumsiness of inexpertise was accompanied by a certain disregard of preestablished goals or standards of perfection in artistic terms.

John Vaccaro, the director of the Play-House of the Ridiculous, never made a mystery of having welcomed in his company whoever wanted to participate, without any standard form of recruitment, and to have particularly enjoyed working with untrained actors, some of whom were also regular drug consumers. As he explains in an interview in 1969:

> The most important thing about these people is that they are not ACTORS. No auditions. See them on the street . . . hear about them from a member of the group—someone has a desire, a NEED to work with us. I give them something to do. We fill a void in our lives—a need to do one THING. There are about forty in my group now. But there is no limit. Can't figure out what holds us together, except that we LOVE EACH OTHER. I'm excited to see that there are people who love and that will accept my love. I do the plays with this particular people, the only worthwhile people. That's the only worthwhile audience, too.[21]

Although in the memory of people who worked with Vaccaro or gravitated around his theater group the atmosphere of the Play-House is remembered mostly as a ferocious environment, one characterized especially by Vaccaro's cantankerous temperament and violent outbursts (which he would direct toward his actors in order to stimulate them to fly into a temper and to "act it out" on stage), it is quite relevant that here, as in conversations I had with him in the last years, Vaccaro emphasizes love as what held the group together. In a sense, more than a sentimental remark, such comments could be read as a precise statement about theater and about the relation between the company and the audience itself. Describing the leisurely performance-making of the Play-House of the Ridiculous, Vaccaro explained: "We are really having a BALL onstage . . . there is an aura of excitement with us all the time . . . There is great joy to what we're doing. We love to get up there. Here's to you, right now! Take it!"

In 1978 Stefan Brecht published a collection of texts entitled *Queer Theatre*, which was intended to be the second volume of the ambitious and never-completed project of a series of books devoted to the broad spectrum of theater experiments in the New York downtown art scene. As I anticipated, these texts (encompassing essays on the work of Jack Smith, John Vaccaro, Charles Ludlam, Ronald Tavel, the Hot Peaches, the Trockadero Gloxinia Ballet Company, and John Waters) constitute an extremely precise survey, as well as a very personal account of Brecht's own participation in and enjoyment of these performances. In other words, Brecht was one of those invited to participate in the "ball," and to take enjoyment in such theatrical "clumsiness." Brecht's impressions on the work of the Play-House (which, he declares, he tried to appreciate by keeping "Freud, Sartre, Artaud, de Sade, Genet, Warhol and la *pataphysique* out of it")[22] are very insightful about the disregard for professionalism that characterized not only the technique but the very idea of theater embodied by John Vaccaro's company.

According to Brecht, the members of the Play-House were all performing and at the same time living a queer mode of existence in performance, and not conceiving of themselves as artists producing professional "artworks":

> This theatre is resolutely opposed to art. It rejects the ideal of a formal integrity of the art-work in abstraction from the artist and his activity; it rejects the ideal of subordination of the artist's personality to his artistry; . . . it invites reaction to its activity rather than to its product.[23]

Brecht read the theater of the ridiculous as a ferocious and derisive attack on the "civilized adult"[24] that we could well consider as synonymous with the "professional" as described by Brakhage: the adult living in the public sphere, admired for her techniques and goals, for her productivity, her commitment to achieving such goals, to crafting such techniques, and mastering her own productive capacities. In this context, the enjoyment described by Vaccaro as a key element of the theatrical operations going on onstage could also be considered in the light of Brakhage's defense of the amateur: the performer of the Play-House was someone who practiced at leisure an activity that others would do professionally as "art," and measured its value by virtue of a continuous private enjoyment.

The autonomy of such amateurism from professional standards, along with the peculiar aura of dilettantism emerging from the work of Tom Eyen, the Play-House, Jack Smith, and Andy Warhol, were interestingly addressed again in 1978 by Philippe R. Perebinossoff (notably, not a theater scholar), who called this distinctive modality a "theatre of stylized amateurism": [25]

> Private theatricals or home entertainments which previously depended on a larger framing work for existence outside of private living rooms, attics, or makeshift club stages have come into their own. Deemed an interference, the frame play has been dropped, resulting in full-length public works which celebrate the flamboyance, dressing up, and role reversals associated with amateur theatricals. Distinctions between amateurism and professionalism blur as private theatricals or essentially "home movies" go public.[26]

In his fascinating analysis, which reveals both attraction and suspicion toward this modality of theater which he calls a "movement," Perebinossoff suggests that groups like the Play-House of the Ridiculous (which he places, among others, alongside the cinema of Andy Warhol and John Waters, the Hot Peaches, the Cockettes, or Tom Eyen's plays) require the redefinition of new critical standards for the discussion of theater as well as for the concept of performance. In fact, the "theatre of stylized amateurism" postulates a cheerful dismissal of what is traditionally considered mastery in professional theater, and conceives itself as a private/public display of "flamboyant style dependent on costuming, spangles, role playing, and an indulgence in excesses."[27] Distancing themselves from the professional, "legitimate" Broadway theater where acting skills are evaluated first of all according to a rigid system of recruitment, the "stylized amateurs"—the author continues—also contrast "sharply with other new theater movements which advocate discipline, ordinary dress, and bare stages,"[28] such as the theatre of Jerzy Grotowski or the Performance Group. For the "stylized amateurs"

> theater . . . would seem to originate in recollections of grade school pageants and fraternity skits. Their aesthetic is grounded in the teachings of popular culture and their concept of performance recalls matinees spent in neighborhood movie houses watching mythic Hollywood idols. Many people make a clear distinction between professional theater, which is serious, and amateur theatricals in grade schools, high schools, neighborhood drama clubs, etc., which are not serious. The two are viewed as entirely different and as having very little influence upon one another. The new movement abolishes this distinction because productions which glorify amateurism are currently being performed publicly by professionals.[29]

It is worth emphasizing that such analysis is dated 1978, and that indeed most of the examples mentioned by the author were at that point circulating beyond the so-called underground, as well as influencing international and mainstream art (among the examples influenced by such style Perebinossoff mentions Luchino Visconti, Ken Russell, Federico Fellini, Sam Shepard, and Bette Midler). What interests Perebinossoff, however, is not so much the loss of innocence or subcultural allure that this stylized amateurism acquired in the late 1970s, but rather the particular technology of theater that it engendered throughout. According to Perebinossoff, the theater of stylized amateurism is particularly significant because "it has freed the theatrical interlude from the confines of the frame play."[30] What he means and goes on to argue is that traditionally, amateur theatricals would function as "interludes" in a broader (literary, filmic, or, for that matter, social) narrative and not be allowed a space and time of their own on the scene. For this reason they would often appear within narrative works as "time-filler":

> Conventionally, the inner play serves a variety of functions designed to complement or illuminate the larger work in which it is contained. Private theatricals within the context of the frame work serve to define the personalities of the individuals participating in the private entertainment, because an inner play often contains characters whose lives parallel those of the individuals in the frame play; similarly, when "actors" in the frame play perform in an inner play, the

> audience tends to forget that these individuals are already performing in a play and the reality of their characters in the frame play is firmly established . . . as in Jean Renoir's *The Rules of the Game*.[31]

Building on Perebinossoff's suggestion, I want to propose that liberating the interlude from its function of time-filler means claiming a sort of self-sufficiency for an activity supposed to be only supplementary. Like the amateur's labor conjured by Brakhage's description, or the leisure performances of Hanna and Arizona, the theatrical activities of "stylized amateurism" acquire autonomy from professionalism almost surreptitiously.

Furthermore, as in the traditional interlude, in this theatre the *personas* who played in films and performances were already known for their social and performance specialties in the public/private sphere of the "frame narrative": the 1960s New York downtown scene. The character of Hanna in Tom Eyen's play, for instance, was modeled partly on the flesh-and-bone actress Helen Hanft, known on the amateur stages and social scene of 1960s Off-Off Broadway for her specific persona of the "sassy dame," recognizable in several performances and crystallized in her main scene in *Why Hanna's Skirt Won't Stay Down*.[32] Likewise, performers like Mario Montez, Beverly Grant, Jackie Curtis, Holly Woodlawn, Penny Arcade, or Ruby Lynn Reyner were all recognizable personas whose performances in specific artistic instances (such as films or shows) were perceived in a continuum with the life of their private/public images in the underground circuit, reproduced through photographs, lived and remembered events, gossip, and other forms of renewal.

An important recent contribution to thinking about amateurism and theater which is useful to bring into this analysis is Nicholas Ridout's book *Passionate Amateurs*, where the figure of the amateur is mobilized as a way to foster a historical materialist reflection on "theatre's occasional capacity to trouble some fundamental assumptions about work and time—about the work of time and the time of work—that have come to shape social and cultural life at least since the consolidation of industrial capitalism."[33] In Ridout's project the "passionate amateur" is a returning figure of (more or less conscious) resistance to the organizing demarcations of work in capitalist modernity. She is a figure that by devoting "her energy to a labor that is its own reward" performs a condition of life and work "to which the revolutionary might aim to in her visions of a humanity liberated from the alienation of wage labor."[34] Crucially, in Ridout's speculation and in the examples supporting it, the passionate amateur is not someone living and working outside capitalism; rather, she is a figure who, from within the organization of labor in which human activity is regulated in capitalism, prefigures a potential for a radically different experience of work, time, and community. Ridout calls such potential "communism," understanding this term both in relation to historical instances of revolutionary utopias and to a "fraught relationship with industry, with institutions, and with capitalism itself, rather than as a flight or freedom from them."[35] It is vital, however, that in Ridout's project the passionate amateurs perform their love labor in and by means of theater: theater's time—intrinsically inscribed into a common space between work and leisure, between production and consumption—offers itself as the space where the present might temporarily negate itself in favor of another temporality, one either projected in a utopian past or future. In Ridout's words, theater

> offers this negation by way of an experience that is not normally experienced as work, but as some kind of nonwork or "play." Of course, there is no such thing: it is work for those who make it, just as the nonpresent past or future summoned into the present by the act of theatre-making is also no such thing, but rather the present itself, experienced otherwise. The detour taken through the theatre leads through a past that is not past and is accomplished through work that looks like it is not work. This is why the theatre is a particularly good place for the passionate amateur or romantic-anticapitalist who wants to find some way of undoing, even if only for a moment, the time of her work and the work of time upon herself.[36]

Ridout's work on the passionate amateur and the particular uses she makes of theater is in interesting dialogue with my argument. In the examples observed in this book, theatre-making stands in ambivalent position "between work and non-work or play,"[37] and precisely by virtue of that I recognize in this praxis a potential for unsettling—at least in the form of leisurely play—the relation between time and work which was hegemonic in both mainstream and experimental theater in 1960s New York. Bringing together Perebinossoff's and Ridout's voices, along with Brakhage's apologia for amateurism, I want to interrogate further the particular technology of time entailed in the claim of autonomy of these amateur theatricals in the scene of foreplay. Namely, throughout this chapter I shall address such "stylized amateurism" as a habitat where theater's temporary transformation of capitalist time appears less as professional show business than an objectified public/private form of *show-idleness*. In the last section of this chapter, I shall discuss the temporality of such form of show-idleness in particular regarding the artistic work of Jack Smith, who could be considered a prime example of what Ridout, as an alternative to passionate amateur, defines as the "romantic anticapitalist," referring to a figure mobilizing her passion against the hegemony of mastery, and mobilizing her private life against the power of public life.

An Immature State of the Artist: Amateur Labor and Training

In *Camera Lucida*, reflecting on the practice of photography, Roland Barthes proposes a definition of the amateur artist's predicament: "usually the amateur is defined as an *immature state of the artist* [emphasis mine]: someone who cannot—or will not—achieve the mastery of a profession".[38] The amateur artist, Barthes seems to suggest, is an eternal adolescent: someone who overstays in a space which is supposed to be temporary, who is frozen in a condition of arrested development, whose practice fails to progress toward a mature state. But what exactly would be a "mature state" for an artist? Should we understand this state merely as an economic category, positing professional artistic work simply as remunerative activity? Or does the mature state rather designate a stage in which the artist will be ready to be considered as such, regardless of an economic determination? And in this case, who—if not the artist herself—will determine whether maturity has been achieved?

In the simplicity of its formulation, Barthes's definition grasps an essential aspect of amateur artistic labor, both with regard to the disparaging way in which this expression is commonly employed, and to the character of difference that this peculiar labor might retain, if thought outside of a direct dichotomy with professional labor. Barthes's formulation points to amateur labor as a concept already embedded in a developmental conception of work, as much as immaturity is commonly intended as the antechamber to adult productivity in a developmental conception of life. In this sense, amateur labor appears as a potentially unproductive practice, where not only is labor performed for free, but it is also exempt from agreed-upon standards of work proficiency. Just as an adolescent is not yet expected to be expert, efficient, focused, precise, and task-oriented, the amateur artist performs in a space of potentiality, where artistic labor might proceed in view of unexpected "mastery."

Question of mastery, development, profession, and efficiency were very much debated in the discursive environment of experimental theater in the New York of the 1960s. Important reflections around these questions were developed in particular by Richard Schechner, in many respects a real "professional," recognized in the public sphere in various professional capacities, in many ways related to theater. In the mid-60s Richard Schechner was active as the theater director of the New York-based theater ensemble The Performance Group, as an academic teacher (first at Tulane University, then from 1967 at the Tisch School of the Arts at New York University), and as the editor of *TDR: The Drama Review*, a leading publication in which the discipline of performance studies took shape. Along with his growing interest in social and cultural anthropology (enhanced, later on, by his field research in Asia and his collaboration with anthropologist Victor Turner), a major influence on his work was the artistic practice of contemporary practitioners whose work Schechner had the chance to witness and study: among them, Jerzy Grotowski, Joe Chaikin, Allan Kaprow, and John Cage. This range of experiments, despite many dissimilarities, all pointed to live art as a practice that happened first and foremost in the here and now of an encounter with an audience. In his writings, Schechner focused especially on the "eventfulness" of this encounter, discussing it in relation to other typologies of events, such as rituals (religious and secular) and sports. In 1970, in a theoretical systematization of his analysis, Schechner proposed (building on Mircea Eliade)[39] the definition of "actual," naming with this term "the simple but altogether upsetting idea of art as an event."[40]

The notion of the actual is presented as a theoretical attempt to bridge the idea of artistic process and final product: "understanding actualizing," Schechner writes, "means understanding both the creative condition and the artwork, the actual."[41] Schechner characterizes the concept of the "actual" through five basic features which pertain to both avant-garde events and tribal and religious performances: processuality ("something happens here and now"),[42] contest (the relation at stake between performers and spectators), irrevocability (including both situations and forms of exchange), initiation (a change of status for participants to the event), and space (the concrete and organic organization of space for a given purpose).[43]

Schechner's idea of "actual" casts the performer's faculty to perform her labor as a distinctive quality of potentiality: it cannot be measured with standard notions of economic productivity, but is characterized by the recognition of its value as "event" by an audience. In fact, performing depends on a public sphere in order to be *actualized* as labor. The term "actual," therefore, stands in specific relation with the *potentiality of performance as labor*: its enactment in public brings the performance into being, realizing its appearance in the world in the form of an event.

Schechner's reflection on and experimentation with the notion of performance also contributed to shape a new horizon of reflection on "theater work," a reflection in which Jerzy Grotowski featured as a prominent figure. In this context, the "outcome" of performance would fall outside the domain of art, and would thus exceed judgment or appreciation, seeking something altogether different from the spectator's consumption. Interestingly, the question of what an event should or could be became caught up in an interrogation of the effect of a given performance in the encounter with an audience, in terms other than those predicated by passive consumption.

In Schechner's writing, the question of effect was reformulated as an inquiry into what he called "efficacy," which he differentiated from "entertainment."[44] In a more recent formulation of the binary opposition between efficacy and entertainment, which Schechner started elaborating since the 1970s, what he calls the "efficacy-entertainment braid" is defined in the following terms:

> Efficacy and entertainment are not binary oppositions, rather they form a pole of a continuum. The opposition is between efficacy and entertainment, not ritual and theatre. Whether one calls a specific kind of performance "ritual" or "theatre" depends on context and

> function. . . . The purpose is the most important factor determining whether a performance is a ritual or not. If the performance purpose is to effect change, then the other qualities under the heading efficacy . . .[45] will also be present, and the performance is a ritual. But if the performance purpose is mostly to give pleasure, to show off, to be beautiful, or to pass time, then the performance is an entertainment. The fact is that no performance is pure efficacy or pure entertainment.[46]

From this passage, it would seem that Schechner associates the idea of efficacy with a capacity to fulfill a task. In this formulation, efficacy is the faculty to make happen, to *actualize* performance as form in purposeful action, as a praxis oriented toward a goal, even if the achievement is not necessarily of economic worth; that is, even if, as in orgasm, the outcome is considered as waste.

As Stephen Bottoms has discussed, the notion of efficacy in Schechner's writings appears in close association with the establishment of the idea of "performance" as a distinctive praxis with regard to theater. "Efficacy"—Bottoms writes—"which Schechner associates strongly with ritual behavior, suggests a performance that accomplishes some actual positive change in the 'real world' of the community—it produces results."[47] According to Bottoms, Schechner's emphasis on efficacy has contributed first of all to the rise of performance as a category understood as more real, authentic, and "potent"[48] than theater. Through the years, this truism has fueled the embrace of performance in academic discourses as a key element in the refashioning of Theater Studies into the new disciplinary field of Performance Studies, contributing to the formation of a new "ruling mythology."[49] Secondly, Bottoms argues that efficacy has served, in both Schechner's artistic and critical praxis of the 1960s, to establish a paradigm for regarding performance work in masculinist terms. Not only, Bottoms claims, did Schechner launch in 1962 his attack on established American theater and his vision for a renewal of theater practice by using a set of highly gendered metaphors (American theater "has been too long the call-girl of money and ambition. In some sense we hope to restore [its] virginity"),[50] but at the beginning of his tenure as director of *TDR* he criticized what he considered the deplorable theatricality of American stages in openly homophobic terms. Notably, with reference to Edward Albee's *Who's Afraid of Virginia Woolf?* Schechner wrote: "I'm tired of morbidity and sexual perversity which are only there to titillate an impotent and homosexual theatre and audience."[51] As Bottoms remarks, on this and other occasions in *TDR* during the early 1960s[52] a well-known homophobic topos (the one associating theatricality and downright effeminacy, considered in most debased terms) is strongly reiterated, and offered precisely as a way of condemning the supposed "inauthentic," "pervert[ed]" and "impotent" trend of American stages. In contrast to this Schechner elaborates his vision of an efficacious performance-making, characterized by "significant leadership" and by successful achievement as *actual* action. Bottoms emphasized that this position favored the establishment of a canon of what a radical and progressive theater should be, grounded in examples of 1960s experimental theater work which appeared as "secular ritual,"[53] such as the work of the Living Theatre, the Open Theatre, the Performance Group in the American context, and the work of Polish director Jerzy Grotowski, discussed for the first time in *TDR* in 1965 in an article signed by Grotowski's pupil and Odin Teatret director Eugenio Barba. At the same time, according to Bottoms, the establishment of this canon through *TDR* corresponded to a significant absence of critical interest in other contemporary alternative theater, such as the Off-Off Broadway scene—a scene which, notably, featured approaches and procedures different than the ones praised in *TDR*, but which was also characterized by the prominence of gay artists, and by an explicit homosexual sensibility.[54]

I am, however, not so interested in the anti-theatrical prejudice Schechner's position expresses, although this point is certainly at stake in the claim of authenticity attributed to efficacious performance, and in the condemnation of artifice, and entertainment. Rather, I am interested in how "efficacy" has functioned, in and beyond Schechner's work, as part of an ideology which on the one hand valorized "theater work" according to a specific vision of what "work" is supposed to be, and on the other hand aimed to secure for performance a position outside productivity, affirmed through a more or less explicit contradistinction with the domain of sex. As we shall see, in this comparison "sex" was also conjured according to a specific vision of what "sex" is supposed to be.

On Preparation: Workshop, Process, Event

Schechner's emphasis on efficacy, along with his formulation of performance as something that produces *results* in "real life," is an attempt to reconfigure the function of theater outside a market rationale. Positing performance as inherently related to its process of production, not separable by the psychophysical qualities of the individual who performs, tries to avoid a commodity status. Likewise, this approach repositions the professional status of the performer as the profferer of a service, and not as the mere producer of an event, understood as something consumable in the entertainment market. However, the idea of mastery is not really put in question, but simply reformulated: whereas the traditional virtuoso, in theater, would achieve an extraordinary result by perfectly mastering her own artistic technique, the performer can also achieve an effective performance by "mastering" a technique directed toward results that transgress the mere artistic domain.[55]

Since "efficacious" performance entails a teleological end, it is a productive activity: the value and circulation of this production exceeds the aesthetic domain, but is certainly relevant in the social sphere. It is productive of social values—such as, for instance, the sense of community (a notion highly valued in the group-based work promoted by *TDR*), political awareness (for instance in the case of the Living Theatre, the Bread and Puppet, the San Francisco Mime Troup), or personal and spiritual growth (especially in Grotowski's work). However, for Schechner, in order to be effective performance labor must depower artistic "virtuosity," leaving space for extraordinary achievements on an anthropogenic level.[56]

Returning to consider the terms of Marx's schema I discussed in the introduction, I want to recall that in every production the consumer (here the audience) features as an *active subject of desire* for art, as the conceptual purpose for its making. Furthermore, according to Marx the amount of this desire also measures the status of the product: the urge to consume the product more than once—"the need for repetition" characterizing consumption—"leads to the perfection of abilities evolved during the first process of production and converts them into skills."[57] The category of perfection (also evoked in Brakhage's text, as one of the arrogant features of professionalism) appears of course problematic when thinking about performing arts, and even more so as a category defining abilities and skills at stake in a production. Clearly, however, the phase of a show's preparation is part and parcel of the production process, and so is the repetition of the show fostered by the audience's desire to consume it more than once.

In theater history, the repetition of theater labor, elaborated and brought to a semi-ultimate state which can be subsequently reproduced, has long been stabilized in the form of rehearsals. As Annemarie Matzke points out in her historico-theoretical discussion of rehearsals as basic units in the grammar of theater labor,[58] rehearsals have historically been an arena of negotiation not only for the status of theater as "product," but also for that of theater-makers as workers. Rehearsals function as a measure for the time and space devoted to work before the event, which constitutes the visible part of theater's working process. Not surprisingly, therefore, the question of a show's preparation became central to the reflection on theater work throughout the twentieth century, and played a crucial role especially in those theater practices developed outside commercial theater, where the status of the activity as well as that of its producers as workers was seemingly less under scrutiny.

Significantly, under the rubric of "preparation" feature not only rehearsals (time-framed as a more or less extended working period projected toward a final theater production) but also educational activities that prepare people for performance-making as a profession, such as the practitioners' training. Experimentation in these two domains often went hand in hand in the work of theater-makers of various kinds who, since the late nineteenth century, had articulated in their theory and praxis an idea of theater-making as a specific and autonomous craft.

Notwithstanding substantial differences in terms of politics and poetics (as well as in the sociocultural contexts in which they operated), the concept of *craft* constitutes a common thread between a number of figures who, at the turn of the century, helped establish the principal terms in which theater work has been discussed during the twentieth century. To name just a small number of examples, the theme of work recurs in the practice and writings of Konstantin Stanislavsky, Jacques Copeau, Rudolf Laban, and Émile Jaques-Dalcroze as well as in the laboratory practice of Vsevolod Meyerhold, whose writings are filled with metaphors referring to the domain of nonartistic work, such as—for instance—the factory.

This emphasis on work was oriented first of all to claim the status and legitimacy of the place of theater in the field of art in opposition to that of entertainment; secondly, it served as the organizing principle of artistic practice, considered as a craft to be developed in a process (both professional and ethical) before and after the moment of performance, which is nevertheless considered and valorized as event. The centrality of work in this approach also implied the establishment of a system for the organization of time and space, so as to provide continuity for the creative process and to not disturb its development.[59]

In the 1960s, this line of thought returned in several theater practices that emphasized the idea of training and placed great value on the practice and poetics of the workshop. Notably, Schechner himself linked his interest in the fundamental features of performance, with an attentive investigation of the procedures of professional theater work. As a preliminary survey, in 1964 he devoted two issues of the *Tulane Drama Review* to an inquiry into established systems and practices for actor training in the United States, inviting scholars and practitioners to discuss the question of training in the American professional theater, with particular reference to the American reception of Stanislavsky's Acting Method.[60] In the introduction to this report, he writes:

> In no other profession is there so little agreement about standards and methods, so little active contact among those doing the work. What is the relationship, if any, between those offering courses at universities, actors "sharing their craft" at the studios in New York, and "faculties" at professional schools? . . . Where in this country might a young and talented would-be actor find continuous work in the sequence of basic training, advanced training, apprenticeship, and professional opportunity? . . . Other professions nurture their young, carefully separating the no-talents from the achievers. Theatre companies have set up schools because trained actors are not "trained"; even worse, many are permanently spoiled by the very process which promised to bring their talent into focus.[61]

The premise of this inquiry, therefore, is the desire to solve a structural problem of American theater by systematizing a sequence in the education of an actor: a trajectory which would bring the craft to "perfection" so as to secure professional opportunities. At the same time, Schechner's interest in training methods extended to the experiments of contemporary theater practitioners working outside mainstream theater, and to his own practice as director of the Performance Group. It is in this context that the landscape of early twentieth-century European practices was often conjured: the word "laboratory" (adopted by Grotowski in the name of his Teatr Laboratorium) became a staple in the language of all those groups which started exploring the procedures of theater work outside of the standard relation between "rehearsals" and "event."

As Theodor Shank has pointed out in his survey of 1960s group theater, especially in the case of the Open Theatre, the idea of preparation was specifically investigated as a way to counter the structure of commercial theater production:

> The workshop, unlike training for commercial theatre, would not try to make the actors "better commodities." The purpose of the Open Theatre was not so much the creation of a product, but investigation through theatre of certain forces in our culture and an attempt to invent new means necessary to express and share the actors' insights through performance.[62]

Significantly, although the idea of a show as an "end product" was evaded by means of the workshop, and the latter was also conceived as pleasurable experimentation, artists considered the workshop as the space of a progressive self-education, as an ongoing testing and expansion of techniques which would allow the performer to master her psychophysical faculties and produce an effect on the audience's life. In the case of the Open Theatre in particular, the use of the workshop coalesced with the strong emphasis placed by the group on research and investigation, addressing both theater and society at large.[63] Most of the techniques explored in the 1960s workshops were neither directly related to standard acting practices nor fashioned after prescribed methodologies: prominent examples of exercises experimented with in the space of the workshop are Indian body techniques, such as yoga, or traditional dance techniques. The exposure of the technique itself, in this context, could acquire, and has in fact later acquired, the status of an event in itself.

This shared interest in the question of the preliminary processes which lead to the actualization of the event can be regarded in light of the idea of *preliminari*, which is a linguistic equivalent to the word "foreplay" in other European languages. Keeping in mind the common feature of sex and theater as encounters in time, the period of training and rehearsals can be considered not only a form of preparation, but also a preliminary phase to the event proper. Furthermore, the expression *preliminari* directly echoes the discussion on "liminality" which featured prominently in early developments of Performance Studies, largely inspired by Victor Turner's work, drawing, for his part, on the theorization of liminality developed by the anthropologist Arnold Van Gennep. According to the latter, "preliminal rites" are those implying a metaphorical death, a radical break from previous practices before "passing" into another regime of event. According to Turner—who took up Gennep's idea of rituals as marking a moment of passage between different phases, regimes, and stages of life—the liminal phase that follows the preliminal one is characterized by a strictly prescribed time sequence, where everyone knows what to do and how. Turner's concept of liminality found extensive resonances in Schechner's performance theory, where "performing" is itself defined as "a paradigm of liminality."[64] The "limen" Schechner posits as the territory on which performance happens is that between life and art, between the performer and her role-playing. In Schechner's words, it is the limen between the *not-me* and the *not-not me*. Liminality is crucial for Schechner as a process of organization of what he called *actual*: the unrepeatable, consequential, irrevocable act of performance.[65] Relatedly, liminality is also the territory of an actor's training, and the process of rehearsals is leading the creative process toward an encounter with spectators, considered in this context more precisely as participants.

In the 1960s the boundaries between performance and its preparation began to shift significantly: artists started opening their workshops to audiences and show performance pieces as *works in progress*. In Schechner's words:

> Since around 1965 what has been shown to the spectators is the very process of developing and staging the performance—the workshops that lead up to the performance, the various means of theatrical production, the ways the audience is brought in and led from the space, and many other previously conventional and/or hidden procedures. These all became problematic, that is, manipulable, subjects of theatrical inquiry. These procedures have to do with theatre-in-itself and are, as regards the theatre, efficacious: that is, they are what makes theatre into theatre regardless of themes, plot, or the usual "elements of drama." . . . All this attention paid to the procedures of making theatre was, I think, an attempt to ritualize performance, to make theatre yield efficacious acts. "This is who we really are and what we really do," and "we can do this together with you" were the key messages sent.[66]

The incorporation of the preparatory phase into the event amounted to a refiguring of the value of artistic work in the logic of theater production, on the base of a conceptual separation between the show understood as a marketable commodity and the process of its making. Schechner's and Chaikin's investigation of theater work in the 1960s figured the time and space of this process as something preliminary, elaborated "before passing into another regime of event," and hence suspended in a potential projection toward an encounter with spectators, during which the culminating moment of the process would occur. On these premises the exposure of the preparation acquires a strong connection with the idea of "efficacy": exposing preparation means to show who the performers "really" are.[67]

The idea of training and preparation is also central in the 1960s work of Grotowski, an important influence for the Open Theatre and the Performance Group.[68] Particularly significant is the terminology Grotowski used to describe what he called the "total act" that the actor should be trained to achieve before encountering the audience: he talked about undertaking an act of "self-penetration," as well as of the ability to learn to give oneself "in one's deepest intimacy, with confidence, as when one gives oneself in love."[69] Such a "love work," however, was supposed to reject "the least trace of egotism or self-enjoyment"[70] on the part of the performer, and it was conceived as a gift to spectators, who were invited to join the fulfillment of theater as a total act. Both actors and spectators were called upon to join this love work toward a common aspiration to fulfillment. According to Grotowski "theatre has certain objective laws and the fulfillment is possible only within them, or, as Thomas Mann said, through a kind of 'high obedience,' to which we give our "dignified attention."[71]

The encounter between performers and spectators is figured as something other than an exchange: in Grotowski's poetics, in fact, it is specifically posited as a "sacrifice." In Lisa Wolford's words, for Grotowski performance entails "a culminating moment in the actor's role in which she/he is able to transcend the performance score and the technical demands of the part, revealing a truth which is paradoxically both personal and universal. It is an act of self-sacrifice."[72] The training procedures are essential to this process, as they serve to remove "blocks" which would otherwise prevent the actor from performing her service. Rather than collecting and accumulating skills, in Grotowski's training, techniques are aimed to convey the actor into a state in which, through performance, she can bring to exposure a hidden truth about life itself.

Significantly, in Grotowski this theater encounter is often accounted for through various sexual metaphors. His prototype of the "holy actor," Ryszard Cieslak, famously prepared the score of his final scene in *The Constant Prince*, improvising on the memory of his first orgasm, although in the scene this memory was translated into an act of martyrdom: the final sacrifice of the Prince's holy destiny. In order for the "total act" to be accomplished, in fact, Grotowski urged that pleasure had to be transcended in order for the theater encounter to be achieved. The audience's role is understood as participation in a ceremony, in which spectators are called upon to offer their "dignified attention."[73] Grotowski's productions were carefully conceived in order to prepare the conditions for this special attention to be paid: from the early years in Poland, Grotowski admitted only small numbers of spectators to his theater. This choice did not respond only to spatial conditions, but it fully informed Grotowski's poetics. In each performance of the Theatre Laboratory the dramaturgy incorporated the audience's point of view, making its position in space a key compositional element, and including it as part of the play, renegotiating it each time. Although the audience was supposed to be willing to engage "the spiritual act" enacted by the actors on their behalf, in his writings Grotowski also makes it clear that the distinction between what he called "holy actors" and suitable spectators ("holy spectators") was a matter of "work": a spectator "only comes to the theatre for a brief moment in order to square off an account with himself, and this is something that does not impose the *hard routine of daily work*" (emphasis mine).[74]

Especially in the latest turn of his experimentation (leading him beyond theater altogether)[75] Grotowski associated theater techniques with the practice of tantra yoga, a body discipline that allows its practitioner to control body faculties in order to prolong and enhance impulses experienced during action. The best-known application of tantra techniques (which became popular in Europe during the 1960s) is the sexual sphere, and the main purpose of tantra sex is a work of deferral of the moment of orgasm, by means of techniques that master pleasure toward its increase and development until the moment of pleasure's own cathartic extinction. This approach to what is "preliminary" differs substantially from the way I have been understanding throughout the dynamic of foreplay, where orgasm is not consciously deferred, but is rather an accident in the course of an enduring pleasure, and forepleasure proceeds and survives outside of any mastering of actions or purpose.

Opening up this very metaphor, the actualization of event itself can be considered as an "orgasm," enhanced by techniques of development and deferral: the release of the performance labor, in the encounter with spectators, is conceived in the logic of a climax, following precisely the androcentric model of sexuality according to which the actualization of pleasure corresponds to a subsequent disappearance of the event itself. In the writings of both Schechner and Grotowski of the 1960s, the idea of performance is strongly associated with that of mastering techniques of *preparation* and *actualization*. The event, designated to disappear as a "form" but actualized as purposeful action on the audience's everyday life, marks also a passing between different regimes of leisure and of work, between producers who are "insiders" of a set of techniques, and consumers, "participants" to a ritual, coming together in the "fulfillment of theater".[76]

The Continuity of "Small Time" Production

In contradistinction to this approach, to both notions of preparation and event, the scene of the "stylized amateurs" existed far apart from a regime of "dignified attention," and even less in a condition of "high obedience." It was a theater of no attention to the process, no intention of self-development, and no intention to produce a positive action toward its audience. Neither training nor an extended period of preparation was involved in such theater practice, nor an ethic of organization of time and work. As Phoebe Wray put it, at the Caffe Cino "we workshopped nothing." Indeed, at least until the Showcase Code was established in 1965, at the Caffe Cino and at La MaMa the shows were not "works in progress" or "showcases," but were conceived as full productions. In Michael Smith's words: "though the stage was minute and there was no money for scenery, the productions there were real theatre, fully staged, completely realized. The audience was hip and eager, if often sparse."[77]

The rhythm in which these productions would follow one another in the two coffeehouses was indeed frenetic, and most of the shows had little time for rehearsals.[78] One of the first things I learned from Ellen Stewart, and which I heard her repeating often with pride was: "at La MaMa, we have always put onstage fantastic shows prepared in only three-day rehearsals!"[79] Some of the shows presented in the coffeehouses were, without doubt, weak: they were loosely structured around a script, put on without rehearsals, and sometimes simply improvised. It was also a theater where shows were not clearly identifiable as individual events, not so much because they were not specific units of performances, but because they were often presented in double-bill productions, crowding the weekly programming of the coffeehouses, galleries, and performance spaces at a vertiginous rhythm of production. The double bill featured two one-act plays: the short plays (often less than an hour long) were presented to the audience in a more or less coherent diptych. As Bottoms remarks, the establishment of the one-act play in 1960s Off-Off Broadway playwriting corresponds to a confluence between the strategic use of material conditions of production and a choice of poetics:

> Initially the necessary result of practical considerations, this priorization of short plays had liberated writers from the conventional expectation that they stretch their material over two or three acts to create a "full evening's entertainment"—an expectation that tends necessarily to place emphasis on a play's linear trajectory, in terms of cause-and-effect narrative and developing "themes." By contrast, the one-act form relies less on linear dramatic development than on the presentation of an immediate, theatrical "moment"—staging not so much a story but a *single act*.[80]

Bottoms identifies the emphasis on the one-act form as one of the reasons for the critical neglect of Off-Off Broadway playwriting. He associates this with the fact that "one-act plays have always tended to be underrecognized and underanalyzed, simply because they are rarely produced professionally."[81] In a way, therefore, the one-act form is itself haunted by the specter of amateurism, as an ideal basic unit of "small time" theater.

Indeed, the frenetic amateur theater production produced in the early years of Off-Off Broadway was a distinctive example of "small time" production. The category of "small time" is especially significant when thinking about the vaudeville tradition which flourished in the late nineteenth century in New York, where this expression originated. According to Cullen:

> Originally, the term derived from managers' reports and trade-papers reviews that decreed that an act had the potential for bigger theatres or, alternately, was deemed suitable only for small theatres. Although big-time vaudeville was well-defined—playing two-a-day (one matinee, one evening performance) at reserved seat prices—small time vaudeville was best described as everything else, and everything else varied widely . . . Small time acts were paid less, allowing for lower ticket prices (the entrepreneurs were compensated by the greater number of shows). Small time vaudeville mostly appealed to local neighborhoods, often those of working class or immigrant New Yorkers.[82]

As in the nineteenth-century vaudeville circuit, this small time production functioned as well as a form of "preparation" for a potential professional production. As Brecht describes in great detail, especially the Play-House of the Ridiculous's theater work proceeded almost in a fluid form, although developed through a number of different plays, and it was presented not so much as finished "artworks" but as sketches for collective improvisation, always rewritten, transformed and "camped out" on the stage each evening, with very little previous preparation:

> While in the framework of reference of conventional theatre experience is the individual presentation of "the" play, in this theatre it is the production of the play—the series of presentations, rehearsals, compositions of the script: its making in development defines the individual evening's experience. The composition of the script appears as mere preparation of the *mise-en-scene*, almost incidental. Script and set are essentially by-products of the developing performance, collapsing into the activity of making the play.[83]

Significantly Ronald Tavel, one of the prominent playwrights working with the Play-House and the author of the first two plays directed by Vaccaro in 1965 in the Coda Gallery, clearly specified on the script of *The Life of Juanita Castro*: "This play must never be rehearsed."[84] Tavel had written both the plays that would mark the beginning of Vaccaro's directing of the group that would later become the Play-House of the Ridiculous—*Shower* and *The Life of Juanita*

Castro—as screenplays for Andy Warhol, with whom Tavel had started collaborating as in-house dramatist in Warhol's more recent films (*Kitchen*, *Screen Test I* and *Screen Test II*). *The Life of Juanita Castro*, in fact, exists also as a film, shot by Warhol a few months before Vaccaro's play premiered.

Participating in performances of the Play-House was not a matter of rehearsal, nor of preparation. Crucially, the casual recruitment of Vaccaro's "non-actors" would not follow a course of training, and the time of rehearsal for the shows was minimal. In the recollection of Ruby Lynn Reyner, who would later become a star on the stage of the Play-House, her encounter with Vaccaro coincided with her immediate entrance into the company: "I went to NYC, and on 7th Avenue I met this woman and later we were modeling together, and she said: you have to come, we are rehearsing a play. So I went down to John Vaccaro's loft, I walked into this circus, this world I have always dreamt about, and I walked into the play that very day: it was *The Conquest of the Universe*."[85] The "awful talent" Vaccaro would foresee in actors like Ruby Lynn Reyner, Jackie Curtis, Frank Dudley, and Sierra Bandit (who "could all make a big mark commercially," he still recalls today)[86] was in a sense a matter of immediacy, rather than of preparation: it was a capacity of exposure and improvisation, which in a sense could be compared precisely to what Robert Snyder has called the "synthetic quality" of amateur vaudevillians.[87]

Keeping busy was another form of "hyperproductivity" characterizing this anomalous form of small production. In Vaccaro's terms: "you don't just come and do one play with us, you do a lot. There is no stoppage in doing plays, we keep doing them. We get paid by the amount that we make. There are no contracts: you are free to leave whenever you want."[88] Such frenetic production was a distinctive form of foreplay: a love labor prolonging as an engine of theatrical pleasure. Recalling Brakhage's words, I see in such loitering in performance, in such resistance to giving shape to a "work," a mode of "experiencing the work while working," a private gauging of amateur labor, outside of preestablished standards of achievement. At least, the achievement to be valued here in terms of virtuosity or body technique, neither in the encounter with the audience (as a ritual event in space and time).

In the novel *Temple Slave*, Robert Patrick recounts that initially, most of the performances presented at the Caffe Cino not only lacked recognition in New York show business but also, at least in principle, lacked the attention of an audience. The famous phrase "Play it for the Walls!" attributed to Joe Cino encouraged artists to put on a play in his café even when there were no spectators to attend it. It clearly exemplifies the extent to which the pleasure of performing, in places like Caffe Cino, was accorded a value exceeding immediate "consummation": theater was welcomed in the space outside of a prospective encounter with spectators. Such an encounter, however, was longed for: one of the crucial features of Off-Off Broadway was that it provided the possibility for unknown plays to encounter an audience, constituting as well a tryout for artists who elsewhere had no chance to access means of production for their performances, nor a response to their artistic labor. Not only did the "producers" of these shows—for instance, Ellen Stewart or Joe Cino—invest a sum of money (however low) to provide basic conditions for the shows to take place (at the beginning, little more than the rent for a space, a wooden platform as a stage, and some cheap lighting devices), but the artists themselves contributed to the costs of the performance-making they offered to spectators, by laboring for free. Especially in the early 1960s, most of the venues were operating without an entertainment license, and shows were not widely advertised: the audience would come to know about a show mainly via word of mouth, reading an ad in the listings of the *Village Voice*, or encountering someone distributing leaflets advertising the show on the street, just around the corner from where the performance was going to take place that same evening. At least in premise, therefore, we could imagine that artists were always in the condition of "playing for the walls," or simply for a small group of friends, or for casual spectators who had just happened to pass by with no expectation of entertainment. Somehow by chance, and more frequently as the 1960s proceeded and the downtown scene grew in popularity, audiences of Off-Off Broadway shows also started to feature "professional spectators," that is, critics, and producers who developed an interest in seeing these plays, which were put on stage gratuitously at first, and produced again later in a more legitimate theater venue, and for profit. Furthermore, in the course of the 1960s Off-Off Broadway stages also became increasingly attended by aspiring professional artists, coming out of acting schools but not having the chance to practice their craft in proper theaters, and who were yearning for both theater apprenticeship and a potential access to "big time" production.[89] Regardless of whether a horizon of recognition was later achieved or not, however, in the coffeehouses, apartments, clubs, and social spaces of downtown New York in the 1960s, performance production did take place, and leisurely. As Patrick puts it: "Every bloody week of the year you could come and see experimental theatre we were doing for free. We don't care if anybody pays to see it, we have the right to produce it."[90] Small time production, as it were, was both the claim for the right to produce, and the affirmation that such peculiar production would not depend on the value conferred upon it by a paid consumption. It was a production whose value was, in a sense, bestowed by the pleasure of theater as a "doing."

The Pleasure of Show-Idleness

Hanna's performance described at the opening of the chapter, where she stood enjoying herself on the breeze-hole of the fun house in Coney Island, could be read as a metaphor for the queer temporality of such small time production. To a certain extent, in fact, the fluid form of the theatre pleasure discussed in these pages could be regarded as a dynamic akin to the specific intensities and leisurely rhythms of female sexuality: a dynamic in which foreplay is neither preliminary, nor preparatory, nor subsidiary to orgasm, but is rather a bodily disposition to a multiplicity of orgasms, none of which exercises sovereignty over either the pleasure or the temporality of love-making. As with Hanna's continuing enjoyment, multiplied in her persistent acts of exposure, so also in the small time production of the "stylized amateurs": the enjoyment of "doing" theatre produced a continuing incandescence of events, none of which was "prepared," nor completely disappeared in the fulfillment of an act, none of which constituted the actualization of *work as an event*. Interestingly, the plays staged in this scene of "stylized amateurism" are crowded with flirtatious characters such as Hanna, or ambitious starlets like Noola Noonan in Jackie Curtis's *Glory, Glamour and Gold*, whom we will encounter later on; the prostitute Heaven in Jackie Curtis's *Heaven Grand in Amber Orbit*, which will be the object of the next chapter and whose story is staged, in fact, in a "pleasure house"; or the would-be starlet Mario Montez in *Screen Test*, both Andy Warhol's movie and Vaccaro's show, based on the script of Ronald Tavel.

Considered all together as part of a common theatrical pantheon, these figures—neighboring, courting, alluding to or embodying prostitution as they do in their relation with the exposure and "selling" of their bodies—are key not only as signifiers of an explicit relation to pleasure and self-enjoyment, but also to the camp relation adopted by the plays in question with regard to mainstream show business. The appropriation of tropes, references, music, and performance styles from mainstream and popular culture also corresponded, on the part of the "stylized amateurs," to a significant *détournement* (rerouting) of the very grammar of such theatricality. The domain of show business, described by Off-Broadway and Off-Off Broadway practitioners and critics as characterized by both a dynamic of "selling out" and by "faking, artificiality, and non-authenticity," was joyfully embraced by the stylized amateurs as a framing device for their "inner play" (evoking Perisbinoff's term) recouping along the way the shame of pleasure that meretriciousness entails.

But these references also seem to suggest a significant *détournement* of what Jennifer Doyle has named a certain "rhetoric of prostitution"[91] which has old roots and especially in the 1960s was pervasive in art criticism. It is a discourse expressing an anxiety toward exchange exceeding the domain of theater and performance and which, interestingly, occupies a central role also in the reflections Grotowski developed around the same time, theorizing what the actor's vocation is supposed to be:

> The actor is a man who works in public with his body, offering it publicly. If this body restricts itself to demonstrating what it is—something that an average person can do—then it is not an obedient instrument capable of performing a spiritual act. If it is exploited

> for money and to win the favour of the audience, then the art of acting borders on prostitution. It is a fact that for many centuries the theatre has been associated with prostitution in one sense of the word or another. The words "actress" and "courtesan" were once synonymous. Today they are separated by a somehow clearer line, not through any change in the actor's world but because society has changed. Today it is the difference between the respectable woman and the courtesan which has become blurred.[92]

Grotowski condemns playing for the audience as "flirtation," recommending however that the actor should also escape the pleasure of playing theater for herself, in a narcissistic way, "for the satisfaction of being accepted, loved, affirmed."[93] In fact, his definition of "holy actor" ("a metaphor defining a person who, through his art, climbs upon the stake and performs an act of self-sacrifice")[94] is fashioned precisely in contradistinction to the notion of "courtesan actor": "the difference between the 'courtesan actor' and the 'holy actor' is the same as the difference between the skill of a courtesan and the attitude of giving and receiving which springs from true love."[95]

Grotowski's metaphors postulate a precise body politics, according to which on the one hand the body is supposed to be annihilated in the act of performance, while on the other it must be trained, by means of hard work, to achieve a climax, after which, for performers and spectators, a relief of sort ensues, as in a post-orgasmic state. The contradistinction with the "courtesan" attitude functions to establish a sensual discourse which would eradicate the threat of exchange, and, in the end, remove the body itself from the picture. On closer observation, Grotowski's contempt for the "courtesan artist," and the abstraction of enjoyment from the act of performing, reformulates the cultural anxiety which, at least since the nineteenth century, was widespread in relation to those practices deemed not supposed to be exchanged: among them art, intellectual activity, and sex. As Jennifer Doyle has explained, the development of an art market, in replacing the aristocratic system of patronage, "set in motion a nostalgic longing for a time when the artist's relationship to his work was (or at least appeared to be) less mediated."[96]

Whereas this rhetoric is grounded in the twofold premise according to which the prostitute is the epitome of someone selling pleasure (something not supposed to have a price) and having a passive attitude toward her work (finding no pleasure in it), in the theatre of stylized amateurism the figure of the prostitute appears first of all as a body of pleasure, which interestingly problematizes the very relation of pleasure with the market, as well as with the notion of production all together. I argue that it also points to the intrinsically uneasy position of working for pleasure, outside of labor's recognition as profession (as in amateur work) and having the necessity, the desire, or the fatal destiny of having this pleasure projected toward its potential becoming value in a market. In contradistinction to Grotowski's conception of the "hard work routine" which would sustain the performer in eradicating self-enjoyment and becoming "someone working in public with her body" providing a "service" radically different to that offered in prostitution, the performance work of the "stylized amateurs" took place in conditions of free time, far away from both the *busy-ness* of professional Broadway theater, as well as from the dignified craftsmanship of experimental theater. Such conditions, I suggest, could be considered a specific form of *idleness,* which was at the core of the particular production at stake in such theatre context.

The notion of idleness I am conjuring here refers to something radically different from leisure, insofar as it is not conceived in a dialectical relation with the time regime regulating work in the system of productivity. The particular idleness I am pointing to is the one explored by Walter Benjamin especially in his *Arcades Project.* "Idleness" Benjamin writes, "seeks to avoid any sort of tie with the idler's line of work, and ultimately to the labor process in general. That distinguishes it from leisure."[97] Whereas the very idea of leisure in modernity relies on the organizational demarcations of work-time, Benjamin looks at idleness as an attitude and a praxis of "an unlimited duration, which fundamentally distinguishes it from simple sensuous pleasure of whatever variety."[98] The idea of idleness explored by Benjamin presents itself as characterized by a profound ambivalence. The apparently inoperative labor of the idler, in fact, may well be regarded as perfectly functional to the exploitation process at work in the domain of *busy-ness*, in the context of capitalism where the category of what can be considered "labor" is continuously shifting. In other words, another way to look at idleness could be as the theatrical mask of what, in more recent times, has been called precarious labor, sheer free time offering itself to be appropriated and retrospectively evaluated as such, in an always-adapting capitalist economic system. Benjamin already recognized this process in specific instances of his own culture, as well as in the culture of the late nineteenth century he researched and analyzed in *The Arcades Project.*

Crucially, Benjamin's theorization of idleness goes hand in hand, in *the Arcades Project,* with his interest in a series of figures which, in different ways, prefigured in the Paris of nineteenth century the "fungibility of people and things"[99] which became predominant in mass society in the twentieth century: among them, the flaneur, the sandwichman, and the prostitute. As Susan Buck-Morss has insightfully suggested, all these figures function in Benjamin's investigation as instances of "loitering," trading their "free time" on the marketplace of sociability, standing at the same time as both instances of marginality, in the productivity of industrial capitalism, and embodied examples of attractions in search of a buyer, prototypical of the condition of intellectual work in twentieth-century capitalism. Significantly, however, "while the figure of the flaneur embodies the transformation of perception characteristic of modern subjectivity, the figure of the whore is the allegory for the transformation of objects, the world of things,"[100] in that in her trade she is both the seller and the commodity. Not only, as Doyle suggested, does the prostitute appear in Benjamin's thought as a melancholic allegory of the condition of the artist, but her place of pride as the most prominent female figure in the *Arcades Project* is haunted by the distinctive gendered equivalence Benjamin posits between the female body and the domain of objects: "the image of the whore . . . is the embodiment of objectivity, not subjectivity."[101]

While I am not intending to undermine Benjamin's masculinist deployment of the figure of the prostitute, it is worth observing, however, that the equivalence between bodies and objects also appears elsewhere in Benjamin's later writings as a connection productive of an even deeper understanding of the destiny of workers in capitalism. As Rollerston suggested, especially in the wake of the 1930s economic depression, Benjamin's reflection on the disposability of time and labor under capitalism ends up delineating a substantial equivalence between the figure of the "unemployed" and that of the "discarded commodity": items which are out of use, which no longer bear a commodity status.[102] In a logic according to which the capacity to produce, hence to consume, is crucial to existence itself, the "unemployed" becomes a further figure of "loitering," but one making especially apparent how "free time" that does not coincide with leisure is understood in capitalism as "empty time," a time full of desires for consumption but deprived of the capacity for production which would make possible any form of consumption. As Buck-Morss suggests, in Benjamin

> the gesture of loitering points in two directions. It is a condemnation of capitalism to which exploitative labor and unemployment are intrinsic. But it is also the hellish, negative image within existing society of that which could become positive within a radically different one. It looks to a regime in which cutbacks in labor-time, automated production, and the saturation of markets would be, not the cause of crisis, but the intended, humane result.[103]

In other words, crucial to Benjamin's analysis of the ambiguity of loitering is the simultaneous acknowledgment of idleness as both the disuse to which the unemployed is condemned, which makes her equivalent to a discarded commodity, and the potentiality for the idler to experiment, in this empty time, with a different modality of relation with activity itself. Profoundly connected with the capitalist economic order in which, over time, it flourishes, idleness for Benjamin is also a specific form of engagement with activity. Hence, it is not a condition defined only by the absence of labor, but rather a scenario enabling and temporarily hosting forms of labor—and, I would like to add, forms of production—not yet recognized as proper.[104]

It is precisely in this sense that I regard the theater experiments performed by the "stylized amateurs" of the 1960s New York scene during the time in which they were not, or not yet, employed in the professional entertainment industry, as standing for a distinctive form of *show-idleness*. In this show-idleness, those cast aside, or "discarded" by professional theater would reconfigure amateur theater-making as a space of loitering, of dwelling, of entertaining relations with theater work which exceeded standard notions of efficiency, productivity, and expertise. Benjamin, in fact, already suggested that the distinctive "work preparedness"[105] characterizing idleness could be the precondition for *resisting* proper forms of work in the present, and proposing a different duration for labor itself, outside of a time-oriented sequence in the production process. Furthermore, and queering Benjamin's own formulation, the "work preparedness" of the stylized amateurs performed such resistance precisely by positing pleasure as a productive force of endurance in work, one which reclaimed a crucial place for the body and its sensual experience in both production and consumption, phases significantly coinciding in theater. In this sense, the figure of the prostitute repeatedly appearing in the theatrical pantheon of the scene of foreplay, could be read as a radical allegory of the complex relations at stake in the status of the performer as a worker, so often suspended between the curse of her passion, supposedly sustaining the self-investment of time in unpaid labor, and the paradoxical horizon of redemption entailed in the recognition of the right to be paid in order to perform a service, either conceived as professional entertainment or as a spiritual act. Rather than a figure embodying "a pathology of agency"[106] (someone having a passive attitude towards her own labor praxis and who finds no pleasure in it) the figure of the prostitute appears in this context as winking toward other ways to address the artist's subjectivity, other ways to figure the place of pleasure in the complex scenario of any form of production.

It is useful, then, returning to consider Ridout's research on theater as one of the sites where "passionate amateurs" have experimented, throughout the twentieth century, with alternative modes of temporality which, precisely by virtue of their occupying a space intrinsically in between production and consumption, could figure "some way of undoing, even if only for a moment, the time of [the laborer's] work and the work of time upon herself."[107] Interestingly, not only does Benjamin himself feature in Ridout's constellation of figures,[108] but theater's capacity to open a time-space in which "the present is experienced otherwise"[109] is explored by Ridout precisely in its uneasy utopian dimension: one experienced by both performers and spectators as a possibility glimpsed in theater's time to figure a future temporality of liberated work, from within a capitalist productive system which seems to intrinsically negate this very possibility. This utopian dimension is similar to the queer futurity explored by José Muñoz as a force of potentiality at work in instances of queer art produced in the 1960s, and projected toward a future of otherworldliness: a future in which the "not yet" of life possibilities is nurtured precisely by the failure of past experiences to conform with the demands, norms, and productivity predicated by the present.

Interestingly, thinking Ridout's and Muñoz's research alongside each other offers especially useful insights for the reading of the work of one particular artist active in the scene of stylized amateurism, an artist who, not by chance, has been central to Muñoz's reflection on the utopian possibility of queer futurity: Jack Smith. Furthermore, Benjamin's own poetic and theoretical inquiry into the early forms of capitalism deposited in the imagery of nineteenth-century Paris provides images which resonate strikingly in Smith's artistic work, whose multifaceted development through film, photography, performance, and writing can be itself considered a distinctive form of poetic and theoretical inquiry into the workings of capitalism. Keeping the echoes of all these voices, in what follows I shall look at the way Jack Smith's work (or more precisely: at the way it was received, *consumed*, by his contemporary spectators) was an exemplary form of *show-idleness*: an attitude to theater-making capable of enacting an alternative temporality, one capable of resisting its always already forthcoming incorporation into capitalist production.

Toward an Idle Theater: Jack Smith and the Absence of Hurry

Jack Smith's artistic work developed from the mid-1950s in a multiplicity of forms: starting as a photographer, and as a performer in underground films such as Ken Jacobs's *Saturday Afternoon Blood Sacrifice* and *Little Cobra Dance* (1956), *Little Stabs at Happiness* (1958–63), and *Blonde Cobra* (1959–63), he was the author of the legendary and controversial film *Flaming Creatures* (1962–63) as well as of a number of other films (including *Normal Love*) which were often screened during the artist's lifetime in different versions, but never presented as finished artworks. He also features in the film work of Andy Warhol (for instance, he starred in *Camp,* 1965), whose work Smith clearly influenced and with whom he entertained throughout a complicated relation, which included a failed collaboration around the never-finished film project *Batman/Dracula* (1964). As performer, Smith participated in theater plays by a number of artists, such as John Vaccaro, Charles Ludlam, Robert Wilson, and he collaborated as costume and set designer for various theater productions of the Play-House of the Ridiculous. Throughout his life, Smith has also realized numerous performance pieces, such as *Rehearsal for the Destruction of Atlantis: A Dream Weapon Ritual* (1965), *Brassieres of Atlantis* (1969), *Gas Stations of the Cross Religious Spectacle* (1970), *Withdrawal from Orchid Lagoon* (1970), and *Claptailism of Palmola Christmas Spectacle* (1970–71), to name just a few of his early works. Most of these performances were presented, at the turn of the 1970s, in Jack Smith's home, a loft he used to call "the Plaster Foundation."[110]

Smith's multifaceted artistic production has been documented and discussed, in the last decades, by a number of writers,[111] and most recently and thoroughly in Dominic Johnson's book *Glorious Catastrophe: Jack Smith, Performance and Visual Culture*.[112] It is not the intention of these pages to replicate these important scholarly efforts, nor to provide an account of Smith's performance work in its specificity. Rather, I shall advance some reflections on the particular temporality of Smith's performance work from the late 1960s and early 1970s in light of the line of thinking so far outlined, and in specific relation to the idea of foreplay. I shall do so by relying on the accounts of a few spectators and their responses to Smith's performance work, in the attempt to glimpse, through their reports, features of the particular consumption which Smith's show-idleness seemed to summon: a consumption which, in a sense, resembled the performance production witnessed to.

It is important to introduce these reflections by emphasizing how the idea of capitalism, and the struggle against the social and symbolic system named capitalism, occupies a central place in Smith's imagery, or to be more precise, in Smith's phantasmagoria. Capitalism appears in Smith's work translated into the terms of a highly evocative fantasy world, and in the space of this world this concept finds its most powerful incarnation in the notion of "landlordism." Described as "the central social evil of our time,"[113] landlordism was understood by Smith as the diabolic principle of rent-paying, enslaving humanity by means of the seemingly inescapable demand to have to pay to occupy a space in the world. The phenomenon of landlordism is characterized in Smith's rant as the interminable and seemingly illogical event of "pay[ing] the rent that can never be paid," as a correlative to the museological practice of flattening differences between works to strip them of their critical capacity.[114]

Smith's contempt for landlordism, in fact, was deeply related to his problematic relation with the art establishment, and more precisely with the internal dynamic of valorization and incorporation it embodied. The struggle against landlordism, in its various incarnations, informed almost the entirety of the artist's creative invention, which might be regarded as a quixotic attempt to build an alternative reality to what he called "the rented world." In the face of the domain of space, colonized by the capitalist diktat of property, Smith's artistic practice sought to construct this alternative reality by remaking time.

Most reports describing the experience of witnessing Smith's performances describe a distinctive temporality, characterized not only by an incredible slowness in movement and speech, but moreover by the fact that such slowness did not correspond to meticulousness or precision, but rather to "the continual (and somewhat calculated) going wrong of every performance."[115] Johnson discusses this sensation of continual failure, in Smith's work, in the accomplishment of theatrical tasks, as well as in the management of his own artistic career, as a distinctively queer experiment in excess: as the refusal or impossibility of and disgust at the idea of complying with the skills normally required of a theater-maker, and the urge to exceed a manageable set of creative possibilities. This relation with failure was also connected with Smith's unabashed appreciation of icons of "bad acting" such as Maria Montez, whose reputation as "the World's Worst Actress"[116] became in Smith's phantasmagoria the epitome of the world's own failure to recognize "magic."[117]

In contradistinction with the 1960s experimental theater practiced and theorized by Schechner and Grotowski, Smith's performance practice refused the idea of training, as well as the development of theater as technique. Furthermore, his theatre refused the very idea of performance as "event": in the extended duration of Smith's performances, often extending well into the night and having no clearly identified points of beginning and end, the eventfulness of performance dissolved in the unraveling of performing as an experience that would never culminate in a climax.

In *Queer Theatre*, Stefan Brecht writes about Smith's midnight series of performances in his loft on Mercer Street, involving an extremely slow and protracted setting-up of a scene which continued into the early morning. The preparation of the scene was actually the show itself, which would end, simply, with the completion of the preparation. That is, the idle anticipation was the point, and the spectacle of the completed preparation (an enormous accumulation of junk in a massive pile in the center of the stage) was the *end*—although this end was not presented to spectators in its final form, nor as the point of the piece, although the effort of performing such completion would seem to be of enormous importance for Smith, while performing. Brecht describes friends/spectators entering the room, passing by, falling asleep on the sofa, helping Smith organize the huge heap of junk at the center of the scene—as a sort of *rag picker*, a figure so dear to Walter Benjamin and very prominent in the the *Arcades Project*, committed to the collection of traces of everything that is disregarded by history, and by the modern city. Interestingly, in Smith's text *Capitalism of Lotusland*, the reuse of what Benjamin would have named "discarded commodities" is evoked by Smith with a powerful image: the utopian "Free Paradise of abandoned objects,"[118] where commodities which have lost their sway, and are considered trash, would form a precarious sort of architecture in the middle of the city. It is almost inevitable to recognize such an image glittering in the junkpile which Brecht described being slowly constructed (and constantly unmade, at the same time) during Smith's performance. Brecht describes friends and spectators chatting among themselves and smoking marijuana during the performance. He recalls himself falling asleep, smoking, helping Smith organize the junkpile, finding himself part of an enchantment within a *longue-durée* (long lasting) labor of desire sustaining a performance which was constantly denying itself, or deferring itself, as an event—but which could be encountered in precise moments of attraction, in striking images glimpsed from the chaos of rejected and discarded images. The sort of production/consumption emerging from Brecht's writing is one that allows Smith's labor to *become* itself, but to do so in an absolute absence of hurry:

> Sleepiness, boredom—in the case of many [spectators] probably irritation or anger—alternate with mild hilarity and a trancelike appreciation of the beauty of the form of time displayed as object—this last feeling strengthening in intensity as this object is progressively constituted. The only real feeling of objection that I have noticed in myself might be put: why the fuck am I not fucking instead?[119]

An insight into the particular "unhurry" which emerges from Brecht's description of Smith's performance is offered again by Walter Benjamin, in some notes not included in the *Arcades Project* despite being composed during roughly the same period: the writings documenting his experiences with hashish and mescaline. In one of those texts, Benjamin notes down some reflections on the verb *Säumen*, literally meaning to linger on, to loiter, to dawdle, and connected by Benjamin to a specific attitude in children's activity. The best part of children's happiness, Benjamin writes, is its *Saumseligkeit*, that is: an *absolute absence of hurry*.[120] This peculiar attitude to time, which Benjamin describes as a sort of unraveling of experience, is considered as proper to childhood insofar as the latter can be regarded as a life period not directly embedded in the time regime of adult productivity—even if it is projected toward it in a developmental conception of life. This peculiar sense of time, however, can also be compared to the temporality at stake in certain acts of lovemaking: an absolute absence of hurry, in fact, can characterize the enjoyment of gestures which are both implicated in, but yet somehow also avoid, the teleology of a merely productive desire. In a sense, it can be compared to the temporality of foreplay, understood as a labor of pleasure not rushing toward an accomplishment, not consciously deferring a climax, but rather multiplying itself toward a multiplicity of articulations, enduring beyond the recognition of a climax of pleasure. It is in this sense, perhaps, that we can regard Brecht's comment on Smith's performance, interestingly conjuring the author's sexual desire (the possibility of fucking, rather than witnessing Smith's performance) as the only possible desirable alternative to the peculiar condition and time perception experienced during this performance.

Considering the widespread consumption of drugs that circulated around the theatre of "stylized amateurism" and often referred to especially in connection with Smith's work,[121] the reference to Benjamin's notes on hashish and to the particular "absence of hurry" that this substance induces in time perception appears quite suitable. And it helps in clarifying further, in fact, the potential which Benjamin recognized in idleness: the potential (echoing Ridout's terms) to "experience the present otherwise," entailing as well the capacity to conceive the work and its temporality otherwise. It is relevant, in this respect, that Benjamin's notes on his own experience with drugs also functioned for the philosopher as instruments to learn how to reproduce, without the assistance of drugs (hence, in the future that would follow each experiment) a peculiar modality of thinking and apprehension, as well as a relation with the labor of writing, experienced by Benjamin in his induced states of intoxication: a condition of nonfunctioning pregnant with "*profane illumination*, materialist, anthropological inspiration."[122] Significantly, one of the powerful "lessons"[123] which Benjamin notes having learned from his experience with hashish has to do with a peculiar relation between creation and temporality, which he summarizes with the powerful image of Ariadne's thread:

> What joy in the mere act of unrolling a ball of thread! And this joy is very deeply related to the joy of intoxication, just as it is to the joy of creation. We go forward; but in so doing, we not only discover the twists and turns of the cave into which we're venturing, but also enjoy this pleasure of discovery against the background of the other, rhythmic bliss of unwinding the thread. The certainty of unrolling artfully wound skein—isn't that the joy of all productivity, at least in prose?[124]

What emerges from this metaphor is a distinctive quality of doing, translated into a longing for a temporality of creation proceeding on the one hand unconstrained by the horizon of finality, and on the other nurtured by its own continuous "twists and turns." Just as significant is that such a joy of doing, which Benjamin directly relates to his own work as a writer, is defined as "productivity."

Returning to consider Smith's unhurry in light of these thoughts allows a recognition of his theater-making as a peculiar form of "unrolling an artfully wound skein," a peculiar "joy of productivity." Such productivity, enabled precisely by the state of idleness in which creation took place, denied the normative requirements that productivity would imply, in its standard understanding as a crafting of skills and techniques toward a given purpose. Smith's "theatre of the bored body"[125] was an intoxication of progressive time, an alteration of time perception which was productive of a specific form of "profane illumination" for those spectators called upon to complete, through their act of consumption, Smith's peculiar form of production.

Such productivity, as in Benjamin's metaphor of Ariadne's thread, had to do with creating the conditions for the consumer to experience in the space of theater precisely this "rhythmic bliss of unwinding the thread," and to imagine that this alternative temporality could perform a traction upon future time, a traction from within the seeming inescapability of capitalist time. Richard Foreman's recollection of his experience as a spectator of Smith's performances describes quite precisely this radical deflection from normal time, and the entrance, for spectators and performers alike, into a common and alternative rhythm:

> The great slowness informed by a feeling that "everything was going wrong," . . . made it hard for the audience to remember what was happening at the same time that it was fascinated by what was, indeed, happening in a time rhythm that both spectator and performer were experiencing in sync.[126]

On the other hand, as Jonas Mekas reports, while perceiving such alternative rhythms, while being intoxicated by Smith's show-idleness, spectators also had the constant feeling that the performance being unwound before them was something longer, larger than the narrow space of theater production, the sense that it was something going on anyway, beyond their presence, in Smith's phantasmagoric private life:

> Jack didn't need any audience, he would do it anyway, and I had a feeling that he did it anyway, many nights like this, many Saturdays, by himself, audience or not audience, actors or non actors, he reenacted his ceremony, the last man who was still around and above it all and not part of it but at the same time conscious of it all, very painfully conscious of it all.[127]

Mekas's feeling, of course, interests me beyond his plausibility; the image of Smith "playing for the walls" (recalling Joe Cino's invitation to the artists playing in his coffee-theater) is, however, a powerful image of the amateur as described by Brakhage, as someone "forever learning and growing thru his work into all his living 'clumsiness' of continual discovery,"[128] and gauging the work's value beyond the measures and recognition of public life. Smith's stylized, "passionate" amateurism, along with his mobilization of private life as a different habitat of artistic creation, was far from a privileged escape, far from a leisurely pastime: it was a force of idleness "around and above" capitalism and "not part of it but at the same time conscious of it all, very painfully conscious of it all."[129] It was from the deep cave of such a painful consciousness that the force of idleness could perform its temporary intoxication of temporality, projecting itself, as in Benjamin's experiments with hashish, into the afterlife of the theater experiment, as a sensation of time to be learned from, as a horizon of work to be imagined (echoing Muñoz's formulation) as potentiality, even if not yet experienced as possibility.

I propose to call Smith's theater production, as consumed by Brecht, Foreman, and Mekas as much as by the other spectators who had the privilege to witness this labor—an *idle theater*, insofar as it proceeds with the prospect of an unlimited duration, even if it is projected toward meeting the attention of specific consumers, who did in fact confer upon it a peculiar use value: the critical "appreciation of the beauty of the form of time displayed as object."[130] These consumers were called upon to mobilize their own pleasure so as to sustain their act of witnessing. Borrowing a term proposed by Joe Kelleher, the consumers of Smith's amateur theater might be considered as "latecomer spectators," spectators who had "to crawl to encounter the image, and crawl over the representation in a way that's not going to be comfortable in any sense of the word."[131] Latecomer spectators, in a sense, are consumers who also defer the accomplishment of their attention, along with the pleasure at stake in their participation—as a labor of persistence that seems itself mimetic of the precarious condition in which this theater labor took place, beyond and above the incorporation which Smith feared and against which he struggled in his lifetime in "the rented world." Latecomer spectators, in a sense, are all of us here, still "around and above" capitalism, imagining ways to alterate time, and imagining the alteration of a time we did not experience, the uneventfulness of a performance which never quite had a beginning, and perhaps will therefore never quite have an end.

Chapter 2

✦

A Coney Island of the Mind

Toward a Genealogy of Leisure Performance

The penny candystore beyond the El, is where I first fell in love with unreality.

—Lawrence Ferlinghetti, "A Coney Island of the Mind"

There is the sea! Who shall exhaust the sea?

—Classie Gravesend in *Heaven Grand in Amber Orbit*

Heaven Grand in Amber Orbit

I was not surprised to hear John Vaccaro, when asked which was his favorite play among the many he directed for the Play-House of the Ridiculous, answering me with *Heaven Grand in Amber Orbit.* Written by Jackie Curtis and presented for the first time in New York in autumn 1969 at the Gotham Arts Center (45 W. 43rd Street), and later at La MaMa in February 1970, the play was also taken on tour in France, Belgium, and the Netherlands, and subsequently had another successful revival at La MaMa in 1976.[1] I was not surprised because I consider this play a sort of manifesto of the particular theatrical fascination that characterized the productions of the Play-House of the Ridiculous from their beginning in the mid-1960s with plays such as *Shower* (1965), *The Life of Lady Godiva* (1966), and *The Conquest of the Universe* (1967), when Vaccaro worked in close collaboration with Ronald Tavel, Jack Smith, and Charles Ludlam, to later productions such as *The Moke-Eater* (1969), *Nightclub* (1970), *The Magic Show of Dr. Magico* (1973) by Kenneth Bernard, and *Cockstrong* (1969) written by Tim Murrin.[2] To be more precise: the production of *Heaven Grand* seems to me to be distinctively Vaccaro's/Curtis's brainchild; and yet its phantasmagoric carousel conveys recurring obsessions, figures, and procedures which could also be observed, in embryo or in further articulations, in other performances, as if sharing a common theatrical grammar. As Dick Brukenfeld put it, *Heaven Grand* is "Ridiculous at its best."[3] Reviewed internationally in newspapers such as *Le Monde*, *Le Figaro*, *Newsweek,* and the *New York Times*,[4] *Heaven Grand in Amber Orbit* also condenses in a nutshell the deep tribute that Vaccaro's theater paid to the queer, disenfranchised, and amusing past of American fairground spectacle. The show mobilizes the figure of the freak in a number of directions, troubling any comforting distinction between deviance and normality, mirrored in the relation between performers and the audience, and it does so first of all by queering the standard conditions of the freak show as a genre.

Vaccaro recalled when I spoke with him in 2014, as he had done before in our conversations, that Jackie Curtis started writing *Heaven Grand* on the train, while the whole company was traveling to South Bend, Indiana, to take part in the Obscenity Festival hosted by the University of Notre Dame. And that day was the first time—or so Vaccaro's recollection goes—that Curtis showed up in public in female drag.[5] All the names of the characters chosen by Curtis for this play, starting with the eponymous heroine Heaven Grand (a role performed to great acclaim by Ruby Lynn Reyner, but possibly written by Curtis in the hope of performing it in his own drag persona)[6] were names of racehorses, listed in the sports column of the newspaper Curtis was browsing on the train: Rhumba Line Sam, Ninga Flinga Dung, Lady Galaxy, Nightcloud, Crystal Palace, Madcap Betty, and Terra Rubra, to name just a few. The play, written following that first inspiration, was to present the heights of an acid trip: during the completion of the script, Curtis had taken acid every three days for three months, and attempted to convey his state of alteration into the composition of the material. The result was a script devoid of any sequential logic, crowded with characters sketched in bright colors, somehow suspended between the domain of fairy tales and that of nightmares: a troupe "dressed in carnival clothes, dressed as freaks, idiots, cripples"[7] wandering over the script and "each going in his own direction."[8]

The loose plot of *Heaven Grand* is a horror story: set in a bordello, the play pivots around actions of childish violence perpetrated by the colorful characters on the protagonist, Heaven Grand, the "star" of the pleasure house managed by Lady Galaxy, who finally (well, a "final" moment which lasts at least half of the play) dies of syphilis, sacrificing her life for the sake of her beloved Nightcloud. In a sense, as one review pointed out, "*Heaven* could have billed itself as a musical version of the great film *Freaks* and gotten away with it."[9] As in Tod Browning's movie, in the play the whole point of the theatrical plot is heading toward the reproduction of the freak body: the mutilation of Heaven Grand's beauty through collective sexual abuse, humiliation, and contempt. As we shall see, however, as in Tod Browning's movie, the whole point of the exposure of the freaks, in Vaccaro's play, is also to display a collective body of pleasure and its excess.

Throughout Curtis's script, the characters repeat obsessively the same lines, mostly quotes (ranging from old Hollywood movies and comic books to Aeschylus's *Agamennon*),[10] interpolated with inventive sexual innuendo, and with several songs, to be performed while dancing in individual numbers and in a chorus.[11] Curtis's script specifies that the action should start with "carnival music"[12] and be inaugurated with a prologue, which features a "henchman," Classie Gravesend, and a "mad menace," The Rouge Frolic (a character that in the second run of the play, in 1976, was played by Curtis himself)[13] loudly addressing the public on entering with the line: "There is the sea! Who shall exhaust the sea?,"[14] suggesting that the action is taking place somewhere on the waterfront—we could imagine it, for example, as taking place in Coney Island. (See figures 4, 5, 6, and 7.)

Furthermore, in this prelude the two characters also cast a spell of sorts on the show that they inaugurate: they have a magic word for it, proclaiming the beginning of the exceptional time of their performance with the formula: "Fascination!!!"[15] This is the sentence that The Rouge Frolic would go on to shout almost every time he entered the stage, accompanied by another characteristic gesture: throwing red glitter at the other performers, and at the audience. Perhaps I could also say: every time *she* enters the space. In Vaccaro's production, in fact, The Rouge Frolic shares with all characters of *Heaven Grand in Amber Orbit* an appearance of androgyneity which makes it impossible to regard them in terms of any gender distinctions whatsoever. Just as in the films and performances of Jack Smith (an "incredible influence"[16] on Vaccaro's work), the characters of *Heaven Grand* are "creatures" of desire, existing beyond any gender identity in a queer phantasmagoria.[17] (See figures 8 and 9.)

John Vaccaro smiled when thinking back about this particular play, which—he said—he "immediately turned into a sideshow. It reminded me of the sideshows where my father used to bring me during my childhood in Ohio, even before I visited Coney Island for the first time, and then again in Coney Island, when they were almost disappearing."[18] For one, *Heaven Grand* brings back sideshow to its traditional spectatorial setting: it is organized through the chaotic appearance of short performances which happen simultaneously, literally side by side, without any narrative logic, as "a sequence of non-sequiturs."[19] In an interview about the show, Vaccaro explained that his interest, in theater, was "to break focus—something constantly going on, somewhere, all the time. I want the audience presented with the opportunity to choose. If they missed something, they haven't missed anything. THEY CHOSE. . . . Not lines, but there is SOUND, constantly."[20]

Very much like in the saloons, fairgrounds, and early vaudeville theaters in the New York Bowery area at the turn of the century, or in the amusement parks of Coney Island, the performances of the Play-House of the Ridiculous would go on as a carnival of activities, and the audience was confronted with a multiplicity of "attractions" rather than with a unique climax of event.[21]

The experience of the show, in this context, was part of the night out of an individual, who, in some respects, couldn't even be called "a spectator": the spectacles on the stage of places like the Miner Bowery Theatre, or Steeplechase and Luna Park, were part of the experience of hanging out at a given venue and witnessing performance acts similar to walking through a museum or attending a parade.[22] Accordingly, attention was not granted in advance by the audience, and "showtime" was an expanded period available for potential theater encounters with attractions in a leisure atmosphere.

A Counter-Laboratory for Queer Pleasure and Performance

This chapter proposes to read *Heaven Grand in Amber Orbit*, and more generally the theater of John Vaccaro's Play-House of the Ridiculous, against the background of a universe of references, images, and quotes drawn from turn-of-the-century American fairground amusements. This play can be considered in a constellation with other works from the 1960s underground scene which in different ways carries on a specific urban tradition of New York popular entertainment, one which materially took place in Coney Island and on the Bowery, in the golden age of popular entertainment, but resurfaced in Manhattan in the 1960s on the stages, texts, and films of a specific artistic circuit.

While browsing archival remains of the 1960s and 1970s New York Off-Off Broadway theater, I have often encountered such urban "tradition": for instance, posters and pictures from the show feature explicit visual references to the world of early vaudeville, sideshows, and burlesque of the kind which was distinctive of turn-of-the century Coney Island. (See figure 9.) I am thinking, for example, about Tom Eyen's play *Why Hanna's Skirt Won't Stay Down* discussed in the previous chapter, in which the imagery of Coney Island pop up, functioning as a familiar repertoire for both performers and spectators, as a magic lantern to conjure a forgotten time of performance.

Such tradition seems to be kindred to the Coney Island evoked by Lawrence Ferlinghetti in the title of his 1958 collection of poems, which I borrow for this chapter: *A Coney Island of the Mind*. An expression which, on his part, Ferlinghetti had borrowed from Henry Miller's text *Into the Night Life* (1947), subsequently published as part of *Black Spring*.[23] An expression which might be suitable, as well, for Djuna Barnes's suggestive reportages of Coney Island in the 1910s.[24] All these authors reference Coney Island as a landmark of New York carnival life, and also as a fantasy repository for enchanting forms of nocturnal sociability. They look at Coney Island as an experience of bizarre pleasure and—to borrow Ferlinghetti's own terms—"unreality."[25]

The Coney Island described by Barnes and Miller had transformed but not yet disappeared at the time of Ferlinghetti's poems, at the end of the 1960s. It was agonizing, in terms of productive economy, in that its leisure structures—the amusement parks, the fairground facilities—were no longer having their sway in New York's productive economy, had fallen out of fashion and had become regarded as obsolete. But the persistence of its image in the performance culture of the 1960s brought forth specific resonances. Taking cues from this "Coney Island of the mind," surfacing out of works composed long after the turn of the century, I am interested to ask: what is entailed in the survival of images from turn-of-the-century fairground amusement in works such as *Heaven Grand in Amber Orbit*? What sort of temporality does this particular performance culture bring about? What does the deployment of forms such as sideshows, vaudeville, and one-act plays in the 1960s New York scene add to the reflection on pleasure, *show-idleness*, and unproductivity articulated so far?

Whereas in the previous chapter I discussed the centrality of the "workshop" in avant-garde and ensemble-based groups in 1960s New York (and their forebears in theater history), here I shall consider Coney Island as a counter-laboratory for images, behaviors, and temporality "re-performed"[26] in the 1960s queer theater, of which the Play-House of the Ridiculous stands as a definitive example. Coney Island is taken here as the icon of such a leisure performance scene, but also stands for a broader set of entertainment forms which flourished in turn-of-the-century New York, such as the array of spectacular activities enacted in the downtown Manhattan area known as the Bowery. What I call "a Coney Island of the mind" is a particular theatrical attitude that returns, on the stages of the Play-House of the Ridiculous, not only as a "repertoire"[27] but as a counter-laboratory for queer pleasure, visual imagery, and temporality, *dragging itself* onto another scene, the 1960s, which is by now itself history. Also in this case, there is at stake a technology of theater, although not systematized in a method or in a tradition, neither transmitted nor recognized as such. In this return, I see not a traditional lineage of genealogy, but rather a movement of *becoming*: a becoming of bodily engagements, images, and forms of exposure. This return is a becoming turned backwards: a "becoming Coney Island," so to say, performed in the 1960s scene, rather than a *development* of that scene into 1960s downtown Manhattan. This becoming is not synonymous with evolution, nor does it inhabit a progressive conception of history. Like foreplay, it is a becoming which does not aim at a certain accomplishment, but rather a movement of pleasure prolonging itself over time. To say with Deleuze and Guattari, in this becoming I do not look for resemblances, but for cross-temporal forms of "alliance";[28] I do not envision a filiation, but recognize a foreplay held in common with performance-making, and a queer mode of being together in performance.

Crucially, this peculiar becoming does not inhabit a history of performance *work* (such as the one accounted for in theater history, tracing the subsequent developments of performance as a craft) but rather a history of *leisure*. What I am suggesting is *a genealogy of leisure* in New York performance history, a narrative in which a condition of leisure, rather than one of committed work, has enabled peculiar modalities of performance labor to take place, in different historical phases, circumstances, and locations on the New York map. This labor was indeed "work" for the performers who made the material history of fairground amusement such as those of turn-of-the-century Coney Island, but has not always been considered as such in theater history. I am thinking about the exposure of performers in freak shows, about the "attractions" in the amusement parks, and about the community permanently inhabiting the phantasmagoria of leisure of Coney Island, including those spectators and tourists taking part in Coney Island's ongoing performance. I am also thinking about vaudeville performers performing for a cash prize in the amateur nights of the late nineteenth-century Bowery area.[29]

In conjuring the "Coney Island of the mind" of 1960s New York, I explore the politics of use at stake in this particular performance repertoire: one passing first of all through a precise mobilization of disparaging attributes, which in one way or another have characterized the performance culture of Coney Island. In the next section, I shall examine these attributes and the context of their employment in the 1960s, trying to follow their stratified cultural history. Later on, I shall return to *Heaven Grand in Amber Orbit*, where this nonlinear genealogy of anomalous practices of performance-making is literally dragged on in a ferocious and cheerful enactment, as a forgotten tradition starring in the firmament of another leisure scene. In *Heaven Grand in Amber Orbit*, such disparaging attributes are not advocated in an explicit political agenda, but are mobilized within a technology of theater which functions, however, as a phantasmagorical political critique. Finally, the last part of the chapter and the following interlude will cast the spotlight on two of the actresses who have performed in *Heaven Grand in Amber Orbit*: Ruby Lynn Reyner and Penny Arcade, following them both, as it were, until the landscape of the future. I shall focus in particular on some threads related to the life stories and work of the two women (who, in different ways and for different reasons, have rarely occupied a central place in scholarly discussion of the 1960s queer theater) which in my view can be seen in a peculiar continuity with the counter-laboratory of queer pleasure and performance experimented with, and in a sense embodied by, the Play-House of the Ridiculous's *Heaven Grand in Amber Orbit*.

Amateur, Freak, Queer: Appropriating Disparagement

I have already pointed out how the definition of "amateur" has been historically detached from its etymological relation to the notion of love, and has progressively acquired a disparaging sense, marking amateur activities as superfluous and immature versions of labor praxis done professionally. I have also discussed how the figure of the "amateur" has been recouped and reappropriated in the 1960s New York tradition in a specific sense, and through a distinctive form of stylization. Here, it is important to emphasize also the association of amateur theater with a particular New York institution: the late nineteenth-century amateur night, which emerged in the Bowery vaudeville culture, and where aspiring vaudevillians were competing for a cash price and, if failing to entertain, were dragged offstage by the impresario, and rejected into the underclass of unemployment.[30]

The second category of disparagement productively appropriated by the "stylized amateurs" was the term "freak," historically associated with the praxis of exhibiting human oddities and—borrowing Garland Thomson's expression—"extraordinary bodies"[31] in fairs, traveling circuses, and permanent amusement installments in or close by the metropolis. This praxis was grounded in the self-exploitation of performers offering their labor of appearance for a paying audience, and in the exploitation of this labor on the part of impresarios, who would organize and display these performances of exposure to amuse the public.[32] The decades leading to the 1960s marked the decay of the "freak show" as a spectacular genre,[33] also due to the ethical campaigns against the exploitation for profit of the mentally and physically ill, as well as of racialized bodies and sexual curiosities (such as transvestites, hermaphrodites, bearded women, and the like). By the 1960s, the term "freak" was inevitably related to a history of shame: the shameful past of American performing art history, its original sin. Hence, the term had acquired a derogatory sense, pointing to an abnormality which was perceived, now, as *obscene* (no longer welcomed on the scene),[34] as well as to the memory of an entertainment form that had been removed from the public sphere of American amusement.

The use of the term "freak" was also dismissed in the 1960s as a signifier of physical and mental anomalies in medicine, science, and common language. As Leslie Fiedler points out,[35] in the 1960s

> the name "freak" was being rejected by the kind of physiologically deviant humans to whom it has traditionally been applied. . . . Meanwhile, the name Freak that they abandoned [was] being claimed as an honorific title by the kind of physiologically normal but dissident people who use hallucinogenic drugs and are otherwise known as "hippies," "long hair," and "heads."[36]

The resurfacing of turn-of-the-century sideshow culture in the scene of foreplay participates in that process through which, in the course of the 1960s, the term "freak" underwent a reevaluation in language and collective imagery, significantly operating a *détournement* on the supposed "original" meaning of this word, as well as on the derogatory use it had acquired precisely due to such origin. As Fiedler explains, although the use of the term can be traced back to very old times, and is linked specifically to turn-of-the-century American entertainment, in the 1960s it returned to occupy a central position in society and language, especially in the youth counterculture. Fiedler suggests that this was also an effect of the widespread consumption, among the young people, of certain products of mass culture. Both in E.C. Comics horror comics (accused by Frederic Wertham of "seducing the innocents")[37] and in the underground press,[38] since the late 1950s there had started to proliferate peculiar, anomalous, and wondrous bodies, quoting more or less explicitly the iconography of the turn-of-the-century freak show. At the same time, the image of the freak was mobilized in the 1960s counterculture as an "antithesis of normality,"[39] and transformed from "a brand of misfortune and suffering to a mode of affirmative self-identification"[40] against law and societal convention postulating norms on sexuality and social behaviors. Claiming back the word "freak" for its own purposes, the counterculture would position itself outside of the domain of normality, praising deviance and extraordinariness against formal societal obligations. In the 1960s, the word "freak" started identifying both a condition and a series of activities, becoming "an active verb"[41] employed to challenge a standard judgment about induced states of alteration, such as drug-taking, and also participating in subcultural communities.[42] The term also appears prominently in the writings of two of the prophets of the "psychedelic revolution," Jerry Rubin and Abbie Hoffman; it appears as well in Andy Warhol's 1960s diaries to refer to a group of Factory regulars who made large use of amphetamines, referred to by Warhol as "speed freaks" (such as Ondine or Brigid Berlin aka Brigid Polk).[43] In the same period, the term "freak" also entered the jargon of rock music (famously as the title of Frank Zappa and The Mothers of Invention's 1967 album *Freak Out*) as well as the domain of fashion and style.

This countercultural recouping of the word "freak," Fiedler points out, was immediately valorized in a series of books written in the early 1970s by authors defined by Fiedler as "apologists of the cultural revolution,"[44] in the attempt to support an awareness of the counterculture's difference from mainstream values and its marking of a radical break from the past of American culture *tout court*. Fiedler's study stages itself as somewhat skeptical regarding the political relevance of such countercultural appropriation (going so far as to express rather misogynist reproaches, especially against feminist appropriations of the figure of the "freak" in the struggle over body politics). As Rachel Adams points out, however, Fiedler's study shares the countercultural tendency to substantially reinscribe the concept of freak in fixed categories in which "deviance," "abnormality," "marginality," and "excess" are affirmed as "essential attributes" and less as matters of agency. Fiedler's psychoanalytical reading of the freak show as display of the radical "Other" nostalgically reinserts the author's childhood memories in an irremediable past of American culture, a period which hosted performance praxis functional to a society capable of confronting its own traumatic forms of identification. In the case of the counterculture, the claiming of the freak as a metaphor of radical "Otherness" was likewise detached from a more rigorous consideration of the social stigma which has historically supported the practice of displaying "otherness" in the American spectacular tradition, hence overlooking the complexity of the freak show phenomenon and reducing the figure of the freak to little more than an imprecise signifier. As Adams puts it:

> In the 1960s, the term "freak" acquired meanings as contradictory as the counterculture itself. Identifying oneself as a countercultural freak could be both a serious quest for alternatives to the conformity of the dominant culture and a gesture of self-indulgence. . . . Despite the professed radicalism of the countercultural freaks, they often failed to introduce progressive solutions to the social order they condemned while remaining ignorant of the contradictions of their own attitudes.[45]

Adams goes on to point out that some of these "countercultural freaks" also mimetically reproduced standard behaviors in terms of gender relations, unfair division of labor, as well as a large exploitation of the gratuitous labor of reproduction that made the countercultural "scene." There is, however, another kind of cultural appropriation of the term "freak" which started taking place at the same time within that very counterculture that had grown up consuming comic books and psychedelic drugs. It is a cultural appropriation that participated in such consumption, and also passed through a specific form of movie consumption. As Rosenbaum and Hobermann point out,[46] Tod Browning's 1933 movie *Freaks* achieved in the 1960s a cult status on the same circuit of "midnight movies" where films of Jack Smith, Andy Warhol, and John Waters first circulated.[47] Shot with a cast of performers who, in the early 1930s, were still employed in the vanishing institutions of the freak show and sideshow, Browning's movie is a horror story, opposing the group of freaks ("human oddities" such as midgets, pinheads, hermaphrodites, clowns, various sideshow actors featuring body deformities, and a couple of conjoined twins) and the "normal" trapeze artist Cleopatra, who marries the midget Hans (heir of a large fortune) and then tries to poison him (with the help of the muscle man Hercules). The macabre story displays an ethos of solidarity between freaks that not only encompasses moments of leisure, material support, and friendship, but also a code of revenge, activating a specific form of reproduction: the reproduction of the freak body, so that at the end of the movie the beautiful Cleopatra is turned into a human oddity.[48] The movie displays several forms of queer bodies, exposed in their materiality, in their ease, in their condition of exploitation, in their pleasures and desires. Almost none of the actors in Browning's movie played characters, but rather they all—so to say—performed themselves; and yet, they all played specific characters in terms of performance specialties of exposure. They were the performance laborers of their own free time. They were professionally employed in the entertainment industry not for the technique of their acting, but for their sheer performance of appearance: in a sense, an amateur performance par excellence.

The film also stages and emphasizes several forms of queer sexuality, featuring sequences in which the bodies of the "freaks" are activated for spectators to confront such sexuality directly: this is clear, for example, every time the film hints at the sexual body of the conjoined twins Daisy and Violet Hilton, a body that perceives pleasure all over, when they are courted by their lovers. Theirs is a body of excess: if one of the twins is touched, that is, the other is able to feel it, and several gags of the film play with this bizarre circumstance: that pleasure is able to expand beyond the body as singularity, that pleasure moves within a body with different limits, particularities, and configurations of desire than the supposed "barbs of normality."[49]

It is first of all on the level of the body and its extraordinary possibilities, then, that the performance of the freak was always already distinctively kindred to queerness. And this becomes even more clear around the end of the 1960s, when both "queerness" and "freakness" within and around the counterculture started being claimed back in the frame of an increasingly explicit political project. Even if not always or not yet inscribed in an explicit political agenda, such a project involved appropriating unlimited possibilities of desire and pleasure, claiming the potentiality of transformation, embracing the right to practice same-sex desire, multiple configuration of love relations, peculiar kinship ties, as well as modes of labor and reproduction.

Adams's book *Sideshow U.S.A* claims that "far from marginal, freak shows have exerted a strong grip on the form, as well as the content, of American arts and letters throughout the course of twentieth century"[50] and that an understanding of their survival in peculiar loci of that artistic landscape might offer important insights into an alternative history of the American cultural imagination and into modes of "politically efficacious appropriation."[51] Averting a purely metaphorical or psychoanalytic reading, which has often eluded the "material history of the sideshow and its performers,"[52] Adams reads the appropriation of the sideshow within the arts as something aligned with the political project of queer theory, which likewise wrestled over the recouping of marginal historical instances and pejorative terminological connotations, explicitly refusing "a logic of identity politics, and the irreconcilable problems of inclusion and exclusion that necessarily accompany identitarian categories."[53] For instance observing how the categories of "freak" and "queer" function as overlapping terms in Carson McCullers's writing, Adams notices that these words

> do not connote any fixed identity, but a broad opposition to normative behaviors and social distinctions. Put very simply, queer refers loosely to acts and desires that cannot be described as heterosexual, whereas freaks, who appear first at the sideshow and then wander

> at large through her fiction, are beings who make all kind of queer tendencies visible on the body's surface.[54]

Overall, Adams interrogates the category of freak as a stratified deposit of historical memory (a memory of marginality, but also of self-empowerment, of difference, of transformation) and as a challenge to "a comforting fiction that there is a permanent, qualitative difference between deviance and normality, projected spatially in the distance between spectators and the body onstage."[55] In an earlier study of the freak show, Robert Bogdan had already pointed out that "freak is a frame of mind, a set of practices, a way of thinking about and presenting people. It is the enactment of a tradition, the performance of a stylized presentation."[56] Adams reads the category of "performance" employed by Bogdan in light of Judith Butler's description of gendered performance in order to suggest that we might read the figure of the freak as a non-fixed identity "instituted through a stylized repetition of acts."[57]

I am interested to conjure both Bogdan's and Adam's definitions in my analysis of *Heaven Grand in Amber Orbit*. If not exactly "the enactment of a tradition," in the play we can however recognize "a way of thinking about and presenting people"[58] which framed theatrically stylized personas and acts, challenging—at least on a rhetorical level—a permanent distinction between normality and deviance. As in the 1950s prose of Carson McCullers, "freak" and "queer" seem to form the grammar for a playful linguistic subversion of sexual, cultural norms and margins of visibility. A further conceptual mobilization of the category of freak in relation to queerness and to the specific social and artistic context of *Heaven Grand in Amber Orbit* has been developed recently by Dominic Johnson, in his study of Jack Smith's work and in particular of his 1962 movie *Normal Love*. "Imagining the queer as freak,"[59] Johnsons suggests, is a way to address the peculiar creatures populating Smith's phantasmagorias as outside of a "coherent polarization between conformity and deviance,"[60] and at the same time is a way to account for Smith's specific appropriation of a historical stratification of exclusion. Such history, Johnson reminds us, building on the work of Marybeth Hamilton, was first of all one in which already by the mid-1950s "freak was not simply pejorative, but also a 'historically specific social identity' taken up by lesbians and gay men as a means of appropriating the subcultural tradition of carnival sideshow."[61] Furthermore, it was a history which marked a particular positioning in the dialectics between assimilation and difference which characterized the representation of lesbian and gay subjects in the dominant culture of the time. Along these lines, Johnson offers two other pointers for our own argument, which interestingly complicate the 1960s appropriation of "freakishness" and more specifically its relation to queerness.

First of all, reading Jack Smith's freakishness against the grain of other 1960s mainstream works which mobilized the dyad queer-freak in a rather "essentialist" dimension (such as Edward Albee's and Mart Crowley's),[62] Johnson suggests that Smith's work does not immunize the history of freak from the materiality of its experience of shame and marginality but rather

> borrows and soothes the ugly history of those unfamiliar bodies that have, historically, been labeled as freakish by a frightening majority. The assumption of freakishness by non-normative subjects assumes the burden of difference, stripping it of its obscenity and laying claim to it as an unfamiliar state of dignity. Smith's freaks are therefore a compensatory invention, produced by minority subjects in response to a desire or to be different from the majority, coloured by a need to do so together. Freakishness conjures a peculiar form of sociality, as a temporary release from marginalization and persecution, which is revoked as one returns to other modes of social participation.[63]

Such "joy of freakishness" was embedded in a specific mode of sociality and togetherness, which was also an affirmation and "sexual self-designation"[64] against majoritarian ways of life, and representation. Secondly, such joyful inhabitation of freakishness welcomed in what Johnson calls an "unfamiliar state of dignity"[65] and was a precarious shelter of imagination and belonging which outlived the 1960s as the ambivalent period when "potentialities inaugurated in freakishness"[66] were tamed and normalized in the contact with mainstream culture. As Johnson explains:

> By the end of the 1960s, the short-lived possibilities of queerness as a lived personification of innocent monstrosity had simply run its course. Contained by the mainstream, queers could be represented as freaks, with amusing results, but at the risk of re-inscribing the subjective crises that the phenomenon set out to challenge.[67]

Smith's work, however, always defers this reassuring dimension, and evades such appropriation both fully inhabiting its queer present of bodies and affective relations, and projecting itself into the future. A future, Johnson suggests, in which Smith's work hands itself over as an ever-renewing mode of "self-sustenance"[68] for unconventional bodies, sexual possibilities, and modes of being and working together.

The freakiness of *Heaven Grand in Amber Orbit* seems to acquire precisely such a character of complexity. And not by chance: in fact, the Play-House of the Ridiculous stood in close proximity with the imagery of Jack Smith, who collaborated on the company's first productions. Furthermore, in 1964 the play's director, John Vaccaro, had himself participated in the "innocent monstrosity"[69] portrayed in *Normal Love*, starring in Smith's pasty phantasmagoria while participating with the group of friends involved in the production during a freakish long weekend, in the summer house of the painter Wynn Chamberlain in Old Lyme. What is more, the filming of *Normal Love* proceeded, afterwards, in John Vaccaro's loft on Great Jones Street.[70]

John Vaccaro participated from 1962 in the erotic, polymorphous, hallucinated world of pre-Stonewall queer New York, and in the adolescent theater economy of mid-1960s Off-Off Broadway, and also outlived as an artist such a "golden age." In his 1970s work, Vaccaro's praxis continued to bear the burden and the delight of just such a queer legacy, a joyful pleasure of freakishness without claims of normality, although the very freakishness displayed as "compensatory invention" had, by that time, already entered a market circulation of sorts.

"Freaking on in": Focus, Attractions and Show Time

Turn-of-the century amusement presented to Vaccaro an immediate reference point for his intention to "break focus." As Tom Gunning has pointed out, such a typology of amusement was characterized by "attractions," understood as "units of impressions" that "aggressively subjected the spectator with sensual and psychological impact."[71] Discussing the fascination of the avant-garde, and especially of Sergei Eisenstein (who first employed the term "attraction" speaking of theater) for the "exhibitionist quality" of turn-of-the-century popular art, Gunning points out that narrative film imposed itself on the pre-1907 "cinema of attraction" reproducing the models of legitimate theater, hence incorporating the dramatic form and its conventions, and contributing to progressively detach film from its shameful origin in a space neighboring fairground amusements. John Vaccaro's work gleefully inhabits such a shameful space of proximity between cinema and fairground amusements: not only does it not neglect it, but it emphasizes it.

Vaccaro's work also shares with the "cinema of the attractions" its belonging to a noisy, chaotic, and immersive space characterized by sensual fascination, enthusiasm, and arousal, as well as by a drive to an "exhibitionist confrontation rather than diegetive absorption"[72] regarding the audience. Bringing the fascination for 1940s Hollywood movies grounded in gay subculture and camp imagery on the stage alongside a carnivalesque parade of freaks therefore contributed to rewriting cinema's own "illegitimate" history, restoring its proximity with the actors' live presence by virtue of their respective performances of exposure.[73]

Such embodiment of fairground theatricality was also a precise statement in terms of theater, a praxis understood by Vaccaro as not only kindred, but almost synonymous with fairground attractions. Sharing with Sergei Eisenstein also a passionate admiration for the world of circus, Vaccaro had in mind a circus of a particular sort: "For me, art is the circus. That's what excites me. Go into the streets—look at one block—that's the circus. To me, that's THEATRE. Something going on all the time, not just one isolated scene."[74]

Circus fascinated Vaccaro not so much as a perfect technique, as it appears in the later work of Eisenstein (who will finally channel his fascination for the fairground's attractions into a more rigorous experimental calculation, in his theory of montage);[75] but as a framing device for a certain circus-like quality that he recognized in his everyday life and social space. The latter was a space characterized, as Sally Banes has carefully mapped out, by a lively artistic scene, where boundaries between art and life were indeed blurred, not least because of the appearance and affirmation, in art and life, of "effervescent bodies."[76] Borrowing her terminology from Mikhail Bakhtin, Banes characterizes the "effervescent, grotesque body" as a recurring topos in the artistic production of the mid-1960s New York scene, and discusses this figure as one profoundly embedded in the everyday life of the social and political community that was producing it:

> The effervescent body is seen as literally open to the world, blending easily with animals, objects and other bodies. Its boundaries are permeable; its parts are surprisingly autonomous; it is everywhere open to the world. It freely indulges in excessive eating, drinking, sexual activity, and every other imaginable sort of licentious behavior. . . . The effervescent body is first and foremost a body of carnivalesque performance . . . And more importantly, the effervescent, grotesque body challenges the new "bodily canon"—the close, private, psyschologized, and singular body—of the modern Renaissance world of individual self-sufficiency. For it speaks of the body as a historical as well as a collective entity.[77]

The social scene where the "effervescent bodies" described by Banes proliferated is the "street scene" Vaccaro referred to in his interview: the "circus" that inspired his theater work was a social scene where indeed "something was going on all the time," and spontaneous "numbers' were rapidly incorporated into film or performances.[78] For example, the famous backroom of the restaurant Max's Kansas City (where the Play-House presented *The Moke-Eater* in 1969) used to host not only the flamboyant social appearance and interaction of Andy Warhol's entourage (many of whom featured as actors in productions of the Play-House)[79] and the most eccentric characters of the downtown art scene, but was also the stage of impromptu performances, such as the famous "show time" launched by Andrea "Whips" Feldman, and Eric Emerson. "Showtime," very much like The Rouge Frolic's "Fascination!," was a spell of sorts, and it served to catch the attention of the people gathered in the space, who would become spectators (and potential performers) of performances of exposure that did not demand specific skills or capacities, but consisted in the presentation of their personas in highly theatrical terms:[80] "show time" consisted mainly in improvised exhibitionist numbers of theatrical presentation, pivoting first and foremost on the personality on display in that particular moment. As Penny Arcade describes, and Johnson reports in his book:

> Everybody performed all the time. It was a way of entertaining yourself and entertaining your friends. But it wasn't self-conscious, it wasn't like somebody was *on* all the time, it was a way of mediating your own personality. We didn't have any model for the people we were. We were freaks in the real sense that we were not normal and we were pegged as not being normal, in school and by our families, and we were here in New York being not-normal together.[81]

According to Adams's definition of "freak performance" recalled earlier, this too was in a sense a "stylized presentation," where recognizable identities were instituted by virtue of a repetition of acts, witnessed by a distracted audience.[82] However, differently from the traditional audience of the freak show, the spectators here were all potential participants, and therefore the very reenactment of the "freak performance" would tactically reconfigure what in the traditional freak show was the distance of spectators-consumers. In other words, the common affective, social, and artistic space of the downtown art scene, in places like Max's Kansas City, would allow a stepping beyond narrow distinctions between performers and spectators, as well as between supposed normality and deviance; and the relation between the impromptu "freak performers" who were performing for free in front of an improvised audience—both in social spaces, and on the stage of the Ridiculous—was not a relation of distance, but rather of "flirtation." I borrow this term from Stefan Brecht, who describes the relation between performers and the audience of the Play-House of the Ridiculous as follows:

> The performers' attitude toward the audience at first seems to be indifference—no warmth or projection. An occasional address to the audience has the effect of an aside. This self-centredness sets the tone for a subsidiary intent to charm the audience (Woronow: "I want to take the audience on a trip—as one might a small kid by telling it a story which fascinates it even though perhaps it does not understand or like the story"). This tentative domination relates to a relatively inoffensive vanity and runs the gamut from intents to be attractive to ideas of being offensive (by imposing a repulsive personality). This approach combines unfocused eroticism (flirtatiousness) with unfocused social self-assertion.[83]

The "unfocused eroticism" described by Brecht could be considered another way to think about the performance mode that I call foreplay. Flirtation was a dynamic that was productive of attention which Vaccaro borrowed from the very social scene in which these performances took shape—and it was a dynamic productive of attention also in the widespread distraction of Vaccaro's stage. Significantly, the flirtatious scene which Vaccaro had in mind, describing his idea of "circus," was also a scene where queer sexuality flourished and the relation of intimacy between bodies was very strong, not least because of the widespread habit of sharing, among other things, sexual partners, clothes, spaces, objects, artistic projects, apartments, money, and drugs. It was also a scene where the eccentric play with gender identity involved a collective elaboration of costumes, recognizable personas that would exceed the individual stage appearance, and constituted in flexible but "fixed types" returning in different stage and filmic performances.[84]

The space of transhistorical proximity between the 1960s underground scene, and turn-of-the-century sideshow entertainment was also a space of shame: just as the performances of exposures of human oddities constituted a taboo in the 1960s culture, so homosexuality, cross-dressing, polyamory, and drug use were all life practices existing in a marginal place in American society. In mainstream culture these choices and habits were still reasons of shame even after the so-called sexual liberation advocated by the 1960s counterculture, and after the 1969 Stonewall Riots which had initiated the long route toward an open claim of "pride" for homosexuals. Likewise, even though Timothy Leary's experiments with drugs, hosted by prestigious universities like Harvard, had been widely discussed in the mainstream press, drug consuming was still considered a taboo topic in the American public sphere.

Rather than the precision and the technique of the trapeze artist, which fascinated Eisenstein, Vaccaro was fascinated by the circus as the space of nonconformity with established norms of behavior, and with peculiar conditions of shame. The "bad acting" of the Play-House members was the first among the reasons of shame that Vaccaro welcomed in his group. Likewise, it was no mystery that many of the members of the Play-House of the Ridiculous were regular drug consumers: "speed freaks" and "heads," recouping Andy Warhol's terminology, or heroin addicts.[85] Vaccaro himself specified that he would welcome people with drug addictions in his plays in the hope to engage them in theater work as a way to "focus." It is not irrelevant, furthermore, that Vaccaro himself had been a heroin addict for many years before moving to New York, and was still consuming a lot of grass throughout the 1960s and 1970s. Furthermore, Vaccaro himself performed in his shows, such as in the memorable role of Mother Super Viva in *The Life of Lady Godiva* (1966) or as Princess Ninga Flinga Dung (the queen of song) in *Heaven Grand*, in both cases in an eccentric, "freakish" semi-drag.

Obviously, the presence of drugs, emphasized as well in many biographical and scholarly accounts of the Play-House of the Ridiculous, has a precise relation with the very temporality of their performances: drugs, as well, engender a particular quality of "focus," shifting between very intense durational moments of focus and a constantly distracted attitude. It should also be remembered that the author of *Heaven Grand* had written the play having experimented with LSD for three months, and that the "attractions" already embedded in the structure of the text could be read as translated forms of "highs" of Jackie Curtis's ongoing acid trip. Vaccaro's direction activated such "highs," turning the polymorphous potentiality of his troupe into a parade of exhausted clowns, grotesque beauties, excessive bodies, and sounds.

"Fully-Fledged Freaks": Surviving the 1960s

The Barnumesque quality of *Heaven Grand in Amber Orbit* appears immediately when we consider some of the characters in the production: the circus barker Rhumba Line Sam (already present in the script, played in 1969 by Francis William Dudley), a set of Siamese triplets (Midnite Mary, Madcap Betty, and Millie Mae, three actresses wrapped together and naked underneath, played in 1969 by Elsene Sorrentino, Penny Arcade, and Tina Krakow),[85] a couple of identical twins wearing a tuxedo and moving simultaneously during the performance, and first and foremost the Thalidomide Baby (played by Baby Bettie Moses, and then by Delia Sorrentino), a character doubled by the "stump-armed"[86] grown-up thalidomide baby and ex-chanteuse Princess Ninga Flinga Dung, played by Vaccaro himself in both runs of the play. Beyond particularities, however, all characters of *Heaven Grand* are freaks: to make this clear from the very beginning, the show starts with a parade of the actors singing in a choir the song "Freaking On In," whose lyrics are worth taking into consideration here:

> We were exceptional children
> Under-achievers so it seems
> Now we are fully-fledged freaks, folks
> Guilt fears in nine-months dreams
>
> We were born to be looked at
> Street stars at side-show screen
> Now we are full-fledged freaks, folks
> Our Christmas is your Halloween
> Your ghoulishly gleeful curiosities
> Your guaranteed monstrosities
> We are fully fledged freaks
>
> Your perfectly weird curiosities
> Your privately feared monstrosities
> We are fully-fledged freaks

We're movin' on in
We're comin' on in
We're freakin' on in, folks!

We were children of the sixties
Moon-men babies and napalmed skin
Now we are fully fledged freaks
The door has been opened and we are coming on' in

. . .[87]

A number of reviewers described *Heaven Grand* as a "story of what happened to those who survived the 1960s," as "a retrospective revival of what happened to 'exceptional children' who become 'gleeful curiosities.' "[88] Michael Feingold, writing in 1976, went so far as to talk about the show as a "nostalgia musical," even if nostalgic for a period that was "scarcely five years past": "the characters in *Heaven Grand in Amber Orbit*" he writes "are '60s people—mutilated, ugly, screaming, street freaks—not so much glossed as glittered over by the Play-House of the Ridiculous and aggrandized with elaborate meaningless names."[89]

The Thalidomide baby was indeed a "fully fledged" 1960s freak: the expression had come into use during the 1960s after the massive international scandal in the pharmaceutical industry which involved the production and distribution of Thalomide, an immunomodulatory drug (produced in West Germany by the company Contergan) which was handed out over the counter for curing several forms of mild illness, and in particular morning sickness for pregnant women, and was subsequently proved to be the cause of a large number of infants born with deformities, such as phocomelia. If "John Vaccaro's scenic fantasy is his own true underground comics,"[90] the Thalidomide Baby features in this show as a distinctive type of 1960s freak super-heroine: like the Spider-Man, or the Hulk, her extraordinary body was produced because of science's mistakes. Likewise, the "moon-men babies and napalmed skin" are powerful images of another sort of deformity, caused by 1960s U.S. military violence, and supported by science: the disfigured bodies hit by napalm bombs, which the United States military had been using first in Japan, and then Korea and even more systematically during the Vietnam War, which was still going on at the time of *Heaven Grand*. In these monstrous images—evoked on the stage with no pity, no seriousness, and seemingly no compassion either—the scene of "shame" of the freak show was turned upside down: here it was "the self-governed, iterable subject of democracy, the American cultural self,"[91] which was exposed as a monster. It was "the man on the moon," the American man highly visible to mainstream audiences in his imperialistic gesture broadcast on television in 1969, who, in other spaces, outside of visibility, was capable of monstrosity. The moon-men babies were evoked and exhibited side-by-side with the napalmed-skin, with those born with phocomelia, all of them extraordinary enterprises produced by science and by the 1960s economic boom—moon-landing, imperialistic conquering, improvements in the medical industry—which had, as well, the "side effect" of producing along the way teratogenic deformities. In *Heaven Grand* these side effects were turned, so to say, into sideshow. Political critique, in Vaccaro's theater, is never self-indulgent, never "correct": it is rough, morbid, and often cruel. But its critical mobilization of attractions might well be regarded in the lucid terms used by Stefan Brecht, when he wrote that "ridiculous theatre approaches the effects, if not the status, of a popular revolutionary art."[92]

The Monster of Unproductivity

Perhaps the most revolutionary aspect of Vaccaro's *Heaven Grand* is, however, the exposure and celebration of another "monster," fully embodied by the 1960s exceptional children in his company (those described by Penny Arcade as people "not being normal together"), a monster of which the very Play-House of the Ridiculous was in a sense a side effect: the *monster of unproductivity*.

Amongst the very first information that the troupe offers to the audience, in its cheerful embrace of freakiness, is the intimate connection between being "exceptional children" and being "under-achievers." Interestingly, whereas the expression "fully fledged" conveys a sense of completeness, as in a mature stage of development, its association with the word "freaks" throughout the show seems to ridicule the very idea of training or status expressed by the adjective: on this particular stage, "fully fledged" resonates more in relation to the acquisition of feathers than to the acquisition of skills. The "under-achievers," the song seems to suggest, are those who throughout the 1960s acquired feathers—taking feathers as signifiers of the glittering flamboyance characterizing costumes, props, and stage design in *Heaven Grand*—instead of skills.

However, the "fully-fledged freak" is also a self-conscious reference to the counterculture's progressive normalization into a brand, precisely in line with the scenario described by Rachel Adams and also hinted at by Dominic Johnson, in which already by the end of the 1960s "freakishness" had reached a precise market value. Hence, the song 'Freaking On In' itself plays around the ambivalent positions performed by the underground theater freaks in the show, and seems well aware of possible comments such as the one formulated by Michael Feingold reviewing *Heaven Grand* in 1976: "It is curious, these few years after, how placid the Ridiculous style now seems. Many of its devices—the glitter, the sexual interpretation of everything, the use of two actors playing one character—have been absorbed by mainstream theatre, and with this defusing, Vaccaro's work seems to take a mellow charm."[93]

However, Vaccaro's ridiculing of training, skills, and proper theater achievement does not amount only to a satirical remark, but constitutes the core of his theater practice: as already discussed, none of Vaccaro's actors were professionals, and most of them were brought on the stage simply for their exhibitionist drive, for their participation in a common scene in which "showtime" was one among many leisure possibilities. As Ruggero Bianchi has insightfully explained, the "bad acting" of the Play-House marks a crucial difference between the Ridiculous of John Vaccaro and that of Charles Ludlam, which became especially evident in the 1970s. Although drawing from very similar materials and cultural obsessions, Ludlam's Ridiculous Theatrical Company elaborated over the years a distinctive, elegant form of *craftsmanship*, encompassing acting as well as dramaturgical technologies,[94] whereas Vaccaro's theater maintained well into the 1970s the roughness, imprecision, and accidental flair which was distinctive of the 1960s Off-Off Broadway theater.[95]

In the 1976 production of *Heaven Grand*, almost all actors were featured on the program with their real names, whereas in the 1960s productions of the Play-House they used to be listed with "extravagant pseudonyms invented by Vaccaro like Otto Erotica and Bela Box."[96] But Vaccaro (and La MaMa, which hosted the play) also had to rely on the participation of three actors "for gentle concession of the Actors' Equity," a required clause introduced with the Showcase Code in the second half of the 1960s in the scenario of the progressive professionalization of the "underground" that Stephen Bottoms has so painstakingly reconstructed in his book.

The undisciplined amateurism of the 1960s seems to function in *Heaven Grand* very much like Perebinossoff had described "interludes" to function in traditional narrative: exposing hidden, unspoken features of the characters' personas in the frame narrative or "frame condition." What would it mean, however, that the "stylized amateurism" of the Play-House of the Ridiculous had "liberated the time-filler" from the confines of its function? What would it mean, for *Heaven Grand*'s supposed "frame play" to be dropped, and for the theatrical interruption to become autonomous, without having formulated any alternative form of "mastery"?

What *Heaven Grand* Drags On: Potentialities of Mutation

The "freakishness" welcomed as safe amusement in the 1970s public sphere, and previously allowed as underground, superfluous, amateur play during the 1960s, was itself enabled by the wealthy American society which in the same years was founding its resources on capitalist exploitation, as well as on the military and imperialist politics evoked by *Heaven Grand*'s fully-fledged 1960s freaks. Dropping the "frame play" of professional theater work would mean to display, on the stage, *time itself as a monster*: the "unfocused eroticism" of performers and spectators, the drugs' temporality and exhibitionist showtime of Max's Kansas City, the bedlam of circus performance without virtuosic bravura. It would mean displaying the enjoyment of living (and having lived) in "a queer time and space"[97] not only temporarily, but as a continuous state; it meant to affirm that the particular mode of performance production experimented with in the 1960s was not simply a prelude to what came after (such as professional success), but a possible mode of performance production and reproduction exceeding what Elisabeth Freeman has termed "chrononormativity, or the use of time to organize individual human bodies toward maximum productivity."[98]

Having dropped its "frame play," the amateur theatricality of *Heaven Grand* dragged on a specific temporality, both in terms of history and in terms of time perception, playfully subverting the very "logic of time-as-productive."[99] First of all, *Heaven Grand* carried on itself the memory of the plays put on in front of a few friends and spectators in the early 1960s in places with no license for entertainment, such as the Caffe Cino or La MaMa, or in private spaces, where voluntary labor, taking place in leisure time, was the first material base of theater production. *Heaven Grand* also dragged on, in a stylized presentation, the frenzy of production of these early times, when plays were churned out at Cino or La MaMa at an exhausting weekly rhythm, with little or no rehearsals, in a merry-go-round of theatrical attempts, rather than in a coherent and concentrated trajectory. This unfocused hyper-productivity, collectively elaborated over the 1960s, survived in the Play-House's work as a stylized reference, beyond the "underground" beginnings, affirming a persistence of this mode of production even when the shows had entered into broader circulation. Liberating private entertainments from the "frame play" would mean, in this case, also undermining what both professional theater and alternative experimental theater groups, from very different perspectives, used to recognize as "valuable" in the 1960s: the presentation of performance as "event," as the climax of a work preparation entailing discipline, training, forms of (however experimental) regulation of time and creativity. As Brecht pointed out, in his reading of the work of the Play-House:

> The action-style of the play and performance so sharpen our awareness of the passage of time and the problem of its use that we become resentful of the foolishness and sterility as wasteful. We are confronted with time by: the lack of direction; the absence of a sense of progress or continuity or development or achievement; inarticulation (no well-marked sections or changes of direction in the line of action; deliberately slow-motion or speeded-up passages; frequent changes of rhythms and speed). . . . The basis of such boredom is anxiety, compulsiveness, the frenzy to keep busy so as to face oneself, the habit of allocating time to particular purposes (tangible gains), tension or frustration, a general sense that one is wasting one's life—in short, an inability to play.[100]

Such confrontation with time, and with the compulsory necessity to put it into use, typical of capitalism and of the conception of professional work ingrained in capitalism, can be seen as one of the targets of the rampant non-purposefulness of the Play-House's theatricality at the turn of the 1960s. Their "professional" theater labor reproduced modalities of theater production pertaining to leisure sociability and amateurism, and did not claim a direct genealogy in theater history in terms of technique,[101] nor of privileged places of transmission, such as the experimental form of the workshop. Rather, the theater of the Play-House located itself in a discontinuous genealogy, articulating a belonging to turn-of-the-century leisure sociability which did not understand itself as filiation, nor progeny. Such leisure sociability did not ridicule work as such (Vaccaro used to say: "I don't think people realize how much work we do: twenty-four hours a day we are living the Play-House of the Ridiculous!"),[102] but rather a certain conception of "professional work," of "adult life" and "normality," which were exposed on the stage as abject, as "monstrous."

Such a conception of work and life, postulating a narrow distinction between leisure and labor, as well as between amateurs and professionals, had been elaborated in the first decades of the twentieth century with the development of urban, industrial capitalism in the United States. The heyday of Coney Island and its fairground amusement, as John Kasson has emphasized, hosted a leisure culture in its becoming, "when the nation came of age as an urban-industrial society and its citizens eagerly but painfully adjusted to the new terms of American life."[103] At the same time, it hosted the hard work of those who—likewise—"lived in performance twenty-four hours a day": the attractions of the freak shows, amusement parks, fairgrounds. In dragging on the fairground attractions which were the stars of the leisure firmament of turn-of-the-century Coney Island, *Heaven Grand* turned the stigma of deformity and exceptionality into an affirmative statement. As Kasson explains, in Coney Island

> midgets, giants, fat ladies, and ape-men were both stigmatized and honored as freaks. They fascinated spectators in the way they displayed themselves openly as exceptions to the rules of conventional world. Their grotesque presences heightened the visitors' sense that they had penetrated a marvelous realm of transformation, subject to laws on its own. The popular distorting mirrors furnished the illusion that the spectators themselves had become freaks. Thus Coney Island seemed charged with a magical power to transmute customary appearances into fluid new possibilities.[104]

The mode of production and reproduction experimented with by Vaccaro's theater (with no auditions, no contracts, with all artists involved being "paid by the amount they make") was one bringing back the stylized presentation of the freak but reversing its logic of exploitation, according to which the freak was only the object of consumption and not the producer of her own labor.[105] More important, encountering the freak show again in the present meant to mobilize precisely the shameful history of the freak as professional amateur in view of new possibilities.

Heaven Grand, in fact, "moils and roils around the theme of mutation,"[106] which constitutes the gist of the Play-House's Ridiculous's poetics. Vaccaro once described the Play-House as a theater "beyond Freud, a theatre of simultaneous activities, of perpetual transformations, of inversion of sexes and characters in a climate of humor and sanity."[107] Significantly, whereas Browning's sordid story ended with the mutilation of the beautiful Cleopatra, whose body was turned into a freak, the "enfreakment"[108] (echoing David Hevey's term) of Heaven Grand happens as a sheer mutation: her loose and deferred agony happens simultaneously with the transformation of her lover, Nightcloud, into her own drag persona:

> (As NIGHTCLOUD steps forward SACRA VIA begins dressing him up to look like HEAVEN GRAND IN AMBER ORBIT)
>
> . . .
>
> HEAVEN: Nightcloud, what are you doing?
>
> NIGHTCLOUD: If you go away Heaven Grand in Amber Orbit someone must take your place.
>
> . . .
>
> I will carry your name for you.
>
> HEAVEN: You will? Oh Nightcloud what more could a girl ask from her man, Oh Nightcloud . . . you look like an usherette from the Roxy![109]

On the stage of *Heaven Grand*, of course, there is no space for love or sacrifice: Nightcloud's gesture is portrayed as a useless masquerade, and his drag persona immediately becomes an object of denigration: he is mocked as the "painted lady," on the part of the other characters, although as a matter of fact most of them are in drag. The mutation of Heaven Grand/Nightcloud is a pure act of theatrical transformation: the 'passing on' of an identity as a matter of choice, not as an essence.

Likewise, this gesture also stages desire as the engine for the persistence of memory, in theatrical terms. Such mutation could, of course, also be read as intimately related to the very transformation that Jackie Curtis was going through in the period in which he composed *Heaven Grand*, during which he started living and performing alternatively in both genders.[110] Significantly, Curtis started writing the play the first day he wore female drag in public and was hoping to perform the part of Heaven Grand; subsequently, in 1976, Curtis played The Rouge Frolic as a boy, during the period in which he had dismissed female drag and—as the next chapter discusses—he was living and performing in "male drag." In a sense, Curtis's perpetual transformations mirrored the magic lantern that Vaccaro's theater orchestrated.

On the stage of *Heaven Grand* not only performers, but spectators alike would experiment with the monster of time as engine of mutation, rather than progression. As in Kasson's description of turn-of-the-century Coney Island, here too spectators were not immunized and in this distorted mirror they would end up recognizing, imagining, hoping, even, to see themselves as freaks: as part of this perpetual movement of mutation, as inhabiting a temporality out of capitalist productivity. Such a recognition, such a hope, was strongly connected with a dynamic of desire, one beautifully described, for instance, in Ricardo Castillo's spectator response to the show. Resisting describing the performance, lamenting the insufficiency of writing as a mean to convey the bodily affect perceived as a spectator, Castillo recalls in visceral terms this particular theatrical experience, conjoining the description of his desiring body with the account of the way such a body was hailed, so to say, to prolong such freak temporality beyond the duration of the show:

> It was a kind of theatre experienced through the eyes, and ears and pores, but they left one like an unsatisfied lover, always asking for more; an insatiable desire to laugh out of frustration, to ejaculate through guttural sounds and find a way out of a stale existence and step on solid ground for at least an ephemeral moment. How slow and painful is the process of starting out a freak and slowly work your way up to a fully fledged human being only to then find out that in the end you have to withdraw back into yourself, the point you had originally started out from. In going through you skidded from glitter fantasy and endless fucking to cursing the life you carry within.[111]

The monster of unproductivity, so to say, demanded more space, demanded more time. The temporality of this performance attacked the spectators' "normal time," making them wish it to be prolonged, deferred, reconfigured as a space of loitering, returning, "tripling your pleasure," echoing the title of one of the songs performed by the freakish triplet twins, and possibly referring also to Curtis's three-months-every-three-days acid consumption. The monster of unproductivity, performed in *Heaven Grand*, was the monster of a *contagious* time: a time affecting productivity and demanding alteration, a time confronting normality with shame and with excessive desire, a time reminding of the guilty leisure of the sideshow, a pleasure which the masses were enabled to enjoy precisely by virtue of the monster of early twentieth-century industrial capitalism, ferocious and exploitative as the American imperialism embodied by the man on the moon in the early 1970s.

Heaven Wants Out: Ruby Lynn Reyner, and the Unpunctuality of Promises

In 1970–71 Ruby Lynn Reyner, the protagonist of *Heaven Grand*, starred in the movie *Heaven Wants Out*, directed by 22-year-old Robert Feinberg, her lover at the time. More precisely, she participated in the "making of" this movie: first of all because besides starring in it, she was involved in its conception and realization, and secondly in the sense that the "making of" the movie turned out, in the end, to be the entire outcome of that year of shooting. In fact, the movie remained unedited for thirty-eight years, and it was released only in 2009, preceded by the documentary *Finishing Heaven*, which reconstructs the long course of the movie's "unfinishability."[112] Conceived as a portrait of Bowery life in the early 1970s, *Heaven Wants Out* features a remarkable cast: besides Reyner, the movie features superstars Holly Woodlawn, Mary Woronov, and Ondine, as well as photographer Francesco Scavullo, performing as himself in intense photographic sessions with Reyner, dressed, in the movie (as in everyday life, Reyner recalls) in female drag, inspired by her love for actress Barbara Stanwyck. The film also offers a glimpse of Sammy's Bowery Follies, "the quintessential 20th century New York nightclub,"[113] a legendary hotspot of Bowery life. Located in the Lower East Side at 267 Bowery between Houston and Stanton and active from 1934 to 1970 (it closed shortly after the death of its founder, Sammy Fuchs), the Bowery Follies carried on the vaudeville tradition, hosting the last vestiges of the entertainment that once lit up Bowery stages. Through the years, the nightclub also became a hub for drinkers and people from all walks of life, and yet its fame also drew celebrities, politicians, and Broadway stars. At the moment of filming, however, the Bowery Follies was living its last days, hosting the amateur hour of a mixed, intergenerational community of New York "freaks," among whom featured "painted ladies," midgets, third-class vaudevillians, as well as artists active in the downtown scene. The film is named after the protagonist, Heaven (Ruby Lynn Reyner), who desperately wants to get out of the small, decadent time of this Bowery circus, but finds herself again and again on its dirty stage, singing in front of a seemingly hopeless community. The film was conceived as a double narrative, featuring scenes from Heaven's life and a variety show, with improbable numbers performed by amateurs from the Bowery Follies scene. Considering the temporal proximity of the Play-House of the Ridiculous's *Heaven Grand*, and Reyner's involvement in both enterprises, it is clear that Feinberg's movie also carried an echo of the performance persona Reyner had so powerfully embodied in the New York scene of the previous year.

The movie, however, never became public, but remained for thirty-eight years an unfinished, private product of amateurism. In the documentary which accompanied the recent release of the movie, realized by Mark Mann for HBO, we learn the story of Feinberg, who had grown up—in his own words—as "a boy wonder," always believing he would become, one day, a successful film director.[114] When he went to study film at New York University he soon got in touch with the lively underground scene of the time, as well as with other film directors, such as Martin Scorsese, who were then breaking into the American film industry. The New York period, however, was for Feinberg also a period of intense idleness: he made much use of drugs, and he failed ever to complete a single movie. Unlike Jack Smith with his movies, failing to complete *Heaven Wants Out* was for Feinberg not a political nor a poetic choice, but arose rather from the impossibility of properly editing an undisciplined accumulation of materials, shot in leisure circumstances, among friends, often under the influence of drugs. In a sense, Feinberg never finished his movie because he was caught in a tower of idleness by the monster of unproductivity: he never succeeded in giving a form to the scenes he had filmed back then, and kept carrying around the world the heavy film reels he had accumulated after the shooting, haunted by those intense New York years, until they ended up in his current home, in North Carolina. He ended up embodying the destiny of those "exceptional children" (echoing the lyric of "Freaking On In") who were both "unachievers" and "gleeful curiosities," simultaneously pampered and deceived by the turn of the 1970s New York.

Ruby Lynn Reyner never forgave Feinberg for this sin of idleness: for having surrendered to the monster of unproductivity and not being "on time" with his own life, with his own success. The movie, in 1971, could have been the vehicle for launching Reyner's career. She was working as an actress in downtown theater, she was modeling for Francesco Scavullo and other fashion photographers, she was the front woman of the band Ruby and the Rednecks, who were regulars at Max's Kansas City. *Heaven Wants Out* was just the thing she needed to acquire the visibility, but most importantly the memorability she deserved. The movie would have been *just in time*.

Alas, the movie arrived late for its appointment with fame: it never got to be completed. Reyner and Feinberg split up, and they both had intense years of travels, drug addiction, and precarious employment in and around show business.[115] Neither of them became a star, outside of the intense years of show-idleness in New York at the turn of the 1970s. "At that time, when I was twenty-two, it was great to have a film; when you are fifty-eight with an unfinished film you made when you were twenty-two it is not so great," as Feinberg put it.[116] Both figures survived, however, in the affectionate oral history of the underground scene and Reyner in particular has been involved, in the last decade, in many initiatives commemorating the 1960s and 1970s performance scene such as revivals of the Max's Kansas City scene, the Coffehouse Chronicles organized at La MaMa, or other homages and reenactments of legendary Off-Off Broadway performances at the Theatre for the New City.

When Reyner told me the story of the movie's long deferral, in 2008, the documentary *Finishing Heaven* had just been shot. The documentary was itself a spin-off of the attempt to complete *Heaven Wants Out* that was triggered again by the interest of Mark Mann, who saw in Feinberg's story the potential to film a "portrait of the would-be artist as a young and aging procrastinator."[117] The documentary stages the reencounter of Reyner and Feinberg in 2007, with the intention to finally finish the movie. In their dialogues, the completion of this project comes to signify both an "act of love"[118] and the improbable accomplishment of a project which, at this point, is well beyond its possible horizon in terms of value. Or rather, it has entered another order of value: that of memorability. "I don't expect to become famous," Reyner says; but she takes this "trip on memory lane"[119] enthusiastically, agreeing to participate in the completion of the movie, even if her future of success—which the ambitious flair of the shooting in the film, the beauty of her old-fashion styled image, her lively and charismatic performances and exposure all seem to promise—has not, eventually, taken place.

With the help of an editor, *Heaven Wants Out* would finally be completed in 2009, but will forever have arrived late in the lives of its producers, in the career of its protagonists. Today, its value is more that of a document than that of a movie, understood as a unit of artistic labor in its own right. It is the document of an era, the 1960s, of a place and a practice, the Bowery Follies' amateur hour, and of love labor in a state of artistic potentiality. Even its technology, the material substance of the film reels, as well as the quality of sound and images, are out of sync with contemporary film technique. In many ways, *Heaven Wants Out* seems to have arrived too late on its own future, while being at the same time a document of this very appointment.

It is interesting, in this respect, that before the movie was released, Mark Mann realized a documentary about this story. In *Finishing Heaven*, Feinberg and Reyner are portrayed as the authors of a movie which does not yet exist, which never became famous: the documentary uses film sequences from *Heaven Wants Out*, but also contextualizes it with archive materials from 1960s New York. Relatives and friends of Reyner and Feinberg are interviewed about the authors' youth and their dreams of fame, and the latter are portrayed in their homes, telling the story of their lives, while the narrative accompanies Feinberg into the last steps toward the editing and montage of *Heaven Wants Out*.

Finishing Heaven resembles many of the documentaries produced in the last decade around protagonists of the 1960s underground scene.[120] The way the protagonists are staged against the background of their past, recollected through documents and oral history, is inscribed in this genre, but it also has something peculiar to it. The documentary has a distinctive nostalgia about it, a melancholy for a past which reclaims its pride of place in the lives of Reyner and Feinberg as an anticipation of the future, even though this future somehow got lost along the way. For Feinberg and Reyner, the prelude of this future, one might say, lasted a bit too long, suspended in the state of procrastination which prolonged itself beyond the 1970s, in a monstrous unproductivity forever sabotaging the possibility of transforming an "amateur" into a "professional."

Still, in *Finishing Heaven* Reyner and Feinberg are finally portrayed as "underground stars": beyond the market value of their own work, their document has therefore entered in a specific economy of attention and memorability, participating in the "coming over-ground" of the underground, a resurfacing to which major commercial operations, such as HBO, are currently turning their interest. On the one hand, Mark Mann, the professional filmmaker who made possible (productively and technically) the completion of *Heaven Wants Out* and made the documentary about it, presents the story as that of two artists who finally "achieve the dreams of their youth," and packages it commercially as "a look at what it is to grow old in kind of a New York frame of mind."[121] On the other hand, the potentiality of *Finishing Heaven* and *Heaven Wants Out* as documents has come to substitute for the film itself, in its accomplished form: its potentiality has become itself value, although beyond its actualization as capital in the lives of its producers. One thing is sure: the *Heaven Wants Out* finished in 2009 was not the film it could or would have been thirty-eight years ago. That film will never exist. But at the same time, paying careful attention to this story, we can perceive an echo of that film, we can grasp its phantasmatic presence, we can perhaps linger a moment on the glimpse of its inspiration.

Such inspiration, Feinberg explains, had been in 1969 a series of images shot by Francesco Scavullo while Ruby Lynn Reyner was performing in *Heaven Grand in Amber Orbit*. The section of Scavullo photographing Reyner is apparently the first scene Feinberg shot for his movie, trying out poses that would become, then, the grammar of the movie itself, largely staging Reyner in 1940s-style poses such as the one immortalized in the pictures. The latter, then, became part of Scavullo's photographic work. Significantly, although I had the chance to see copies of these photographs in Reyner's private collection, these images are not included in this book: the fee which the Scavullo Foundation, holding today the rights on these images, asked me for reproducing them, was way too expensive, especially for an independent researcher (or to say it otherwise, for a precarious academic) like myself. This inconvenience, however, adds another interesting dimension to the story of the posthumous valorization of this moment, and its remains. Therefore, I shall ask the reader to rely on my description and follow me in an effort of imagination.

In these pictures, Reyner appears in character as Heaven Grand wearing silver gloves and a red dress punctuated with white stars, with hair arranged in a 1940s style and gathered at the neck in a fishnet. She embodies the image which was described in detail in most reviews of the show, where Reyner was presented as a "musical comedy find,"[122] and whose wit, performance talent, and personality were marked out for praise by many critics who saw the performance both in New York and in the Play-House's international tour.

Looking at these images, we can glimpse as well Reyner/Heaven's personality, and imagine it standing out as an attraction on the stage of the Play-House of the Ridiculous. But what is more, we can also glimpse in these images a specific temporality which seems kindred with both the tempo of *Heaven Grand in Amber Orbit* and the monster of unproductivity which characterized the faith of *Heaven Wants Out*. It is a temporality of deferral, of prolongation, of accumulation, of distracted potentiality.

The pose of the actress, clearly dragging in pictures of golden era Hollywood stars such as Jean Harlow or Barbara Stanwyck, is still, and she looks beyond the picture frame. The makeup crowning her beautiful star image is, however, disproportionate. It is glittering, shining, and powerful, but also slightly disturbing, slightly oversized. Not only does Reyner's beauty border on monstrosity,[123] but she also participates in a peculiar sort of *show-idleness*. It is as if the actress, while getting into costume, had grown distracted in front of the mirror, had kept passing the lipstick over her lips well beyond the contours of her mouth, and had enjoyed applying the glitter on her eyelids and eyelashes well beyond what was needed. It looks as though in doing so, the actress had involuntarily achieved another kind of "perfection" in her star image: a monster/beauty of unproductivity.

Looking at these images, I recalled an episode Reyner told me about in one of our conversations. At the time the film was shot, she was very close friends with Jackie Curtis, with whom she had shared apartments, money, drugs, and also a strong attachment to 1940s Hollywood movies, which they would watch again and again over seemingly endless days, while reproducing on their bodies and in their postures the images they saw on the screen, most of which return in the free-form of Feinberg's film. Ruby recalls the way she and Jackie were working and living around that time, and described it with a particular image: "Sometimes we were ready to go out only in early morning, and walking down the streets completely high on drugs, with our wigs and gowns, we would meet people walking out from their houses and going to work. I always thought this was the perfect metaphor for our condition at the time."[124] Reyner recalled that one of those nights she and Curtis had spent hours getting into costume, and applying makeup to their faces, aiming to reach the perfection of their image, whose "making of" lasted a bit too long to be exhibited in public, in the nightlife or in a theatrical performance. This body image, which had been constructed all night long, would then erupt into the orderly morning of productivity, bringing its own evident unproductivity, glittering from the old-fashioned clothes, as a cosmetic sign on the skin among the productive adults of the city.

In these photographs, the monster of unproductivity is dragged on in a specific fashion. It is condensed in the typically camp effect according to which the person appearing in the image is in a perpetual state of incandescence, is "one very intense thing" (echoing one of Sontag's famous notes)[125] such as the 1940s Hollywood star icons to whom the image paid homage.

It is also a performance *in potentia*: the performance of Heaven, in *Heaven Grand in Amber Orbit*, and again of Heaven, in *Heaven Wants Out*. The images are also a piece of work in their own right: the staged photographs of a woman looking like a man dressed like a woman, shot in a collaboration between a photographer and an actress, inspired by a particular theater work that the actress was participating in, at the time, and that the photographer had witnessed as spectator. The performative synthesis the images embody, that of Reyner's memorable stage performance and that of Reyner's film performance *in potentia*, is the detonator of a series of historical echoes which in their flamboyance, in their idle appearance, expect no validation through future development: they stand still, in the grip of their promise.

Interlude II

✦

Longing Lasts Longer

Penny Arcade and the Radical Value of Pleasure

In 2014 at Joe's Pub in New York Penny Arcade presented her latest piece, entitled *Longing Lasts Longer*, a solo performance realized in collaboration with her longtime friend Steve Zehentner, who co-directed and designed the show.[1] The piece is both an act of mourning and a political claim of resistance: it is a performance about New York, and the way the city (and in particular downtown Manhattan, where Arcade still lives and works) has transformed in the last forty years, more or less since the time of *Heaven Grand in Amber Orbit*. Rhythmically scanned by a variety of musical themes, the performance has a simple structure: it is a long monologue, which Arcade reads aloud from white sheets of paper she throws on stage around her as the piece advances, and which she enriches substantially drifting into improvisation. Arcade addresses the audience directly, drawing from a repertoire which is familiar to her regular spectators. The long monologue is made of a repertoire of figures and stories from Arcade's life and from a New York past which some members of the audience share with the performer, some others might remember from previous shows, and yet some others do not—Arcade seems to suggest—but must listen to, must learn about, and might decide to carry on, at least as an antidote to the "cultural amnesia" (borrowing Arcade's own expression) which has been affecting the social and urban fabric of her beloved city in the last decades. *Longing Lasts Longer*, however, is not a piece about nostalgia, and it is not even merely about memory. As the title suggests, it is a piece about longing: a longing coming from far back, but turned onward. Indeed, although Arcade's raging presence on the stage and the disappointment she expresses toward contemporary New York, as well as contemporary arts, might seem pessimistic at first glance, the particular longing she conjures in her storytelling is a dynamic force of transformation which, eventually, she still believes theater is capable of hosting, of producing, of mobilizing. The endurance of such longing, and its relation to theater, is key not only to this piece, but to the very repertoire populating the long (and until recently overlooked in scholarly accounts)[2] course of Arcade's artistic work.

In the late 1960s Penny Arcade (at the time still known by her birth name, Susana Carmen Ventura) was a run-away adolescent, coming from a working-class Italian family who lived in Connecticut, and had immigrated to the United States from Basilicata, a region in southern Italy. After spending some time in a reform school, she arrived in New York and lived on the street for a year before being rescued, in 1968, by some of the young artists gravitating around the Play-House of the Ridiculous. She soon became a spectator at these performances and then joined the group, even if at the beginning appearing only in minor roles. While Reyner was placed by Vaccaro as "the star" in most productions, in the Play-House of the Ridiculous Arcade mainly performed as part of the chorus, so that, she recalls, she had to "always improvise her way into a starring role," but at the same time she was put in the position to learn "how to make art atom-by-atom."[3] As I anticipated, in *Heaven Grand in Amber Orbit* she was one of the three conjoined sisters who, however, received great attention in many of the reviews, some of which drew particular attention to Arcade's role in the trio. Among the many remarkable works in which Arcade featured in the 1970s, it suffices to mention Warhol's movie *Women in Revolt* (1972), Jackie Curtis's 1970 play *Femme Fatale*, in which she performed with Patti Smith, as well as many photographs by Peter Hujar or Leee Black Childers.

Penny Arcade also "survived" the 1960s and 1970s, and in many ways she bears the memory of what got lost on the way: of the many friends of hers who died during the cruel decade of the 1980s, especially because of the massive impact of the AIDS epidemic on the downtown art scene, or because of drug overdoses. Penny has taken care in one way or another of the many archives of her disappeared friends, such as Jack Smith,[4] or of those still alive but very old, like John Vaccaro, who a few years ago was temporarily evicted from the loft where he lived for the last forty years, because a bank purchased the building on 1st Street, and entirely renovated the apartment, forcing the artist to remove all his accumulated memorabilia, which Arcade helped organize and then stored in her basement, before Vaccaro's archive was eventually sold to the Downtown Collection. Arcade also bears the memory of the way the city has changed and given itself over to real estate investment, financial speculation, and gentrification. Besides being actively involved in political actions fighting against urban development in the Lower East Side (mobilizing in various ways the local community in order to raise awareness of the transformation there, and contributing to support local businesses and historical venues of the downtown art scene facing the danger of disappearance), she has also tried to counter the "cultural amnesia" of the particular history of New York in which she took an active part by means of her multifaceted cultural work. In 1999 she started with Steve Zehentner an oral history series called *The Lower East Side Biography Project*, aiming at "bridging the cultural gap between long time residents of New York's Lower East Side and newcomers to the rapidly gentrifying neighborhood."[5] The biography project, consisting of video interviews screened weekly in New York and making up an ever-growing archive (comprising today more than 1,300 entries), pays homage to the scene in which Arcade took part, but also to the rich cultural tradition of the Lower East Side. As one significant line of *Longing Lasts Longer* puts it, today in Arcade's opinion "gentrification is over. . . . We've been colonised. It's not just about gentrification of buildings, but gentrification of ideas. When ideas get taken over, what do you have left?"[6] Her whole work, in a sense, can be read as an enduring revolt against the rampant absorption and domestication into the grammar of capitalist valorization which today (paraphrasing the title of Currid's book discussed in the introductory chapter) "drives New York City," of all transgression and countercultural modes of living and working.[7] Interestingly, this revolt is also addressed to the politics of art, which in Arcade's view is hardly ever the subject of artists' critique, even when art is presented as politically engaged.[8] It is a revolt, therefore, against a pervasive dynamic of self-investment and posthumous valorization in terms of success which has led to the progressive incorporation of experimental work practices developed beyond the market in the 1960s and 1970s into contemporary structures of academic education (Arcade especially attacks art education in the university) and which have thereby ended up modeling the contemporary "corporatization of the arts."[9]

Aware and proud to be from a working-class, immigrant background, Arcade emphasizes how questions of class and origin have been long removed from the narratives of performing arts, as well as in the posthumous valorization of artists in terms of success in the "avant-garde" and later "performance art" scene. Not only is the case that "the 1960s were spearheaded by a working-class, entrepreneurial bunch of artists—Warhol, John Vaccaro, Jack Smith and so on,"[10] but some of those artists had, just like Arcade, also grown up in a hybridized context characterized by the mixture (not always easy) between customs and habits from other places, and the attempt to make them conform them with the American way of life. To name just a few of these artists, Andy Warhol was a second-generation American with Ruthenian origins, and Joe Cino was Italian American with Sicilian origins, just like John Vaccaro and Jackie Curtis. The grandmother of Curtis, a daughter of Italian immigrants, managed a famous bar in the Lower East Side, Slugger Ann's Bar and Grill, on 12th Street and Second Avenue, after having worked for years in Times Square, together with her two daughters, as a dime-a-dancer (dancers hired with wages for the hour).[11] Their family lived and worked for generations on the same block where Joe Preston, Curtis's cousin and the affectionate executor of his archive, still lives today. Jackie Curtis too grew up on the same block, surrounded by his mother's and grandmother's feather boas, glossy lipstick, and burlesque paraphernalia. It seems clear how this imagery directly flew into the drag fantasias staged in his plays, along with the memory of a nightlife he had only slightly experienced, nor directly inherited, but fantasized about and made his own.

The nightclub tradition of the Lower East Side, in which both Slugger Ann's Bar and Grill and the Bowery Follies (pictured in *Heaven Wants Out*) participated, was also interlocked, in many ways, with the history of American variety and popular entertainment which, since the late nineteenth century, has developed as part and parcel of the social and artistic interaction of people living in the area, and coming from different countries, making up in the street and on the stage what Sabine Haenni has named "the immigrant scene."[12] As I have already suggested, although it would not make sense to speak of a linear tradition, considering the urban and historical proximity of the Lower East Side "immigrant scene" to the artistic experiments of the 1960s can be helpful to reflect further on certain characteristics of performance work developed in this context, and which are interestingly carried on in Arcade's later performance practice.

Curiously, the stage name Susana Ventura chose for herself in the late 1960s (which, as the artist told me, was chosen by accident rather than programmatically) itself echoes a certain typology of popular entertainment: "penny arcades" were the cheap amusement devices operating at the turn of the century in fairgrounds, allowing the spectator to insert a few coins in a machine and have access to a short phantasmagoria of images and objects. Furthermore, as Arcade has repeatedly declared, a crucial influence for her performance-making were the practices of storytelling and imitating recurring figures: a practice which she connects with both her family background in childhood years and with her social experience as a young artist in the 1960s downtown art scene. Such a tradition of storytelling would inform her work as a playwright—she is the author of a various plays, such as *La Miseria* (1991) and *Bad Reputation* (1999)—as well as the distinctive style of performance art she developed through the years, where she features always as a narrator, as well as the resonator of a multiplicity of voices which speak through her and around her on the stage.

Arcade started developing her own performance work in the early 1980s by re-creating on stage the personalities she and many spectators of the downtown New York art scene of the time could recognize as a repertoire of familiar references: among them, Andrea "Whips" Feldman, the Warhol superstar who initiated the "show-time" at Max's Kansas City, or Margot Howard-Howard, a drag queen from Queens who was still alive at the time Arcade would re-create her character onstage, and who reportedly enjoyed watching her do it.[13] These characters were the first "attractions" of Arcade's theater, functioning in her performative invention very much like the personalities performing in the 1960s social scene had done as a distinctive inspiration for the Play-House's theatricality.

Penny Arcade is also the bearer of the memory of a particular way of making theater and being together, the one she experienced when she arrived in New York, especially in relation to Jack Smith and John Vaccaro, two figures she recognizes had a tremendous impact on her work, even if—she is at pains to emphasize—they were never her "mentors,"[14] in that they never transmitted to her a method or a system of knowledge or techniques. This way of making theater is one she learned by doing, before what she calls the "the professionalization of the arts."[15] It is a way of making theater in which improvisation goes alongside the written text, nourishes it and gives it a body, escaping both the mystique of drama and of the actor's "presence" onstage.[16] It is also a theater where various actions take place at the same time, and where most of the performers are nonprofessional actors.[17] It is a theater in which the relation with the audience is direct, unmediated, and often relies precisely on the sort of "unfocused eroticism"[18] which Brecht described as distinctive of the Play-House's performances. Furthermore, it is a relation with the audience which calls for a sustenance of performance production beyond critical validation: in Arcade's words, today as in the good old days, her theater can persist only if each spectator "replaces herself"[19] with a friend, if the spectator acts not simply as a theater consumer, but as the partner in crime of a certain theater, the producer of a certain possibility of its renewal by means of producing new audience, new conditions for performance.

Arcade's artistic and material engagement with the legacy of the New York underground amounts not only to a distinctive form of reproduction, but to a distinctive way of making history. Arcade's labor of reproduction, that is, is at the same time the passionate reading of such a history outside of a progressive course of value realization, and the defense of such a praxis beyond the politics of "entitlement."[20] More precisely, it is the insertion of the history of the 1960s–1970s theater she took part in into a radically different order of value. It is the reactivation of its burning core. I propose to read Arcade's artistic and political praxis in terms of what Elisabeth Freeman has called "erotohistoriography." In Freeman's terms:

> Erotohistoriography is distinct from the desire for a fully present past, a restoration of bygone times. . . . Erotohistoriography admits that contact with historical materials can be precipitated by particular body dispositions, and that these connections may elicit bodily responses, even pleasurable ones, that are themselves a form of understanding. It sees the body as a method, and historical consciousness as something intimately involved with the corporeal sensations.[21]

Freeman proposes her notion of erotohistoriography as an explicit challenge to the idea that "eroticism and material history" are "theoretical foils,"[22] claiming that "various queer social practices, especially those involving enjoyable bodily sensations, produce form(s) of time consciousness, even historical consciousness, that can intervene upon the material damage done in the name of development."[23] The potential of such a notion is not only to undermine the standard gendered logic that codes "history as male" and "reproduction as female,"[24] but to figure a different configuration of "binding," queering not only standard notions of progeny or progress, but also hegemonic views on the productivity of pleasure and pain.

In very much the same line, Arcade's mourning of the New York scene which had welcomed and nourished her as a young artist in the 1960s, although carrying the burden of loss and the bitterness of disappearance (of people, of places, of life possibilities), is a sentiment drenched with pleasure: it is an affect which is at pains to recoup the thrill of a certain intimacy, as well as the pleasure of sharing it off and on the stage. Indeed, according to Arcade, what her own story (not devoid of sorrow, humiliation, hardship) has taught her is that "pleasure is a radical value,"[25] and that this is something which should be carried on against the generalized "gentrification of ideas" which has affected even the history she herself contributed to make: the history of the 1960s New York underground, of the birth of performance art, of the gay movement after Stonewall. Affirming that she is "so queer that she is not even gay," in her work and theatrical rage Arcade has also long challenged a certain glamorization of identity politics, along with the "straightness"[26] which she saw taking over gay culture and lifestyle since the 1970s. Stubbornly affirming her own queer politics, Arcade's work reproduces in her magic lantern at the same time a mode of making theater, and of being in life: inhabiting a city, establishing friendly relations, taking care of friends' memories and archives, having sex and talking about it.

Indeed, Arcade's own narrative (romanticized, and not devoid of narcissism, like any autobiographical account) seems to offer a rich example of the peculiar configuration which "erotohistoriography" might engender: a runaway girl rescued from the street in the Lower East Side by a group of gay men, who not only supported her but also introduced her to a certain way of making theater; who subsequently survived the 1970s and made her way into "what came after" as a professional artist beyond "entitlement," although struggling to maintain, throughout, amateurism (at least in the understanding of amateurism I propose throughout these pages) as the burning core of her work. Then she took on herself the function to take care, materially and artistically, of the legacy of people like Smith or Vaccaro who, back then, had taken care of her, for their part, without ever taking on the paternalistic role of mentors. After all this, as she proudly declares at the end of *Longing Lasts Longer*, at sixty years old she found out that she had finally become capable of "giving birth to herself."[27]

In the multiple layers of generative connections outside of progeny, the labor of reproduction accounted for in Arcade's narrative is reminiscent in a curious way of the story of the little girl narrated by Freeman as a figure of "erotohistoriography": a little girl growing tomatoes in the earth fertilized by the monstrous dead body of Frankenstein, which Freeman picks up from a contemporary variant of the famous Frankenstein story.[28] In Freeman's reading, "the digestive work the little girl's body will eventually do upon the tomatoes"[29] becomes the example of many queer bodily practices which, binding pain and pleasure together over time, figures forms of reproduction which are not only outside of genealogical progeny, but cannot be foreseen, nor recognized in advance. Just like Penny Arcade, what the little girl receives "is not a transmission of authority or custom but a transmission of receptivity itself, of a certain pleasurably porous relation to new configurations of the past and unpredictable futures."[30]

We encounter an image of a little girl of just this sort in one very significant scene from Arcade's work: her legendary performance *Bitch! Dyke! Faghag! Whore!* It is an image Arcade uses to explain to her audience what she means by eroticism:

> There is just one energy and it is sexual. And the thing that is kind of funny and kind of sad is that none of us, not one single person in this room including me, is ever going to be as sexual as we were when we were two and half years old. Have you ever been with a two-and-a-half-year-old that likes you? They're just ah, ah, ah, ah, ah . . . (*Penny raises her arms and jumps around, imitating a child who wants to be picked up*). They want you with every little cell in their body. They're not trying to figure out what they're gonna get you to do in bed later.[31]

As Stephen Bottoms emphasized in an essay about Arcade's work, this image also condenses the deep influence on Arcade's work of the thinking of the psychoanalyst Wilhelm Reich, who famously advocated the crucial place of the energy liberated by sexuality for life, and the necessity that this force not be domesticated.[32] Even more crucially, however, what this image and Arcade's notion of eroticism conveys is the idea of a force of pleasure which does not imply a development, nor an accomplishment. It is a force of pleasure whose "radical value" is, in a sense, precisely its not being "entitled" to be considered sexual, and still, its persisting as pleasure, without a prescribed measurement of value, nor of productivity: a force of pleasure so intense which does not need a climax, as it is itself a continuing climax. Such force, in my view, can also be considered a powerful metaphor for the idea of theater advocated by Arcade's work: a *dispositif* of pleasure proceeding beyond any horizon of "entitlement," a non-domesticated memory of resistance against the diktat of value which presides over artistic work in contemporary capitalism.

Curiously, then, conjuring the figure of Frankenstein, we came back to confront, again, the theme of the monster. *Heaven Grand in Amber Orbit*, in which Arcade took part in 1969, staged at the same time the monster of unproductivity and a vision of theater as a magic lantern of mutation. Arcade's latest show, *Longing Lasts Longer*, constitutes the endurance and queer reproduction of precisely such a monstrous unproductivity, and the unpredictable offspring of its potentiality of mutation. In her pink dress and hair, in her passionate defense of the "joy of freakishness"[33] in which she grew up as an artist, Arcade appears just as significant for this queer history as the little girl evoked by Freeman, growing and then eating tomatoes drenched by the bodily fluids of previous bodies, reinventing in her gestures possibilities for new encounters of pleasure, and figuring new images of little girls shouting and jumping on forever-multiplying stages in order to defend the radical value of pleasure, and its long-lasting force.

Fig. 1. *Why Hanna's Skirt Won't Stay Down.* Written by Tom Eyen, directed by Neil Flanagan, and produced by the Theatre of the Eye Repertory Company at La MaMa Experimental Theatre Club, June 1969. Actors in the photo: Helen Hanft and Steven Davis.

Photographer unknown. Courtesy of La MaMa Archive / Ellen Stewart Private Collection.

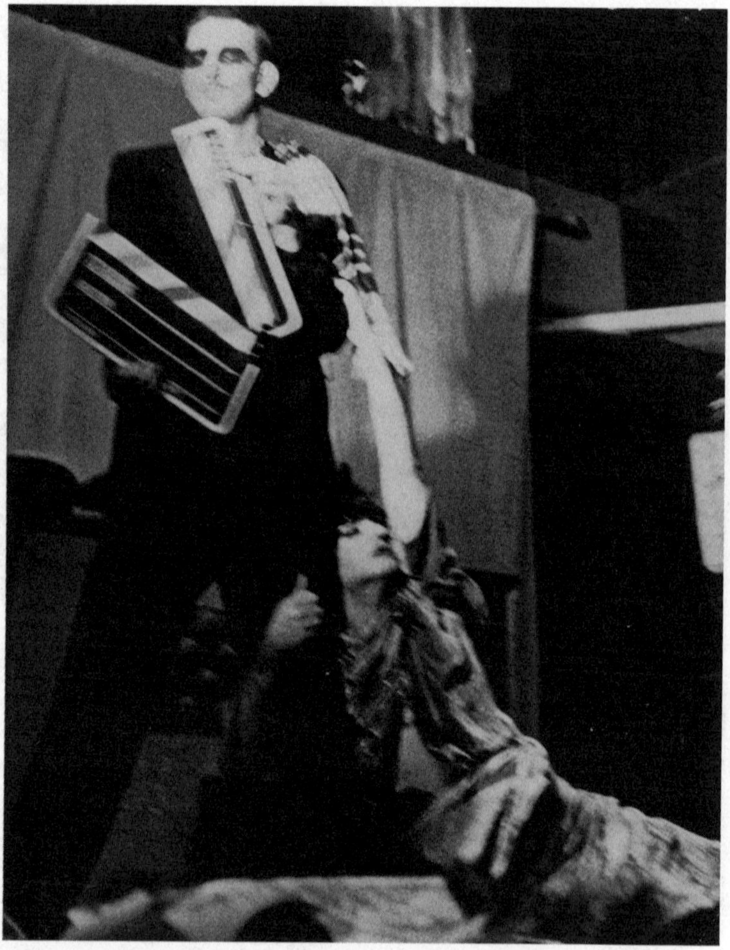

Fig. 2. *Untitled* (from *Brassieres of Atlantis*), c. 1970.
Black-and-white photograph, 9⅝ × 7¾ inches (24.4 × 19.7 cm).

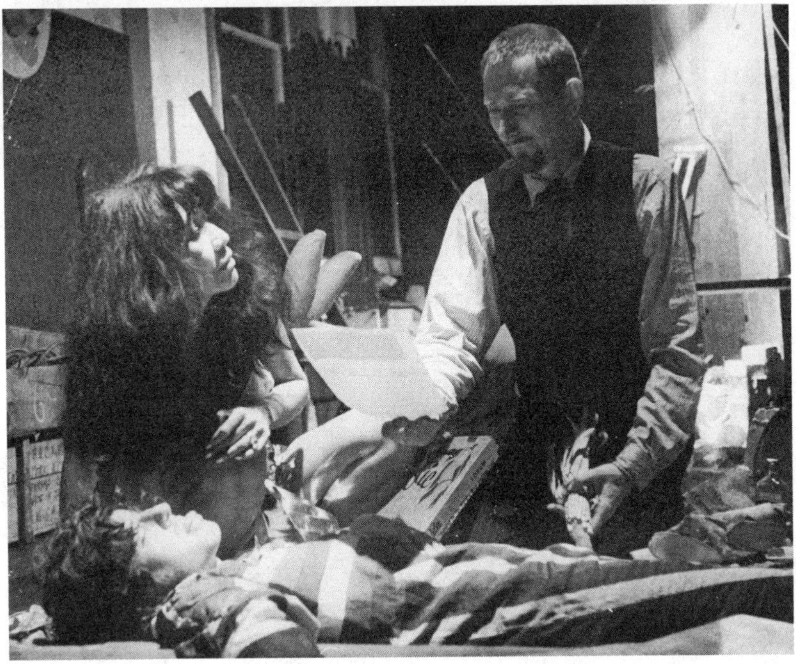

Fig. 3. *Untitled* (Jack Smith in *Brassieres of Atlantis*), c. 1970. Black-and-white photograph with Tosh Carillo and Maria Antoinette Rodgers, 7½ × 9½ inches (19.1 × 24.1 cm).

Photograph by Edwin Ruda. Copyright Jack Smith. Courtesy Gladstone Gallery, New York and Brussels.

THE MONGOLOID
PRINCESS
FLINGA

Figs. 4, 5, 6, and 7. *Heaven Grand in Amber Orbit*, performance of September 25, 1976: 76_0925-1-frames 20a, 29, 31, 33.

Fig. 8. *Heaven Grand in Amber Orbit*, at La MaMa Experimental Theatre Club, February 1970. Written by Jackie Curtis, directed by John Vaccaro. Actors in the photo: Ruby Lynn Reyner as Heaven Grand and Jaime de Carlo Lotts as Rouge Frolic in the foreground, with Michael Abrams as Classic Gravesend behind them.

Photograph by Dagmar.
Courtesy of La MaMa Archive / Ellen Stewart Private Collection.

Fig. 9. Flyer for *Heaven Grand in Amber Orbit*, at La MaMa Experimental Theatre Club, September 23–October 17, 1976.

Artist unknown.
Courtesy of La MaMa Archive / Ellen Stewart Private Collection.

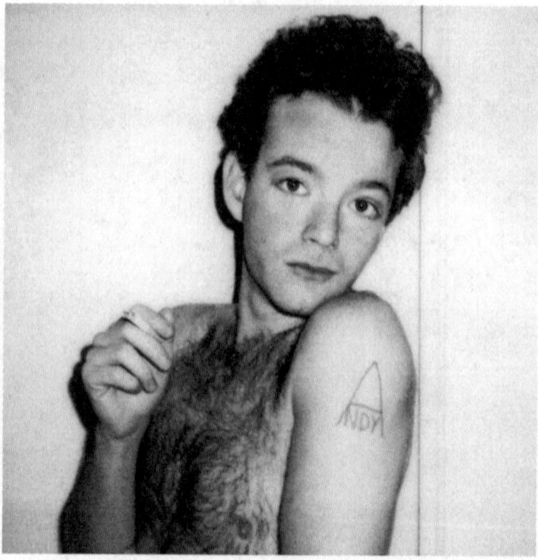

Fig. 10. Photograph of Jackie Curtis as a boy by Craig Highberger, 1973.

Copyright Craig Highberger. Courtesy of Craig Highberger.

Fig. 11. Photograph of Jackie Curtis as a girl by Craig Highberger, 1973.

Fig. 12. Jackie Curtis's first wedding, with Tony Ingrassia and unidentified friend, July 21, 1969.

Photographer unknown. Courtesy of the Estate of Jackie Curtis.

Fig. 13. Jackie Curtis's first wedding, with the groom "Stuart Eagle Speed" and unidentified friend dressed as a priest, July 21, 1969.

Photographer unknown. Courtesy of the Estate of Jackie Curtis.

Fig. 14. Jackie Curtis's last wedding, with his aunt Josephine Preston and groom Gary Majchrzak, May 1984.

Photographer unknown. Courtesy of the Estate of Jackie Curtis.

Chapter 3

✦

The Bride, the Mother, and the Star

Queer Kinship and Memorability in Jackie Curtis's and Ellen Stewart's Life and Legend

My next husband will be a beauty.

—Tom Eyen

La MaMa is a lot of people.

—Ellen Stewart

It's a poor sort of memory that only works backwards.

—Lewis Carroll

Two Promising Scenes

(1) According to the legend, the origins of La MaMa Experimental Theatre Club rest on the image of a pushcart belonging to a man called Abraham Diamond. Ellen Stewart moved to New York in the 1950s, planning to attend fashion school, an opportunity she was denied as a black woman in Chicago, where she grew up. She knew nothing about theater, and the only "performances" familiar from her youth were the radio dramas broadcast to her kitchen, which her mother would listen to during the afternoon.

Once in New York, Ellen realized she could not afford to pay for her education up front, and in order to support her future studies she started working as a porter at Saks Fifth Avenue. There, like all the other black employees, she was required to wear a blue smock over her dress. It was during this time that Stewart met Abraham Diamond, a Jewish stallholder who had immigrated to the United States at the turn of the century, and who had started a retail business from a pushcart on Orchard Street, in the Lower East Side. Diamond's pushcart—or so Stewart's recollection goes—was the impetus for other Lower East Side immigrants to establish a street market on

Orchard Street. It was at this market, one Sunday, that Stewart met Diamond, who "adopted" the young woman as a protégée: every Sunday, Diamond would donate a piece of fabric to Stewart that she would use during the week to realize a dress, exercising her creativity. The following Sunday, she would come back to Orchard Street and show her creation to Diamond, who would give her a new piece of cloth to work with, and as a gift he would also read her a poem, or a piece from the Torah.

According to the legend, one lunchtime when Stewart wasn't wearing her blue smock, one of her self-designed items was spotted by the fashion manager Edith Lances, who promoted Stewart right away to the role of executive designer for her company. Almost overnight, Stewart was provided with her own workroom, and had fifteen women working under her. Most of these women were survivors from concentration camps, recently arrived in the United States: no other white people in 1950s New York—Stewart recalls—were willing to work for a black woman. It was those women, it seems, who first started to call Ellen Stewart "Mama," for they saw in her a human and maternal relation, not just a boss.

For several years Stewart worked as a successful designer, collaborating with international firms. At some point she fell ill, and decided to make a trip to Tangier to recover. It is during this trip, Stewart says, that she "encountered" again the image of Abraham Diamond, who had died several years earlier. "Appearing" to Stewart in Tangier's casbah, Diamond suggested to her a brand-new path to follow: stop feeling sorry for herself, go back to New York, and build up her pushcart so as to allow other people to exercise their creativity. Stewart's pushcart, once she got back to New York, became Café La MaMa. With her own income, she rented a basement on East 9th Street, intending to run it as her own boutique during the day, and at night offer it as a venue for presenting her friends' work, beginning with that of playwrights Fred Lights and Paul Foster. Shortly after the programming of the small theater started, Stewart found herself without time to sew, and began working full-time as a producer.

Repeatedly told by Stewart through the years, the story of the pushcart is a well-known legend for the La MaMa regulars, and has been reiterated in most biographical and autobiographical accounts that I have come across about Stewart and La MaMa.[1] I have listened to Ellen telling many variations of this story, which I integrate with details I've gathered from listening to the same story told by others in New York, as recalled in conversation by her friends or employees. It goes without saying that it is a story hybridized by many voices, by many echoes, and whose "originality" (if it makes sense to look for one in a narrative encompassing miraculous encounters, "magical agents or helpers,"[2] visions, and all the like) is lost in the waves of storytelling.

As a foundation narrative, this legend must have been a familiar tale in the La MaMa environment by the early 1960s, since its central image could be spotted in a play produced at La MaMa in 1963, Paul Foster's *Hurrah for the Bridge*. In the meantime, the figure of Ellen Stewart started to perform a recognizable form of "motherhood," which she put to work to generate, or more precisely to produce, a specific artistic scene. Accordingly, she also started crafting the means of production for the scene itself. She not only built her pushcart, she also started taking care of fashioning its wheels, negotiating its position in the city, and establishing its distinctive style and identity. During this time, the legend functioned as a leitmotif that connected the very long history of La MaMa (continuing to this day, after Stewart's death) to its very point of departure, in 1963. Apparently, Stewart herself immediately recognized the power of this legend: it is hardly by chance that the only decorative element on the bare walls of the first La MaMa venue, at 321 East 9th Street, was the wooden wheel of a pushcart.

(2) There is a black-and-white picture of two men holding in their arms a glamorous bride in her white dress. She stands at the center of the picture, her hair adorned with a white ribbon, with a bright sky behind her curly hair. All three characters are smiling and seemingly looking beyond the camera, participating in an exposure offered to what one can imagine to be a broader wedding crowd surrounding the photographer. This picture was shot, one might guess, after the wedding vows were spoken, in the moment when souvenir photographs are usually shot, and witnessed by the group of guests in a spirit of cheerfulness, awaiting their turn to be "immortalized" in a picture for the wedding album. The gesture performed by the two male friends, therefore, might be taken to be both for the sake of the moment and for future amusement, for when the bride will linger over her wedding pictures, and smile again remembering the happy moment, even though, or if, as it happens, she is no longer in touch with those friends of her youth who held her up back then, in celebration. (See figure 12.)

In the picture, the bride holds up one of her hands, her fingers covered with rings, and brandishes a milk carton, showing it for the photographer. There are no clues as to what the milk carton is there for, and again one might guess that it is a souvenir of some sort for an activity transpiring behind the camera. Perhaps the milk added to the overall cheerfulness of the staged picture, or one might go as far as to imagine that the carton was part of a nuptial ritual prepared by friends (represented in the picture by the two men) for the newly wed bride. Indeed, such a guess wouldn't be too wide of the mark, since it's quite common, even in many secularized cultures, that in wedding celebrations close friends organize jokes or tricks involving one or both spouses performing funny or symbolic actions, which figuratively cement the newborn couple, including of course actions involving sexual innuendo, to which a tacit agreement assures that even relatives in attendance give their consent.

Milk, indeed, has an ancient history in nuptial symbology, which might even be linked back to what is considered a seminal text on human love and the marriage relationship, not least on the powerful force of sexuality: the Song of Songs. "Your lips are honey, honey and milk are under your tongue, your clothes holds the scent of Lebanon,"[3] the groom famously says to his woman in the biblical text. He continues: "I've come into my garden, my sister, my bride, I have gathered my myrrh and my spices, I have eaten from the honeycomb, I have drunk the milk and the wine. Feast, friends, and drink, till you are drunk with love."[4] And in the bride's response, milk is again a metaphor of appreciation and sensual attachment: "My beloved is milk and wine, he towers above ten thousands. . . . His eyes like doves by the rivers of milk and plenty" (87).[5] Milk stands here for fertility and prosperity, but also for taste, specifically the taste of each spouse's body, which henceforth—in the marriage liaison—will be available for full enjoyment. This (future) enjoyment is celebrated with friends, who are invited to "feast and drink, till they are drunk with love." During the wedding ceremony friends often provide the bride with a glass of milk, which she then offers to the groom before the first night.

Our picture is drawn upon with a number of little stars in blue and red ink, which frame the upper part of the image as a sort of posthumous festoon, or else as a theatrical drape standing over the heads of three actors. It might also be seen as a penciled burst of stardust, since the little stars are connected by curved, ink lines, resembling clouds coming down in infantile fashion from the bright summer sky in the background. It might have been the bride herself who added the stars to the picture while looking back at it in the years that followed, since it was collected among her other memorabilia.[6] Or it might have been the photographer, who wanted to add a graphic comment to the picture itself, enhancing its quality, before donating it to the bride. In any case, looking closer, one might notice that the bride has a little heart painted on her face, which seems to wink at the viewer almost as a foretaste of the graphic ornament to follow. What was to follow, in fact, was the gist of that very picture: not a future of marital sexual intercourse, nor one of honey and milk, but, rather, a future of wedding photographs. No matter how consciously welcomed by the bride's friends, the milk's stratified symbology appears as a metaphor for the nuptials of that particular bride. This is a bride who, at the same time, offered and drank from her own milk carton, before what could barely be called a first night. The name of the bride was Jackie Curtis, and the picture was taken on the occasion of *his* first wedding.

From 1969 to 1984 Jackie Curtis performed as a bride in eight weddings which he organized around New York City. None of them was a celebration of an actual relationship with any of the men he chose to wed, nor did they involve the beginning of a legal marriage. The series of weddings Curtis performed may be considered as the most long-term performance project he conceived and, at the same time, the expression of a peculiar affective attachment, which not only exceeded the notion of the "couple," but also affirmed the collective nature of the relationships that sustained this performance gesture. The social intimacy that hosted Curtis's bridal appearances through the years, involving the New York artistic scene in a happening-like mode of participation, nourished at the same time a distinctive form of queer kinship, and Curtis's inhabitancy of a small-scale star system, finding in such events the stage for its own celebration.

Modes of Production and Reproduction: Femininity as a Performative Movement

The life and legend of Ellen Stewart, and her "theatrical motherhood," and that of Jackie Curtis, and his long-term "bride project," are the subject of this chapter, which explores, through these two significant examples, peculiar modes of production and reproduction in the 1960s scene. I begin by considering these stories from a photograph and a family tale: fundamental tokens of memorability, understood both as vehicles of renewal (the renewal of affect, and that of attention) and as potential bearers of future value. These items, and the stories which surround them, are interlocking traces of a broader archive extending beyond their materiality as remains, and making up the "being-memorable" of the specific social time and space in which these stories took place.

The two "scenes" of the opening section have something in common, besides their proximity in the history of 1960s downtown New York. First of all, they both display kinship as an image, which comes to the spectator—the listener, the viewer—with great immediacy; they both construct kinship as a praxis, recognizable from the outside, and conjure a story, which the spectator doesn't know, but is invoked to imagine. In both cases, however, the conjured story is not so much the one behind the image, but the one which follows it: the story which the image itself, in a sense, is set up to generate, or more precisely, to produce. Both scenes function as a promise for a story to come. In one case, the story of the theater activities of La MaMa and of the role which Ellen Stewart will play within them, and in the other the story of Jackie Curtis's multifaceted career. As in any promise, what is at stake in these scenes is a performance of seduction, casting a spell on one's attention and bringing it along, in the future. It is perhaps the sort of seduction that every image, every story, performs by means of its exposure, by means of its "being in the world" to be looked at or listened to, for whoever might be there to recognize it.

Both these items are also traces of a way of living and remembering, which strongly resonates with the particular idea of reproduction discussed in the preceding pages on Penny Arcade's work: a reproduction enabled by, and enabling in its turn, the production of a certain potentiality of theater. Interestingly, both items bear witness to the way in which, from the beginning, Stewart and Curtis consciously chose—borrowing Arcade's own expression—to "give birth to themselves." In these two cases, this amounted first and foremost to the construction of personas upon which their own future would be built: each persona enabling a particular future to take place. In both cases, when this persona was first exposed for the world to see, there was no guarantee that such a future would actually take place. And yet, a certain projection toward the future seems intrinsic in the promise which these scenes make to whoever might be there, one day, to recognize that such future has indeed happened. In this sense, these scenes are themselves distinctive instances of foreplay, insofar as they configure a desire for continuation with no guarantee of arrival.

As in the poetics of Penny Arcade, the renewal of the promise at stake in the stories of Ellen Stewart and Jackie Curtis is also grounded in a distinctive politics of insistence, which, as I shall argue throughout the chapter, interestingly troubles the idea of reproduction as a genealogical process. In the cases of Jackie Curtis and Ellen Stewart, reproduction is not only the material labor sustaining the enactment of their life and artistic projects, but also the stubborn and reiterated gesture of taking care of the memory at each step along the way: marking its happening, producing resonances for it into the future, and securing a place for it in a legendary past.

From the point of view of "production," Curtis and Stewart share another common trait: both of their profiles exceed categories of artistic production, although they are commonly recognized as central figures *in the memory* of the 1960s and 1970s New York art scene. They are, in a sense, the ultimate figures of *amateur* producers.

From 1967 up to his death in 1985, Jackie Curtis was active in the New York downtown art scene in a number of respects, through many different forms and media. The author of a remarkable number of plays staged on the Off-Off Broadway scene (many, but not all, by the Play-House of the Ridiculous), he also performed as an actor in both stage and film productions and became known as one of the prominent Warhol superstars of the 1970s. Furthermore, he composed poems, journal articles, and a script for a television soap opera, which was never broadcast. Curtis's multifaceted artistic production, however, has generally been overlooked in scholarly considerations of the "New York underground," and until recently his presence was acknowledged only as a token role in the widely explored Warhol-based world, as well as in most accounts of the Off-Off Broadway theater. A possible reason for this oversight might be identified in the scattered forms of Jackie's work. Although he experimented with his own artistic vision in a number of ways, Jackie's figure was never fully articulated as a distinct "professional identity." Indeed, Curtis seems to have evaded such categorization throughout his life, aiming instead to open up his creativity across as many platforms as he could access. On the other hand, the lack of scholarship on Jackie Curtis might also be explained by the limited circulation of his work. Until very recently his plays had never been fully published, and the manuscripts kept in the

Curtis Estate are covered with handwritten notes, and are hardly identifiable as "final versions." Even when some of these plays have been referred to by scholars who have explored drag and cross-gendered performance texts, they have usually been dismissed as little other than amateurish "put-ons," and considered scarcely original in their contribution to a distinctive style of playwriting, as opposed to the more elegant productions of New York playwrights such as Charles Ludlam,[7] or to the most famous Play-House of the Ridiculous authors such as Ronald Tavel and Kenneth Bernard.[8] Curiously, though, the interest in Jackie's artistic life remains vivid in the memory of many artists, who acknowledge the influence of his work on the developments of both theater-making and social performativity.[9] In most accounts of people who have worked with Curtis, this influence—as it emerges, for instance, in Craig Highberger's important documentary *Superstar in a Housedress* (2005)—is explained precisely in terms of the kaleidoscopic quality of his artistic persona, involving a slippery personality whose complexity certainly exceeded the famous frame of Andy Warhol's Factory.[10]

The identity of Ellen Stewart is slippery, too, when measured against specific categories of work in theater. She was neither a director nor a playwright, nor a dramaturge, much less an actress or a set designer—although in the very long course of her life she did, in one way or another (and even more systematically in her old age) undertake all these practices.[11] It would be quite narrow, even, to define her as a "theatre producer," which would perhaps be the more accurate definition for her role at La MaMa. That is, unless one is willing to put the term "production" under scrutiny, and take it to encompass the various ways in which, beyond the materiality of the stage, theater is indeed socially produced and reproduced.

Among the many accounts of the early 1960s, perhaps the most recurrent image describing the figure of "Stewart as a producer" is the one offered by Paul Foster and reported in Sally Banes's research:

> Ellen Stewart cooked soup to feed her actors and playwrights. Her salary went into the communal kitty . . . She rang a cowbell at the beginning of each performance and welcomed the audience to the theater with her now famous, "welcome to La Mama; dedicated to the playwrights and all aspects of the theater." They were her life and she was their mother.[12]

Clearly what is at stake in this "production" (which Foster recalls in explicitly gendered terms) is not only the personal investment of Ellen's salary, which enabled the theater activities to take place, but also her domestic labor of renewing the labor force, as well as the affective labor of making La MaMa a home for theater, and presenting it to the public.[13]

With great precision, Claudio Meldolesi once called Ellen Stewart "una donna-teatro," a "woman-theater," borrowing and adapting for her the beautiful definition employed by Jean-Louis Barrault with reference to Antonin Artaud (that of a "*homme-théâtre*"):[14] by that, he meant that not only had Stewart strongly interwoven her own existence with theater, but somehow her own persona might "embody and display theatre itself."[15] What I take from this definition is an interesting use of the word "theater," one which seems to exceed the practice of theater-making in its particularities. "Theater" here stands for the essential features *belonging* to theater as a habitat: an environment and a practice, before and beyond any other quality. Paradoxically, it stands for *a theater without qualities*. Hence, La MaMa's persona embodied and displayed, in a way, theater as such: a habitat recognizable from the outside for a particular quality of attention, and for its hospitality to encounters between friends and strangers, a temporary polis bringing together and negotiating in that space a multiplicity of desires, rights, and life possibilities.

In light of this definition, the "producer" role performed by Stewart since the early 1960s may be more accurately grasped. Since the birth of La MaMa, she started producing and sustaining, like a mother, like a worker, like a producer, a theater to be invented anew, without plays, program, or future. This theater to be imagined, then, was in a sense hosted by the very scene of imagination Stewart had produced for herself, with the powerful image of the pushcart at its center. This image can be considered Ellen's first investment in the kinship which would sustain La MaMa's activities. On a different note, as I discussed in the first interlude, "Paying Homage to the 'Underground,'" Stewart also constitutes a distinctive entrepreneurial figure, and one of those who survived the 1960s and were able to turn into capital the love labor initiated back then, primarily by taking care of its heritage.

Likewise, the establishment of Jackie Curtis's persona, from his debut on the underground stage in the early 1960s to the picture portraying her in bridal dress on July 31, 1969, was the production of a distinctive scene of imagination, in and by virtue of which Curtis's particular artistic production would take shape. Curtis died of a heroin overdose in May 1985 and did not achieve, in his lifetime, mainstream success. On the other hand, as I shall discuss in more detail later on, the whole course of his life since the early 1960s is characterized by a relentless pursuit of fame, in and outside the downtown art scene, as well as by a productive mobilization of affects and by powerful strategies of self-promotion which might well suggest a consideration of Curtis's figure as a model or precursor of precisely the typology of "self-entrepreneur" seemingly central in today's creative economy.

In a sense, then, the lives and legends of Stewart and Curtis constitute significant examples of the potentiality, as well as the ambiguity, of foreplay. Their stories speak about a tension between the promise of love labor as an engine for artistic production and the unforeseeable future of its actualization. Furthermore, both stories mobilize, in diverse and yet similar ways, the social and artistic habitat in which both Stewart and Curtis operated at the same time as a system of queer kinship, and as a small-scale star system. In the grammar of both systems, Stewart and Curtis deployed an image of femininity which, while winking at the narrative and symbolic codes pertaining to both kinship and stardom, radically detached it from its assigned roles in terms of production and reproduction. In the case of kinship, both Stewart and Curtis detached femininity from an idea of progressive time, traditionally associated with women's position in a relation of conjugality as well as women's biological capacity to give birth. As I have already noted, from the beginning of their lives and legends Curtis and Stewart "gave birth to themselves"; yet such a "birth" was later put to work to generate a social and artistic environment in which their own figures did not perform traditional functions associated with either the figure of the "mother," which Stewart's moniker would seem to announce, or the "wife," which the bride costume would seem to promise. In the case of the star system, both figures constructed for themselves the role of a "star" but put this role to work reversing the position of the star herself in the system of production. Whereas in traditional star systems, the "star" was produced by an external orchestration of elements and agents, in these cases it was "the star" herself who conceived and pursued the production of her own image in order to allow an external orchestration of elements and agents to take place. The star, as it were, was her own producer.

For all these reasons, in the pages that follow I choose to read Curtis's and Stewart's stories in parallel and in the light of the three stereotypical female figures—the bride, the mother, and the star—with the additional aim of suggesting a particular use of femininity as a performative movement related to securing conditions for art-making, rather than as a destination. In this sense, this constitutes yet another instance of foreplay. Beginning with staging these stories in the background of what I consider the broader system of queer kinship on which the 1960s New York scene was founded, I shall later direct the spotlight toward some significant moments of Stewart's and Curtis' stories, which follow up the scenes previewed in the opening section, and give added depth to the figures' peculiar modes of production and reproduction.

Queer Kinship in the New York Scene of the 1960s

Crucial, for both these stories, were the affective relationships and forms of memorability which in 1960s New York informed artistic and social practices, and which I propose to regard as a distinctive form of queer kinship. These functioned as confirmation of a common belonging but also extended relations into the future of their actual disappearance as "live presence," in the form of survival in memory, as well as in the form of value. Relations of love, solidarity, and nontraditional coalition in this scene also reconfigured standard relations of production and reproduction, and passed them on by means of a common grammar of images, stories, and names.

The starting point for my own conceptualization of queer kinship is underscored in the ideas elaborated by Elizabeth Freeman, who suggests that the notion of kinship can be mobilized to discuss queer bonds of solidarity outside of genealogical connections, by first understanding kinship as a set of "techniques of renewal":

> as the process by which bodies and the potential for physical and emotional attachment are created, transformed, and sustained over time. The largest and most systematized example of kinship as a technique of renewal, of course, is the domestic labor that women are expected to do to transform the raw material of a worker's wages into what he needs to labour for another day: a bed, food, clean clothes, etc. This kind of bodily renewal literally reproduces the labor force. But kinship also . . . recreates and recharges bodies toward ends other than labor, such as play, love, and even violence.[16]

Freeman's argument, on its own, builds upon a great amount of scholarship which, since the early twentieth century, has contributed to a more complex understanding of kinship outside the paradigm of biological reproduction, making clear that its essential function consists in alliances that enable reciprocal support and exchange among individuals.[17] Crucial to this scholarly context is the work of Pierre Bourdieu, who introduced the notion of practical kinship for describing those connections founded on assistance, care, and reciprocal dependency, which, he claims, are entirely comparable with those relations traditionally referred to as *family* relations.[18] Whereas historically the emphasis on sexual reproduction has overshadowed the value of cultural reproduction, the latter has in fact always been crucial to the functioning of kinship, making forms of social solidarity other than those based on consanguinity absolutely integrated into people's everyday lives. Social solidarity is thus recognized as even more powerful than official kinship ties, not least because the very existence of such connections depends upon their continual renewal. Bourdieu describes the distinctively social nature of bodily dispositions, collectively elaborated and transmitted, in practical kinship, not as abilities but rather as faculties, employing and extending Marcel Mauss's idea of habitus. In Bourdieu's sense, habitus, on which any *habitat* is founded, is "a product of history" that "produces individual and collective practices—more history. . . . It ensures the active presence of past experiences."[19] Freeman further develops such thinking on peculiar modes of passing on relations beyond the present, queering the notion of "belonging" so central to the very ideology of kinship. The etymology of belonging incorporates an idea of proximity, of closeness;[20] Freeman goes so far as to suggest a "false etymology" for the term "belonging" (in which *belong* would contain the sense of "*being long*"), forcing the language to express both the social function of belonging and its temporal dimension. In this respect, she downplays and appropriates the dominant ideology of official kinship, unraveling the way in which belonging is supposedly represented, for instance, by photographs or by family tales, usually understood as metonymies of reproduction. Instead, kinship's ideology can also read back reflexively: if the very notion of kinship is itself elaborated through visual reproduction, this simply makes evident that "all kinship may, indeed, be a matter of poses, gestures, performance."[21] The circulation of family photographs beyond the private sphere has been a way of suturing kin relations in the history of the modern, privatized but geographically dispersed family. Freeman suggests that in queer liaisons photographs function similarly as evidence of forms of attachment and loving gestures, but also as means of establishing new connections through time, projected toward a future renewal of queer kinship embodiments.

In our two examples, such appropriation of the ideological performance of kinship operates in particularly interesting ways. First of all, both the life and legend of Jackie Curtis and that of Ellen Stewart were made possible by their being embedded and exposed in a specific social and affective environment which not only secured their enactment and renewal in memory, but also constitutes—resonating with Bourdieu's words—their common *habitat*: the social and artistic scene of 1960s New York. As previous studies usefully pointed out (most remarkably Brecht and Banes), the downtown art scene of New York in the 1960s was founded on a system of relationships radically distinct from those of the family, which mainstream society still understood as the base from which a life beyond the home could be experienced.[22] Rather than a community (in the traditional sense in which it is imagined as a "given" situation), the social intimacy experienced in this context might rather be considered as the *performative invention* of a community, founded on a shared familiarity with specific images and behaviors.

Participants in the New York scene engaged in behavioral patterns that literally reproduced the "elementary structures" and rituals on which the idea of family was traditionally based, but did so in ways such that those very same structures were also, and at the same time, contested and debunked. Several artists became reference figures, recognized as such by interconnected groups of people, and routinely referred to as "parent figures" by those artists gravitating toward them. Besides the key example of Ellen Stewart,[23] a number of other figures can be considered in this perspective, such as Andy Warhol, Jonas Mekas, Diane di Prima, and Al Carmines. In fact, these figures performed for sustained periods the role of "concierges" in relation to several "homes," but did so in a context where the idea of the concierge, together with the idea of home itself, was constantly renegotiated. Home was not a given place but rather an assumed one, adopted, as it were, for the purposes of making things happen. Home became a way of asserting one's *be-longing* in the present and in the future.

If the normative domain of language determined the employment of labels like parent figures, in the actuality of behaviors the function performed by those same figures with their assumed "family" of artists featured few of the characteristics traditionally associated with what is thought as a "parent role." Those concierges were rather those who guaranteed the permanence of that kinship in the New York social and art scene. The linguistic burden of family labels enabled the concierges to wear a "second nature," playing with the (supposed) "restored behaviors" of the kinship code.[24] Hence, kinship labels were abstracted from the domain of progeny in order to value some functions commonly attributed to kinship roles (such as economic support, cohabitation, assistance) while denying others (such as power, control, punishment).

Artistic work was not extraneous to the dynamic of such peculiar kinship. Stefan Brecht, for instance, describes the performance style of the Play-House of the Ridiculous as a private/public staging of familiar obsessions, where the spectator constantly has the impression that "the evening's performance is a meaningful event in, and a product of, their ongoing family life and history" and that each play, ultimately, defined first and foremost a particular "epoch in the history of the family"[25] as a sort of self-reflexive measurement of time. Likewise, Sally Banes points out that many plays and performances in 1963 staged the breakdown of the family, which was "a sociopolitical shift internal to American postwar economics and demographies."[26] She underscores that the social intimacy of the downtown art scene supplied images of a diverse community model while also challenging power relations in familiar contexts. An outstanding example of this was the social space of the Caffe Cino, where many such plays were staged, and which was "mythologized more as a family than as a collective":[27]

> The liberating privacy that its participants identified as feeling at home—even though this was a home whose peace was constantly threatened by police busts, since the theater was unlicensed, and even though domesticity in real life never guaranteed privacy—was key to the creative ferment at Caffe Cino. People could try things out informally for a supportive audience that was practically at the actors' fingertips, and, most important (unlike at home), anything was allowed. This was a liberated home, a party with parents perennially out of town and a generous uncle, rather than a father, at the helm. (It was also a family where homosexuality rather than heterosexuality was the norm.) Even the fact that "the room," as Cino referred to it, was not a true theater, but a space handmade anew for each production, without any budget, added the feeling of imaginative freedom and cooperative, domestic warmth.[28]

This model of community could be compared—weirdly enough—to that presented in Walt Disney's classic Ducks cartoons: a universe where "parents" are not present in the narrative, but where there are instead only "uncles," "aunts," "great-uncles," "cousins," "boyfriends," "girlfriends," "nephews," and "friends."[29] In Duckburg the absence of parents seems to reflect a desire to exclude sexuality from the picture (since the cartoons were designed for children),[30] including even the exclusion of any evidence of reproduction. On the other hand, the pervasive nature of kinship in Duckburg contributes to the creation of an atmosphere of intimacy among characters who interact, support, and help each other out even though they're not related by explicit, direct family ties; or rather, even though family ties don't involve the establishment of households along the lines of the standard American family.[31]

If in Duckburg this eccentric form of queer kinship can be read as a device for removing active sexuality from the scene, in the 1960s New York scene the widespread kinship-like intimacy functioned the other way around: in these queer (anti-)families, sexuality was if anything overexposed, and formed a vital dimension of everyday life. It was something people talked about, looked at, embodied in creative forms, and it was of course spectacularized. Andy Warhol's movies are exemplary in this respect: in his films, sexuality is typically overexposed and presented as a childish, often cruel form of play, conducted by people related to one another by explicit forms of belonging.

In the cases of Jackie Curtis and Ellen Stewart, the performative play on the ideological function attributed to sexuality in the traditional family appears striking: the choice of their "second nature"—the one they invented and embodied in the continuity of their life and work—addressed directly the kinship figures which, supposedly, secure the reproduction of society: "the bride" and "the mother." Interestingly, in both cases these figures were strategically detached from a discourse of biological reproduction and put at work, instead, as producers and reproducers of social and artistic life.

Fairy Tales and Insistence: The Metonymic Crystal of *Hurrah for the Bridge*

Ellen Stewart's pushcart story is clearly both a family narrative, and a fairy tale. The seduction of the tale is in the promise of development, which—as in classical fairy tales—enables the story to happen and to become crystallized especially in one image: in this case, the pushcart. In the line of thought of Italo Calvino, fairy tales are the deposit of potentiality: they enact imagination as a "repertoire of what is potential, what is hypothetical, of what does not exist and has never existed, and perhaps will never exist but might have existed."[32] Belonging to the territory of what "might happen," they also portray potential destinies, or more precisely, destinies while they are taking place. They don't contain introspective storytelling, nor formation narratives; they host figures who are totally apparent, whose existences are exposed in their full unity of appearance. Such that, at the end of her pushcart tale, *Ellen Stewart* appears *as La Mama*. Curiously, such is also the mechanism according to which the star image is synthetically constructed and presented to the public.

Ellen Stewart's fairy tale pertains to the oral tradition: as I anticipated, it has been recounted in various forms in the La MaMa theater building (as well as in all the international affiliations of La MaMa) for forty years.[33] As a classical family tale, this story pivots around an anecdote featuring a (present or dead) family member performing an identity that will afterwards be recognized as founding that family unit: just like the story of grandparents being "fiancés," of how the family house was bought, the tale of one's birth, the narrative of difficult moments and how they were overcome. In a way, every family narrative accounts for an origin, and it is narrated to others—the "offspring" of the narrated family, or those who are outside of the family unit—both to confirm the story and to foster its continuation.

The labor of reiterating such anecdotes through the years, typical of the oral tradition of family tales, is characterized by a habit of repetition of a certain kind, which Gertrude Stein gracefully describes as a work of "insistence": a practice different and somehow opposed to repetition.[34] Stein recalls having become conscious of this difference when, as a seventeen-year-old visiting her aunts in Baltimore, she would sit and listen to them talking about the same life episodes over and over again: "no matter how often what had happened had happened any time one told anything there was no repetition."[35] Insistence, Stein suggests, has to do with something that exists, that is alive and recognized as such in narration; it has to do with "listening and talking at the same time."[36] There can only be repetition when things are described, not when someone is listening to and talking through a life story, even if—especially if—the story is already known. The same sort of insistence, in a sense, can be recognized at work in Penny Arcade's performance texts, where many voices return and overlap, but never as "past": on the contrary, the people and stories remembered onstage always appear alive and present in the practice of storytelling, according to a particular use of repetition avoiding the narrative mode of description, and translating a quality of oral history into the distinctive space of theater.

Also in the La MaMa queer family, the work of insistence did not encompass only storytelling but also the production of artistic works, which interestingly performed precisely such practices of "listening and talking," such longing for memorability to take place in the present. An outstanding example of this work of insistence is Paul Foster's play *Hurrah for the Bridge*. First performed on September 15, 1963, at the Caffe Cino, and repeated a few days later at La MaMa,[37] *Hurrah for the Bridge* is described by Stephen Bottoms as one of the "homegrown plays from La Mama."[38] Paul Foster was, in fact, one of the first playwrights to be associated with Café La MaMa and also featured in the core group of artists whose work was presented in La MaMa's second location, on Second Avenue. There, a slight shift occurred in the theater's activities, not least because its café status was legally converted into that of *a club*. Following complaints from neighbors, in April 1963 the New York Building Department had evicted Café La MaMa from the East 9th Street basement where it was founded (in October 1961), arguing that it was located in an area zoned against cafés. Although the legal claim subsequently proved to be in error, in June 1963 La MaMa had already managed to relocate to a second-floor loft on Second Avenue. In March 1964, however, Stewart was informed that the new area was also off-limits for cafés: the theater was closed by the Fire Department and Stewart was arrested and held in jail for a night. Instead of moving again to a different place, or attempting to get a theater license to meet the city regulations, Stewart's subsequent resolution was to "make do" with the theater activities previously taking place in the café, only in a different legal frame: one of a club. Membership cards were issued and the name was changed to 'La MaMa Experimental Theatre Club" (La MaMa E.T.C.). Interestingly, not only did Stewart's tactical move not affect the profile of her theater, but it asserted what La MaMa had been from its foundation (although disguised as a café)—"a permanent private party."[39] The different space of the Second Avenue location, however, did foster a cast of different features for La MaMa: whereas the first basement was suitable for only 30 spectators, the second venue accommodated 74 seats (and often more than 74 people); the larger room allowed a bigger and slightly raised stage,[40] as well as the presence of dressing rooms, located in the rear opposite the coffee bar.

Hurrah for the Bridge, Foster's first play staged at La MaMa, embodies the continuity of the La MaMa theater practice, from the human and familiar environment of its beginnings to the more articulated possibilities offered by the new venue, shortly before its café status was going to be turned into that of a club. But upon closer observation, the play does more than that: its plot dramatizes and puts on stage the very image of which La MaMa's family is crystallized. Conrad Ward's photographs of *Hurrah for the Bridge* kept intact such crystal and display it for those who have not witnessed the performance live, in 1963. In most of the pictures a big pushcart, filled with all sort of rags, takes up a great part of the stage. Standing beside it, a man (the actor Paul Boesing) holds a sheet of white paper that states: "shut up and push." In *Hurrah for the Bridge* the pushcart belongs to Rover, the tragic protagonist of the play. Somewhere offstage, a bridge is being built, and apparently its construction requires that human bodies are embedded in the stanchions. Accordingly, a group of criminals organizes to take over the city in search of people to kill, and of more bodies to support the pillars. The play conveys an atmosphere of continuous emergency and urban violence, even war. The Rover character is a beggar, helplessly defending his life and his pushcart that contains all his belongings (mainly rags and junk objects) as well as his beloved female companion, who is hidden beneath the rags. The woman, named Ruby, apparently doesn't reciprocate Rover's devotion, and her presence is expressed throughout the play only by means of harsh messages delivered to Rover from inside the pushcart. The end of the play sees the gang eventually succeed in killing Rover: only at this point does Ruby emerge from the pushcart and laugh at Rover's corpse before abandoning the scene and the play's dead protagonist.

From the standpoint of a theater historian, the most immediate iconographic reference for Rover's image would be that of Brecht's *Mother Courage*: there too a pushcart is a central prop, pushed by a woman in a constant state of emergency provoked by war. Likewise, Mother Courage's cart contains objects: merchandise that she sells to the soldiers, to profit from the war. Also in Brecht's play, the pushcart sometime carries human beings—Mother Courage, her children—but rather than defending her beloved at her own risk, the protagonist ends up merchandising their lives, just as she had merchandised the other items filling her pushcart from the beginning of the play. For many among the 1963 La MaMa audience, however, the image of the pushcart will have evoked most powerfully the image of another sort of mother: one existing outside of a theater tradition, but whose presence was crucial for *Hurrah for the Bridge* to take place. It was a mother produced, as it were, by her own children, and whose motherhood was invented and anticipated by the pushcart's fairy tale.

Hurrah for the Bridge, of course, offered its own particular version of the pushcart image: one which even encompassed a possible playful subversion, on the part of Foster, of Stewart's rhetoric: after all, the play is not celebratory and the woman inhabiting the pushcart is a rather ambivalent figure. Even so, the very grammar on which such potential subversion could take place was the one established by Stewart's legend and deeds, which the audience knew and could recognize. Hence, *Hurrah for the Bridge* was in any case a powerful vehicle for this tale; but even more significantly, its staging was also the articulation of a further episode in the family narrative.

Crucially, in fact, one of the stage objects employed in the show (a bell, attached to Rover's pushcart, ringing every time the character appeared on stage) also became a familiar symbol of La MaMa, and since 1963 it has remained associated with the figure of Ellen Stewart. Since that date, showtime at La MaMa would be announced by Ellen Stewart appearing on stage and ringing the bell, to capture the attention of the audience, and introduce the show with the standard formula: "Good evening ladies and gentlemen, and welcome to La MaMa, dedicated to the playwright and to all aspects of theater."

As Freeman suggests, in kinship relations objects always function as a mode of passing on human relations "in the form of secondary possessions rather than some primary personhood, or as substance rather than form. . . . Objects imperfectly express as metaphor a more properly metonymic flow of corporeal material between people."[41] In *Hurrah for the Bridge* such metonymic flow was reproduced by means of a theater of metaphors: Stewart's familiar legacy with Abraham—a non-consanguineous relation of affects binding two individuals in what was for both a foreign city—in oral storytelling came to be epitomized by the image of the pushcart, hence turning a real object into an image deliberately employed as a vehicle for renewal. La MaMa's founder made that image stand as a platform for enhancing collective achievements, and allowing the gist of her own attachment to Diamond to persist. The metaphor of the pushcart, then, bounced back and forth among artists associated with La MaMa, most of whom were personally related to Stewart, either living in her home or benefiting one way or another from her economic support, as well as from her domestic and affective labor. In Foster's play, the pushcart returned to be an object, which on its part became the engine for the production of another metaphor, passed on by means of a metonymic flow: a bell.

Therefore, Foster's play was not only an homage to Stewart, or a playful subversion of her mythology, but an *affective archive* of her project in its enactment.[42] The 1963 *Hurrah for the Bridge* performance archived both the story of Stewart's pushcart and a particular epoch in the history of the family defined by Foster's play (the Second Avenue period in 1963/1964). The bell, which endured in the history of the theater, carried on the story of the first production of *Hurrah for the Bridge* as a "metonymic flow" of corporeal materials in the La MaMa kinship system. Furthermore, not only did Foster's play archive the La MaMa story, but its performance was itself a *mode of production* for the La MaMa archive, depositing photographs, objects, and words to be returned to afterwards.[43] No less importantly, what enabled the performance to happen—the spatiotemporal conditions for its taking place—was the narrated story: Ellen Stewart's project to make La MaMa endure. The mode of production of *Hurrah for the Bridge* was itself imbricated in the exposure of La MaMa kinship: a theater labor which was not a product in market conditions, but was consumed by a familiar audience, which therefore participated in its image economy. Spectators were called upon to witness the "listening and talking" of this family narrative, to host its image economy, and to let its memory crystallize into episodes through the work of insistence (going on beyond the show, for instance in conversation).

The memorability of Ellen's story is interlocked with the production of documents (whether they are plays, photographs, or stage props) to the extent that "documents" don't pertain exclusively to what *actually happened*, but in the attempt to transmit its memory, to what could have happened, or could still happen. Again, we return to think about the basic dynamic of fairy tales, converging with that of family narratives insofar as they both host the potentiality of development and the crystallization of significant images. The narrated episode—being an extraordinary event (such as Stewart's miraculous success, and her subsequent magic encounters with Diamond) or efforts and sacrifices (such as the hardship of her work as a porter, as well as her struggle with the city regulations, as a producer)—establishes the order of possibility for imagination and for theater actions. This generates a net of images which deposit around this "fact" like a crystal.[44] The figure of the crystal is central to Italo Calvino's analysis of the order of fantastic imagination: the crystal is presented as a system of organization of narratability, as well as "a mode of growth in time."[45]

The production of documents, however, might also posthumously assert the actuality of a performance of kinship whose value—in life, as much as in art—was precisely being exposed at the scene of a familiar recognition. Orchestrating performative documents of one's private life was a strategy long practiced in the New York performing art system, from the stars' biographies for the press, in the vaudeville era, to the full blossoming of the gossip and celebrity industry. Exploring the notion of kinship alongside the idea of the 1960s New York small-scale star system helps us understand how the affective narrative making up its memories is also a *play* of renewal, life in search of a "memorable scene."

The life and legend of Jackie Curtis brings into focus this dynamic quite precisely, and further translates the issues discussed so far into a specific convergence toward the figure of the star: memorability achieved through images and names; queer kinship and the performative invention of community; and moreover, the importance of photographs as a way of suturing kin relations and as the visual elaboration of a habitat. Jackie Curtis's archive, moreover, is the affective archive of her own life and legend, inhabited as it was by Curtis in its making.

Glamour, Glory and Gold: The Prelude of Jackie Curtis's Memorability

In September 1967 at Bastiano's Theater in New York City a play opened entitled *Glamour, Glory and Gold: The Life and Legend of Nola Noonan, Goddess and Star*. The script had been written in 1965 by an eighteen-year-old boy from the Lower East Side named John Holder Jr., but it was signed Jackie Curtis. *Glamour, Glory and Gold* was the story of the rise and fall of the ambitious Nola Noonan, who makes her way to Sunset Boulevard through a long series of love affairs, which she exploits so as to advance herself "up the ladder of success, wrong by wrong,"[46] in pursuit of a glamorous status that, once achieved, brings about her headlong decline through burnout to destruction. Nola's story is one of a woman who is exploited by men, but she quickly learns to exploit men in return by means of her powerful sex appeal. Therefore, even the tragic, brutal rape she recalls having suffered at the age of seven at the hands of a door-to-door salesman turns immediately in Nola's words into a precocious (and grotesque) discovery of full sexual pleasure. It also provides her with the possibility of leaving home. Nola persuades the salesman to take her to Chicago, to pursue his dream of "bringing back vaudeville" with her music performances.[47] Shifting thereafter from man to man—from the salesman to a married politician, then a mobster, and an officer of the law—Nola grew up as a stripper and burlesque performer, cultivating the dream of finally getting to "Hollywood. While there is still a Hollywood."[48] Throughout the play she embodies every man's secret desires but actually only pursues her own, that of her metamorphosis into the goddess that she believes she was born to be. After all, as she recalls before leaning on the proscenium and pretending to start a burlesque act, "every goddess does stock,"[49] and she eventually makes it to the big time of motion pictures, to the point of being unable ever to leave. The entire play is in fact a continuous blur between Nola's life and movie scenes (most of them resounding with interlocking quotations from famous movies) with Nola as author, spectator, and actress of her own glamorous and disastrous destiny. The play closes with a campy, heartbreaking monologue, performed to the accompaniment of the Warsaw Concerto,[50] desperately calling on all the disappeared characters of the play, trying to figure out whether she is indeed living her life or playing, instead, in a terribly authentic film set. Trying to figure out, after all, whether it's still possible to "be a good girl, and even finish the picture." But "what picture?"[51]

This narrative stood as a real topos in the American imagery: a story often told by Hollywood movies, a narrative which haunted Hollywood and its mythology. Many stars' biographies were dramatic and scandalous stories of this kind, with their more morbid aspects often deeply interlocked with the experience of stardom.[52] From the start of the American movie industry the fictionalized lives of stars had provided valuable material for advertising: they were publicized in fan magazines, became part of movie launches, and helped attract a community of followers, who were interested as much in the scandals and publicity surrounding the movies as they were in the movies themselves, a fact which the studios orchestrated as part of their commercial strategies.[53] An exemplary case is the movie *Cleopatra* (Joseph Mankiewicz, 1963), starring Liz Taylor in the title role: the entire movie production was publicized along with a detailed account of the star's divorce, as well as with an account of her brand-new relationship with Richard Burton, who—no surprise—in *Cleopatra* played the role of Mark Antony. Undoubtedly, Liz Taylor's numerous weddings and breakups, constantly covered by the media, were crucial to the establishment of her femme fatale persona.

Glamour, Glory and Gold—the legend of the beautiful girl "from the wrong side of the tracks"—was the New York scene's first encounter with Jackie Curtis's imagery, modeled on American movies of the 1940s and nourished by spicy gossip columns about Hollywood stars' lives and behavior. Curtis's mother, Anna Maria Uglialoro, the daughter of an Italian-American family, had moved to New York after her divorce and raised her two children in her mother's house, which was located upstairs from Slugger Ann's Bar, the nightclub which Curtis's grandmother ran. Jackie's fandom was thus developed amidst his grandmother Slugger Ann's glittering garments and in the smoky atmosphere of her New York club at Second Avenue and 12th Street. This glamorous ideal had been before the young boy's eyes, available for his worship, dramatization, and desire, for a year before he adopted it as his own for the first time. At the time of writing *Glamour, Glory and Gold* the fabulous star-image that was later to be projected into the underground galaxy as Jackie Curtis's female drag persona was still unshaped, embryonic, hidden—but Jackie Curtis's "Life and Legend" was already under construction.

The goddess, first of all, had been named. And in the brave gesture of undertaking the ineffable naming of the deity, the young boy established himself as the creator of his own religion, as the prime mover and foundation of his own project of glamorous divinity. The memory of the names of other gods and goddesses resonated simultaneously in the name that John Holder Jr. chose for himself when, as a boy, he started imagining his immeasurably self-conscious display of cross-gender identity. Jackie was of course the name of the first lady who had acquired genuine "superstar" status in American pop culture, as portrayed by Warhol in his late 1950s colored silkscreened paintings and later, in her grief over Kennedy's death, in the famous 1960s series. And just a few years earlier the movie *Some Like It Hot* (Billy Wilder, 1959) had offered to the mass audience the unforgettable image of Tony Curtis in drag, who would seduce Marilyn while "passing" at the same time for a pretty female musician. In perfect accordance, then, with the "stars as gods" equation,[54] Jackie Curtis's name was born before the Jackie Curtis persona. And yet the name seems to convey with immediate efficacy the whole ambiguity of the public image he chose to build thereafter. Jackie Curtis was Jackie Curtis in his immediate appearance: his not-yet-imagined image stood already in that very first dream of glamorous divinity in 1965.

Jackie Curtis in between Genders

Throughout his life, Jackie Curtis's use of drag was intimately related to the establishment of a public persona among the New York art community of the 1960s and 1970s. This was a persona which not only transcended the boundaries of a specifically gendered drag image, but in the practice of going back and forth in different disguises on and off stage, established its own exceptional features. The performative invention of Jackie Curtis's female drag queen was to be reinforced by the simultaneous presentation of his male drag counterpart, each of them being part of what we might call the "ur-image" of Jackie Curtis which the underground community could recognize.

The synthesis embodied in Jackie Curtis's appearance was rooted in the fact that his drag act was first of all an image-making gesture belonging to a specific, historically and geographically determined queer kinship. From his first appearance in full female drag at a 1966 Halloween party, one of the main concerns of Curtis's performative self-display was the construction of his body as a visual image. To some extent, indeed, the entire life and career of Jackie Curtis pivots around the setting to work of visual images. If his experience of fandom, deeply rooted in pre-Stonewall gay culture, was consistently mixed up with the consumption and collection of 1940s Hollywood glamour photographs from magazines and mainstream media, Curtis's achievement of the status of superstar both within and beyond the Warhol-based underground scene was also systematically pursued by means of the production of an extensive body of pictures. The "perfect appositeness"[55] of Jackie Curtis's star quality emerges from the series of exposures he continued to make throughout his life, intended not just as a sideline or side effect of his artistic career, but rather as a central strategy that entered into a profitable exchange with his performances.

Curtis's drag was modeled on the look he observed in Hollywood's manufactured icons: a larger-than-life kind of beauty, a cleverly orchestrated close-up mode, a layout of fashionable gestures. Even so, the shining surface of the body-icon was liable to be overturned by the very attitude that produced it. Curtis's glamour ideal did not crystallize in a single, unique visual image—such as that, for instance, pursued in Candy Darling's 1950s blonde bombshell drag image[56]—but rather functioned as an ongoing inflection of the diva-type of fabulousness, and in so doing produced the conditions for its own transgression. Throughout his presentation of the persona through pictures, Jackie Curtis was not only red-haired, blond-haired, aggressive, sophisticated, bitchy, homely and funny, he was also a perfectly constructed image of a fashionable man. Alongside his obsession with golden-age Hollywood female beauty, Curtis entertained a constant attraction to Hollywood's male stars, particularly the graceful and strong type of male persona conveyed by stars like James Dean (an ongoing idol for Curtis), Montgomery Clift, or the early Marlon Brando. That is, a 1950s male type which, while giving off a tough masculine allure, also embodied a subtle, almost androgynous grace and vulnerability. Openly playing with the "imitative structure of gender itself"[57] Jackie Curtis's male drag was never John Holder Jr., nor did it attempt to be so: it was indeed always the ur-image of Jackie Curtis. (See figures 10 and 11.)

Jackie's entrance into Warhol's world (an objective the boy had pursued systematically) was immediately registered and literally made part of his image. In December 1968 (just two months after the debut of *Flesh*, the first Warhol-Morrissey movie starring Jackie, in a very androgynous drag) Curtis tattooed the name-label "Andy" on his shoulder. The pop gesture of brand-naming his own skin was at the same time a cunning promotional strategy for himself (to be brand-named "Andy Warhol" in late 1960s/1970s New York was a way of opening numerous doors) as well as a specific declension of his own image. Unsurprisingly, many photographs from this period portray Jackie exhibiting the tattoo, as if through this detail one could temporally locate the picture in the star's career.

Observing the series of Jackie's pictures collected in the Jackie Curtis Estate, it seems as though the star was offering several pointers to his "real" life to observers: the obsession with fan magazines, the imprecision of his drag outfit (Jackie often posed unshaven, with torn panty hose or greasy wigs, and he is said to have been very scruffy even if the overall image was constructed as glamorous),[58] the association with partners currently involved in his artistic enterprises (i.e., Holly Woodlawn, Ron Link, Penny Arcade, Patti Smith, etc.), the homage to his current favorite movies. Photographs circulated among friends, were published in underground magazines, and hung from the walls of clubs and venues in the scene (for instance Max's Kansas City, La MaMa, the Factory, the Chelsea Hotel). Jackie Curtis's biography was thus systematically exposed in order to orchestrate the dramatization of his persona's "Life and Legend." The main materials for this "drama" were Curtis's obsessions, mixed up with a strong camp humor; the main attraction was his gender, continuously renegotiated in a dynamic swing of becoming states. All his artistic works (from his film and stage productions to his scripts and poems) were thought of as so many pieces of a puzzle which could be assembled to compose a unique picture: a life-performance. The project begins to sound like a realization of Oscar Wilde's idea that "one should either be a work of art, or wear a work of art," an idea that Wilde had presented as one of his key "Phrases and Philosophies for the Use of the Young," and which Susan Sontag was later to choose as one of the epigraphs for her 1964 "Notes on 'Camp.' "

Jackie's life-performance seems to articulate itself as a theater play, beginning with his early 1960s dream of glamour and followed by his subsequent rise as an underground star on the New York circuit. In this play, then, the time would eventually come for a "big scene," one of those scenes a star leaves to posterity and for which the star will always be remembered. It would have to be a remarkable scene, like Marlon Brando's 'Hey Stella!" scene in *A Streetcar Named Desire* (Elia Kazan, 1951) or, even more precisely, like Gloria Swanson's unforgettable monologue in front of Cecil B. DeMille, before fading out in her *Salome* pose (*Sunset Boulevard*, Billy Wilder, 1950). The big scene of Jackie Curtis's life-performance was to be the wedding scene.

The Womanless Wedding: Camp Parody and Ritual Practice

As Jill Dolan has pointed out, traditional drama is based on gender opposition, hence the convention of placing the heterosexual wedding as the finale of classical plays functions as a powerful statement of the reconciliation of opposites, supporting the heteronormativity upon which society is assumed to be founded.[59] This is of course only possible because of the way in which the wedding ceremony itself already clearly functions, within society at large, as a central celebration of the structure of the society in question, and one which has developed its own specific and powerful symbology, and which has, in turn, endured in spite of the secularization of the ritual. Susan Stewart writes:

> The wedding as marriage ritual marks the transformation of the self from physical body to a network of social and property relations, from play to production, from circularity to linearity. Of all bourgeois rituals, it is the most significant, the most emblematic of class relations; and perhaps this is why, at least since the Renaissance, it has been the ritual most commonly chosen for exaggeration within the realm of imaginary. A lived tableau, the wedding commonly forms the closure of Renaissance comedies. Out of the grotesque antics of the characters comes the wedding scene, which puts proportions at the center stage; the grotesque is forced into the margins of closure.[60]

In its symbology, the wedding ritual brings about a convergence between the complex ties embedding the couple in their society, in a system that seeks to guarantee its perpetuation (through sexual reproduction) and an economy that channels most of its resources through the family structure. The wedding ritual is therefore an event of absolute "seriousness" for the maintenance of the prevailing social contract, even if this seriousness is often glossed over with the seemingly frivolous celebration of love in the very form of the wedding.

The performative exaggeration of the wedding outlined by Stewart goes back to ancient times and might perhaps persuasively be linked to carnivalesque culture.[61] I am thinking especially of the practice of *mock weddings*, clearly born within the *charivari* tradition, and widespread in particular in fifteenth- and sixteenth-century Europe.[62] Brought to the United States and Canada with European colonization,[63] the practice of mock weddings was soon incorporated into American folk tradition. In this context, the practice of the *womanless wedding* was particularly successful, and of particular relevance when thinking about the genealogy of Jackie Curtis wedding-performances.

The womanless wedding was a celebration which took place especially in small, rural towns[64] and which involved the entire population in setting up a fake wedding ceremony in which all the "female roles" were played by men. It seems that cross-dressing in this kind of practice was not connected to the participants' sexuality: on the contrary, men "played" the female roles precisely because the practice was clearly located in the state of exception of "festivity."[65] Therefore, the social function of womanless weddings appears to be the same as that of the final wedding scene in the traditional drama, reconfirming order and appropriately harmonious relations between genders in society. Basically, the cross-dressing element was treated in a similar way to the final "unmasking" in nineteenth-century female impersonator shows: at the end of the show the actor would take off his wig in front of the audience, bringing affairs back to the "norm" for the reassurance of heterosexual spectators.

Although womanless weddings started to die out during the twentieth century, there are still examples of them taking place both before and after the Second World War in Pennsylvania. Significantly, in these latest developments of the practice, men dressed as women (performing as brides, flower girls, and female guests) wore long dresses and straw hats evocative of turn-of-the-century styles of women's clothing, instead of those of contemporary women. Commenting on this, Susan Stewart suggests that "it might be argued that just as the Victorian chair is more likely than a modern one to be a signifier of 'chairness' in the dollhouse, so this antiquated style of dress is more likely to be a signifier of the feminine in the womanless wedding."[66]

Stewart's comment invites a cross-reference to Susan Sontag's "Notes on 'Camp,'" where Sontag states that "camp sees everything in quotation marks," so that "it's not a lamp, but 'a lamp'; not a woman but 'a woman.'"[67] The emphasis on a stereotyped model of femininity points to the inherently camp dynamic at work in the womanless wedding, a practice which plays with the artificiality of the feminine, even if it involves no conscious effort to question normative assumptions about gender or to critique or destructure the traditional notion of marriage. Secondly, this habit of wearing old-fashioned women's clothes brings us back to the etymology of "drag" as having strong associations with "retrogression, delay and the pull of the past upon the present."[68] In this respect, the twentieth-century development of the womanless wedding suggests a gradual shift of this practice into the form of a proper *drag wedding*. One might consider this shift in relation to a similar transformation of the notion of feminine in the wider society: in the 1940s and 1950s, the very idea of the "feminine" was still epitomized by the figure of the long dress and the straw hat, even as "actual women" were enacting a substantial transformation of public behavior and a powerful renegotiation of their assigned roles in society.

In this respect, significant is a passage from Warhol's writings which appears in *The Philosophy of Andy Warhol* at the point at which he is commenting on his 1971 *Women in Revolt* film, starring Jackie Curtis, Candy Darling, and Holly Woodlawn as three women's liberationists:

> Among other things, drag queens are living testimony to the way women used to be, the way some people still want them to be, and the way some women still actually want to be. Drag queens are living archives of ideal movie star womanhood. They perform a documentary service, usually consecrating their lives to keeping the glittering alternative alive and available for (not-too-close) inspection. . . . It's *hard work* [emphasis mine] to look like the complete opposite of what nature made you and then to be an imitation woman of what was only a fantasy woman in the first place. When they took

> the movie stars and stuck them in the kitchen, they weren't movie stars any more—they were just like you and me. Drag queens are the reminders that some stars still aren't just like you and me.[69]

The 1972 New York premiere of *Women in Revolt* at a movie house on East 59th Street was picketed by a group from the (actual) women's liberation movement, and at the time the movie was harshly criticized for making a mockery of sexual revolution. Not only did the film portray its three protagonists as naively involved in what was significantly called the PIGs movement (Politically Involved Girls),[70] but one of the main points of the movie was the impossibility (or inability) for the three women to reconcile their urge for political engagement in the women's cause with their emotional and sexual needs. Overall, the movie was critiqued as a merciless parody of women's bodies and desires, which appeared all the more offensive as it was performed by male actors "pretending" to pass as women. To play with the title of Joan Riviere's famous text, "Womanliness as Masquerade," in Andy Warhol's movie it was women's liberation, not just womanliness, which came out as a masquerade.[71]

Nevertheless, the same comment by Warhol that I referred to earlier points to drag as a demystificatory device, one which we might interestingly connect to a shift in understandings of the politics of drag within later feminist thought. First, the reenactment of an old-fashioned star femininity clearly expresses the artificiality of "what was only a fantasy woman in the first place" but also points toward what Judith Butler calls the "melancholy of gender."[72] Considering the drag image as an archive of "ideal movie star womanhood" also entails consideration of the temporal quality of the cross-dressing gesture, bringing into play the question of the time lag between what is normatively conceived to be "standard womanhood" (always nostalgically projected in the past and in the untouchability of the screen) and "contemporary womanhood" (taken to be that same standard simply brought up to date). But the figure of the ideal movie star brings into the picture issues of attachment directly connected to a process of gender formation as experienced personally by the generation of gay men who came of age in the 1960s (like Jackie, Candy, and Holly) and engrained in a specific habitus of filmgoing and mutual self-recognition.[73]

There is no evidence of Jackie Curtis being aware of the womanless wedding tradition, nor is it possible to establish a continuity between his wedding performances and such a legacy existing in the United States. But it is nonetheless worth recalling that such a practice existed in American culture and moreover that it had once been widespread, especially in small towns. The womanless wedding was an event involving the whole community, and despite its inherent carnivalesque normativity, it also functioned as a camp festival reaffirming the community itself. One might perhaps argue that the womanless wedding functioned as a camp ritual practice.

The Bride Project

The image of the bride in a white dress is an iconographically powerful assertion of the bright promise of a future of love based on the heterosexual couple. Besides displaying a heteronormative relationship model, it also presents the constructed beauty of kinship imagery, celebrating the shining preciousness of the female in the newly married couple. In the wedding itself the bride is clearly the star: she is the main character walking in triumph to the altar, winning the admiring looks of the assembled company; it is she who carries the floral bouquet, and it is she who unveils her face at the very last minute, deliberately delaying the exhibition of her beauty. While the groom's suit is usually just a minor variation on the regular male suit, the bride's dress is traditionally granted a far greater margin of exaggeration. Sumptuousness, a major feature of the wedding in terms of status, also finds in the image of the bride its privileged site of exhibition.

Such sumptuousness, according to Roland Barthes, is deeply engrained in the whole representational function of a *grand mariage*. The spectacular symbology Barthes described as one of his 1957 *Mythologies* is not too far from that inherited by Jackie's imagery: it should come as no surprise that Barthes begins his text about *le grand mariage* by addressing the media reverberation of celebrity weddings:

> What a lot of marrying going on in our illustrated papers: grand marriages (Marshall Juin's son and the daughter of an Inspector of the Fisc, the daughter of the Duc de Castries and Baron de Vitrolles), marriages for love (Miss Europe '53 and her childhood sweetheart), projected star marriages (Marlon Brando and Josiane Mariani). Naturally all these marriages are not apprehended at the same time, for their mythological virtue is not the same.[74]

While in Curtis's everyday life marriage as *ménage* or as the foundation of a family unit was basically lacking, a recurring image in the illustrated papers he collected was that of the wedding, given as the immediate depiction of marriage. His own notion of "marriage," we might therefore suggest, was modeled more on the images of the lives and love affairs of stars than it was on an actual experience of marriage relationships. But "a Star's marriage (to another star)"—wrote Barthes—"is almost never presented except in its future aspect. What it develops is the virtually pure myth of the Couple . . . Conjugality is therefore at the limit of superfluous, relegated without precautions to a problematic future."[75]

In Jackie's weddings, indeed, conjugality is beyond superfluous. The future projection, that is, is disavowed from the start; the groom himself appears negligible. The ceremony is by no stretch of the imagination the promise of a future married couplehood. Instead the couple is "consummated" in the wedding performance itself. The ceremonies were thus events systematically arranged to enhance attention and visibility for Jackie Curtis as a star, and for the artistic outcomes of his career. Ultimately, they functioned as what Richard Dyer has called a "vehicle," a pivotal element in the construction of a star, "important as much for what conventions [it] set[s] up as for how [it] develop[s] them, for their ingredients as for their realization," providing "continuity of iconography, visual style and structure"[76] to the figure of the star. Just like the Hollywood stars whose biographies he followed in the gossip columns of fan magazines, Curtis intended the weddings as the juicy events of his "Life and Legend," attracting press and audience attention by means of their fabulousness. In this respect, the first wedding is exemplary. (See figures 12 and 13.)

The ceremony took place on July 21, 1969, on a rooftop at 211 East Eleventh Street. The choice of the groom was part of a clever promotional strategy: Eric Emerson, a well-known "superstar," had made his way into the New York underground hall of fame through his seductive dancing during the *Exploding Plastic Inevitable*, and his rise reached its climax in the famous self-love sequence in *Chelsea Girls*. Furthermore, in 1969 he was working as a waiter at Max's Kansas City, a position of absolute social visibility.[77] At the time of the ceremony, however, with everything in place and guests gathered on the rooftop, Eric didn't show up. Jackie therefore sought a stand-in groom ("Stuart Eagle Speed") who was on the rooftop among the guests and who therefore performed the role in the ceremony. Apart from this minor detail, the ceremony, which was planned and staged by Curtis's friend and theater director Tony Ingrassia, turned out to be a great success: Holly Woodlawn and Ruby Lynn Rainer, two of Curtis's ongoing associate performers, stood as the bridesmaids, the Larry Rivers jazz band played for the ceremony, and Andy Warhol shot pictures of the whole event. Melba LaRose Jr., who had taken the role of Nola Noonan in the first run of the play *Glamour, Glory and Gold* (the title role was later performed by Jackie herself), was also a prominent presence at the event. The wedding party had been planned for Max's Kansas City, to coincide with the launch party for Warhol's *Blue Movie*, which opened the same night at the New Andy Warhol Garrick Theatre. When the wedding crowd reached the restaurant, where Eric (who was working) attempted to apologize to Jackie for having failed to appear at the ceremony, Jackie, in her shining wedding garment, promptly replied: "Yes I know, Eric. But I have a show to do now—my reception."[78]

The event achieved the media resonance to which Jackie aspired: the following week, the event was covered by the press and a major article appeared on the first page of the *Village Voice*.[79] Interestingly, the article appeared alongside news related to one of the most significant events of that 1969 New York summer: the development of the Gay Liberation Front, which had emerged and grown in the aftermath of the Stonewall riots only a month before and just a few blocks from the rooftop where Jackie's wedding was held. The combination is worth noticing: on the one hand, Jackie's wedding might suggest a continuity with the claims for gay rights being made by the movement inflamed after Stonewall, and could be considered as openly aligned with the "coming out" of the movement itself. However, closer observation discloses divergences in tactics and procedures between Jackie's performance and those of the Gay Liberation Front.

Curtis's wedding performances made no claim for gay marriage rights, nor did they openly contest the form of heteronormative nuptial symbology. On the contrary, they played on the given language of normative culture and employed its own codes as the parameters for a performative *détournement*. By sticking as closely as possible to the normative wedding model, Jackie's wedding performances thus function as modes of "disidentification." Muñoz's notion of disidentification suggests that recycling images and objects already charged with ideological power might be considered a tactical "reformatting" employed by minoritarian subjects in order to challenge ideological power from within. Jackie's employment of wedding symbology might usefully be read as a mode of disidentification insofar as it debunks the ideological interpellation of the wedding by overturning its very "naturalness," which ideology seeks to produce as a characteristic of all its institutions.

First of all, of course, the bride was a man. And in any case, the drag persona Jackie was developing at the time was not even identifiable with a decisively female appearance, but existed in a complex dynamic of interplay between gender positions which also involved the putting on of "male drag." Beyond the wedding performances, from 1969 up to his death in 1985 Jackie's persona continued to operate in this dynamic state, and for long periods he totally abandoned female drag, and lived and performed only in male drag. He even went so far as to spread rumors of his imminent marriage with the actress Sandy Dennis. In any case, he never made a wedding performance featuring himself as the groom, while the "bride project" continued to exist even after Jackie abandoned female drag in his everyday life.

Secondly, in detaching the notion of wedding from that of marriage, Jackie emphasized the inherent artificiality of the nuptial celebration as the immediate and natural representation of a "future of love." The wedding ceremony traditionally communicates, as part of its symbology, a powerful temporal projection which is assumed to mirror the standard model of couplehood in society: the flower girls are "little brides" embodying an apparently inevitable future in which they will grow up to be brides; the newly married couple performs a public kiss in front of the audience, marking their entrance into a domain of "active sexuality" which the state apparatus allows and attests, on condition that this sexuality is expressed within the married couple and for the purpose of the sexual reproduction on which the future nuclear family will be founded; a nuclear family which will accordingly be the foundation for the further continuation of the social order.

In Jackie's weddings such a temporal projection is denied, and the focus is on the event of the wedding itself. Returning to Barthes's account, I suggest that Jackie's weddings are apprehended in their "event-nature" because of their very "mythological virtue": as for every star, conjugality is "a possibility given as assured insofar as its importance is marginal, subject to that very general convention which insists that publicly marriage is always the 'natural' finality of coupling. What counts, under the guarantee of a hypothetical marriage, is to make acceptable the couple's carnal reality."[80] In this respect, Jackie's use of bridal imagery in the underground was a means of affirming a "carnal reality," at the same time as making herself visible and himself adorable (or the other way around). Furthermore, separating weddings from the idea of marriage—as Elizabeth Freeman suggests in her book *The Wedding Complex*[81]—discloses their performative nature as forms of "social intimacy," attesting to the function of such forms as sites of recognition and for the display of a whole range of relationships and ways of belonging that might turn out to be radically different from heteronormative ones. Jackie Curtis's weddings involved the artistic community as both witness and participant in the ritual-like practice, and in so doing they functioned precisely as a "rite of confirmation" of its modes of social belonging. The weddings—which took place in different New York sites, that is, rooftops, clubs, and public spaces—were first of all parties, attended in the continuum of the community's leisure time. Secondly, given the presence of press and photographers, largely encouraged by Curtis, they were occasions of visibility and publicity for the ongoing exposure-oriented attitude of the members of the group. But most significantly, the weddings performed a network of relationships and roles that clearly exceeded the occasion, encompassing the life and artistic performances happening at that particular period of time. In this respect, this recalls the tradition of the womanless wedding, which, as we observed, was meant to confirm the belonging-together of a specific community, and to confirm roles within a given society. In the case of the New York underground scene, then, Jackie's image was confirmed in its ongoing cross-gender dynamism, founded on a shared familiarity with the modes of appearance and the habitus of a practical kinship. That is, the powerful symbology of the wedding was on the one hand detached from its normative ideological mission, and on the other employed to confirm a queer politics of relations and affects. (See figure 14.)

The 1969 *Village Voice* article dedicated to Jackie's first wedding was entitled "Twilight of a Tribe: The Wedding That Wasn't."[82] The reporter Dotson Rader tauntingly reported on the event, presenting it as a failure. According to Rader, the nonparticipation of Emerson made it "the wedding that wasn't." The journalist suggested that the nuptial dream of the drag queen Jackie Curtis—whose existence was supposedly allowed only by margins of visibility granted by the 1960s pop/underground galaxy—was miserably crushed, revealing "the illusion" behind the dream. Overall the article seems to have wanted to bear witness to "the end of an era"—that of the Warhol 1960s—a time when every drag queen was allowed her nuptial dream performance.

The *Voice* article was clearly misleading, but it's worth noticing its sarcastic and somehow reactionary emphasis. Although it failed to grasp the meaning of the event, it nonetheless pinpointed one of its key features. The word "tribe" employed in the article's title underscores the collective nature of the wedding performance, which was absolutely essential to Jackie's performative operation. It is significant, then, that while the *Village Voice* readily understood the significance of the Gay Liberation Front, it clearly misunderstood the inherent dynamic of queer kinship at work in Jackie's performance, which clearly had no need of the "chosen" groom in order to be enacted.

Throughout the 1970s this "tribe" went through a long process of transformation involving the departures of some members, the deaths of others, and the mainstream success of still others. Over this time Jackie's weddings functioned as a sort of barometer of the mood of the tribe. All the guests gathered for the performance/ceremonies between 1969 and 1985 gathered in order to celebrate an ongoing image—perhaps itself a crystal, recalling Calvino's formulation previously examined: the image of Jackie-as-a-bride. The bride was thus the star of the event she herself orchestrated, a star who performed as an ongoing quotation of herself, hence undermining the very "eventfulness" of each of those events. Each wedding performance involved new guests, each event welcomed new grooms, performing the role formerly taken by Emerson, and actually performed by someone else. Every wedding was followed, after a short period, by the announcement of a "divorce" in order to make room for a new groom/event.

Through the years other grooms would also function as publicity stunts for Jackie. Lance Loud, who wed Jackie on June 9, 1973, would appear a few months later in the first reality show ever produced on American television, *An American Family*, which aired on PBS. Based on the life of the Louds, a Californian family, the second episode of the TV show follows the mother on her trip to New York, where she visits her eldest son Lance, who moved to the city in order to start a career as a writer. Loud, who later became a satiric columnist and the lead singer of Mumps, a 1970s pop-punk band often playing at Max's Kansas City, was living at the time at the Chelsea Hotel and actively participating in the gay subculture of the time: the episode was clearly an attempt to offer a glimpse of the "New York underground" to a mass TV audience, at that moment in the early 1970s when it had started to become a trendy attraction. During the episode (shot in September 1973) Loud took his mother on a tour of New York, culminating in an evening attending a show at La MaMa: the show in question was *Vain Victory: The Vicissitudes of the Damned*, written and performed by Jackie Curtis. Although the TV cameras caught just a small fragment of the show, Jackie (as well as La MaMa) had achieved his objective of gaining access to the small screen, a goal Curtis had systematically pursued throughout the 1970s.

Likewise, the 1972 wedding with Hiram Keller (celebrated on Valentine's Day) also contributed to Jackie's image in another domain. Having starred in

Federico Fellini's *Satyricon* (1969) and appearing frequently in the illustrated pages of journals like *Afterdark*, Keller was a major gay sex symbol of the time. Although there was never a relationship of love between Jackie and Keller, Jackie's connecting his image to Keller's can still be defined as a publicity stunt genuinely comparable to those orchestrated by the Hollywood studios: "rumors" about the Curtis-Keller liason were deliberately spread by Jackie to the press long before the wedding,[83] and to no one's surprise the event was widely covered, especially by the gay newspapers. On May 1, 1972, Jackie succeeded in hitting the cover page of *Gay Power*, which published a sepia-toned Leee Black Childers photograph in which Jackie posed as a 1930s diva.[84]

In 1970 the Yugoslav director Dusan Makavejev shot scenes with Jackie Curtis for the movie *WR: Mysteries of the Organism* (released in 1971). Constructed through the juxtaposition of blocks of fictional and documentary materials shot in Belgrade and New York, Makavejev's movie is a radical investigation of "the sexuality of politics"[85] and takes as its starting point the work of the controversial Austrian psychologist Wilhelm Reich. The fictional segment of the movie follows the narrative of Milena, a young girl who starts claiming the need for sexual liberation in the context of Soviet-style communism. The movie alternated this story with documentary footage shot in the United States. Part of this material follows the legacy of Reich's late 1930s experiments on "orgone," the mysterious life energy produced by orgasm (which was the radical development of Reich's study of the contribution of orgasm to physical and mental health, carried out in the United States before he was prosecuted and died in 1957), while another part is made up of encounters with several New York characters, all somehow involved in the countercultural scene of the time. In addition to Jackie Curtis, the movie features the poet and musician Tuli Kupferberg, the feminist artist and activist Betty Dodson, the artist Nancy Godfrey, and the *Screw* editor Jim Buckley. Makavejev shot Curtis in female drag as she walks eating an ice cream in Times Square along with Eric Emerson and later talks about her love life, mentioning in the process the wedding with Emerson, whom, she said, she had agreed to marry because she didn't want to be "a girl who was never asked."

While I don't wish to embark on a close examination of the complex dialectics explored by Makavejev's movie, I would still like to suggest that Jackie's presence in *WR* (contemporary to *Women in Revolt*) appears itself to function dialectically in relation to various major ideological discourses: not only those employed by heteronormative structures of state power, but also those entailed in some of the more dogmatic approaches of contemporary progressive political movements. Jackie stands as a foreplay of sorts in the orgasmic dynamic which Makavejev's *WR*, by playfully emphasizing orgasm revolutionary power, itself troubles and undermines.

Insomuch as his 1969 wedding ceremony was not aligned with the agenda of the post-Stonewall Gay Liberation Front (actually Jackie is said to have been criticized by gay activists for not being openly involved in political activism),[86] Jackie's drag persona emerges from the landscape of *WR* as an opening towards a complex approach to the politics of sexuality, suggesting ways in which a queer persona might be assimilated into an all-American mythology. This possibility surfaces most clearly especially when related to the scenes of the movie in which Tuli Kupferberg clearly makes sexual innuendo around weapons and talks about capitalistic ownership in American society. While Jackie is portrayed as a female in her dark outfit and scruffy hair, the Fugs founder Kupferberg plays with guns and talks about American private property, suggesting a complex relationship between American mainstream imagery and the countercultural domain, and offering clues to a rather ambiguous sexual politics already at work in the culture of the United States.

In this respect, I am suggesting that New York City's queer culture of the 1960s developed several "ways of making queer differences and singularities visible,"[87] and that while these contributed to creating the urban utopianism which allowed the Stonewall riots to take place, they were founded more on a body politics than on a political agenda of claims for gay life. In other words, Curtis's employment of openly camp strategies of visibility resists or at least stands to one side of the critical discourses of 1970s gay rights insofar as it cannot be framed as a demand for legitimacy. Instead it entails a powerful display of actual queer embodiment, involving affects and relationships rooted in the everyday life of individuals, already capable of sustaining themselves over time, and in so doing projecting their memory into a future potentiality, without the formal mechanisms that might be afforded by legitimacy.[88]

The Last Image, or the First

In moving towards a conclusion of this chapter, I wish to turn again to the images which gave a foretaste to the direction of my reading of Ellen Stewart and Jackie Curtis's life and legend: the image of Ellen Stewart as La Mama, appearing in the legend of the pushcart, and the image of Curtis in his bridal dress, in July 1969.

I am interested in interrogating further the ways in which photography and storytelling operate as media through which the performative invention of queer kinship and its community is achieved. But I am also interested in considering the gaps in the narratives which ensue from such remains, which speak of both the actuality of queer kinship dynamics and the possibility for their future reactivation, first of all, as images made out of memory.

Siegfried Kracauer begins his reflections on photography by arguing that "memory images are at odds with photographic representation,"[89] since the spatial or temporal continuum that photography retains cannot convey the fragmentary nature of memory. According to Kracauer, images held in the memory retain "what is given only insofar as it has significance";[90] this significance is made visible by means of "traits" recollected by a "liberated consciousness" based upon what the subject once perceived as "true" in relation to an image:

> The image in which these traits appear is distinguished from all other memory images, for unlike the latter it preserves not a multitude of opaque recollections but elements that touch upon what has been recognized as true. All memory images are bound to be reduced to this type of image, which might rightly be called the last image, since it alone preserves the unforgettable. The last image of a person is his actual *history*. . . . How a person represents this history does not depend purely on his or her natural constitution or on the pseudo-coherence of his or her individuality; thus, only fragments of these assets are included in his or her history. This history is like a *monogram* that condenses the name into a single graphic figure which is meaningful as an ornament. . . . In authentic fairy tales, the imagination has intuitively deposited typical monograms. In a photograph, a person's history is buried under a layer of snow.[91]

The history of the person photographed, that is, can't be presented by the image the photograph depicts, since the person is fixed in a present time and space, and what appears ends up being only a block of features subtracted from that history. In other words, the objecthood of the photograph makes the person visible. But without many of her attributes, she is thus liable to reification, and as a result, is forgotten. Developing the argument further, Kracauer notes two different sorts of photographic images, and their relationship with the viewer's memory: these are the photograph of "the film diva" and that of "the grandmother." According to Kracauer, everybody recognizes the image of the diva because she looks just as she did on the screen. The grandmother, on the contrary, is a subject which the viewer "knows" in a different way and in whom she can therefore distinguish between the image depicted and that produced in her own imagination. In other words, the recognition of the likeness satisfies the desire to create a historical continuum between the image we are looking at and the person we know. "Were it not for the oral tradition, the image alone would not have sufficed to reconstruct the grandmother."[92] That is, memory conjures up the image of a person we know and detaches it from a mere representation, of a kind that can not be reduced to a photographic image; but the photograph can also foster an appearance that extends beyond the affective recollection, making visible elements of the supposedly "known" that had previously escaped attention. In this respect, Kracauer does not dismiss photography for its inability to convey "significance," but rather reads its function in relation to the labor of history itself. In photography's limited surface and spatial coherence the history of an object cannot be presented, but a disintegrated unit can be conjured up, capable of being retrieved from the snow by memory and reconstituted in the drive to establish a historical continuum.

Through Kracauer's insight and recalling Calvino's thinking about fairy tales, I am interested in considering how Stewart's legendary image of motherhood and Curtis's performative embodiment of the bride figure both converge into a *monogram*, which interestingly conflates into the image of "the star." In his wedding photographs, Curtis appears as a recognizable image—that of a star—whose representation points to specific forms of presentness. She "looks like" we might see him in other photographs, or movies and stage pictures. On the other hand, even for me—a viewer who never met Curtis, looking at those images forty years later—the multitude of details and information about his "Life and Legend" inevitably conjures up a range of additional associations, which come together to offer me the *history* of this person in the form of a *monogram*. This monogram might well be an ornament, if we consider Jackie Curtis's name in relation to the "masquerade" of both Curtis's femininity and masculinity. In any case, what makes Jackie Curtis's monograph visible—to me, for instance, as I write this book—is the existence of a collective memory in which it remains attached to events and records which photographs alone do not retain. In the legend of La MaMa, likewise, Stewart's existence is exposed in its full unity of appearance: the *monogram* in which her history is condensed is sustained by the possibility that collective memory might reactivate the story in relation to other instances which, like Foster's play *Hurrah for the Bridge*, touch upon the gist of the tale, and expand it in ever-new specific forms of presentness for the image of Ellen Stewart: the star of the La MaMa firmament.

Just like "the grandmother," Curtis's and Stewart's images could not be recollected had not the oral tradition of the New York scene "passed them on." Jackie's bridal image, then, is, on the one hand, a perfectly composed image of "the diva" and recognizable as such by a viewer who saw Curtis's female drag on the screen. At the same time, its encoding in the standard language of stardom was equally relevant as a means of "disidentification," insofar as Jackie could be "tactically recognized" in a shared politics of representations and affects. Such a politics constitutes the affective basis for the memorial recollection of Curtis' traits, making the image much more like that of "the grandmother." This is what allows his monogram to resurface in the continuum of history. And so the image of Ellen, in the particular "mode of growth" of her fairy tale, is not only recognizable as the mother who works in the background, in an unrecognized affective labor enabling others to occupy the central stage, but displays herself, through her politics of insistence, as a "woman-theater," in the unique form of stardom she produced for herself and her theater.

Jackie's wedding photographs are, in one respect, wholly artificial, since they pretend to depict a fake ritual where there is no couple to affirm, nor marriage to witness. On the other hand, the affective relationships between the participants have, in Kracauer's words, "significance": the postures and gestures were "made for the camera" just as much as in any family photograph, but in a way that exceeds the power of conventional family photographs, they serve as memoranda for a future renewal of the assembled family. Even if the labor of kinship—entailing assistance, care, and reciprocal support—can not be made visible in photographs, the wedding guests nonetheless appear in Curtis's wedding photographs "in drag"—dragging in both a shared past and a possibility for future embodiment. As Roland Barthes wrote, a few years after his text on the *grand mariage*, "a code cannot be destroyed, only 'played off.'"[93] Jackie Curtis's wedding performances and Ellen Stewart's theatrical motherhood constituted a collective performance, which "played off" both stardom and kinship codes. In both cases an affective attachment—a form of love, indeed—is crucial to the symbology of these codes, but an inherent quality of resistance is expressed by means of asserting both a peculiar star system and a habitat of queer liaisons understood and experienced as kinship.

Before letting these monograms fade away into the surface of their many photographs, into the echo of their many tales, I shall linger a moment on the particular way in which, in the present, they continue to crystallize, passionately, in their *last image*, the one which "alone preserves the unforgettable."[94] I shall do so by offering a short account of my own encounter with Curtis's and Stewart's "last image." Or else, as I have suggested throughout the chapter, I shall perhaps conjure again their "first image": the image in which the promise of their story stood still, awaiting to be realized.

In Stewart's case, as I have already indicated, I was able to encounter the image more than once: first in the encounter with Stewart, for the first time in Italy in 2004, and then again in New York, on other public and private occasions, and then also through the accounts of other people who had listened to the story, told by Stewart herself or by someone else, who had been—echoing Gertrude Stein's expression—"listening and talking" to the La MaMa family tale over the last forty-five years. Every time I heard the story, I have tried to remember the precise words Stewart used to describe to me the events in the first place. How much was she earning as a fashion designer? Did she keep records of her work as a fashion designer, or did her passion for collecting archival remains only start when she initiated her theater activities? Did she realize costumes for the first shows, or did she radically detach her own professional expertise from her new, amateur work as a theater producer? Were these questions relevant to the story I was going to tell about her?

When Stewart died, in 2011, I felt sorry that I had not been able to write about her story and have her read it before it was published. I felt that it would have been fair to let her have a say in the authenticity of the information I was going to offer, and that my affective relation with her would bind me to a certain loyalty to her story, whatever interpretation of it I intended to offer. Years later, during the completion of this book, I found myself misremembering whether I had, in fact, asked these questions of Stewart, and then possibly forgotten the answers along the way; whether in the waves of storytelling and recollecting, the first and the last image of her story—the one which promised it, and the one which appears to me, today, under a layer of snow—have ended up collapsing into her monogram. Almost as if, long after Stewart herself had ceased to tell it, her story has constructed its very mode of narration, resisting in a sense the particularities of questions in a continuing labor of self-crystallization.

Also in the case of Curtis, who I never met, I have encountered the image more than once. I first encountered the wedding picture as a photograph kept in the Jackie Curtis Estate, carefully looked after by Curtis's cousin Joseph Preston. At that time, at the beginning of my research in New York in 2007, I was also told that someone had shot some film footage of Curtis's first wedding. Several artists, including Ruby Lynn Reyner and John Vaccaro, remembered having seen it, but, alas, no one seemed to remember who had shot it. During the following years I made several attempts to get hold of the footage, but all of them were unsuccessful. I contacted Jonas Mekas, who also remembered that the film existed, but could not help me identify where it was or whom to ask. At some point, I came across the information that the film had been shot by the Maysles brothers, at the time two underground filmmakers and later authors of the legendary documentary film *Grey Gardens* (1975). In 2008 I got in touch with Albert Maysles, asking for the film, and he said he remembered shooting it, but had no idea where it was now. A few months later, his secretary contacted me asking if I had got hold of the film, but unfortunately there seemed to be no traces of it around. After this episode, I assumed that the footage had been lost, gave up my search, and worked for years with the materials of the Jackie Curtis Estate, including numerous photographs of the 1969 wedding. In 2014 I went back to New York and I came across a line in a book on Max's Kansas City[95] which mentioned again the film of Curtis's wedding, as well as the name of the woman who had shot it: Elspeth Leacock. With the help of Penny Arcade, who had herself fortuitously got in touch again with Leacock only recently, I finally met Leacock, who had recently digitized her footage and kindly invited me to have a look at it the following day in her apartment in Brooklyn.

Watching the footage was a beautiful and strange experience. After all these years, I realized that in a sense Jackie is for me a familiar figure. I know his obsessions, his way of speaking, his postures, and also the names of his friends, as well as the places where he walked and performed. But I have, of course, not actually been there. Leacock, however, was one of Jackie's best friends, and when she heard that Jackie wanted "to get married," she decided to borrow $5,000 from a Chinese millionaire who was her acquaintance and to film the whole thing, with no plan of making anything out of it afterwards, as, indeed, she never did. As in any wedding, she filmed the rehearsal, the preparation of the bride in her apartment, the arrival on the rooftop, the friends taking pictures of each other, and the crowd waiting for the groom, who never showed up. There I also learned that the stand-in-groom was Elspeth's short-time boyfriend of the time, who had chosen not to make his name public for the press. I saw in the footage the affective labor of the friends putting together Jackie's wedding, the bridesmaid Ruby Lynn Reyner combing her hair with Jackie in the bathroom before the ceremony, the passionate work of Toni Ingrassia, the theater director who was asked by Jackie to stage the whole event, and was rehearsing the order of theatrical numbers like tap dancing, singing, and playing music before the whole thing started: numbers which in some cases never got to be performed and anyway never got documented in the pictures. Ingrassia's presence itself, in fact, had passed almost unnoticed in most narratives of the event.

The most uncanny experience, however, was that while watching people taking pictures, I realized that I had seen the pictures before. I was seeing the gestures which were producing the images I had grown familiar with, and which I could recognize, such as the one with Jackie holding the milk carton with the two friends, one of whom was Toni Ingrassia. So now, I had in front of me the background to familiar images—images of a family of sorts, and found myself recognizing the images as familiar to me, as if I had developed an intimacy with them, as if I had been in proximity with them, as indeed I had. While I was watching the movie Leacock was sitting close to me, commenting on her friends like a friend does, with anecdotes, details, and sometimes sadness when the friends were long passed away. At some point, she smiled and said "What I like about it is that there was a certain innocence in all this."

Watching the movie, I found many imprecisions in the story I had reconstructed for myself, starting with the stand-in-groom, whom I had identified as a "porno producer," perhaps because he had been introduced with a fake identity to the press which reported on the event, like the *Village Voice*. I also found out that the Maysles brothers were in fact good friends with Leacock, and had collaborated with her own brother on other projects. But she doubts that they ever shot a film of Jackie's first wedding. So the question remains open: did Albert Maysles imagine having shot this film? Was he at the wedding and remembers Leacock filming it, and had he come over time to think he had shot it himself? Or else, as Leacock suggested, he was not at the wedding at all, but he heard her telling the story of the wedding, imagined it in pictures and, over time, he misremembered himself as having shot this movie? Alternatively, the Maysles brothers could have shot a home movie of another of Jackie's weddings, since there were eight overall. Hence, while thinking that seeing the footage would finally close for me this particular archive, it ended up opening further questions, further possible lines of inquiry.

One thing is certain: as Gertude Stein put it, "no matter how often what had happened had happened any time one told anything there was no repetition."[96] The first and the last image, in other words, are never as such, and in a sense they always are: they promise and preserve the unforgettable, against the future in which images and stories will be forgotten, then resurface, then be forgotten again. Such insistence, in other words, is the inner labor of memorability.

Chapter 4

✦

Larger Than Life

Andy Warhol's Screen Tests, and the Distracted Potentiality of Performance

"Will you be getting any money for your ride, Lady Godiva?"
"No: I am doing it for the exposure."

—Ronald Tavel, *The Life of Lady Godiva*

That's, uh, all television is, my dear, nothing but auditions.
—Addison De Witt in *All About Eve* (Mankiewicz, 1950)

Bleeding Tears

On the screen, in black and white, there is the image of a woman's head. She stands still, her dark long hair framing her face, which is pale, almost the same color as the wall behind her head. Her image persists in its contours, in its stillness. The face becomes familiar after the first minute one endures in watching it, during the first minute which it endures in being exposed. At some point there seems to be a trembling in the image, as if the portrait was swallowing, or about to swallow. But it is just an impression: the image, in fact, remains motionless, like a photograph. Until at some point, enduring in looking, one might notice that the eyes of the woman in the image are starting to be filled with tears. One of the tears becomes bigger in the woman's right eye, and very quickly falls down the cheek, reaching the chin, then disappearing outside the screen. After a few seconds, a second tear reaches the edge of the eye, directing itself, very slowly this time, down the same cheek. Now the other eye, too, starts shedding tears that appear in the image at first as small pearls on the edge of the eye, and then follow their course, irrigating the face. Both eyes, however, remain open, even after the image has revealed itself to be a long pose in front of a camera, rather than a photograph. Some of the tears stop for a second on the edge of the chin before disappearing offscreen, again in the form of small pearls of water. After three minutes or so, the image dissolves, with eyes still open.

When the first tear started falling, the image of the face seemed relieved, almost slipping into another state of appearing. On a more attentive observation, however, we should acknowledge that the face has kept exactly the same expression—one of absolute quiet, indifference, serenity—from the very beginning. Even so, we might retain that misremembering of a sense of change, of relief. This is maybe because the most immediate response to the appearing of tears, the first glimpse of awareness that the image is not completely still, and that it records in fact the presence of a person in duration amid her living, comes to the spectator with the realization: "this is not a photograph but a film, starring a woman who is crying."

The woman, of course, is not precisely "crying," not—at least—if we understand this verb as synonymous with "weeping," and associate it with sorrow, or other kinds of emotions which might foster the shedding of tears. These particular tears are not a signifier of emotions. They are, in a sense, a form of bleeding, to employ a term used in botany to designate the flow of lymph from plants. They stir from the face as a physical phenomenon: as an effect of the effort to keep the eyes open for three minutes. They are part of the surface of the image, they share the tempo of the image. But they do not participate in the emotional life of the subject. In a sense, the tears of the image we are observing are a form of bleeding very much like the "crying" of certain madonnas whose tears of blood are believed to appear on the statues as magical attributes. The object—the statue, the image—is not supposed to produce tears. But sometimes it is claimed to do so. And in these cases—when "crying," a distinctively human body praxis, is attributed to an inanimate object such as the statue of a madonna—the bleeding of tears from the eyes of these images is considered an event, or more precisely "a miracle."

For the spectator, the experience of observing the portrait of the woman "bleeding" tears has indeed something miraculous about it: until the first tear appears on the woman's face, in fact, the image is absolutely immobile and the impression is of observing a photographic portrait, which is not supposed to start producing tears. But as soon as the first drop introduces movement into the image, there comes the awareness that the image was, in fact, always already in movement, and that stillness was an effort of stasis, rather than a permanent condition. Such a small revelation is not devoid of impact for the spectator, and the affective suggestion of being a witness to the incursion of a miraculous element from within the image itself is a small event in this short performance of exposure.

The first spectator of this image, as well as the eye which set up the camera for the exposure of Ann Buchannan, the weeping woman, immediately recognized the extraordinariness of this event: in a 1965 interview for the

New York Herald Tribune Andy Warhol, the author of this portrait, defined Buchannan's as one of his favorites among his collection of film portraits, since "she did something wonderful, marvelous. She cried."[1]

The Ambiguity of Foreplay

Buchannan's portrait and the small event that both I and Warhol recognized it to be bothers me. This is because it is an example of the slippery and ambiguous terrain which the notion of foreplay inhabits. It can be seen as embodying, in a visual image, the flirtation with capital which foreplay necessarily entertains, projecting love labor toward a posthumous valorization.

In this chapter, I shall confront directly the ambiguity of foreplay as something supplementary to capital and yet also forcing its logic from within, and shall regard the paradigmatic stage of such ambiguity: Andy Warhol's Factory. I shall regard the collection of *Screen Tests*, of which Buchannan's image was part, as the particular visual archive of such ambiguity. In the end, I shall return to Buchannan's portrait and to my awe in front of the small event her tears brought forth for myself, and question what kind of value we can imagine for this image in the posthumous encounter with this particular spectator.

But I shall start here by looking more closely at the reasons why my awe in front of this portrait bothers me. Warhol was a spectator of the social and artistic scene I have discussed throughout the book, and he participated in the particular idleness characterizing its labors and productions. However, in participating in such a scene of familiar recognition, Warhol seems to have had a particular intuition about its distinctive dynamic of posthumous valorization, about its potential as pleasure and as capital. Warhol's comment on Buchannan's portrait is the expression of such powerful intuition: that any amateur labor of idleness is pregnant with eventfulness, and that the event of appearing can be commodified *as such*.

Andy Warhol was fascinated by the forms of value that I call foreplay, by their capacity to interrupt, at least for a short while, the progressive course of productive economy and professional work. He was fascinated by the force of such overstaying in the time of foreplay, rather than rushing out to develop a career, to actualize one's own labor in professional modes of production. In his work, he chose to record and to portray such moments of idleness, to make a catalog of them for the world to see. At the same time, his work functioned as an exemplary site of the accumulation of "attentive capital" for the artists offering their amateur labor in Warhol's productions, a symbolic capital which was the precondition for potential posthumous value realization. Furthermore, in his work Warhol seems to have understood, and put to work, the performance labor of foreplay as a distinctive "surplus" in the production of capital: he understood that memory participated in and enhanced the actualization of value, it functioned as something creating a surplus of "attention."

Whereas in the same years artists like Grotowski and Schechner were experimenting with new forms and techniques of performance "work" to foster the actualization of performance labor as event, in performance, Warhol's film work was an affirmation that a valuable "event" can be likewise a labor or idleness. Warhol's cinema was an homage to the "inefficiency" of "stylized amateurism," sharing its lack of technique, its dilettantistic nonpurposefulness. But Warhol's work, and the collection of *Screen Tests* in particular, seems to have done more than that. They seem to have affirmed that it is a labor of idleness, rather than hard work, that is more profitable as material for a posthumous value realization: that such love labor is the potential site of accumulation of the surplus value of attention.

The portrait of Buchannan, appearing before me forty years after its recording, is the condensation of the unease and fascination I have confronted in my research on the scene of foreplay, and not by chance is it a product of Warhol's work. Its accidental "eventfulness" speaks to me about the becoming-value of performances of exposures offered for free in such a social and artistic scene, a value I encountered in the professional cultural institution of the MoMA film archive. And yet my fascination, my own attraction for this exposed performance also accounts for what I call the potential of foreplay to exceed its own becoming-value, crystallized in a form of appearance. The particular labor of my familiar recognition, in my scholarly consumption of this image, is crucial to this account. My encounter with this image was in fact not simply a spectator's appreciation: it was the *longue durée* of a study, the sedimentation of a scholarly gesture of getting familiar, of imagining "inhabiting" the space and time of pleasure of 1960s New York by observing its traces forty years after. My familiar recognition of such an event had also to do with my own pleasurable "learning" of the particular technology of camp, which I have observed throughout the book as an engine at work in the scene of foreplay, a key to the alternative economy of the scene.

Warhol's work, and the *Screen Tests* collection in particular, is a peculiar archive of the distracted potentiality of the scene I have been studying, and a distinctive example of camp as a technology which, as suggested by Andrew Ross, "re-creates surplus value from forgotten forms of labor."[2] The following paragraphs reconstruct my own loitering in the traces of the productive context of the *Screen Tests* collection. Discussing the place of the collection in Warhol's body of work, I shall suggest that the intrinsic ambiguity of Warhol's storing of the human capital of appearance in the film portraits is a form of *camp production*: it shares camp's ambiguous projection toward capital, as well as its surreptitious appropriation of marginality. My loitering in the study of the collection was in a sense a prelude to my encounter with Buchannan's image: she was not one of the performers active in the artistic scene I have mapped out, she was not a star in the firmament of my research. She was, however, "hanging out" in the scene of familiar recognition I had been tracing and reconstructing for myself as an archival habitat.

Andy Warhol's *Screen Tests* Collection: Portrait Filming

Between 1964 and 1966 Andy Warhol shot a series of 472 film portraits, which were later referred to by the artist as *Screen Tests*. The film portrait of Ann Buchannan was one of them. The screen test was based on simple rules: a motionless camera, a three-minute duration, a plain background, and a centered subject in the frame who was asked to sit as still as possible.

Considered in its entirety, the *Screen Tests* series represents the most long-term project Warhol ever realized, although one of the least demanding from a technical and authorial point of view. The recording of the first screen tests started in December 1963, shortly before Warhol moved to his new studio at 231 East 47th Street, a former industrial space renovated with the help of his assistant, Gerard Malanga, and his friend Billy Linich, which soon came to be known as the Factory. Seemingly, the first portraits were shot with the intention, on Warhol's part, to produce a selection for a film portrait series entitled *The Thirteen Most Beautiful Boys*. Echoing the title of the controversial project Warhol would propose in April 1964 for the New York World's Fair—*The Most Wanted Men*,[3] a mural featuring a blown-up representation of thirteen infamous criminals' pictures reproduced from New York Police Department brochures[4]—the idea of realizing portraits of the *Thirteen Most Beautiful Boys* might well be read as an explicit homage to homoerotic desire. It is along these lines that Douglas Crimp proposes reading as double entendre the adjective "wanted" in the mural's title.[5]

Soon enough, however, the series *The Thirteen Most Beautiful* became only a cue to a much larger project, itself a sort of spin-off of the *Screen Tests* collection rather than its ultimate aim.[6] Alongside the film portraits of male posers, Warhol started realizing an all-female series, *The Thirteen Most Beautiful Women*, as well as other film portraits not purposefully conceived for any of the two series. What is more, the recording of the portraits ended up becoming a major attraction of the Factory in its double function of studio and social space, and a major appeal for Warhol himself, as it embodied two of his most recent obsessions: portraiture and film.

Warhol's success as an artist had been characterized especially by the pop, silk-screened paintings realized in the previous years, reproducing serial portraits of celebrities from various walks of fame: from Marilyn Monroe to Elizabeth Taylor and Marlon Brando, from Elvis Presley to Jackie Kennedy. Furthermore, in August 1963 Warhol had adopted the same silk-screening technique and approach to realize his first commissioned portrait: that of art collector Ethel Scull. Differently from the previous ones, Warhol realized the silk screen *Ethel Scull Thirty-Six Times* by reproducing Scull's image in a series using a photo booth, which constituted an important source of inspiration for the *Screen Tests* series. As Callie Angell remarks:

> The photobooth mechanism—a small room or booth in which a seated poser faces a camera for a predetermined length of time—is remarkably similar to the *Screen Test* setup at the Factory: both devices produce mechanical photographic portraits *over time,* which therefore can record change or movement.[7]

Such an urge to visualize time, in and by means of portraiture, can be detected as well in Warhol's early film work, which started in the same period. After the purchase of his first Bolex camera in June 1963 (the same he would use to shoot the *Screen Tests*) Warhol began to make films, having simple, everyday actions of his closest friends as the one and only subject. These films were silent, even if realized on sound film. The first two were *Sleep*, a long camerawork filming the poet John Giorno sleeping, and *Kiss*, featuring a long series of kisses between variously assorted couples from among Warhol's friends. The third was *Haircut*, featuring a number of subjects (light-designer Johnny Dodd, dancer and choreographer Freddie Herko, choreographer James Waring) in the act of getting their hair cut by Billy Name. Significantly, besides erasing any narrative structure, in these films Warhol decided to focus not only on a sole extended action, but on activities commonly considered nonproductive. If such an aspect appears quite obvious in the case of *Sleep*, the nonproductivity acquires a less obvious nuance in the case of *Kiss*. Whereas in classical Hollywood films kisses usually mark a climax, here they are made in series and stand outside of a plot, as a multiplication of climaxes, hence losing their very climax-like quality: they do not mark the accomplishment of a romance, or the beginning of it.[8] These scenes, in a sense, appear as leftovers or cut parts from films: as in the legendary final scene of *Nuovo Cinema Paradiso* (Tornatore, 1988), where the protagonist returns to his childhood memories as he sits all alone in a (soon to be demolished) movie theater. There he watches the series of kisses and other "obscene" sequences of foreplay that in earlier times used to be removed from films in Italy for censorship reasons, and which have been collected in one reel by the projectionist, as a gift for this particular once-upon-a-time child spectator returning to the small town after many years.

For Warhol—who as a child grew up falling in love with cinema, but then became a professional painter—to return to cinema as a maker of these leftover scenes, encompassing all that was left out of the Hollywood industry (such as same-sex foreplay, as well the intrinsic boredom of physical intimacy, or the boredom of sleep that knows no necessity of climax), was in a sense love labor. It was an exercise in cinema, a learning to do film according to a necessity of desire: the desire to look at those scenes, to make a sequence of them. The desire to produce them, while consuming them—or to consume them again, later.

As for *Haircut*, portraying in a sense a productive action, the particular reference standing behind it is quite telling about the character of such productivity. The film portrayed a specific social habit, which for years had been taking place in Name's flat, on East 7th Street in the East Village: the haircutting parties, during which guests—most of whom were artists active in the theater and dance scene, such as Herko, Dodd, and Waring—would get their hair cut by the householder.[9] The haircuts, in this context, were ascribed to a domestic environment, and hence removed from a paid professional activity. Warhol's filming of this habit therefore portrays a fragment of the autarchic economy of the downtown art community, and gives a glimpse of the economy of reproduction and mutual support that is founded on amateur techniques rather than professional skills.

Ultimately, the very setting of Warhol's first films (characterized by a wise use of lights, and a scrupulous focus on the faces' details) reveals an approach to cinema deeply indebted to a pictorial tradition, and these films can be considered the first step towards Warhol's subsequent exploration of the potentiality of a genre that, until then, was extraneous to cinema practice: portraiture. In Steven Watson's words:

> Andy's obsession with portraiture immediately surfaced in his filmmaking. He revived a tradition that appeared in America's first avant-garde to not only create portrait likeness, but to reconceive the form. In the case of Warhol, a portrait usually focused on a single characteristic action. The result was part gossip, part plastic expression, and all absolute likeness.[10]

Not unlike Gertrude Stein's "portrait writing," the *Screen Tests* collection discloses Warhol's desire to portray his friends while they were alive, not to remember them as a repetition of what they had been.

A Family Album, a Portrait Gallery

In the introductory essay to the *Screen Tests* catalogue raisonné, Callie Angell refers to the overall *Screen Tests* series as a "unique map of the New York downtown scene in a watershed period" and the series of film frames appearing in the catalog as a geography of connections functioning as an archive for a specific belonging:

> Like a yearbook of the mid-1960s avant-garde, the Screen Tests contain photographic portraits of a diverse population of cultural figures, all linked through their shared connection, however brief, with Warhol and his camera: poets, artists, writers, filmmakers, musicians, dancers, models, speed freaks, opera queens, street people,

> performers, a smattering of celebrities and the wealthy as well as all grades of the Factory personnel, from anonymous freshmen to superstars and other seniors.[11]

The 472 portraits identified as *Screen Tests* feature a number of poets, theater and film practitioners, as well as a number of folk and rock musicians. In the collection there is a large sampling of intellectuals variously active in the field of New York journalism, and others especially linked to the art world, of art collectors, as well as of wealthy socialites (who played the role of patrons toward Warhol and often supported some of the Factory regulars) and of personalities from the world of fashion and advertising; the latter were acquaintances of Warhol from the 1950s period, in which he used to work as a commercial artist.

The succession of photographic portraits suggests a consideration of the catalog itself as a form of family album. All the more so, given that the gesture of detaching individual film frames from the duration of each screen test and presenting them as photographic portraits is not only embedded in Angell's catalog, but had already been done back at the time they were made. In 1967, in fact, Andy Warhol and Gerard Malanga had published with Kulchur Press a limited-edition book entitled *Screen Tests/A Diary*, featuring film frames from the *Screen Tests* series as photographic portraits, along with a number of poems especially written by Malanga. One of those poems, located on the page facing Billy Name's portrait, features the following lines:

> what are the relationships between swapped destinies?
> what light does
> the use of the diary text reveals the crucial ideas,
> and the loss of heaven in life is authentic
> the rain becomes rain again-
> the friends are forever involved in the "family photo."[12]

The idea of kinship suggested in Malanga's poem is something discussed at length in the previous chapter. And indeed, the proximity of portraits in Andy Warhol's *Screen Tests* collection, along with its fruition in collective circumstances, could itself be read as a habitat (in Bourdieu's sense) in which people produced bodily resemblances to one another, and expressed the affinities of these relations through forms of visibility rooted in the socially determined sharing of habitus. Images and behaviors asserted the insistance of identities, collectively elaborated and available to be recognized. In the three-minute duration of the screen test, particular identities were archived as a familiar trace.

During the period in which the *Screen Tests* were realized, Andy Warhol's Factory was a peculiar demimonde in between uptown and downtown, between the productive economy of New York "pop society"[13] and the "underground" of the Film-Makers' Cooperative and the Off-Off Broadway theater observed throughout this book. It was during the two year period of 1964–1966 that Warhol got closer to the underground scene (especially thanks to his friendship with Gerard Malanga and Billy Linich) and made a number of "home movies"[14] starring some of his friends as performers, most of whom were involved in the Off-Off Broadway theater and performance productions: among them Gerard Malanga himself, Beverly Grant, Mario Montez, Ronald Tavel (who worked as a screen player for all of Warhol's first sound films), Jack Smith, Taylor Mead, Mary Woronov, Jackie Curtis, Penny Arcade, Holly Woodlawn and many others. At the end of this two-year period Warhol's film work moved to uptown movie theaters, and this move was marked by the succès de scandale of *Chelsea Girls* in 1966, which not only reached a larger audience but also provoked some indignation, as expressed for instance by Bosley Crowther, in a *New York Times* review, who lamented the "underground overflow" and warned the art world and the intellectual community ("permissive adults") to stop "winking at their too-precocious pranks." [15]

Throughout 1964–1966 Warhol's filmmaking was entirely amateur work, independently produced and sustained economically by his work as a professional artist, as well as by the voluntary participation of actors, playwrights, and collaborators of other sorts. Such amateur collaborators clearly benefited from their participation in Warhol's world and imagery, if not in economic terms then certainly in terms of visibility and enhanced possibilities of future success, of making it some day to the "big time" in cinema or other fields. Warhol, on his part, benefited from the crowding of his studio and from his own participation in underground film and performance, not least because the entrance into this world allowed him to imagine and to experiment with what Ross called an "alternative studio system geared to regular and rapid productions, with its own stable of homegrown Superstars (with their own steady stage names), its own casting system, screen tests, and publicity stunts to stimulate media attention."[16]

The Counter-Field of Camp Production: Portraits of a Theatrical Imagination

Something else, however, seems to have been going on in the artistic collaboration between Warhol and these amateur performers. The intimacy of work and life expressed by Warhol's cinema can be read as a collective creation of a counter-field of production within the broader New York productive economy, a counter-field of reproduction and intimacy "represented" in his movies as another mode of living and working. As significant scholarship has already explored and as Jennifer Doyle argues in particular in her essay "Between Friends,"[17] the collaborative nature of Warhol's film work obliges us to consider not only the complex status of Warhol as "author" but also the peculiar relations which emerge from the making of his movies, relations of work and sex, of trust and negotiation—relations which, Doyle suggests, might well be understood in terms of friendship. Echoing Michel Foucault's interview "Friendship as a Way of Life"[18] (in which the philosopher notably remarked that homosexuality threatens people as a mode of life, rather than as a way of having sex), Doyle reflects on friendship[19] as a mode of relation that queers standard notions of intimacy, attachment, and collaboration, to the extent that even forms of exchange are figured as participating in a culture of sexual generosity exceeding any prescribed social, gender, or economic role. In her analysis of Warhol's *Blue Movie* (1969), "a lazy portrait of lovers spending an afternoon 'in,'"[20] Doyle emphasizes the many ways in which the relation between Viva and Warhol, mirrored and extended in the intimate screen relation between Viva and Louis Waldon (playing couplehood as "an act, not as a destination"),[21] explores friendship as a space in which it is possible to experiment with "other forms of intimacy"[22] involving not only sex, but also artistic work. In fact, in Warhol's movies collaboration entails a continuing shift in the "authoriality" of the movie, of the action and of the agency, and in this shift even the presence of spectators seems to be called upon.[23] Along the same lines, Mark Siegel has suggested that the people involved in Warhol's movies might be regarded as all linked in cooperation toward a "project of aesthetically and erotically publicizing their way of life,"[24] and thus enacting a political promise of a sort. Such a space of collaboration and desire in Warhol's work has been further explored in Muñoz's research on the traces of a forthcoming, queer futurity emerging from specific works of 1960s New York art, such as Warhol's. It has also been addressed by Douglas Crimp in his effective and affective analysis of the movie *Screen Test*, which Crimp reads in light of the collaboration between Warhol, Tavel, and Montez. All these studies, in different ways, nourish the historiographical image of the Factory as a habitat for an intimacy that playfully subverted standard modes of production in filmmaking, and the reproduction of social life. They look at Warhol's cinema as productive of affective bonds and solidarity, as friendly labor rather than professional work.

Along the same lines, I argue that the collection of *Screen Tests* was a peculiar experiment in reconfiguring notions of labor, production, consumption, and waste, particular expressions of what I suggest calling a form of *camp production*. On the one hand the *Screen Tests* constitute stored-up labor, available exposures for posthumous realization that are grounded in the self-exploitation of the exposed subjects; on the other, they are also a queer unit of value actualizing itself in the potentiality of its own futurity, in a particular economy of attention. Each of the posers in the *Screen Tests* collection appears "in a state of continual incandescence—a person being one, very intense thing,"[25] the crucial characteristic that Susan Sontag attributes to camp. They are incandescent because these images are self-consummating: they are simply a promise of performance, and in this promise they appear *as* performance. The three-minute-long exposures were conceived as leftovers of a time yet to come: the future in which the promise enacted in the *Screen Tests* selection would be realized, the moment in which, in the future, they will be recognizable as valuable. In the form of the screen test, however, such value stands still, in the grip of its potentiality.

An important insight for my analysis is offered by the excellent study developed by Matthew Tinkom, who has interrogated Warhol's work in the frame of his broader inquiry into the relation between camp and capital in the work of four gay American filmmakers.[26] Confronting notions of labor and value in Marx with the cultural politics of camp, Tinkom's analysis holds that "Marxism and camp intellectual practices derive their energies from similar but hardly identical interests in upending, in their disparate ways, the world that capital has brought about."[27] More specifically, Tinkom interrogates camp as the point of surfacing of the "unstable status of value"[28] with a particular relation to human labor:

> One might read the history of capital as, in fact, the overpowering insistence that all humans make themselves adequate for their abstraction and insertion into processes of production. Arguing in a contrary direction, I wonder if the commodity's status as an object with some undisclosed feature of its historical moment of production that might be revealed in a movement through exchange might not be, at least sometimes, the fact of its having been shaped by some anomalous labor and laborer, and at this point camp emerges as an expression of such concealed efforts.[29]

I am interested in Tinkom's articulation of the promise that camp, in Warhol's cinema, points to a particular reflection on labor, and also—I add—on the very "being adequate" for labor that capitalist production requires. In the *Screen Tests* collection such camp production functioned as an homage and a critical engagement with the mode of performance labor elaborated in the 1960s underground theater that we have been observing throughout this book. Such performance labor, as I emphasized, was not developed out of a prescribed course of training, discipline, and craftsmanship. At the least it was a labor expressing a shallow attitude regarding the accomplishment of an efficacious performance, either understood as a piece of theatrical bravura or as an effective encounter with an audience. It was a labor based on the mobilization of theatrical personalities constructed out of onstage and offstage forms of interaction. According to Stefan Brecht, for example, the work of the Play-House of the Ridiculous is populated by "stock fantasy figures,"[30] personalities whose display was to be understood in specific terms:

> Personality is like the make-believe identity a child assumes in play with others or an actor assumes in the theatre and is as real as these—accepted (felt by him and projected outward in activity), real not in

> the sense of corresponding to any true given nature but as being his free product expressed in Action.[31]

Warhol's work is usually the main lens through which, and in relation to which, the 1960s underground theater and performances are discussed. Here I propose a shift in perspective, looking at things the other way around. I like to think about Warhol as a professional painter who became acquainted with a particular theater scene—the one inhabited by the Play-House of the Ridiculous, contiguous to Tom Eyen's and Jackie Curtis's camp plays staged at La MaMa and at Caffe Cino (as well as to the much broader downtown art and performance scene, such as the one grown around the Judson Memorial Church)—and who developed a desire to portray these personalities in his personal portrait gallery. Along this line of thinking, I see Warhol occupying a peculiar place in the long tradition of artists who, in different historical epochs, offered their canvas to the images of actors, captured in the particular character that had contributed to their memorability on stage. Among them, for instance, Jean-Francoise Watteau, who left remarkable portraits of actors who played at the Comédie-Française, or Johann Zoffany, who famously portrayed the Shakespearean actor David Garrick as *Macbeth*, or Otto Dix, who painted in the 1920s the legendary portrait of Anita Berber in Weimar Berlin. Besides, in Warhol's case, very much as in Dix/Berber's case, the performers would not appear "in character," but rather visually reaffirmed their recognizable personalities in the broader stage of social and artistic life.

Long debated in theatre iconography,[32] the status of the actor's portrait has been theoretically reconfigured beyond documentary exactitude and is currently considered, also in theater historiography, as the index of a set of social practices of reception, rather than as evidence of a particular theatrical event. Even more specifically, the very genre of the actors' iconography is regarded as a symptom of the particular circulation of images in a given society, rather than as a document of theatrical performance. As Maria Ines Aliverti summarizes:

> The value of a theatrical image is not that of an illustration or a source; . . . Both on a structural and historical level . . . the image of theatrical content . . . can be interrogated regarding the specific way in which a particular theatre is expressed in the image. That is, more than real information about the image itself, what can emerge is something of the contemporary theatrical imagination: not only what the audience in a particular time thought they were seeing, but what in that particular cultural system the audience could, in fact, see.[33]

Along the same lines, Warhol's portraits are symptoms of the particular theatricality of an expanded stage where gestures, recurring habits, forms of imitation, and spontaneous moments of exhibitionism were all potential "highs" of performance. In a sense, as in the work of the Play-House of the Ridiculous, the continuum between the shows and the occasional moments of "showtime," such as the ones regularly put on at Max's Kansas City, made it difficult to separate particular forms of "performance work" from generally theatrical behaviors enacted (echoing Doyle's essay) *among friends*.

In Vaccaro's words, the directions he would give to the Play-House actors were significant of a particular, shared imagery:

> Within an hour and a half you do anything you like. I call it PRECISE SPONTANEITY. I tell them—"camera's got a close up on you, and you've got to keep doing something at all times. Keep busy, staying with the character". The type of acting we do is very early movies. We INDICATE. Bette Davis, Joan Crawford, silent movies are all INDICATORS.[34]

Ironically, then, portraying the personalities of the actors taking place in Vaccaro's shows meant not only capturing their recognizable images, but also capturing the very sense of such theatricality, which (as Vaccaro's quote makes clear) was already organized according to a logic of "close-up" in performance. Vaccaro's frenetic theater, like Warhol's filmmaking, was made of rapid productions, mobilizing a self-affirmed pantheon of stars with steady names and features; it was likewise practiced by amateurs.

Warhol's portraiture, then, offered an iconography of such theater which might well be considered in the terms in which theater historians like Balme or Aliverti have proposed regarding actors' portraits: as image-deposits of the particular theatrical imagination of a certain moment in time. Warhol's portraits, likewise, are not loyal reproductions of "personalities": they are deposits, not only of "what the audience in a particular time thought they were seeing, but what in that particular cultural system the audience could, in fact, see."[35]

The Factory Court

A reading of the figure of Andy Warhol as the peculiar heir of a long tradition of "court painters" is carried out with interesting results in an analysis by Peter Wollen, who has proposed reading Warhol's entire career as somehow associated with the model of the court.[36] I am not sure I agree with Wollen's hypothesis, but I find it useful in speculative terms for questioning how the foreplay of the 1960s underground functioned in the demimonde of the Factory.

Wollen reconstructs the various phases of Warhol's career, dating back to his work in fashion as a commercial illustrator in the 1950s, and holds that even during this first phase Warhol played the role of the courtier, bustling to demonstrate his talent to please the power holders of commercial enterprises. Afterwards, when he became mainly a professional painter, he was able to invert the terms of the court-mechanism, building a form of court into the Factory.[37] Then in the last phase of the artist's work, in a further inversion, Wollen sees Warhol returning to the position of courtier, but this time as court artist, eager to satisfy the taste and the vanity of New York high society of the 1980s, for whom he produced portraits on commission, using the style which became famous as the screen-printing *à la Warhol*.

Wollen also compares Warhol's multifaceted artistic production to the model of a "Renaissance man" (as defined by Jacob Burckhardt)[38] and to artists like Michelangelo or Leonardo, who achieved excellence in several activities, widening their interest to painting, writing, architecture, literature, and music, as well as to science and technology. Warhol inherited this humanistic approach, since his work took diverse forms over his life: painting, sculpture, cinema, staging, music, literature and theater, but also fashion, and television. It is crucial to add to Wollen's considerations that whereas for the Renaissance artist practicing various art fields entailed a wide "education" (understood as apprenticeship in the specific technique of the medium), in Warhol this aspect is reduced to a zero degree: amateurism seems for Warhol a basic condition of self-learning.[39] The question of technique is also curiously reconfigured in Warhol's practice: the famous phrase, "I want to be a machine,"[40] ascribed to Warhol, was a radical denial of the strongly humanist, Renaissance concept of "invention," which is first rooted in the author's mind, and only secondly in the technical possibilities.

The affinity between Warhol and the model of the Renaissance man, in Wollen's view, also involves a cultural reassessment process. During the Renaissance there was a general rediscovery of classical culture as iconographic material, fostering a renewal of the grammar of visual art imagery: the mythological figures populating the work of Raphael, Michelangelo, Leonardo, and Donatello. Similarly, during the 1960s, Warhol took part in the general process of popular culture revaluation, with a particular attention to the mass culture of his recent past. According to Wollen, Warhol's iconography from the beginning drew from icons of classical Hollywood, building into his work an outright pantheon of recurring divinities. On this basis, Wollen compares the images of Marilyn Monroe or Elvis Presley to the figures of classical mythology, who were for Renaissance artists a source of inspiration and an iconographic paradigm. Another remark has to be added to Wollen's analysis, again related to modes of production: ancient classical art became an object of study and inspiration in Renaissance art, where many artists (in particular Brunelleschi, Alberti, Michelangelo, and Leonardo) devoted attention not only to the iconography, but to classical art's modus operandi and grammar of composition. The interest in classical mythology in Italian Renaissance art was also accompanied by an interest in the ancient techniques, language, and style: the fascination in classical culture was also a form of knowledge. The work of artists like Michelangelo or Raphael was of course not only a recouping of classical mythology and techniques; it was a reformulation of modes of composition through quotes, through devotion to proportion and form, and compositional invention.[41]

I also believe that for Warhol the interest in the mythology produced in the Hollywood studios was not limited to iconography, but involved a valorization of the modus operandi typical of the golden age of the American cinema. It suffices to reflect on the way Warhol describes his approach to filmmaking:

> I made my earliest films using, for several hours just one actor on the screen doing the same thing . . . I did this because people usually go to the movies to see only the star, to eat him up, so here at least is a chance to look only at the star for as long as you like, no matter what he does and to eat him up all you want to.[42]

The *Screen Tests* might be read as an experiment in such extraction of the star from the movie. Again, this brings us back to the sequence of *Nuovo Cinema Paradiso* earlier recalled, where the kisses were extracted from movies, in an arbitrary sequence, and to Warhol's *Kiss* where, likewise, the kisses had full legitimacy of appearance, not as teleological elements in a broader narrative, but as self-accomplished cinematic units. According to Andrew Ross, "Warhol copied all of the institutions of the legitimate studio system in a way which traded directly on the camp appeal of faded star quality but which also made no attempt to conceal the celebrity-making process which manufactured 'star quality.' "[43] In the *Screen Tests* collection Warhol recouped golden-age Hollywood's modus operandi not only as a quote or a homage, but in a theatrical appropriation of the ways of doing of that very Hollywood. The homage to a faded Hollywood was also an appropriation of its waste of production: namely, the auditions, which never got to have value as a movie.

Screen Tests as Cinematic Foreplay

In the *Screen Tests*, the close-up of the star coincides with the form of the audition. Hence, Warhol captured the overlapping of a desire to access Hollywood production, on the part of the poser, with an appearance of stardom which was not only produced, but immediately consumed by Warhol, as a spectator, desiring to see the star take shape before him. It was later kept in the grip of portraiture, on the reels of the collection of film portraits that Warhol himself withdrew from distribution and circulation in the 1970s, handing over to posthumous spectators the whole corpus of his 1960s films.[44]

Belying the expectations aroused by the term "screen test" as an audition for a movie to come, Warhol's *Screen Tests* are self-accomplishing. As the film scholar Homay King pointed out:

> Warhol does not seem to evaluate the silent, immobile subject for any of the abilities or traits a screen test would normally measure. . . . The test form has been de-teleologized; these films are neither preparatory nor subordinate to a final work. Warhol allows the trial-and-error aesthetics a cinematic life of its own, and the series of Screen Tests remains perpetually open-ended.[45]

Naming the film portraits *Screen Tests*, Warhol plays with the standard language of Hollywood cinema, promising to enact a core process of the entertainment industry: the audition. The latter is the moment of access to a paid job in film, and traditionally a chance to verify—in performance—a subject's potential as a laborer in the show business industry: it is a form of recruitment, which ritually marks the passage from "free time" to "work time" for the aspiring performer. The performance labor in the audition, in fact, is usually not paid for up front, but this gratuity is functional to the formulation of a promise of paid labor in a future work. The brief time of the audition is the space to realize, for a performer, her potential value, crystallized in a form of appearance. Since only some of the performers auditioning for a movie will be hired to work, however, the screen test is also a basic unit of unpaid labor hoping to realize itself in the future.

Such labor of appearance is literally "like a railway where no trains run,"[46] which Marx offered as an example of labor not yet recognized or recognizable as exchangeable. Hence, the screen test is a pure form of foreplay: it is both the promise for a future value realization and the possible waste of production, if the production in question would not happen in the end, or if the performer would not be hired for the role. The form of the screen test is a very suitable site to observe how Marx's scheme of the creation of value functions in the particular contest of performance production. In the screen test a performer is "tested" to be adequate for labor. There, the labor expected of the performer coincides with a set of body behaviors, capacities of movement and speech, as well as a potential ability to perform a particular role. The labor of appearance, in the screen test, constitutes the moment in which—in Marx's scheme—labor is not yet objectified, but is only the bearer of its potential use.

The *Screen Tests* are also a particularly good site to observe what Marx defines as the origin of the economic chain of value: labor power, which Marx considers the fundamental commodity. Marx considers labor power as potentially bearing a use-value and defines it as *the possibility for a subject to be adequate for labor*. Labor power "distinguishes itself from the ordinary crowd of commodities in that its use value creates value, and a greater value than it costs itself."[47] Therefore value stands both inside and outside value determination, as it precedes the actual labor and also partakes in the exchange process.

At the same time, the audition normally participates in a phase of work-preparation, and is only a process on the way to a movie to come: a process in which the judges—those in charge of evaluating the performance—are both consumers of the images produced in the audition, and producers of a selection. In Warhol's case, however, none of the skills of the sitter were evaluated for future purposes. The three-minute duration of a screen test is literally a "strip of behaviour" (referring to Schechner's terminology) where the subject's exposure is offered as material for both social and stage performances. It is at the same time what Georges Bataille would name a *dépense*: "nonproductive expenditure" of the labor of appearing, framed as performance. The word "expenditure" is employed by Bataille

> for the designation of all the modes of consumption that serve as a means to the end of production. Even though it is always possible to set the various forms of expenditure in opposition to each other, they constitute a group characterized by the fact that in each case the accent is placed on a loss that must be as great as possible in order for that activity to take its own true meaning.[48]

The horizon of loss, in the case of the *Screen Tests*, resided in the waste of such labor of appearance, in the fact that while performing at being evaluated, in the gratuitous exposure of the film portrait, the value of such labor was necessarily to be forgotten. In the screen test, the labor power of performance is exposed in a distinctive state of potentiality. This reading seems to be further supported by Warhol's own conception of work, proving that he understood far too well that such labor of appearance was a bearer of potential value:

> I suppose I have a very loose interpretation of "work" because I think that just being alive is so much work at something you don't always want to do. Being born is like being kidnapped. And then sold into slavery. People are working every minute. The machine is always going, even when you sleep.[49]

Here it is where, in my view, the entire *Screen Tests* collection can be regarded as a sheer form of camp production. Warhol's desire to work with leftovers produced in the *Screen Tests* collection is a fascinating interplay between different phases of production and consumption. In principle, the labor of appearance in the *Screen Tests* is disguised as a waste of production, as it would be for an audience: a "waste" of labor intrinsic to film production itself. At the same time, such waste was recouped for production: the production of the film portraits, objects of consumption. What would be consumed, regardless of the "adequacy for labor" of the subjects, was the particular theatricality, a mode of appearing that Warhol had observed so many times on the stages of the social and artistic scene of downtown New York, and which he observed being donated gratuitously around him.

Warhol's mimetic enactment of a core process of the entertainment industry, the work-preparation, outside of a project of productive work (the film to come) leaves us with 472 images of performance labor hoping to realize themselves in the future. Such labor of appearing seemed to have no intention of realizing itself in an immediate outcome. The posers were not asked to play a role, but were conscious of participating in a "nonproductive expenditure." They knew that those images could also have remained "just exposures." Yet, they were also aware of participating in a secondary market of sorts which the Factory art world embodied: an economy of attention.

The Long History of the Attention Income

The fact that Warhol had adopted such cinematic foreplay in his work over the course of two years also interests me as an expression of a specific technology of attention borrowed by the artist from a tradition which preexisted his work: the tradition of vaudeville and variety which, as already suggested, had a close proximity with the birth of Hollywood cinema, and substantially marked its style: vaudeville, in fact, also handed over to cinema a number of stars, who—like Buster Keaton, the Marx Brothers, and Mae West—started out in low vaudeville circuits, then made it to the "big time" of the pictures. The mechanism of the audition in a sense replicated the performances of talent contests, where, as I have argued elsewhere, in the brief time span allowed by the contest, the vaudevillian had to prove her abilities and performance value, which very often coincided with the construction of a recognizable persona.[50]

The idea of an economy of attention was usefully developed by Georg Franck, who has termed "attentive capital" the nonmonetary, accountable, gratuitously donated attention, functioning as a secondary economy of sorts.[51] With this definition, Franck refers to a specific form of "attention income" corresponding to the ability, by various means, of catching other people's attention and hence acquiring social credit or recognition. According to Franck, the "economy of attention" has always worked as a secondary market exceeding (or rather, developing alongside) the monetized one. Although Franck's analysis focuses especially on the crucial role of attention in the social functioning of today's media-driven economy, he also emphasizes that what he considers the more recent phase of "full industrialization" of the tangle between money income and attention income is in fact a process which started to develop long before the media acquired full power in the economic sphere. Furthermore, since their establishment this tangle has already passed through several different phases:

> The economy of attention not only looks back on an ancient pre-history, it also has a long industrial history. It was pre-industrial as long as publication technologies were either of the handicraft type or, respectively, had not yet permeated the entire economy. Attention economy reached its early industrial phase when the first, relatively simple information and communication technologies developed. The technology of printing, radio broadcasting and sound film for the first time assembled critical amounts of anonymously donated attention, turning the star cult into a mass phenomenon. It was then that the business of attraction became professionalised, that deliberate eye-catching became industrial in advertising. We may speak of a phase of full industrialisation since the advent of television.[52]

This analysis touches upon some important aspects of my study, especially considering the prominence which the early industrial media technologies played in the context of nineteenth-century American spectacle. The historical development of variety, as well as of the sideshow and dime museum, benefited enormously from the expansion of a popular press, distributed broadly and available at a lower price for working-class audiences, in the same years making its way into American society as a powerful new social media.[53] Significantly, in his autobiography P. T. Barnum emphasizes, as evidence of his entrepreneurial capacity, his immediate understanding of the power of advertisement and publication technology for launching and promoting the attractions of his American Museum.[54] Likewise, in the mature development of the vaudeville industry the media construction of the performers' personalities (often highly fictional and carefully constructed by impresarios) proved crucial in fostering interest and attraction on the audience's part. As Trav. S. D. repeatedly spells out in his study of vaudeville history, one of the basic features of variety was the presentation of the personality in the media and on advertising leaflets, as well as on the stage:

> The vaudevillian was not just creating an onstage character: he was creating a persona that would appear to have a life on its own from performance to performance, and offstage as well. The most successfully wrought of these personas had an absolutely mythic power. The character W. C. Fields created, for example, was so irresistible that it seems to live on to this day, even without the living presence of the man who inhabited it.[55]

On the one hand, the established course of celebrity creation seems to have first been rehearsed in vaudeville, and then applied in its full potentiality in the film industry, which capitalized on the industrially manufactured aura of the actors in order to establish the Hollywood star system. On the other, vaudeville also suggested a modus operandi which was deemed to be long-lasting in the industry of American show business: the exposure of personalities also encompassed details of the performer's private life entailing aspects often considered taboo in American society. The larger-than-life personas proposed on stage were nourished by the questionable lifestyles of the performers, whose private/public lives also encompassed—for instance in the cases of Sophie Tucker or Mae West—hard drinking, sex outside of marriage, or—in the case of female impersonator Bert Savoy—flamboyant homosexuality. According to the same logic, as Kenneth Anger's 1959 book *Hollywood Babylon* morbidly explores,[56] the Hollywood industry in its golden years turned the ambiguous coincidence between the star persona's fictional life and her biography into a profitable and spicy media spectacle, which contributed to the construction of a following for the stars themselves, which was of course a guarantee of profit for the studios. In a very similar logic, the vaudeville impresario would invest in advertising the vaudevillian's constructed persona, as this would secure an economic return in terms of box office revenues.

This dynamic can also be recognized in the 1960s scene, where not only were performers socially recognized personalities in the downtown art world (and then since the mid-1960s also in the mainstream press) and were often conflated with their stage characters, but the blurred boundaries between private and public life, as vehicles of attractions, were consciously experimented with in artistic terms, as in the case of Jackie Curtis previously discussed. Hence, Franck's industrial history of the economy of attention could be summarized as follows: the dynamic of attention-catching was first elaborated in the context of variety (developed at the same time as the "relatively simple information and communication technologies"), then refined during the Hollywood era "turning the star cult into a mass phenomenon," and eventually found its ultimate expression in television, where the attention-catching mechanism found an even wider dissemination. Interestingly, this narrative traces a trajectory of development that has its point of arrival in the late 1950s and early 1960s: the moment at which television became a widespread medium in American society. Significantly, this is also the moment in which most of the protagonists of this book first participated. They did so first as consumers of the economy of attention entailed in the personality-driven economy, developing a particular fascination for a form of stardom which, by then, was fading out in terms of immediate economic profit, but was again entering a secondary market of attention: the domain of *memorability*. Movie theaters first and television afterward constituted pivotal vehicles for prolonging the charm of a Hollywood that in the 1950s was already fading out, and also for creating the longing for performance which was being experimented with in the 1960s scene of foreplay.

Me, Myself, and the *Screen Tests*: An Attention *Démesurée*

I encountered the *Screen Tests* in a circumstance that had never occurred before in my life. I was sitting in a movie theater and I was the only spectator, like in the last scene of *Nuovo Cinema Paradiso* earlier recalled. I was at the Celeste Bartos Film Center at MoMA during the series of screenings of Andy Warhol's film portraits organized by appointment during my research in New York between January and June 2008. I would reach MoMA by the subway, arriving from the Lower East Side, where I lived, and in the small movie theater of the museum I was the only person watching those film portraits, forty years after they were shot. Every now and then the screening would interrupt, giving the projectionist time to prepare the showing of the next film portraits I wanted to see, from different reels.

I spent in that small movie theater several afternoons throughout these months, and on my last day I entered the cabin of the projectionist, who I would see every now and then, in between different reels, in order to say goodbye and to thank him for his work. He smiled, under his white beard, and told me: "I am glad it is your last day here, that this is over. I don't think it is very healthy for you to be watching these faces *all this time*." What I took from this comment was that the attention and the time I was giving to Andy Warhol's film portraits was, according to the projectionist, disproportionate.

As a matter of fact, mine was an absolutely disproportionate act of attention toward these film portraits, especially considering the conditions of production and of consumption characterizing the time and space in which the *Screen Tests* were first realized and then seen, in the mid-1960s. These portraits were in fact not supposed to be consumed in a condition of focused attention, but rather in a state of distraction. Nor were the *Screen Tests* produced by Warhol in a state of labored concentration either, but amidst the leisurely and work activities of the Factory. Warhol is said to have often set up the camera in front of his posers and then left to attend to other duties, such as silk-screening, or conversations with collaborators and guests, and then to have come back to turn the camera off after three minutes or so.

Likewise, often the posing was not planned in advance, and subsequently the portraits were not to be presented to spectators in a condition of labored attention: during Warhol's life they were screened almost exclusively during parties, or at multimedia art events such as the *Exploding Plastic Inevitable*, and the like; watching the portraits was accompanied by music and conversation, as well as by the consumption of drugs and alcohol; it was also not supposed to happen in a traditional spectatorial setting. Furthermore, most of the subjects of the film portraits were also the spectators of the *Screen Tests*: the appearing of the spectators' images on the screen, during parties, created a complex short circuit of recognition, a loop of images which worked as an engine for the overall circulation of images among different art pieces and social spaces around the Factory.

In the movie theater of MoMA I was not surrounded by faces I could recognize, nor was I consuming food, alcohol, or drugs, nor was I dancing or talking with friends. My attention was completely directed toward these faces appearing before me, literally starring—being the stars of my consumption—in the firmament of my research. These images were for me images of strangers. Besides, for months before these screenings I had studied the social scene in which most of these persons had lived and worked. Hence, I knew some of their addresses in the mid-1960s from previous archival research, and I had read about the performances they were involved in during the period in which the portraits were shot. I had encountered some of them, or had met their friends who were still living in New York. I could recognize some details, and relate them to their stories. Names and faces tied to stories.

The proximity of these presences in the collection also spoke to me about a set of relations of collaboration, friendship, love, kinship, hatred, or jealousy which were part of the narrative of the scene through which these personas had moved in the 1960s New York art world. Obviously, not all of the subjects were—so to say—acquaintances of my research: I had constructed my own constellation of faces on the basis of my study of the beautiful catalog of Warhol's *Screen Tests* that Callie Angell had realized and published a few years earlier, and in the collection I had chosen to see the portraits of a number of artists whose artistic practices were part of my mapping of the 1960s New York "scene of foreplay." In those portraits I was therefore able to recognize a few distinctive signs, which were hints for me toward other stories, connections, and attributes contributing to the formation of specific personas.

I could recognize Beverly Grant, the "Queen of the Underground,"[57] who appears in three screen tests in the recognizable persona in which she starred in a number of films, photographs, and performances realized shortly before or very soon after that moment in which the film portraits were shot in 1964.[58] Among these works, I remembered Jack Smith's photographic series *The Beautiful Book* (1962) and the film *Normal Love* (1964), Ron Rice's *Chumlum* (1963), Warhol's unfinished project *Batman/Dracula* (1964), and the Play-House of the Ridiculous's theater piece *Shower* (1965). In all these works Grant appears as a vampiric figure, with long dark hair often transformed in scenic props by the actress, emphasizing the contrast with her white skin and pale blue eyes. Looking at one of Grant's portraits, I could remember that the poster of *Shower*, presented at the Coda Gallery in a double bill with *The Life of Juanita Castro* as the first production of the Play-House of the Ridiculous, was designed by Jack Smith, and featured Grant holding a fan with her characteristic long black hair, resembling very much the way she was portrayed by Jack Smith in a photograph collected in the 1962 *The Beautiful Book*.[59]

I could recognize Susan Sontag in seven portraits shot in 1964 the same year the writer published her famous "Notes on 'Camp.'" Sontag's attendance at the Factory studio during 1964 obviously documents the direct connection between her landmark essay and the contemporary aesthetic sensibility enacted in the underground cinema and theater. Furthermore, this contiguity can be regarded as connecting to the recent circulation of the word "camp" itself, which around 1964–66 became a keyword of the underground artistic firmament.[60] Warhol himself gave the title *Camp* to a 1965 film starring "various examples of camp in performances by Paul Swan, Jack Smith, Tally Brown, Mario Montez, Donyale Luna, and others."[61]

The performer Rene Rivera, who appeared in *Camp* with a small vaudeville number, appeared again in a screen test in the drag persona of Mario Montez, a personality Rivera had been building through his appearances in a body of filmic and theatrical performances since 1962. The screen test of Mario Montez is another crossroads of important intersections: in the same year of 1965 Montez appears as the main character of a Warhol movie and a Play-House of the Ridiculous theater production, both based on a script by Ronald Tavel and both significantly entitled *Screen Test*.[62] In the movie and in the show, the form of the screen test is manifestly brought back to its original use, that is, an audition reel. But from the very beginning it is evident that the audition (standing as the final work) is indeed a gimmick to focus and play on Montez's long take. The exposure section is intended to expose Montez in a progressive unmasking process, revealing, at the very end, the ambiguous, cynical gaze of the camera, as Montez is asked by a voice offscreen to show his genitals to the camera. The audience of the film and theater performance, though, was mainly the same one attending the Factory studio and was certainly aware of the *Screen Tests* project Warhol was developing at the time. On a multiple level, therefore, the overturning of the function of the screen test form in these works was meaningful as a meta-comment of the *Screen Tests* production among the community.

The attention I was giving to these film portraits in the solitude of my scholarly consumption was *démesurée* (disproportionate), over-labored in my pursuit of visual images of the 1960s New York scene, rather than received in a state of distraction. I was watching the portraits in a different temporality than the one in which they were produced and consumed. And yet, in confronting the collection I was aware of this other temporality precluded for me, having arrived forty years after the present in which they were produced and consumed in the 1960s.

The exposure of the posers in front of me was itself somehow *démesurée*: the performers appeared, in the film portraits, "larger than life." They were blown up, not only on the screen, but in a territory of possible recognition pertaining to their social and artistic exposure, in the present and in the future of their memorability. The accumulation of all their potential attentive capital was suddenly realized in the endurance of my labored attention. The singular incandescence of the characters was actualized in my recollection of the leftovers of that particular tempo, where my own narrative contributes to

Warhol's posthumous camp project to "re-create surplus value from forgotten forms of labor."[63]

My disproportionate act of attention toward these performances of exposure had indeed something to do with the special economy, the domestic habitat of images and personalities characterizing the scene of foreplay I have explored throughout this book. Interestingly, in 1964, a few months before her film portraits were shot, Susan Sontag had written that "in Camp there is often something *démesurée* in the quality of the ambition, not only in the style of the work."[64] If the ambition of memorability in Warhol's film portrait gallery was disproportionate, its solitary actualization as value in my disproportionate, labored attention was indeed another form of camp production—or maybe more appropriately, of reproduction.

In the process during which the image becomes a persona in Warhol's *Screen Tests*, it acquires a distinctive value in the economy of attention of its audience, either contemporary or, like me, posthumous. Today, in their luxurious archival position in the Film Center of the MoMA, they have achieved a recognizable form of appearance in and beyond a proper market of attention: these images are often part of art exhibitions, they are the object of scholarly study and appreciation, and they have a value as art objects and as archival remains.

My appreciation of Ann Buchannan's weeping image, happening in the posthumous landscape of such valorization, was not directed toward her performance technique, which lured me into believing that the bleeding of her image was a performance of weeping. But her performance came about, to me, as self-consummating: as an artistic gesture in its own right, with no sequence whatsoever in any narrative frame, existing in the interval of my attention. Ann Buchannan was a *figurante* (an extra) in the social and artistic scene I have been studying. She is described as "a young bohemian with connections to Beat writers and poets of both coasts; she lived with and then married the Kansas-born poet and writer Charles Plymell in 1963."[65] She was definitely a footnote in most narratives of the particular scene in which she apparently took part.[66] I did not know anything about Ann Buchannan before encountering the *Screen Tests* collection, and I have not come across further information about her later life. In other words, she did not become a star, outside of this very portrait. Or more precisely: "she was a star not called upon to be a star." Echoing Philip Core's famous definition of camp as the "heroism of those not called upon to be heroes,"[67] I'd like to come to a conclusion thinking about Buchannan's portrait as the form of appearance of her value, realized precariously in the focus of my attention, but again suspended outside of value judgment, in a quintessentially camp operation. In fact, her disproportionate endurance in appearing was itself *démesurée;* we might fantasize that her focused tension to "become" something more than a footnote in this narrative accidentally provoked the performance which I, forty years later, recognized as a small event. Her tears can be regarded as the *excess* of her labor of appearing: the consumption of her own act of attention, in enduring to look at the camera, a consumption which is not reducible, that exceeds what is necessary for the production of her image to endure.

She, of course, did not *do* anything extraordinary during her three-minute pose. She simply followed a rule which was given to all the posers, especially in the first phase of the shooting of the *Screen Tests*: the demand not to blink, for the duration of the portrait. She, as well as a few others, succeeded in enduring this performance.[68] The miraculous element, therefore, seems at first glance to have been produced by the image itself. Or we could imagine, perhaps, that the endurance of the subject in front of the camera, Ann Buchannan's becoming-image in an effort of stasis, was capable of producing a small event in the encounter with the spectator, precisely because of her absolute lack of muscular effort toward the achievement of performance. We could consider her performance of exposure as a counter-technique developed out of idleness, as a queer unit of value in a distracted potentiality of performance.

Studying the collection of *Screen Tests* during the years which led to the long completion of this book, I have progressively turned my scholarly attention to the distinctive quality of exploitation which, in a sense, the performance of exposure in the collection prefigures: to what I could ironically call "the dark side of foreplay," corresponding to the projective temporality of contemporary precarious labor. That is, thinking about the dynamic of posthumous valorization of foreplay, I have progressively become interested to research the "nameless" performers who, like Buchannan, remained *figurantes* in the scene of foreplay and its historical returns in the past and in the present, perpetually offering their labor for free and hoping to make it to the big time: hence offering their performance of exposure in a condition of self-exploitation, without the guarantee of reciprocal payment, but simply in the hope that their personality might eventually acquire an exchange value. My analysis today thinks of itself as a materialist investigation of the creation of value in performance, considering how acts of appearance offered gratuitously during free time, as a labor of idleness, participate nevertheless in the production and accumulation of capital. Regarding my future research, this book has been in a sense a long foreplay: a playful loitering into a fascination, which might well be understood as a "tender feeling," echoing again Sontag's very definition of camp.

Confronting Warhol's *Screen Tests*, in their prominent archival location and in the landscape of my attention, I find myself portrayed, in return, as a "romantic anticapitalist," echoing the figure which Nicholas Ridout has proposed as kindred to the passionate amateur. My focused attention on Buchannan's portrait can also be seen as a form of bleeding: it is not something called for, it is not functional to my research; it is the surplus of my scholarly attention, the excess of its desire. It is a form of attraction, a valorization of her appearance as "event." My "tender feeling" (echoing Sontag's definition of camp) toward this portrait bleeds through its posthumous valorization as the surplus value of the attentive capital produced by Buchannan's gratuitous exposure.

The sense of unease, therefore, might well have to do with recognizing my own attention as the place of actualization and accumulation of Buchannan's "attentive capital"[69] as event. My own fascination with the capacity of this image to exceed, through appearing, the frozen state of its possible becoming value is mimetic to my "romantic anticapitalist" research on the emancipatory potential of camp as a technology of pleasure, and my elaboration of foreplay as a playful subversion of productive economy. My pleasure in visualizing Buchannan's labor of appearing arrested in a state of potentiality, imagined as a fragment of a leisure scene, accounts in a sense for my own desire, which sustained the completion of this study, to see potentialities of performance, such as those enacted in the 1960s scene of foreplay, not exhausted in their becoming value.

My unease and fascination are that of imagining foreplay as a utopian horizon of pleasure operating within valorization, but resisting the idea that potentiality, along with the pleasure sustaining any form of performance labor, is completely exploitable, in its trajectory toward the future of its possible becoming-capital.

NOTES

Introduction

1. "Foreplay," *Oxford English Dictionary*, online edition, http://www.oed.com/.

2. "Foreplay," *Merriam-Webster's Collegiate Dictionary*, 11th ed. (Springfield, Mass.: Merriam-Webster, 2003). Also available at http://www.merriam-webster.com/.

3. "Foreplay," *Oxford English Dictionary*.

4. Bertolt Brecht, *Brecht on Theatre: The Development of an Aesthetic*, ed. John Willett (New York: Hill and Wang; and London: Methuen, 1964), 180.

5. On the importance of gossip, both as social practice and as a valuable historiographic material for the early 1960s New York scene, see Gavin Butt, *Between You and Me: Queer Disclosures in the New York Art World 1948–1963* (Durham, N.C.: Duke University Press, 2005); Marc Siegel, "Gossip Ist Fabelhaft / Queere Gegenöffentlichkeiten und 'Fabulation,'" *Texte zur Kunste* 61 (March 2006); Marc Siegel, "On Gossip," in *More Than One Tie*, ed. Tom Engels, http://olga0.oralsite.be/oralsite/pages/Marc_Siegel/.

6. Henri Lefebvre, *The Production of Space* (Oxford: Blackwell, 1991). According to Lefebvre, "social space is constituted neither by a collection of things or an aggregate of (sensory) data, nor by a void packed like a parcel with various contents, and that it is irreducible to a 'form' imposed upon phenomena, upon things, upon physical materiality" (27). More importantly, for Lefebvre social signs assign and contain specific relations of production and reproduction, as well as their symbolic representation of both modes of relations, serving the purpose of maintaining these relations "in a state of coexistence and cohesion" (32).

7. Stefan Brecht, *The Original Theatre of the City of New York from Mid-1960s–1970s: Queer Theatre* (Frankfurt am Main: Suhrkamp, 1978).

8. Sally Banes, *Greenwich Village 1963: Avant-Garde Performance and the Effervescent Body* (Durham, N.C.: Duke University Press, 1993).

9. Banes's study also encompasses experiments in visual and performance art, happenings, dance, and film not directly related to the object of my inquiry, but standing in geographical proximity and often operating in the same spaces where the artists I examine also worked.

10. Stephen J. Bottoms, *Playing Underground: A Critical History of the 1960s Off-Off Broadway Movement* (Ann Arbor: University of Michigan Press, 2004); David A. Crespy, *Off-Off-Broadway Explosion: How Provocative Playwrights of the 1960s Ignited a New American Theater* (New York: Backstage Books, 2003).

11. Cindy Rosenthal, "Ellen Stewart La Mama of Us All," *The Drama Review* 50, no. 2 (Summer 2006): 12–51; Dominic Johnson, *Glorious Catastrophe: Jack Smith, Performance and Visual Culture* (Manchester: Manchester University Press, 2012).

12. Judith Halberstam, *In a Queer Time and Space: Transgender Bodies, Subcultural Lives* (New York: New York University Press, 2005).

13. A few of the works by these authors who make up this landscape of scholarship, and that we'll reencounter in the course of the book, are Jennifer Doyle, *Sex Objects: Art and the Dialectic of Desire* (London: University of Minnesota Press, 2006); José E. Muñoz, *Cruising Utopia: The Then and There of Queer Futurity* (New York: New York University Press, 2010); Butt, *Between You and Me*; Douglas Crimp, *"Our Kind of Movie": The Films of Andy Warhol* (Cambridge, Mass.: MIT Press, 2012); Marc Siegel, ed., "Jack Smith: Beyond the Rented World," *Criticism: A Quarterly for Literature and the Arts* 56, no. 2 (2014).

14. Marc Siegel, "Doing It for Andy," *Art Journal* 62 (Spring 2003), 6–13; Jennifer Doyle, "Between Friends," in *A Companion to Lesbian, Gay, Bisexual, Transgender, and Queer Studies*, ed. George E. Haggerty and Molly McGarry (Malden, Mass.: Blackwell, 2007), 325–40.

15. Michel Foucault, *The History of Sexuality,* vol. 2: *The Uses of Pleasure* (London: Penguin, 1992), 9.

16. Richard Florida, *The Rise of the Creative Class: And How It's Transforming Work, Leisure, Community and Everyday Life* (New York: Basic Books, 2002).

17. Elizabeth Currid, *The Warhol Economy: How Fashion, Art & Music Drive New York City* (Princeton, N.J.: Princeton University Press, 2007).

18. Ibid., 35.

19. Ibid., 34.

20. An obvious example of the influence of the Factory's self-display in the contemporary "creative economy" is the centrality of social media in the networking of the creative class, where portraits, and more recently "selfies" are put in circulation, reaffirming the presence in a given scene.

21. Suely Rolnik, "The Geopolitics of Pimping," *European Institute for Progressive Cultural Policies (EIPCP)*, October 2006, http://eipcp.net/transversal/1106/rolnik/en/#_ftn6.

22. Ibid.

23. Ibid.

24. In his book *The Rise of the Creative Class*, Florida explicitly mentions with praise the role of the Castro LGBT movement in the "success" of San Francisco's creative economy.

25. Paolo Virno, *A Grammar of the Multitude: For an Analysis of Contemporary Forms of Life* (New York: Semiotext(e), 2004).

26. Muñoz, *Cruising Utopia*, 1.

27. Ibid., 25.

28. Rolnik, "Geopolitics of Pimping."

29. On the idea of "projective temporality" and the functioning of cultural labor in contemporary neoliberalism according to the logic of "project," see Boris Groys, "The Loneliness of the Project," in Boris Groys, *Going Public* (Berlin: Sternberg, 2010); and Bojana Kunst, *Artist at Work: Proximity of Art and Capitalism* (Winchester, Eng.: Zero Books, 2015).

30. For a detailed account of the different strands of works in philosophy and literary theory which have addressed the theme of free time and its relation to

work, see Martin Jörg Schäfer, *Die Gewalt der Muße: Wechselverhältnisse von Arbeit, Nichtarbeit, Ästhetik* (Berlin: Diaphanes, 2013).

31. See Susan Buck-Morss, "The Flaneur, The Sandwichman and the Whore: The Politics of Loitering," *New German Critique* 39 (Autumn 1986): 99–140. On the figure of the flaneur and Benjamin's research on free time and labor, see also Walter Benajmin, *Charles Baudelaire: Un poeta lirico nell'epoca del captalismo avanzato*, ed. Giorgio Agamben et al. (Vicenza: Neri Pozza Editore, 2012).

32. For a definition of immaterial labor, see Maurizio Lazzarato, *Lavoro immateriale: Forme di vita e produzione di soggettività* (Milan: Ombre Corte, 1997); Yann Moulier-Boutang, *Le Capitalism cognitif: La nouvelle grande transformation* (Paris: Editions Amsterdam, 2007).

33. Virno, *A Grammar of the Multitude.*

34. It would be very complex to discuss the different approaches to the question of "work" in the broad spectrum of experiences in happenings, dance, and performance of the 1960s New York downtown scene, and perhaps this would be worth the subject of another book. In fact, such an artistic landscape was rich and polymorphous, and developed very interesting directions for thinking further about the complex relation between amateurism and professionalism.

35. Silvia Federici, *Wages against Housework* (London: Power of Women Collective, 1975); Mariarosa Dalla Costa and Giovanna Dalla Costa, eds., *Women, Development, and Labor of Reproduction* (Trenton, N.J.: Africa World,1999); Marylin Waring, *If Women Counted: A New Feminist Economics* (San Francisco: Harper and Row, 1988).

36. See, for instance, Diane Elson, ed., *Value: The Representation of Labour in Capitalism* (London: CSE Books, 1979); and Gayatri Spivak, "Scattered Speculations on the Question of Value," in *In Other Worlds: Essays in Cultural Politics* (New York: Methuen, 1987), 212–42.

37. Miranda Joseph, *Against the Romance of Community* (Minneapolis: University of Minnesota Press, 2002).

38. Ibid., 66.

39. Karl Marx, *Grundrisse*, trans. Martin Nicolaus (New York: Penguin Books, 1973), 91.

40. Ibid., 91.

41. Ibid.

42. Ibid., 92.

43. Ibid.

44. Ibid., 93.

45. Ibid., 90.

46. Foucault, *The History of Sexuality*, vol. 1, *An Introduction (La Volonté de savoir)* (New York: Random House, 1978), 107.

47. Foucault's project interrogates the production of sexuality not only in view of the historical organization of sexual practices for the purpose of securing reproduction, but especially regarding the scientific preoccupation with sex as a measure of knowledge and power. In this context, the four figures he identifies as major targets of these preoccupations—the hysterical woman, the masturbating child, the Malthusian couple, and the perverse adult—were at the same time the embodiment of an economic preoccupation in terms of reproduction (i.e., figures of "waste" in terms of labor force) but also of unregulated pleasure.

48. I borrow this wording from Rachel P. Maines, *The Technology of Orgasm:"Hysteria," the Vibrator and Women's Sexual Satisfaction* (Baltimore: Johns Hopkins University Press, 1999).

49. Ibid., 5.

50. Sigmund Freud. *Three Essays on the Theory of Sexuality,* in *The Standard Edition of the Complete Psychological Works*, ed. James Strachey (London: Hogarth Press and the Institute for Psycho-Analysis), 7:1955.

51. Leo Bersani, "Sexuality and Aesthetics," *October*, vol. 28, "Discipleship: A Special Issue on Psychoanalysis" (Spring 1984): 27–42.

52. Ibid., 29.

53. Ibid., 30.

54. Ibid., 30.

55. Rebecca Schneider proposes to understand the idea of "meantime" as a conjunction characterized by an intrinsic doubleness, including both the meaning of "interim, meantime, meanwhile, lag (the time between one event, process, or period and another)" but also "at the same time" (88), conveying therefore a sense of simultaneity. Rebecca Schneider, *Performing Remains: Art and War in Times of Theatrical Reeenactment* (New York: Routledge, 2011), 87–110.

56. The concept of disidentification is developed by José E. Muñoz in *Disidentifications: Queers of Colour and the Performance of Politics* (Madison: University of Minnesota Press, 1999).

Interlude I

1. Robert Patrick, *Temple Slave* (New York: Masquerade Books, 1994), 135–36.

2. Juan A. Suárez, *Bike Boys, Drag Queens and Superstars: Avant-Garde, Mass Culture and Gay Identities in the 1960s Underground Cinema* (Bloomington: Indiana University Press, 1996), 82.

3. Ibid., 82.

4. Jonas Mekas, *Movie Journal: The Rise of the New American Cinema, 1959–1971* (New York: Macmillan, 1972).

5. Quoted in Dominique Noguez, *Une renaissance du cinéma: Le cinéma "underground" américain* (Paris: Klincksieck, 1985), 162.

6. As Farber argues, these movies "found their natural home in caves: the murky, congested theatres, looking like glorifying tattoo parlors on the outside, and located near the bus terminal in big cities." Manny Farber, "Underground Films" (1957), quoted in Suárez, *Bike Boys*, 86.

7. Bottoms, *Playing Underground*, 11.

8. Ibid., 12.

9. Ibid., 11.

10. After *Hair*, O'Horgan also directed *Jesus Christ Superstar* and *Lenny*.

11. Conversation with Tom O'Horgan, in Giulia Palladini, "Ellen Stewart e La Mama: Un'idea di teatro" (M.A. diss., University of Bologna, 2005).

12. Besides the already mentioned Ellen Stewart, I refer to Ozzie Rodriguez, but also John Vaccaro, Ruby Lynn Reyner, Micheal Arian, Agosto Machado, and Joe Preston, Jackie Curtis's cousin and the legal executor of his estate.

13. See, for instance, Crespy, *Off-Off-Broadway Explosion*; and Michael Bronski, *Culture Clash: The Making of Gay Sensibility* (Boston: South End, 1984).

14. Michael Smith and Nick Orzel, eds., *Eight Plays from Off Off-Broadway* (Indianapolis, Ind.: Bobbs-Merrill, 1966), 5.

15. Marshall W. Mason, "To Conquer Broadway," in Susoyev and Birmisa, *Return to the Caffe Cino,* 19.

16. See in particular Jack Smith and Sylvère Lotringer, "Uncle Fishook and the Sacred Baby Poo Poo of Art," *Semiotext(e)* 1, no. 2 (1978); Jack Smith, *Wait for Me at the Bottoms of the Pool: The Writings of Jack Smith*, ed. Jim Hoberman and Edward Leffingwell (New York: High Risk Books, 1997). See also Paul Arthur, "Routines of Emancipations: Alternative Cinema in the Ideology and Politics of the Sixties," in David E. James, *To Free the Cinema: Jonas Mekas and the New York Underground* (Princeton, N.J.: Princeton University Press, 1992).

17. Shot in 1962, *Flaming Creatures* was first screened privately by Smith at the beginning of 1963, and then included by Mekas in his independent program of screenings at New York's Bowery Theater, in the frame of the Film Makers' Cooperative. There, after only a few days, the film was seized, and Jonas Mekas and Ken Jacob, responsible for the screening, were arrested. After this episode, Mekas engaged in a fierce defense of *Flaming Creatures* by all means: in his writings, but especially by organizing further screenings, some of which were meant as benefits to raise funding for defending Smith's movie in court. Eventually, the film was banned in the state of New York. The film also continued to be censored and busted by the police throughout 1964 outside of New York, with the consequence that the fame of the movie was even heightened and the movie—although not legally visible—acquired a cult status precisely while it could not circulate. For the first Mekas review of Smith's film, see Jonas Mekas, "*Flaming Creatures* and the Ecstatic Beauty of the New Cinema," *Village Voice*, March 2, 1963, republished in Jonas Mekas, *Movie Journal*. (New York: Collier Books, 1972), 82–83.

18. The Anthology Film Archive was founded in 1969 as an archive for the repertoire of the underground films, and a theater with a program open to experimental films. See J. Hoberman and Jonathan Rosenbaum, "The Underground," in *Midnight Movies* (New York: Harper and Row, 1983); and Curtis, *To Free the Cinema*.

19. The version of *Normal Love* currently in circulation is the restored work realized by Jerry Tartaglia following the list of sequences which Smith gave to Tony Conrad, who was supposed to work on the movie's soundtrack. On the restoration work on *Normal Love,* see Jerry Tartaglia, "Restoration and Slavery," in *Jack Smith and His Secret Flix,* ed. J. Hoberman (New York: Museum of the Moving Image, 1997).

20. Jonas Mekas, conversation with the author, Lucca, November 2008.

21. Patrick, *Temple Slave*, 314–15.

22. For an account of the first European tour of La MaMa, see Giulia Palladini, "Lo spazio del La Mama," in *La Mama dell'Avanguardia: Il teatro di Ellen Stewart, i rapporti con l'Italia*, ed. Moreno Cerquetelli (Rome: Edizioni Interculturali, 2006), 11–69.

23. Bottoms, *Playing Underground*, 270.

24. See Anonymous, "City to Hear Pro & Cons of NYU Library," *Village Voice*, June 9, 1966; Marlene Nadel, "NYU Attacked: 'Fraud,' Says Mrs Jacobs, 'Library Is Not a Library,'" *Village Voice,* June 23, 1966; M. Nadel, "NYU Shows Plans

to Prove Library Is Really a Library," *Village Voice*, June 30, 1966; D. McNeil, "NYU Campus Erupts, but No Berkeley Develops," *Village Voice*, December 15, 1966.

25. Notable examples are *Caffe Cino and Its Legacy: An American Cultural Landmark*, curated by Richard Buck and Magie Dominic in 1985 in the Vincent Astor Gallery at the Lincoln Center Library and Museum of the Performing Arts; *Flaming Creature: Jack Smith, His Amazing Life and Times,* organized in 1997 by the Institute of Contemporary Art, MoMA, and Ps1 in New York, and curated by the Plaster Foundation; the conference-event *Live Film! Jack Smith! Five Flaming Days in a Rented World*, organized by the Arsenal-Institute for Film and Video Art, Hebbel am Ufer (HAU) in Berlin in October 28–November 1, 2009, and curated by Susanne Sachsse, Stefanie Schulte Strathaus, and Marc Siegel; the exhibition *Jack Smith: A Feast for Open Eyes*, organized at the Institute for Contemporary Art in London in September 2011, in collaboration with Dominic Johnson, LUX, and the Gladstone Gallery.

26. Filmmaker Mary Jordan posted an ad on the Internet looking for Mario Montez, who had lost any contact with his pals from the 1960s New York scene after he had left the city in the late 1970s. Rivera (aka Montez) in person replied to Jordan's ad, and found out, to his great surprise, that in the last twenty years the movies he had starred in (by Andy Warhol, Jack Smith, Ron Rice, and José Rodriguez-Soltero) had circulated widely and acquired a cult status and a large following of fans. Even more surprising for Rivera was to learn that his performances had become an object of interest in academic scholarship: his "comeback," for instance, was welcomed with a large conference held at Columbia University, involving scholars from diverse backgrounds (such as Gender and Ethnicity Studies, Performance Studies, Queer Studies, etc.) in a conversation about Montez's artistic career. The conference, held in March 2010 at the Center for the Study of Ethnicity and Race at Columbia University, was entitled *Superstar! A Tribute to Mario Montez*. On Mario Montez's comeback, see M. Anderson, "The Return of Mario Montez," *Village Voice*, November 9, 2011, http://www.villagevoice.com/.

27. A few relevant examples are Craig Highberger, *Superstar in a Housedress: The Life and Legend of Jackie Curtis*; and Jeremiah Newton, *Beautiful Darling: The Life & Times of Candy Darling, Andy Warhol Superstar*, produced by Jeremiah Newton, Elisabeth Bentley, and Gill Holland, and directed by James Rasin.

Chapter 1

1. Tom Eyen, *Why Hanna's Skirt Won't Stay Down*, in *Ten Plays*, ed. Tom Eyen (New York: Samuel French, 1977), 29–30.

2. *Why Hanna's Skirt Won't Stay Down* might have been presented before at the Caffe Cino: on the listing of the La MaMa Archive, in fact, the debut of the show is recorded in 1962. However, at La MaMa there are no records (posters, photographs, programs) related to the 1962 run but only to the 1965 production, and the archivist Ozzie Rodriguez suggested that this is because the show was perhaps first presented at the Cino in 1962 and then at La MaMa in its more mature articulation. In the early years Joe Cino and Ellen Stewart did not always keep records of the shows presented in their theaters.

3. Michael Feingold, "Introduction" to *Ten Plays*, 3.

4. Eyen, *Why Hanna's Skirt Won't Stay Down*, 30.
5. Ibid., 31.
6. Ibid., 31.
7. Ibid., 10.
8. Muñoz, *Cruising Utopia*.
9. At La MaMa in 1967 Eyen also established his own repertory company, the Theatre of the Eye.
10. The target of Eyen's satire was both the Broadway success of musicals like *Hair* and *Oh! Calcutta!* and countercultural hits such as *Dionysus in 69* or *Paradise Now*.
11. *Dreemgirls*' plot follows the story of a singing trio—roughly fashioned after the Supremes—from the beginning of their youthful dream in 1962 to their becoming "superstars" in 1975. The musical ran on Broadway until 1985, and subsequently toured internationally. In 2006 it was turned into a film, directed by Bill Condon, and produced by Dreamworks and Paramount Pictures, with major American stars such as Beyoncé Knowles and Eddie Murphy.
12. Richard Eyen, "Tom Eyen, the Beginning," in Susoyev and Birmisa, *Return to the Caffe Cino*, 86.
13. See for instance, Leo Skir, unpublished review of *Heaven Grand in Amber Orbit*, John Vaccaro Papers; the *Figaro*'s reporter Pierre Mazars wrote "It is like witnessing an astonishing bacchanal of people in disguise like students of the Beaux Arts": Pierre Mazars, "Le Ridiculous Theatre," *Le Figaro*, June 15, 1971, 2. See also Stefan Brecht, *Queer Theatre*.
14. Stefan Brecht, *Queer Theatre*, 28.
15. On the appreciation for "bad acting," see also Jack Smith's famous essay "The Perfect Appositeness of Maria Montez," *Film Culture* 27 (Winter 1962–63): 28–36.
16. Maya Deren, "Amateurs Versus Professionals," *Film Culture* 39 (Winter 1959): 49.
17. Stan Brakhage, "In Defense of Amateur: Essential Brakhage," in *Essential Brakhage: Selected Writings on Filmmaking*. (New York: McPherson, 2011), 142–43.
18. Ibid., 142.
19. Ibid., 143.
20. Ibid., 144.
21. Paula Cay Pierce, "An Interview with John Vaccaro," John Vaccaro Papers (no date or source).
22. Brecht, *Queer Theatre*, 30.
23. Ibid., 37.
24. Ibid., 30.
25. Philippe R. Perebinossoff, "The Theater of Stylized Amateurism," *Journal of American Culture* 1, no. 1 (Spring 1978): 137–44.
26. Ibid., 137.
27. Ibid., 139.
28. Ibid.
29. Ibid.
30. Ibid.
31. Ibid., 137–38.

32. The association between Helen Hanft and the character of Hanna remains vivid in the collective memory of those who participated in the 1960s scene. Hanft herself speaks about it in George Birmisa and Steve Susoyev, "To Thine Own Self Be True: A Conversation with Helen Hanft," in Susoyev and Birmisa, *Return to the Caffe Cino*, 26–28.

33. Nicholas Ridout, *Passionate Amateurs: Theatre, Communism and Love* (Ann Arbor: University of Michigan Press, 2013), 6.

34. Ibid., 138.

35. Ibid., 6.

36. Ibid., 9.

37. Ibid.

38. Roland Barthes, *Camera Lucida: Reflections on Photography* (New York: Hill and Wang, 1981), 98.

39. Mircea Eliade, *Rites and Symbols of Initiation* (New York: Harper and Row, 1965).

40. Richard Schechner, "Actuals" (1970), in *Performance Theory* (New York: Routledge, 1988), 28.

41. Schechner, "Actuals," 33.

42. Ibid., 46.

43. Ibid.

44. The first and most extensive articulation of what Schechner calls the "efficacy-entertainment" braid appears in "From Ritual to Theater and Back: The Structure/Process of the Efficacy-Entertainment Dyad," first published in *Educational Theatre Journal* 26, no. 4 (Dec., 1974): 455–481, and republished in *Performance Theory* (New York: Routledge, 1988), 112–69.

45. Here Schechner points to the scheme in which, in the following page, he organizes his proposed distinction, listing the qualifying categories for the notions of efficacy and entertainment, *Performance Theory,* p. 72.

46. Richard Schechner, *Performance Studies: An Introduction* (New York: Routledge, 2002), 71.

47. Stephen Bottoms, "The Efficacy/Effeminacy Braid: Unpacking the Performance Studies/Theatre Studies Dichotomy," *Theatre Topics* 3, no. 2 (September 2003): 174.

48. Ibid., 175.

49. Ibid., 174.

50. Richard Schechner, "TDR Comment," *Tulane Drama Review* 7, no. 2 (1962): 8. Quoted in Bottoms, "The Efficacy/Effeminacy Braid," 176.

51. Richard Schechner, "Who's Afraid of Edward Albee?" *Tulane Drama Review* 7, no. 3 (1963): 8.

52. Bottoms reports also about similar homophobic comments by Donald Kaplan (for instance in "Homosexuality and American Theatre: A Psychoanalytic Comment," *Tulane Drama Review* 9, no. 3 [1965]: 25–55) and Stanley Kaufmann of the *New York Times*.

53. Bottoms, "The Efficacy/Effeminacy Braid," 179.

54. As an example of these different approaches, Bottoms discusses the prominent role of playwrights, marginal figures in the context praised by Schechner, which privileged actor-based work over new dramatic texts. See Bottoms, *Playing Underground*.

55. See Gabrielle Brandstetter, "The Virtuoso's Stage: A Theatreical Topos," *Theatre Research International* 32, no. 2 (2007): 178–95.

56. In theater anthropology, and especially in Eugenio Barba's work, the "extraordinary'" behavior has a prominent theoretical position: more commonly called "extra-daily," the performer's behavior is the one trained to exceed "ordinary" gestures and circumstances by means of a training into different performance techniques (in a process of self-development entailing also the study of techniques from other performance cultures). See Eugenio Barba and Nicola Savarese, *A Dictionary of Theatre Anthropology: The Secret Art of the Performer* (New York: Routledge, 2006).

57. Marx, *Grundrisse*, 93.

58. Annemarie Matzke, *Arbeit am Theater: Eine Diskursgeschichte der Probe* (Bielefeld, Ger.: Transcript Verlag, 2012).

59. On the way space and time were addressed and organized by theatermakers in the early twentieth century, see Fabrizio Cruciani, *Lo spazio del teatro* (Bari, Italy: Laterza, 1992) and *Teatro nel Novecento: Registi pedagoghi e comunità teatrali nel XX secolo* (Florence: Sansoni, 1985).

60. Richard Schechner, "Stanislavski at School," *Tulane Drama Review* 9, no. 2 (Fall-Winter 1964): 198–211.

61. Ibid., 198.

62. Theodore Shank. *Beyond the Boundaries: American Alternative Theatre* (Ann Arbor: University of Michigan Press, 2002), 48.

63. For a detailed discussion of the Open Theatre's work see Carol Martin, "The Open Theatre's The Serpent, Terminal, and The Mutation Show," in *Restaging the Sixties: Radical Theaters and Their Legacies*, ed. James Harding and Cindy Rosenthal (Ann Arbor: University of Michigan Press, 2006), 69–105.

64. Richard Schechner, *Between Theater and Anthropology* (Philadelphia: University of Pennsylvania Press, 1985), 295.

65. Schechner, *Performance Theory*.

66. Schechner, "From Ritual to Theatre and Back, in *Performance Theory*, 130.

67. In contradistinction, Stefan Brecht had written that in the Play-House performances "the suppression of the habitual gestures of professionalism makes them seem amateurish. Yet they accrue no credit for sincerity or for being 'interesting' personalities because of the total investment of personality in the histrionic mode which makes the 'action' theater." Brecht, *Queer Theatre*, 37.

68. On Grotowski's relation with the American theatre, see Kermit Dunkelberg, "Grotowski and the North-American Theatre: Translation, Transmission, Dissemination". (Ph.D. diss., Department of Performance Studies, New York University, 2008).

69. Jerzy Grotowski, *Toward a Poor Theatre*, trans. T. K. Wiewiorowski (New York: Simon and Schuster, 1968), 38.

70. Ibid., 24.

71. Ibid., 24.

72. Lisa Wolford, "Grotowski's Vision of the Actor: The Search for Contact," in *Twentieth-Century Actor Training*, ed. Alison Hodge (London: Routledge, 2000), 197.

73. Grotowski, *Toward a Poor Theatre*, 24.

74. Ibid., 43. In the 1960s Grotowski also devoted attention to the audience's attitude toward the show. In fact he clarifies: "Nor do we cater for a man who goes to the theatre to relax after a hard day's work. Everyone has a right to relax after work and there are numerous forms of entertainment for this purpose, ranging from certain types of film to cabaret and music-hall, and many more of the same lines." On the contrary, the spectator to whom Grotowski's theater work was addressed was the one "who undergoes an endless process of self-development, whose unrest is not general but directed towards a search for the truth about himself and his mission in life." Grotowski, *Toward a Poor Theatre*, 40.

75. Since the 1970s, Grotowski stopped directing theater shows and pursued his investigation (increasingly fashioned as a spiritual and shamanic research) on performance outside of the theater. On the long development of Grotowski's career, including his later years, see Lisa Wolford and Richard Schechner, *The Grotowski Sourcebook* (New York: Routledge, 2001).

76. Grotowski, *Toward a Poor Theatre*, 24.

77. Michael T. Smith, "Caffe Cino," http://michaeltownsendsmith.com/caffe-cino.

78. See Roberto Pasolli, "Off-Off e i nuovi autori degli anni '60," *Sipario* 32, no. 272 (December 1968): 22–28.

79. Conversation of Ellen Stewart with the author, Spoleto, August 2004.

80. Bottoms, *Playing Underground*, 125.

81. Ibid., 125.

82. Frank Cullen, *Vaudeville Old & New: An Encyclopedia of Variety Performers in America* (New York: Routledge, 2004), 1040.

83. Brecht, *Queer Theatre*, 37.

84. Ronald Tavel, "The Life of Juanita Castro," Ronald Tavel website. http://www.ronaldtavel.com/documents/the_life_of_juanita_castro.pdf.

85. Conversation of Ruby Lynn Reyner with the author, New York, March 4, 2007.

86. Conversation of John Vaccaro with the author, New York, June 10, 2007.

87. On the synthetic quality of vaudeville performance, see Robert Snyder, *The Voice of the City: Vaudeville and Popular Culture in New York* (New York: Oxford University Press, 1989), 180.

88. Pierce, "An Interview with John Vaccaro."

89. On the dynamic of "investment" on the part of Off-Off Broadway playwrights, actors, and directors, see for instance Pasolli, "Off-Off e i nuovi autori degli anni '60.

90. Robert Patrick in *In the Life: Documentary Stories from the Gay Experience*, http://www.inthelifetv.org/html/episodes/52.html.

91. Doyle, *Sex Objects*, 52.

92. Grotowski, *Toward a Poor Theatre*, 33.

93. Ibid., 246.

94. Ibid., 46.

95. Ibid., 35.

96. Doyle, *Sex Objects*, 52.

97. Walter Benjamin, *The Arcades Project*, ed. Rolf Tiedemann, trans. Howard Eiland and Kevin McLaughlin (Cambridge, Mass.: Harvard University Press, 1999), 803.

98. Ibid., 806.

99. Buck-Morss, "The Flaneur, The Sandwichman and the Whore," 105.

100. Ibid., 120.

101. Ibid., 120.

102. James Rolleston, "The Truth of Unemployment: Walter Benjamin Reads His Own Times," *South Atlantic Review* 61, no. 2 (Spring 1996): 38.

103. Buck-Morss, "The Flaneur, The Sandwichman and the Whore," 137.

104. Interestingly, the German word *Müssiggang* is produced by the conjunction between *die Muße*—leisure—and *Gang*, literally referring to the practice of "walking, passing," and directly echoing the habit of the flaneur. *Müssiggang* stems from the same linguistic root as the word "duty"—*das Müss*—almost to suggest that idleness itself is generated from "duty"; or, alternatively, that it might be a praxis pregnant with necessity, regardless of whether the "idle labor" will eventually "give birth."

105. Benjamin, *The Arcades Project*, 809.

106. Doyle borrows the expression "pathology of agency" from Anne McClintock ("Sex Workers and Sex Work: An Introduction," *Social Text* 37 [1993]), who, on her part is echoing a term developed by Marc Seltzer in "Serial Killers (1)," *differences: A Journal of Feminist Cultural Studies* 5, no. 1 (1993): 92–127.

107. Ridout, *Passionate Amateurs*, 9.

108. Namely, Ridout devotes a chapter of *Passionate Amateurs* to Walter Benjamin and Asja Lacis's *Program for a Proletarian Theatre for Children*. Ridout, *Passionate Amateurs*, 58–85.

109. Ridout, *Passionate Amateurs*, 9.

110. Some of Smith's earlier performances were also staged at the Cinemateque.

111. See at least Leffingwell et al., eds., *Flaming Creature: Jack Smith, His Amazing Life and Times* (New York: Institute for Contemporary Art, PS 1, 1997); J. Hoberman, *On Jack Smith's "Flaming Creatures" and Other Secret-Flix of Cinemaroc* (New York: Granary Books, 2001).

112. Johnson, *Glorious Catastrophe*.

113. Jack Smith, "Actavistic, Action Packed, Action Acting in PFA Hamlet, and the 1001 Psychological Jingoleanism of Pre-Historic Rima-Puu" (1971), in *Wait for Me at the Bottoms of the Pool: The Writings of Jack Smith*, ed. Jim Hoberman and Edward Leffingwell (New York: High Risk Books, 1997), 167.

114. Johnson, *Glorious Catastrophe*, 80–82.

115. Richard Foreman, "In the Second Half of the Sixties," in *Flaming Creature: Jack Smith, His Amazing Life and Times*, 26.

116. Smith, "The Perfect Appositeness of Maria Montez," 25.

117. Ibid., 25.

118. Jack Smith, "Capitalism of Lotusland," *LAICA Journal* 19 (June-July 1978), republished in *Wait for Me at the Bottoms of the Pool: The Writings of Jack Smith*, 11.

119. Brecht, *Queer Theatre*, 17. The performance Brecht is describing here is *Gas Station of the Cross Religious Spectacle*.

120. Walter Benjamin, "Aufzeichnungen zum Meskalinversuch, May 22, 1934," in *Über Haschisch*, ed. Tillman Rexroth (Frankfurt am Main: Suhrkamp Verlag, 1972), 139; Benjamin's writings on hashish have been gathered in an

English translation which, however, does not include the text in question: Walter Benjamin, *On Hashish* (Cambridge, Mass.: Harvard University Press, 2006).

121. See, for instance, Edward Leffingwell, "Jack Smith: The Only Normal Man in Baghdad," in *Flaming Creature: Jack Smith, His Amazing Life and Times*, 71; J. Hoberman, "The Big Heat: Making and Unmaking Flaming Creatures," in *Flaming Creature: Jack Smith, His Amazing Life and Times*, 161.

122. Walter Benjamin, "Surrealism," in *Selected Writing 1927–1930* (Cambridge, Mass.: Harvard University Press, 1999), 209.

123. Benjamin himself uses the world "lessons" with reference to the experiments with drugs in "Surrealism," 209.

124. Benjamin, *On Hashish*, 53.

125. Johnson, *Glorious Catastrophe*, 41.

126. Foreman, "In the Second Half of the Sixties," 26.

127. Jonas Mekas, "Jack Smith or The End of Civilization," in *Flaming Creature: Jack Smith, His Amazing Life and Times*, 49.

128. Brakhage, "In Defense of Amateurism," 140.

129. Mekas, "Jack Smith or The End of Civilization," 49.

130. Brecht, *Queer Theatre*, 17.

131. Joe Kelleher, *On Self-Remembering Theatres*, 2008, http://www.jonathanburrows.info/#/text/?id=18&t=content.

Chapter 2

1. All of the information regarding *Heaven Grand in Amber Orbit* to which I refer in this chapter was sourced from documents collected in John Vaccaro's Papers, in the Downtown Collection at New York University, where I consulted the original script by Jackie Curtis, the press reviews, the director's correspondence with friends, and a series of photographic shots from the performance.

2. For a detailed history of the Play-House of the Ridiculous and a discussion of the plays developed before and after *Heaven Grand in Amber Orbit*, as well as of the complicated relations between Vaccaro, Tavel, and Ludlam (which led to a series of scissions in the group and the subsequent formation of Ludlam's Ridiculous Theatrical Company in 1967), see Ruggero Bianchi. *Off Off and away: Percorsi, processi, spazi del nuovo teatro americano* (Turin: Studioforma, 1981); Gautam Dasgupta and Bonnie Marranca, eds., *Theatre of the Ridiculous* (New York: Performing Arts Journal Publications, 1979); Bottoms, *Playing Underground*, 215–36; Stefan Brecht, *Queer Theatre* 28–55, 60–75.

3. Dick Brukenfeld, "The Wild Bunch," *Village Voice*, March 12, 1970.

4. See Jack Kroll, "Ridiculous! 'Heaven Grand': Super Circus," *Newsweek*, November 3 1969; Rosalyn Regelson, "Not a Boy, Not a Girl, Just Me," *New York Times*, November 2, 1969; Pierre Mazars, "Le Ridiculous Theatre," *Le Figaro*, June 15, 1971; A.F., " Le 'Ridicule de New York,' " *Le Dernier Heure*, April 26, 1971; J. Gerard Maringot, "The Play-House of the Ridiculous," *Le Monde*, June 13–14, 1971.

5. According to other sources, such as Craig Highberger, *Superstar in a Housedress: The Life and Legend of Jackie Curtis* (New York: Chamberlain, 2005), most likely Curtis appeared for the first time in female drag at a Halloween party in 1966. However, Vaccaro's recollection points to Curtis's appearance in female attire in everyday life, rather than in a costume ball. The episode is also

reported, quoting Vaccaro's tale, in Leo Skir's unpublished review of the play as follows: "meeting at 43nd street & taking the train, Jackie, his/her hair not yet long wearing a plastic table-cloth with fringes, going then to South Bend to Howard Johnsons so-dressed and upsetting the natives no end." Leo Skir, unpublished review of *Heaven Grand in Amber Orbit*, John Vaccaro Papers, 11. The manuscript of Skir's article features in Vaccaro's personal correspondence in the John Vaccaro Papers, and it is accompanied by a letter addressed to Vaccaro, in which Skir communicates to the director that he did not pursue the intention to publish the piece after having received negative feedback by a common friend (Bea) who was at the time editor of the *Evergreen Review*, the journal where, I suppose, Skir was planning to publish the article.

6. The performance of Reyner in the role of Heaven Grand is singled out for praise in many reviews of the time. Dick Brukenfeld, for instance, writes that Reyner is "a musical comedy find" and Frank L. Wilde reports that "Ruby Lynn Reyner . . . may well be the funniest thin young woman in the theatre." Frank L. Wilde, "Heaven Grand in Amber Orbit: You Must See It," *Show Business* (no date), 1969, John Vaccaro Papers. Jim Buckley Mel Gussow defined Ruby as "the compact essence of Jean Harlow," in Mel Gussow, "'Heaven Grand,' A Musical, Now Camping at La Mama," *Village Voice*, 1976.

7. Skir, unpublished review of *Heaven Grand in Amber Orbit*, 5.

8. Brukenfeld, "The Wild Bunch," n.p.

9. Uhshur Quietstone, "Heaven Grand in Amber Orbit," *Gay Power* 1, no. 4 (1969).

10. Alongside quotes from Hollywood movies (distinctive of the style of all the "Ridiculous playwrights," from Ronald Tavel and Charles Ludlam to Kenneth Bernard), *Heaven Grand* also features quotes from Greek tragedy, and more precisely from what I identify as Aeschylus's *Agamemnon*: for instance when Heaven reads from a note "A third shall come to raise our cause. A son resolved to kill his mother, honoring his father's blood" (35). In the script, this line introduces the revelation that The Rouge Frolic is in fact Lady Galaxy's son: "He has returned to set the apex on this tower of crime his race has built. I have watched fate unfold her pattern" (the latter is a quote from Aeschylus's text). And again, shortly after the series of characters, speaking in unison as in the Greek chorus, follow up with "Oh, woman deep in wisdom and suffering you have told us much. Yet if you have truth foreknowledge of your own death, why like an Ox for sacrifice, move thus toward the altar with intrepid step? (35). In Leo Skir's unpublished review, Skir repeatedly advances doubts that the script was written by Jackie Curtis, claiming that the erudite level of the quotes and the reference to Greek tragedy was rather a trademark of Vaccaro's own touch; however, Skir reports that Vaccaro has always insisted that the script was purely the work of Jackie Curtis.

11. The song lyrics were written by Jackie Curtis, Tom Murrin, and Kenneth Bernard, and the music was played live by the three-man rock band called The Shell Game. The composers of the music for the songs were Ralph Czitrom, John Madera, and George Basley.

12. Jackie Curtis, *Heaven Grand in Amber Orbit*, John Vaccaro Papers, 1.

13. In the first run of the play, The Rouge Frolic was played by Jaime de Carlo Lotts.

14. Curtis, *Heaven Grand*, 1.

15. Ibid., 1.

16. See Kenneth Bernard, "Confronting the Ridiculous/A Theatrical Review with John Vaccaro," *Confrontations* (Spring/Summer 1976), quoted in Brecht, *Queer Theatre*, 28. Vaccaro has always openly acknowledged to this day Smith's influence on his work, declaring in one of our conversations that he considers Smith the only true genius he ever met.

17. On the "creatures" populating Jack Smith's artistic world, see Leffingwell, Kismaric, and Heiferman, eds., *Flaming Creature: Jack Smith, His Amazing Life and Times*; Johnson, *Glorious Catastrophe*.

18. Conversation with John Vaccaro, New York, November 2014.

19. Brukenfeld, "The Wild Bunch," n.p.

20. Pierce, "An Interview with John Vaccaro."

21. For a more detailed analysis of the nightlife sociability and performance culture of the turn-of-the-century Bowery, see Giulia Palladini, "The Amateur Hour: On Value, Personality and the Form of Appearance in the Economy of Attention," *South Atlantic Review* 75, no. 3 (2011): 59–77.

22. Trav S. D., *No Applause—Just Throw Money, or, The Book that Made Vaudeville Famous* (New York: Faber and Faber, 2005).

23. Henry Miller, *Into the Nightlife* (Berkeley, Calif.: Henry Miller and Bezalel Schatz, 1947).

24. I am referring especially to "The People and the Sea: How They Get Together," *Brooklyn Daily Eagle*, August 3, 1913; "The Tingling, Tangling Tango as 'Tis Tripped at Coney Isle," *Brooklyn Daily Eagle*, August 31, 1913; "If Noise Were Forbidden at Coney Island, a Lot of People Would Lose Their Jobs," *New York Press*, June 7, 1914; all of them are collected in Djuna Barnes, *New York* (Los Angeles: Sun and Moon, 1989).

25. Lawrence Ferlinghetti, *A Coney Island of the Mind: Poems* (New York: New Directions, 1958), 35.

26. I welcome here the sense of the term employed and discussed by Rebecca Schneider in Schneider, *Performing Remains*.

27. I wish to welcome here an echo of the way Diana Taylor has conceptualized the notion of "repertoire" in performance theory. Diana Taylor, *The Archive and the Repertoire: Performing Cultural Memory in the Americas* (Durham, N.C.: Duke University Press, 2003). Regarding our analysis, it seems particularly relevant to recall Taylor's definition of the repertoire as what "enacts embodied memory: performances, gestures, orality, movement, dance signing—in short, all those acts usually thought of as ephemeral, nonreproducible knowledge" (20). In the same context, Taylor advances the idea that working with repertoire also entails a shift in methodology, proposing that research on the repertoire might entail a more attentive consideration of what she calls "scenarios," paradigms of knowledge and transmission understood as both the *setup* and *action* of performance (28). The notion of scenario can be considered kindred to the idea of scene I propose in the book.

28. Gilles Deleuze and Felix Guattari, *A Thousand Plateaus: Capitalism and Schizophrenia*, trans. Brian Massumi (Minneapolis: University of Minnesota Press, 1987), 238.

29. Palladini, "The Amateur Hour."

30. Ibid.

31. I echo here the title of the excellent collection of cultural studies essays on the theme of "freakery": Rosemarie Garland Thompson, ed., *Freakery: Cultural Spectacle of the Extraordinary Body* (New York: New York University Press, 1996).

32. For detailed historical information on the freak show in the United States, see Garland Thompson, *Freakery*; Robert Bogdan, *Freak Show: Presenting Human Oddities for Amusement and Profit* (Chicago: University of Chicago Press, 1988); Andrea Stulman Dennett, *Weird and Wonderful: The Dime Museum in America* (New York: New York University Press, 1997).

33. See Bogdan, *Freak Show*, 62–68.

34. On the meaning of the word "obscene" coming from Latin, *obscenus*, and encompassing a direct reference to the "scene" and its crucial relation with theater and theatricality, see Carmelo Bene, *Opere con l'Autografia di un ritratto* (Milan: Bompiani, 1995).

35. Leslie Fiedler, *Freaks: Myths and Images of the Secret Self* (New York: Simon and Schuster, 1978).

36. Ibid., 13–14.

37. Frederic Wertham, *The Seduction of the Innocents* (New York: Reinhart, 1954). On the polemics against comic books aroused by Wertham's *J'accuse* and on censorship of the comic book industry in the United States in the 1960s, see James B. Gilbert, "Crusade against Mass Culture," in *A Cycle of Outrage: America's Reaction to the Juvenile Delinquency* (New York: Oxford University Press, 1986). It is remarkable also that prominent superhero figures invented or relaunched in the 1960s by mainstream comic books publishers such as Marvel Comics could be read as examples of "freaks," insofar as their superpowers are enabled by body modifications and anomalies, sometimes linked to some dramatic accidents in the superhero's biography or intrinsic to his body. Among them, we can list Spider-Man (having the superpower of body modifications due to an accident in a scientific laboratory), the Fantastic Four, and the Hulk. I am thankful to Federico Pagello for having drawn my attention to the polemics around Wertham's book, and for having discussed with me the recurrence of the figure of the "freak" in the 1960s comic book production of both E.C. Comics and Marvel Comics.

38. See, for instance, the comic books of Robert Crumb, as well as the number of independent publications that were organized later in the Underground Press Syndacate.

39. Rachel Adams, *Sideshow U.S.A.: Freaks and the American Cultural Imagination* (Chicago: University of Chicago Press, 2001), 9.

40. Ibid., 138.

41. Ibid., 41.

42. It is significant that Adams's discussion of the term freak's transformation in the 1960s starts with the reference to a dialogue between an "earnest hippie and a couple of tourists, which takes place in Micheal Wadleigh's film *Woodstock* (1970)" (*Sideshow U.S.A.*, 138), which documented the legendary 1969 music festival that took place outside of the town of Woodstock, New York.

43. Andy Warhol and Pat Hackett, *Popism: The Warhol '60s* (Chicago: Harcourt Brace Jovanovich, 1980).

44. Fiedler, *Freaks*, 315. The texts Fiedler mentions and refers to in this respect are Charles A. Reich, *The Greening of America* (New York: Bantam, 1971);

Philip. E. Slater, *The Pursuit of Loneliness: American Culture at the Breaking Point* (Boston: Beacon Books, 1970); Robert Hunter, *The Storming of the Mind* (New York: Garden City, 1971); and Theodore Roszak, *The Making of a Counterculture: Reflections on the Technocratic Society and Its Youthful Opposition* (New York: Anchor Books, 1968).

45. Adams, *Sideshow U.S.A.*, 139.

46. J. Hoberman and Jonathan Rosenbaum, *Midnight Movies* (New York: Harper and Row, 1983).

47. See also Johnson, *Glorious Catastrophe.*

48. Browning's film itself inhabits a contradiction between the constraints of the movie industry (which censored the queerest parts of the movie) and the desire to display the materiality of these extraordinary bodies and their "authentic life." For a more detailed discussion of the ambiguities of Tod Browning's *Freaks,* see Adams, *Sideshow U.S.A.*; Joan Hawkins, "'One of Us': Tod Browning's Freaks," in Thompson, *Freakery*, 265–76.

49. See Hawkins, "One of Us," 265–75; Adams, *Sideshow U.S.A.*, 72.

50. Adams, *Sideshow U.S.A.*, 3.

51. Ibid., 10.

52. Ibid., 8.

53. Ibid., 10.

54. Ibid., 90.

55. Ibid., 6.

56. Bogdan, *Freak Show,* 3.

57. Adams, *Sideshow U.S.A.*, 6; Judith Butler, "Performance Acts and Gender Constitutions: An Essay in Phenomenology and Feminist Theory," in *Performing Feminism: Feminist Critical Theory and Theatre*, ed. Sue-Ellen Case (Baltimore: John Hopkins University Press, 1990), 270.

58. Bogdan, *Freak Show,* 3.

59. Johnson, *Glorious Catastrophe*, 126.

60. Ibid., 120.

61. Ibid., 128.

62. Namely, Johnson refers to Edward Albee's *Who's Afraid of Virginia Woolf?* and Mart Crowley's *The Boys in the Band* (*Glorious Catastrophe*, 133–37).

63. Johnson, *Glorious Catastrophe*, 127.

64. Ibid., 137.

65. Ibid., 127.

66. Ibid., 135.

67. Ibid., 137.

68. Ibid., 138.

69. I am echoing again Johnson's terminology in Johnson, *Glorious Catastrophe*, 117–41.

70. Vaccaro recalled in our conversation about the filming of *Normal Love* in his apartment: "I accepted to have the rest of the film being shot in my house and I had no idea that these people would continue staying, eating, dancing, and smoking grass in my apartment for weeks. It was great: like living in a fantasy world."

71. Tom Gunning, "The Cinema of Attractions: Early Films, Its Spectator and the Avant-Garde," in *Early Cinema Space, Frame, Narrative*, ed. Thomas Elsaesser (London: British Film Institute Publishing, 1990), 58.

72. Ibid., 66.

73. The character of Heaven Grand is modeled on a distinctive 1940s diva type, and the references in the script also pertain for the most part to golden-era Hollywood.

74. Pierce, "An Interview with John Vaccaro."

75. Sergei Eisenstein, "Montage of Attractions," trans. David Gerould, *The Drama Review* 18, no. 1 (March 1974): 77–84.

76. Banes, *Greenwich Village 1963.*

77. Ibid., 192.

78. It is worth mentioning, as an example, the weekend during which Jack Smith's film *Normal Love* was shot, a weekend of hanging out among friends and "having a ball" performing a movie at Old Lyme, in Connecticut. "Having a ball," Vaccaro insisted on repeating in many of his comments from the 1960s, and in his recent recollections in our conversations, was what the Play-House was all about.

79. Among them, Holly Woodlawn, Ondine, Mary Woronov, and Beverly Grant. Especially after the split of the company during the rehearsals of *The Conquest of the Universe*, and the departure of Charles Ludlam (who took with him many of the actors who would become part of his new Ridiculous Theatrical Company), Vaccaro replaced many of the actors with a number of "Factory regulars" See Brecht, *Queer Theatre*; Bottoms, *Playing Underground.*

80. On the "showtime" at Max's Kansas City, see Yvonne Sewall-Ruskin, ed., *High on Rebellion: Inside the Underground at Max's Kansas City* (New York: Thunder's Mouth, 1998); and Steven Watson, *Factory Made: Warhol and the Sixties* (New York: Pantheon Books, 2003). See also Penny Arcade, *Bad Reputation: Performances, Essays, Interviews* (Los Angeles: Semiotext(e), 2009).

81. Penny Arcade, interview with Dominic Johnson (New York, May 18, 2005), quoted in Johnson, *Glorious Catastrophe*, 131.

82. As I shall discuss more in detail in the next chapter, observing Andy Warhol's *Screen Tests* collection, the creation of the "personality" in this social scene was deeply embedded in the social exposure of a performance conceived as the potentiality of attention-catching.

83. Brecht, *Queer Theatre*, 41.

84. As several scholars have insightfully remarked, most notably Stefan Brecht and Ruggero Bianchi, the actors of the Play-House of the Ridiculous functioned in a sense like a commedia dell'arte troupe, where performers would be playing recurring roles over the years. Bianchi, *Off-Off and away;* Brecht, *Queer Theatre.*

85. In the 1976 production the role of the barker was played by Gordon Bressac, and those featuring in the group of Siamese triplets were Debra Greenfield, Elsene Sorrentino, and Suzanne Smith.

86. Kroll, "Ridiculous! 'Heaven Grand': Super Circus."

87. The texts of the songs from *Heaven Grand in Amber Orbit* do not feature in Jackie Curtis's script but are collected in John Vaccaro's Papers, and they do not have a page number.

88. C.Y. Nakano, "Heaven Grand in Amber Orbit: Punk Hit at La Mama," *Michael's Thing* 6, no. 39 (September 27, 1976): 46.

89. Michael Feingold, "Musicals Are Supposed to Be Silly," *Village Voice*, 1976.

90. Brecht, *Queer Theatre*, 64.

91. Thompson, "Introduction" to Thompson, *Freakery*, 10.
92. Brecht, *Queer Theatre*, 48.
93. Feingold, "Musicals Are Supposed to Be Silly."
94. On the Ridiculous Theatre Company, see David Kaufman, *Ridiculous! The Theatrical Life and Time of Charles Ludlam* (New York: Applause, 2002).
95. Bianchi, *Off-Off and away*, 18.
96. Feingold, "Musicals Are Supposed to Be Silly."
97. Halberstam, *In a Queer Time and Space.*
98. Elizabeth Freeman, *Time Binds: Queer Temporalities, Queer Histories* (Durham, N.C.: Duke University Press, 2010), 3.
99. Freeman, *Time Binds*, 6.
100. Brecht, *Queer Theatre*, 45.
101. A reference to the commedia dell'arte and to the Japanese puppets theater Bunraku, both theater traditions evoked by Vaccaro in his interviews.
102. Pierce, "An Interview with John Vaccaro."
103. John F. Kasson, *Amusing the Million: Coney Island at the Turn of the Century* (New York: Hill and Wang, 1978), 3.
104. Kasson, *Amusing the Million*, 50–53.
105. For the sake of brevity, I am simplifying here the more complex argument regarding the dynamics of work in the sideshow industry. As many scholars have emphasized, the employment in the sideshow was not always a degrading form of exploitation for the performers, and the "agency" of the freak in the freak show production has been a matter of debate in contemporary scholarship, trying to avoid patronizing attitudes in historiographical accounts on the topic. See Garland Thompson, *Freakery*.
106. Kroll, "Ridiculous! 'Heaven Grand': Super Circus."
107. "au-dela de Freud, dans un theatre d'activitées simultanées, de transformation perpétuelles, d'inversion des sexes et des personages dans un climat d'humor et de santé." "L'imagination prende le pouvoir." (No author, no date, journal article collected in John Vaccaro Papers.)
108. David Hevey, *The Creatures That Time Forgot: Photography and Disability Imagery* (New York: Routledge, 1992), 53.
109. Curtis, *Heaven Grand*, 23–24.
110. This particular interpretation was suggested by Vaccaro in a conversation with Leo Skir, as reported in his unpublished review, collected in the Vaccaro Papers.
111. Ricardo Castillo, "Impression on the Play-House of the Ridiculous' production of HEAVEN GRAND IN AMBER ORBIT," brochure (no journal title/no date), John Vaccaro Papers.
112. The documentary *Finishing Heaven* was produced by HBO and presented in 2008 at the Los Angeles Film Festival. From the documentary's presentation on the HBO website: "as a New York City film student in the 1960s, Robert Feinberg showed the potential to become the next big filmmaker. Produced in part by a young Martin Scorsese, and featuring a cast of Warhol and Scorsese players, "Heaven," Feinberg's directorial debut, was to be his ticket to fame": http://www.hbo.com/documentaries/finishing-heaven/synopsis.html.
113. Eric Ferrara, *The Bowery: A History of Grit, Graft and Grandeur* (Charleston, S.C.: History, 2011), 105.

114. This is how Feinberg defines himself in an interview featuring in *Finishing Heaven*.

115. Feinberg today makes a living greeting tourists for day cruises and picking up people at airports, acting like one of the barkers of Coney Island, such as the one who advertised Hanna and Arizona at the end of Tom Eyen's play *Why Hanna's Skirt Won't Stay Down*.

116. Robert Feinberg, from the documentary *Finishing Heaven*.

117. This is the bitter definition used by Robert Koheler in his review of the documentary: Robert Koheler "Review: 'Finishing Heaven,'" *Variety*, July 8, 2008, http://variety.com/2008/film/reviews/finishing-heaven-1200508478.

118. Reyner in the documentary *Finishing Heaven*.

119. Reyner in an interview featuring in the documentary *Finishing Heaven*.

120. For example, Craig Highberger, *Superstar in a Housedress*; Jeremiah Newton, *Beautiful Darling: The Life & Times of Candy Darling, Andy Warhol Superstar*, produced by Jeremiah Newton, Elisabeth Bentley, and Gill Holland, and directed by James Rasin.

121. Interview with Mark Mann, http://www.hbo.com/documentaries/finishing-heaven/interview/mark-mann.html.

122. Brukenfeld, "The Wild Bunch," n.p.

123. On the performative duality monster/beauty, see Joanna Frueh, *Monster/Beauty: Building the Body of Love* (Berkeley: University of California Press, 2001).

124. Conversation between Ruby Lynn Reyner and the author, New York, March 4, 2008.

125. Susan Sontag, "Notes on Camp," in *Against Interpretation and Other Essays* (New York: Farrar, Strauss and Giroux, 1966), 286.

Interlude II

1. *Longing Lasts Longer* was developed throughout 2014–2015 as a work in progress (as it is typical for Arcade's approach) in a series of runs in New York at Joe's Pub, in November 2014 and May 2015, and then toured internationally in 2015.

2. The book by Penny Arcade, *Bad Reputation: Performances, Essays, Interviews* (Los Angeles: Semiotext(e), 2009), constitutes a long overdue documentation and critical account of Arcade's work, which had been previously relegated to the footnotes in overviews of the 1970s New York underground scene and 1980s–1990s performance art, as well as in the main surveys of feminist approaches to art and theater. Published by Arcade herself, the volume includes the texts of three of Arcade's plays—*La Miseria*, *Bitch!Dyke!Faghag!Whore!* (1991), and *Bad Reputation*, along with contributions by a number of other authors such as Ken Bernard, Sarah Schulman, Steve Zehentner, and Stephen Bottoms.

3. Penny Arcade, "The Drag Factor: Penny Arcade and Chris Kraus Live June 28th, 2008," in *Bad Reputation*, 17.

4. Arcade was nominated cotrustee, together with J. Hoberman, of Jack Smith's archive after the artist's death, in 1989. Afterward, Smith's archive became the object of controversies and has recently been purchased by the Gladstone Gallery.

5. From the presentation of the Lower East Side Biography Project on Steve Zehentner's website, at http://www.stevezehentner.com/lower-east-side-biography-project.

6. Penny Arcade in Neil Cooper, "Festival Interview: Penny Arcade—'I Wasted My Youth and I Had a Great Time,'" *The List*, July 1, 2015, https://edinburghfestival.list.co.uk/article/72110-festival-interview-penny-arcade-i-wasted-my-youth-and-i-had-a-great-time/.

7. Currid, *Warhol Economy*.

8. Arcade, "The Drag Factor," 27.

9. Ibid., 21.

10. Ibid., 13.

11. Slugger Ann's nickname was itself a proud memory of these earlier times. As Joe Preston (Jackie Curtis's cousin and executor) recounts in a recent interview contributing to the oral history of the Lower East Side: "The reason she got the moniker 'Slugger' was in the dance hall when men would get fresh with her, she would have to hit them." Joe Preston, "Interviewed in January 2012 at Mr. Preston's Apartment on East Eleventh Street," in *Lower East Side: Oral Histories*, interviews by Nina Howes, edited by Eric Ferrara (Charleston, S.C.: History, 2012).

12. Sabine Haenni, *The Immigrant Scene: Ethnic Amusements in New York 1880–1920* (Minneapolis: University of Minnesota Press, 2008).

13. Arcade, "The Drag Factor," 20–21.

14. Arcade, "The Drag Factor," 30–31.

15. Arcade, *Bad Reputation*, 24.

16. This point is also suggested by Chris Kraus in Arcade, "The Drag Factor," in *Bad Reputation*, 14.

17. See, for instance, the entire cast of the play *La Miseria*, as well as the stripteasers and pool dancers performing with Arcade in her most famous performance, *Bitch! Dyke! Faghag! Whore!*

18. Brecht, *Queer Theatre*, 41.

19. I've heard Arcade pronouncing this line at the end of two of the shows of hers I attended, *Bitch!Dyke!Faghag!Whore!* in 2008 and *Longing Lasts Longer* in 2014, and I believe it is a recurring line she delivers at the end of her performances. The same line, contextualized and explained further, features in the conversation with Chris Kraus included in *Bad Reputation*: Arcade, "The Drag Factor," in *Bad Reputation*, 21–22.

20. Arcade often evokes the notion of "entitlement" when talking about the politics of performing arts, for instance in the following passage: "Entitlement is a very interesting thing. Right now, everybody has entitlement. All through school they've been told 'You're great, everybody gets a gold star, everybody's special, everybody's unique'—it spoils the kids out in a terrible condition . . . I'm 57 years old and I can't find a trace of entitlement in myself anywhere. I don't feel entitled to anything." Arcade, "The Drag Factor," 31.

21. Freeman, *Time Binds*, 95–96.

22. Elizabeth Freeman, "Time Binds, or Erotohistoriography," *Social Text* 84–85.3, nos. 3–4 (Fall-Winter 2005): 59.

23. Ibid., 59.

24. Ibid., 62.

25. Arcade in Cooper, "Festival Interview."

26. Stephen Bottoms, "Critical Exposure: Politics, Erotics and Penny Arcade," in Arcade, *Bad Reputation*, 186.

27. I quote from a sentence Arcade pronounced in a performance of *Longing Lasts Longer* I saw at Joe's Pub in New York on November 2, 2014.

28. Freeman takes this variant from a contemporary version of the Frankestein story: Hillary Brougher's *The Sticky Fingers of Time* (1997; New York: Strand Releasing Home Video DVD, 2001).

29. Freeman, "Time Binds, or Erotohistoriography," 61.

30. Ibid., 64.

31. Penny Arcade, *Bitch!Dyke!Faghag!Whore*, in *Bad Reputation*, 104.

32. Bottoms, "Critical Exposure," 179.

33. Johnson, *Glorious Catastrophe*, 137.

Chapter 3

1. The story is told by Stewart herself in *Ellen Stewart, "Ellen Stewart and La Mama," The Drama Review, 24, no. 2 (1980): 11–22.* It also appears, for instance in Crespy, *Off-Off-Broadway Explosion*; Bottoms, *Playing Underground*; Rosenthal, "Ellen Stewart La Mama of Us All."

2. Here I am referring to the famous terminology introduced by Vladimir Propp for identifying the figures and functions of characters in the fairy tale structure. Vladimir Propp, *Morphology of the Folktale* (Austin: University of Texas Press, 1968).

3. *The Song of Songs: A New Translation*, ed. Ariel Bloch and Chana Bloch (Berkeley: University of California Press, 1995), 77.

4. Ibid., 81.

5. Ibid., 87.

6. The picture is in the Jackie Curtis Estate, held by Joe Preston, who is Jackie Curtis's cousin and the legal executor of his archive.

7. See, for instance, Laurence Senelick, *The Changing Room: Sex, Drag and Theatre* (London: Routledge, 2000). Senelick's book also features a picture of Curtis miscaptioned as "Candy Darling."

8. In Marranca's and Dasgupta's introduction to their collection of plays entitled *Theatre of the Ridiculous* (including works by Jack Smith, Ronald Tavel, Charles Ludlam, and Kenneth Bernard), Curtis's name only appears in an (arguable, in fact) list of artists to which the editors ascribe the label "ridiculous." See Bonnie Marranca and Gautam Dasgupta, *Theatre of the Ridiculous*.

9. In my fieldwork, I had the chance to discuss Jackie's work and influence, for instance, with John Vaccaro, Ruby Lynn Reyner, Ellen Stewart, and Ozzie Rodriguez.

10. Craig Highberger's (Jackie's long-term friend and associate) documentary *Superstar in a Housedress: The Life and Legend of Jackie Curtis* (2005) is an important contribution which offers an account of the multifaceted aspects of Curtis's artistic figure, and a remarkable archival gesture. It is a collection of interviews, footage, and materials from Jackie's plays and from the movies he starred in, as well as a large collection of photographs, most of which were taken by Highberger himself through the years he knew Curtis.

11. On the activity of Ellen Stewart as a director and as a theater organizer, see Palladini, "Lo spazio del La Mama," 11–69; Giulia Palladini, "Com-memorare

Ellen Stewart, La Mama: Invenzione e custodia di una parentela," *Culture Teatrali* 21 (2012): 233–53.

12. Paul Foster, quoted in Banes, *Greenwhich Village 1963*, 50.

13. Stewart's affective labor, in the first years of La MaMa, even backed up the low quality of the theater experiments staged in the café. An interesting episode in this respect is reported by the Italian critic Giuseppe Bartolucci in *America hurrah: Per un teatro di metafora* (Genoa: Edizioni del Teatro Stabile di Genova, 1968), one of the first Italian publications on the Off-Off Broadway theater. Bartolucci describes his first visit to Café La MaMa, where he happened to see a very bad show, after which Stewart, almost with an apologizing tone, entertained herself with Bartolucci, explaining to him the significance of leaving the stage open for experiments that turned out to be failures, since these experiments would not have a chance anywhere else, and inviting him to come back to La MaMa to see other productions. We can, at the same time, spot in this episode a distinctive form of affective labor and a cunning producer's strategy, especially since, by the mid-1960s, Stewart had already understood that it was strategic to enhance the international dimension of her theater, and this later became a central aspect of La MaMa's mission.

14. Barrault's definition of Artaud as a "home theater" features in Jean-Luis Barrault, *Reflections on Theatre* (London: Rockliff, 1951).

15. The sentence in Italian, hardly translatable, is "remanifesta in sé stessa il teatro." It is from the transcript of the speech Claudio Meldolesi gave on December 13, 2003, in the ceremony where Ellen Stewart was conferred honorary citizenship in the city of Spoleto (document consulted in the archive of La Mama Umbria International).

16. Elizabeth Freeman, "Queer Belongings: Kinship Theory and Queer Theory," in *A Companion to Lesbian, Gay, Bisexual, and Transgender Studies*, ed. George E. Haggerty and Molly McGarry (Oxford: Blackwell, 2007), 298.

17. Classical references on the subject include Arnold Van Gennep, *Les Rites de passage* (Paris: Gallimard. 1909) and Claude Lèvi-Strauss, *Les Structures élémentaires de la parentèle* (Paris: Presses Universitaires de France, 1949).

18. Pierre Bourdieu, *The Logic of Practice* (Stanford, Calif.: Stanford University Press, 1990).

19. Ibid., 54.

20. "Even the term 'belong' so central to kinship's basic function of determining who is connected to whom suggests such literal proximity between bodies, for it comes from the Old English *gelang*, translated in the *Oxford English Dictionary* as 'alongside,' or 'at hand.'" Freeman, *Queer Belongings*, 298.

21. Freeman, *Queer Belongings*, 308.

22. Brecht, *Queer Theatre*; Banes, *Greenwich Village 1963*.

23. Significantly, Cino and Stewart were defined as the "mom" and "dad" of the scene already in the first critical account of the Off-Off Broadway theater: Albert Poland and Bruce Mailman, eds., *The Off-Off Broadway Book: Plays, People, Theatre* (Indianapolis, Ind.: Bobbs-Merrill, 1972).

24. See Richard Schechner, *Performative Circumstances from the Avant-Garde to Ramilla* (Calcutta: Seagull Books, 1983).

25. Brecht, *Queer Theatre*, 34.

26. Banes, *Greenwhich Village 1963*, 34. Among the plays mentioned by Banes are Rosalyn Drexler's *Home Movies,* David Starkweather's *You May Go Home Again*, and Lanford Wilson's *Home Free!*

27. Banes, *Greenwhich Village 1963*, 47.

28. Ibid., 48.

29. In the standard Disney story, Scrooge McDuck is Donald Duck's uncle, but it is by no means clear how they are actually related, nor where Donald Duck's parents are supposed to be. Likewise, Donald Duck is Huey Duck's, Dewey Duck's, and Louie Duck's uncle, but the three little ducks' parents are not specified. Everyone in the Duck world is the niece or nephew of Elvira "Grandma" Coot, but she's not Scrooge McDuck's wife. There are also a number of cousins, most famously Gladstone Gander, Fethry Duck, and Gus Goose, who are Donald Duck's cousins. None of these kinship relations imply genealogy. In 1993 the Disney cartoonist Don Rosa attempted a "Duck Family Tree": the structure created by Rosa is an attempt at normalizing the eccentric system of kinship in the Duck world, but nevertheless further demonstrates the difficulty in reconstructing the kinship structure of that world. In any case, direct genealogical kinship relationships never emerge from the stories.

30. The publication of Frederic Wertham's *The Seduction of the Innocents* and the uproar it caused, reaching the Congress's Subcommittee for Juvenile Delinquency, testifies as to how seriously the content of cartoons was taken. The Comic Code issued in the 1950s expresses the establishment of this control by the U.S. government, which had, however, already been effective through the practice of preventive censorship by publishing houses.

31. My reference to Walt Disney's world is not totally accidental, especially given the wide circulation of comic books in the New York underground community. Many references to classic comic book characters feature, for instance, in the work of Jack Smith, Andy Warhol, in the plays of the Play-House of the Ridiculous, as well in several other movies and performances of the time. Finally, at the Caffe Cino, from December 1966 (shortly before Joe Cino's death) it became an established habit to stage semi-improvisational comic book adaptations involving, among others, artists like Robert Patrick, H. M. Koutoukas, Magie Dominic, and Charles Stanley. The show *Chas. Dickens Christmas Carol* was presented at the Caffe, written by Soren Angenoux and directed by Michael Smith, starring Donald Brooks, Jacque-Lynn Colton, Arnold Horton, Robert Patrick, Charles Stanley, and the famous superstar Ondine in the role of Scrooge. Beyond Dickens's novel, the show refers more explicitly to Carl Barks's 1947 comic book adaptation of it (*Donald Duck's Christmas Carol*), where Scrooge McDuck (Barks's brainchild) "plays" the character of the old skinflint Ebenezer Scrooge. Andy Warhol shot a one-reel film of *Chas. Dickens Christmas Carol*, which was later included in his 25-hour movie **** (*Four Stars*), screened in December 1967. On the comic books show at the Caffe Cino, see Bottoms, *Playing Underground*, 283–90.

32. Italo Calvino, *Six Memos for the Next Millennium* (New York: Vintage, 1988), 91.

33. On the international dimension of La MaMa E.T.C. and the activities of La MaMa Umbria International, see Palladini, *Lo spazio del La Mama.*

34. Gertrude Stein, "Portraits and Repetitions," in *Lectures in America* (Boston: Beacon, 1957).
35. Ibid., 169.
36. Ibid., 175.
37. The dates are reported, respectively, in Susoyev and Birmisa, *Return to the Caffe Cino* (293) and in the play list on the website of the La MaMa Archive: http://www.lamama.org/archives/year_lists/1963page.htm.
38. Bottoms, *Playing Underground*, 101.
39. Ibid., 91.
40. In the Cafe La MaMa the stage was approximately 12' × 12' and was not raised. Overall the space was 20' × 30' deep and 10' high, and featured a small hall (where tables were located) and a large fireplace on the right wall. In the second location, the space measured 20' × 50' and the stage was 20' × 8'.
41. Freeman, *Queer Belongings*, 307.
42. I employ the expression "affective archive" with reference to the line of thought I have proposed in my work since 2010. See Giulia Palladini et al., *Affective Archive: A Catalogue* (Vercelli: Edizioni Mercurio, 2013); Giulia Palladini and Marco Pustianaz ed., *Lexicon for an Affective Archive* (Bristol: Intellect, 2017).
43. Most of the information on *Hurrah for the Bridge* comes from my archival researches at the La MaMa Archive and at the Billy Rose Theatre Collection at Lincoln Center in New York.
44. Such a conception, appearing in many of Calvino's texts, is exposed with particular clarity in "Exactitude," in *Six Memos for the Next Millennium*, 70–71.
45. Italo Calvino, "Exactitude," in *Six Memos for the Next Millennium*, 71.
46. Jackie Curtis, *Glamour, Glory and Gold: The Life and Legend of Nola Noonan, Goddess and Star*, original script, the Jackie Curtis Estate, 12.
47. Ibid., 11.
48. Ibid., 26
49. Ibid., 31.
50. The Warsaw Concerto is an explicit reference to the movie *Dangerous Moonlight* (Brian Desmond Hurt, 1941).
51. Jackie Curtis, Glamour, *Glory and Gold*, 58.
52. See Kenneth Anger, *Hollywood Babylon* (Pheonix, Ariz.: Associated Professional Service, 1965).
53. See Samantha Barbas, *Movie Crazy: Fans, Stars and the Cult of Celebrity* (New York: Palgrave, 2001).
54. First introduced in Edgar Morin, *The Stars* (New York: Grove, 1960), 20–32.
55. Jack Smith, "The Perfect Appositeness of Maria Montez," 28–36.
56. Candy Darling—born under the name of James Lawrence Slattery—was one of the most famous drag queens in the 1960s underground scene, and an outstanding Warhol superstar. She was one of Jackie's best friends and performed in three of his plays: *Glamour, Glory and Gold* (1967), *Heaven Grand in Amber Orbit* (1969), and *Vain Victory: The Vicissitudes of the Damned* (1971). Tennesee Williams wrote for her and cast her in the role of Violet in the play *Small Craft Warnings*, which premiered in April 1972 at the Truck and Warehouse Theatre in New York. Candy was portrayed by several famous photographers, such as Francesco Scavullo, Robert Mapplethorpe, Richard Avedon, and Peter Hujar. She

died in 1974 of leukemia (believed to be induced by illegal hormones she had taken for years). Recently the director James Rasin made a documentary film on Candy Darling, which premiered at the 61st Berlin International Film Festival: *Beautiful Darling: The Life and Times of Candy Darling, Andy Warhol Superstar* (2010). See also *My Face for the World to See: The Diaries, Letters and Drawings of Candy Darling*, ed. Jeremiah Newton et al. (San Francisco: Hardy Marks Publications, 1977).

57. Judith Butler, *Gender Trouble: Feminism and Subversion of Identity* (New York: Routledge, 1990), 137.

58. Several recollections by Jackie's friends and associates address Jackie's imprecise and idiosyncratic drag style, as well as his periods of poor personal hygiene, for instance in the above-mentioned documentary *Superstar in a Housedress*.

59. See Jill Dolan, "Women's Theatre Program ATA: Creating a Feminist Forum," *Women and Performance* 1, no. 2 (1984): 5–13.

60. Susan Stewart, *On Longing: Narratives of the Miniature, the Gigantic, the Souvenir, the Collection* (Durham, N.C.: Duke University Press, 1993), 117–18.

61. Mikhail Bakhtin, *Rabelais and His World*, trans. Helene Iswolsky (Bloomington: Indiana University Press, 1984)

62. On *charivari* see Natalie Zemon Davis, *Society and Culture in Early Modern France* (Palo Alto, Calif.: Stanford University Press, 1975), 97–123.

63. On the influence of the English mock weddings tradition on American culture, see Senelick, *The Changing Room*, 350–59.

64. See also Craig Thompson Friend, "The Womanless Wedding: Masculinity, Cross Dressing and Gender Inversions in the Modern South," in *Southern Masculinity: Perspectives on Manhood in the South since Reconstruction*, ed. Craig T. Friend (Athens: University of Georgia Press, 2009), 219–45.

65. On festivity and the "state of exception" in carnivalesque culture (on which the womanless wedding is rooted), see Mikhail Bakhtin, *Rabelais and His World*.

66. Stewart, *On Longing*, 119.

67. Sontag, "Notes on Camp," 280.

68. Elizabeth Freeman, "Packing History, Count(er)ing Generations," *New Literary History* 3 (2000), 728.

69. Andy Warhol, *The Philosophy of Andy Warhol (From A to B and Back Again)* (New York: Harvest Book, 1977), 54–55.

70. In the pre-release reports, *Women in Revolt* was referred to under other titles as *Sex* (a possible homage to Mae West), *Andy Warhol's PIGs*, and *Andy Warhol's Women*. Some scholars have detected in the ironic acronym (Political Involved Girls) a reference to the SCUM (Society for Cutting Up Men), the radical feminist organization founded by Valerie Solanas, who had shot Warhol only two years before the movie was released. On *Women in Revolt*, see Maurice Yacowar, *The Films of Paul Morrissey* (Cambridge: Cambridge University Press, 1993), 55–61.

71. Joan Riviere, "Womanliness as Masquerade," *International Journal of Psychoanalysis* 10 (1929): 303–13.

72. Judith Butler, "Melancholy Gender/Refused Identification," in *The Psychic Life of Power: Theories in Subjection* (Stanford, Calif.: Stanford University Press. 1997), 132–66.

73. Such a process seems to bear out Butler's positing of gender formation as always already fundamentally melancholic, as it features a primary renunciation of a desire for a same-sex partner, which later develops as the melancholic assumption of the body one renounces as one's own.

74. Roland Barthes, *The Eiffel Tower, and Other Mythologies* (Berkeley: University of California Press, 1997), 23.

75. Ibid., 25.

76. Richard Dyer, *Stars* (London: British Film Institute, 1979), 62.

77. On Max's Kansas City and the social dynamic of celebrities, see Yvonne Sewall-Ruskin, ed., *High on Rebellion: Inside the Underground at Max's Kansas City* (New York: Thunder's Mouth, 1998).

78. Steven Watson's comment in Highberger, *Superstar in a Housedress*, 39.

79. Dotson Rader, "Twilight of the Tribe: The Wedding That Wasn't," *Village Voice* 42, July 31, 1969.

80. Barthes, *The Eiffel Tower*, 25.

81. Elizabeth Freeman, *The Wedding Complex: Forms of Belonging in Modern American Culture* (Durham, N.C.: Duke University Press, 2002), 4–5.

82. Rader, 'Twilight of the Tribe."

83. See, for instance, Tom E. Brown, "The Love Life of Jackie Curtis," *Interview* 2, July 4, 1971, 26.

84. See Vichi Richman, "An Interview with Jackie Curtis Part I: 'Even Garbo Rearranged Her Jewels!'" *Gay Power*, May 1, 1972, 16; "An Interview with Jackie Curtis Part II: I Started as a Baby!'" *Gay Power*, May 15, 1972, 18.

85. Jonathan Rosenbaum, *WR, Sex and the Art of Radical Juxtaposition*, June 18, 2007, Criterion DVD collection booklet (http://www.criterion.com).

86. I am here referring mainly to oral accounts by those of Jackie Curtis's associates I encountered in New York, such as Ruby Lynn Reyner, Ellen Stewart, and John Vaccaro. Significant is also the following anecdote provided by Leee Black Childers: "Once Jackie was confronted at a party by one of those intense revolutionaries that were so numerous and vociferous in the late sixties. Wild-eyed, frizzy-haired, and with little droplets of California hearty burgundy spraying as she talked, he pulled at her dress, pointed at the glitter on her eyelids, and shouted, 'What do you think you're doing? Do you realize there's a revolution on?' Jackie looked at him and replied, 'I do more revolution just walking down the street every day than you do with all your leaflets and pamphlets and crap.'" Leee Black Childers in Sewall-Ruskin, ed., *High on Rebellion, 145.*

87. In this respect, I share the reading developed in Douglas Crimp's scholarship. See for example, Crimp, "Mario Montez, For Shame," in *Regarding Sedgwick: Essays on Queer Culture and Critical Theory*, ed. Stephen Barber and David L. Clark (New York: Routledge, 2001), 58.

88. My reading of Jackie's wedding performances in relation to the 1960s queer culture finds an interesting point of dialogue with the conceptualization of "camp effects" developed by Dominic Johnson in relationship to Jack Smith's work, where Johnson suggests that his argument "entails reading camp effects as hieroglyphs" in order to show how "camp practices might retain the thought of some other form of meeting, a precarious speaking, tongues glancing across the surfaces of words, and thoughts, and skins." Dominic Johnson, "The Wound Kept Open: Jack Smith, Queer Performance and Cultural Failure,"

Women and Performance: A Journal of Feminist Theory, 17, no. 1 (March 2007): 6.

89. Siegfried Kracauer, "Photography," in *The Mass Ornament: Weimar Essays*, ed. Thomas Y. Levin (Cambridge, Mass.: Harvard University Press, 1995), 50.

90. Ibid., 50.

91. Ibid., 51.

92. Ibid., 48.

93. Roland Barthes, "The Death of the Author," in *Image-Music-Text*, trans. Stephen Heath (New York: Hill and Wang, 1977), 147.

94. Kracauer, "On Photography," 51.

95. The information appeared in a comment by Leee Black Childers in Sewall-Ruskin, *High on Rebellion, 150.*

96. Stein, "Portraits and Repetitions," 169.

Chapter 4

1. P.T., "Thirteen Most Beautiful . . . ," *New York Herald Tribune*, January 10, 1965, sec. 10.3. Quoted in Callie Angell, *Andy Warhol Screen Tests: The Films of Andy Warhol Catalogue Raisonnè*, 1 (New York: Whitney Museum of American Art, 2006), 45.

2. Andrew Ross, "Uses of Camp," in *No Respect: Intellectuals & Popular Culture* (New York: Routledge, 1989), 151.

3. Significantly, the title was initially *The Thirteen Most Wanted*, making the connection between the two projects explicit.

4. Warhol's project was to be harshly criticized by the press for celebrating images of outlaws, and was ultimately removed by the pavilion. For a glimpse into the polemics, see Richard Barr and Cyril Egan Jr., "Mural Is Something Yegg-Stra," *New York Journal*, April 15, 1964; Emily Genauer, "Fair Mural Taken Off, Artist to Do Another," *New York Herald Tribune*, April 17, 1964.

5. Douglas Crimp, "Getting the Warhol We Deserve: Cultural Studies and Queer Culture," *Invisible Culture* 1, 1999, https://www.rochester.edu/in_visible_culture/issue1/crimp/crimp.html.

6. Angell's examinations of the reels proves that in the collection there are 43 screen tests marked as "Thirteen" or "13" "Beautiful Boy(s)," portraying overall 35 male posers; the collection encompasses 47 other screen tests portraying 30 female posers identified as potential items of *The Thirteen Most Beautiful Women* series.

7. Angell, *Andy Warhol Screen Tests.* 13.

8. On *Kiss* and its relation with American film history, see Linda Williams, "Of Kisses and Ellipses: The Long Adolescence of American Movies," *Critical Inquiry* 32, no. 2 (Winter 2006): 288–340.

9. Warhol took part in one of Name's haircutting parties in December 1963. See Warhol and Hackett, *Popism.*

10. Watson, *Factory Made: Warhol and the Sixties*, 136.

11. Angell, *Andy Warhol Screen Tests*, 13.

12. Gerard Malanga, *Screen Test/A Diary* (New York: Kulchr, 1967). The poem is dated August 26, 1966.

13. Fabio Cleto, "Intrigo internazionale: Spie pop e segreti chic degli anni Sessanta," in *Pop/Camp*, ed. Fabio Cleto (Milan: Marcos y Marcos, 2008).

14. Angell, *Andy Warhol Screen Tests*, 13.

15. Bosley Crowther, "The Underground Overflow," *New York Times*, December 11, 1966.

16. Ross, "Uses of Camp," 167.

17. Doyle, "Between Friends."

18. Michel Foucault, "Friendship as a Way of Life," in *Michel Foucault: Ethics, Subjectivity and Truth*, ed. Paul Rabinow (New York: New, 1994).

19. In the essay Doyle discusses especially examples of friendship between gay men and women, portrayed in Warhol's films and embodied in particular in the relation between Warhol and Viva.

20. Doyle, "Between Friends," 332.

21. Ibid.

22. Ibid., 338.

23. Elsewhere, Doyle writes that the effect of boredom, likewise, in Warhol's movie seems to be explicitly calling upon the spectator's attention and affect. Doyle, *Sex Objects*.

24. Siegel, "Doing It for Andy," 13.

25. Sontag, *Notes on Camp*, 286.

26. Matthew Tinkom, *Working like a Homosexual: Camp, Capital, Cinema* (Durham, N.C.: Duke University Press, 2002). Tinkom's study includes chapters on Vincente Minnelli, John Waters, and Kenneth Anger.

27. Tinkom, *Working like a Homosexual,* 2.

28. Ibid., 8.

29. Ibid., 8.

30. Brecht, *Queer Theatre*, 34.

31. Ibid., 29.

32. Maria Ines Aliverti, *Il ritratto d'attore nel Settecento francese e inglese* (Pisa: Edizioni ETS, 1986); Christopher B. Balme, "Interpreting the Pictorial Record: Theatre Iconography and the Referential Dilemma," *Theatre Research International* 20, no. 3 (Fall 1997); Christopher Balme, "Cultural Anthropology and Theatre Historiography: Notes on a Methodological Rapprochement," *Theatre Survey* 25 (May 1994); Cristopher Balme, Cesare Molinari, et. al., eds., *European Theatre Iconography: Proceedings of European Science Foundation Network* (Rome: Bulzoni, 2002).

33. Aliverti, *Il ritratto d'attore*, 27–28. The quote is translated into English by the author.

34. Pierce, "An Interview with John Vaccaro."

35. Aliverti, *Il ritratto d'attore*, 28.

36. Peter Wollen, "Andy Warhol: Renaissance Man," in *Who Is Andy Warhol?* ed. Peter Wollen et al. (Pittsburgh, Pa.: British Film Institute, Andy Warhol Museum, 1997).

37. See Wollen, *Andy Warhol: Renaissance Man*, 13–14.

38. According to Jacob Burkhardt, the "Renaissance man" is characterized by the typically humanist ambition of a general competence, and operates outside of specialism in one field.

39. Warhol's disattachment from a tradition is fascinatingly discussed in Claudia Castellucci, "Gemme senza rami," in *Affective Archive: A Catalogue*, 22–32.

40. The sentence appears in the first interview Warhol gave to the press, edited by Gene Swenson in *ARTnews* 62 (November 1963). However, like many other aphorisms attributed to Warhol, it might not really have been pronounced by the artist, but rather suggested by his interlocutor. See Matt Wrbican, "The True Story of 'My True Story,'" in *Other Voices, Other Rooms: Andy Warhol: A Guide to 706 Items in Two Hours and 56 Minutes*, ed. Eva Meyer-Herman (Rotterdam: NAi, 2009), 56–57.

41. A discussion of this topic goes beyond the scope of these pages. It suffices to mention, however, a few relevant examples, such as Leonardo's study of classical proportions (in ancient drawing, architecture, and music), as well as the adoption of classical canons and models (such as the column, the arch, etc.) in architecture. Furthermore, pivotal texts of classical art, such as Vitruvius's treatise on architecture, became a crucial reference for artists like Alberti, Brunelleschi, and Michelangelo.

42. Gretchen Berg, "Nothing to Loose," *Cahiers du Cinéma in English* 10 (May 1967): 42–58.

43. Ross, "Uses of Camp," 167.

44. Warhol's 1960s film work, including the *Screen Tests*, was not accessible to the public until the 1990s, when the reels were restored, cataloged, and presented to the public in the context of the Andy Warhol Film Project.

45. Homay King, "Girl Interrupted: The Queer Time of Warhol Cinema," *Discourse* 27, no. 1 (Winter 2006): 102.

46. Marx, *Grundrisse*, 19.

47. Ibid., 342.

48. Georges Bataille, "The Notion of Expenditure," in *Visions of Excess: Selected Writings 1927–1939*, trans. Allan Stoekl (Minneapolis: University of Minnesota Press, 1985), 118.

49. Warhol, *The Philosophy of Andy Warhol*, 96.

50. See Palladini, *The Amateur Hour*.

51. Georg Franck, *Őkonomie der Aufmerksamkeit: Ein Entwurf* (Munich: Hansen, 1998).

52. Georg Franck,. "Ökonomie der Aufmerksamkeit," *Merkur* 47, nos. 534/535 (September/October 1993): 748–61; trans. Silvia Plaza as "The Economy of Attention." http://www.heise.de/tp/r4/artikel/5/5567/1.html.

53. On the development of the popular press, see also Christine Stansell, *American Moderns: Bohemian New York and the Creation of a New Century* (New York: Metropolitan Books, 2000), 18–39.

54. P. T. Barnum, *Struggles and Triumphs* (New York: Penguin American Library, 1981).

55. Trav S. D., *No Applause*, 143.

56. Anger, *Hollywood Babylon*.

57. Angell reports many sources referring to Beverly Grant as "the Queen of the Underground": for example, the journal *Film Culture* devoted a cover to Beverly Grant in 1964. The moniker is also used by Ronald Tavel in the introduction and in a caption of the script of the play *Shower*; see www.ronaldtavel.com. See also Angell, *Andy Warhol Screen Tests*, 85.

58. Referring to Angell's catalog, Beverly Grant's *Screen Tests* are: ST120, n.d.; ST121, Reel 27, n.5, ST122, Reel 3, n.2, ST123 Reel 25, n.1.

59. Jack Smith, *The Beautiful Book* (New York: Dead, 1962). The poster of *Shower* is reproduced on Ronald Tavel's website (www.ronaldtavel.com) and the image appeared also in the *Village Voice* in the advertisement for the show.

60. On the coming into use of the word "camp" in mid-1960s New York, see Cleto, "Intrigo internazionale: Spie pop e segreti chic degli anni Sessanta," 495–538.

61. Angell, *Andy Warhol Screen Tests*, 190.

62. On *Screen Test* and Mario Montez, see Douglas Crimp, "Mario Montez, For Shame." 57–70; Giulia Palladini, "Mario Montez: An Archive of Femininity for the Past, and the Future," *Comunicazioni Sociali* 1 (2012): 136–51.

63. Ross, "Uses of Camp," 151.

64. Sontag, *Notes on Camp*, 283.

65. Angell, *Andy Warhol Screen Tests*, 45.

66. For instance, Buchannan appears in one of Allen Ginsberg's 1960s poems; she is mentioned also in Charles Plymell's memoirs.

67. Philip Core, "Introduction" to *Camp: The Lie that Tells the Truth* (New York: Delilah, 1984).

68. For instance, Lucinda Childs or Marian Zazeela.

69. Franck, "Ökonomie der Aufmerksamkeit."

WORKS CITED

Adams, Rachel. *Sideshow U.S.A.: Freaks and the American Cultural Imagination.* Chicago: University of Chicago Press, 2001.

A.F. "Le 'Ridicule' de New York." *Le Dernier Heure*, April 26, 1971.

Aliverti, Maria Ines. *Il ritratto d'attore nel Settecento francese e inglese.* Pisa, Italy: Edizioni ETS, 1986.

Allard, Laurence. "L'Amateur: Une figure de la modernité esthétique." *Communications* 68 (1999): 9–31.

Anderson, Melissa. "The Return of Mario Montez." *Village Voice*, November 9, 2011.

Angell, Callie. *Andy Warhol Screen Tests: The Films of Andy Warhol Catalogue Raisonné.* New York: Whitney Museum of American Art, 2006.

Anger, Kenneth. *Hollywood Babylon.* Paris: J.J. Pauvert, 1959; Phoenix, Ariz.: Associated Professional Service, 1965; San Francisco: Straight Arrows; New York: Simon and Schuster, 1975.

Anonymous. "City to Hear Pro & Cons of NYU Library." *Village Voice*, June 9, 1966.

Arcade, Penny. *Bad Reputation: Performances, Essays, Interviews.* Los Angeles: Semiotext(e), 2009.

Arthur, Paul. "Routines of Emancipations: Alternative Cinema in the Ideology and Politics of the Sixties." In *To Free Cinema: Jonas Mekas and the New York Underground*, edited by David E. James, 17–48. Princeton, N.J.: Princeton University Press, 1992.

Austin, J. L. *How to Do Things with Words.* Cambridge, Mass.: Harvard University Press, 1962.

Bakhtin, Mikhail. *Rabelais and His World.* Translated by Helene Iswolsky. Cambridge, Mass.: MIT Press, 1968.

Balme, Christopher B. "Cultural Anthropology and Theatre Historiography: Notes on a Methodological Rapprochement." *Theatre Survey* 25, no. 1 (May 1994): 33–53

———. "Interpreting the Pictorial Record: Theatre Iconography and the Referential Dilemma." *Theatre Research International* 20, no. 3 (Fall 1997): 190–201.

Balme, Christopher, Cesare Molinari, et al., eds. *European Theatre Iconography: Proceedings of European Science Foundation Network.* Rome: Bulzoni, 2002.

Banes, Sally. *Greenwich Village 1963: Avant-Garde Performance and the Effervescent Body.* Durham, N.C.: Duke University Press, 1993.

Barba, Eugenio, and Nicola Savarese, eds. *A Dictionary of Theatre Anthropology: The Secret Art of the Performer.* New York: Routledge, 2006.

Barbas, Samantha. *Movie Crazy: Fans, Stars and the Cult of Celebrity.* New York: Palgrave, 2001.

Barnes, Djuna. *New York (1913–1919)*. Los Angeles: Sun and Moon, 1989.
Barnum, Phineas T. *Struggles and Triumphs*. New York: Penguin American Library, 1981.
Barr, Richard, and Cyril Egan, Jr. "Mural Is Something Yegg-Stra." *New York Journal*, April 15, 1964.
Barrault, Jean-Louis. *Reflections on Theatre*. London: Rockliff, 1951.
Barthes, Roland. *Camera Lucida: Reflections on Photography*. New York: Hill and Wang, 1981.
———. "The Death of the Author." In *Image-Music-Text*, translated by Stephen Heath, 142–48. New York: Hill and Wang, 1977.
———. *The Eiffel Tower, and Other Mythologies*. Berkeley: University of California Press, 1997.
Bartolucci, Giuseppe. *America hurrah: Per un teatro di metafora*. Genoa: Edizioni del Teatro Stabile di Genova, 1968.
Bataille, Georges. "The Notion of Expenditure." In *Visions of Excess: Selected Writings, 1927–1939*, translated by Allan Stoekl, 116–29. Minneapolis: University of Minnesota Press, 1985.
Bene, Carmelo. *Opere con l'Autografia di un ritratto*. Milan: Bompiani, 1995.
Benjamin, Walter. *The Arcades Project*. Edited by Rolf Tiedemann, translated by Howard Eiland and Kevin McLaughlin. Cambridge, Mass.: Harvard University Press, 1999.
———. "Aufzeichungen zum Meskalinversuch, May 22, 1934." In *Über Haschisch*, edited by Tillman Rexroth, 133–40. Frankfurt am Main: Suhrkamp Verlag, 1972.
———. *Charles Baudelaire: Un poeta lirico nell'epoca del captalismo avanzato*. Edited by Giorgio Agamben, Barbara Chitussi, and Clements-Carl Härle. Vicenza, Italy: Neri Pozza, 2012.
———. *On Hashish*. Edited and translated by Howard Eiland. Cambridge, Mass.: Harvard University Press, 2006.
———. "Surrealism." In *Selected Writings 1927–1930*, 207–21. Cambridge, Mass.: Harvard University Press, 1999.
———. "The Work of Art in the Age of Mechanical Reproduction." In *Illuminations*, translated by Harry Zohn. New York: Schocken, 1968.
Berg, Gretchen. "Nothing to Loose." *Cahiers du Cinéma in English* 10 (May 1967): 42–58.
Bersani, Leo. "Sexuality and Aesthetics." *October* 28 (Spring 1984): 27–42.
Bianchi, Ruggero. *Off Off and away: Percorsi, processi, spazi del nuovo teatro americano*. Turin: Studioforma, 1981.
Bloch, Ariel, and Chana Bloch, eds. *The Song of Songs: A New Translation*. Berkeley: University of California Press, 1995.
Bogdan, Robert. *Freak Show: Presenting Human Oddities for Amusement and Profit*. Chicago: University of Chicago Press, 1988.
Bottoms, Stephen J. "The Efficacy/Effeminacy Braid: Unpacking the Performance Studies/Theatre Studies Dichotomy." *Theatre Topics* 3, no. 2 (September 2003): 173–87.
———. *Playing Underground: A Critical History of the 1960s Off-Off Broadway Movement*. Ann Arbor: University of Michigan Press, 2004.
Bourdieu, Pierre. *The Logic of Practice*. Stanford, Calif.: Stanford University Press, 1990.

Brakhage, Stan. "In Defense of Amateur." In *Essential Brakhage: Selected Writings on Filmmaking*, 142–50. New York: McPherson, 2011.

Brandstetter, Gabrielle. "The Virtuoso's Stage: A Theatrical Topos." *Theatre Research International* 32, no. 2 (2007): 178–95.

Brecht, Bertolt. *Brecht on Theatre: The Development of an Aesthetic*. Edited by John Willett. New York: Hill and Wang; London: Methuen, 1964.

Brecht, Stefan. *The Original Theatre of the City of New York from Mid-1960s–1970s: Queer Theatre*. Frankfurt am Main: Suhrkamp, 1978.

Bronski, Michael. *Culture Clash: The Making of Gay Sensibility*. Boston: South End, 1984.

Brown, Tom E. "The Love Life of Jackie Curtis." *Interview* 2, July 4, 1971.

Brukenfeld, Dick. "The Wild Bunch." *Village Voice*, March 12, 1970.

Buck-Morss, Susan. *The Dialectics of Seeing: Walter Benjamin and the Arcade Project*. Cambridge, Mass.: MIT Press, 1989.

———. "The Flaneur, The Sandwichman and the Whore: The Politics of Loitering." *New German Critique* 39 (Autumn 1986): 99–140.

Burrows, Edwin G., and Mike Wallace. *Gotham: A History of New York City to 1898*. New York: Oxford University Press, 1999.

Butler, Judith. *Gender Trouble: Feminism and Subversion of Identity.* New York: Routledge, 1990.

———. "Performance Acts and Gender Constitutions: An Essay in Phenomenology and Feminist Theory." In *Performing Feminism: Feminist Critical Theory and Theatre*, edited by Sue-Ellen Case, 270–82. Baltimore: Johns Hopkins University Press, 1990.

———. *The Psychic Life of Power: Theories in Subjection*. Stanford, Calif.: Stanford University Press, 1997.

Butt, Gavin. *Between You and Me: Queer Disclosures in the New York Art World 1948–1963*. Durham, N.C.: Duke University Press, 2005.

Calvino, Italo. *Six Memos for the Next Millennium*. New York: Vintage, 1988.

Carlson, Marvin. *The Haunted Stage: The Theatre as Memory Machine*. Ann Arbor: University of Michigan Press, 2003.

Carsten, Janet. "Substantivism, Antisubstantivism, and Anti-Antisubstantivism." In *Relative Values: Reconfiguring Kinship Studies*, edited by Sarah Franklin and Susan McKinnon, 29–53. Durham, N.C.: Duke University Press, 2001.

Carter, David. *Stonewall: The Riots That Sparked the Gay Revolution*. New York: St. Martin's Griffin, 2004.

Chansky, Dorothy. *Composing Ourselves: The Little Theatre Movement and the American Audience*. Carbondale: Southern Illinois University Press, 2005.

Cleto, Fabio. "Intrigo Interazionale: Spie pop e segreti chic degli anni Sessanta." In *Pop/Camp*, edited by Fabio Cleto, 495–538. Milan: Marcos y Marcos. 2008.

Cooper, Neil. "Festival Interview: Penny Arcade—'I Wasted My Youth and I Had a Great Time.'" *The List*, July 1, 2015, https://edinburghfestival.list.co.uk/article/72110-festival-interview-penny-arcade-i-wasted-my-youth-and-i-had-a-great-time/.

Core, Philip, ed. *Camp: The Lie That Tells the Truth*. New York: Delilah, 1984.

Crespy, David A. *Off-Off-Broadway Explosion: How Provocative Playwrights of the 1960s Ignited a New American Theater*. New York: Backstage Books, 2003.

Crimp, Douglas. "Face Value." In *About Face: Andy Warhol Portraits*, edited by Nicholas Baume. Hartford, Conn.: Wadsworth Atheneum, 1999.

———. "Getting the Warhol We Deserve: Cultural Studies and Queer Culture." *Invisible Culture* 1 (1999), https://www.rochester.edu/in_visible_culture/issue1/crimp/crimp.html.

———. "Mario Montez, For Shame." In *Regarding Sedgwick: Essays on Queer Culture and Critical Theory*, edited by Stephem Barber and David L. Clark, 57–70. New York: Routledge, 2001.

———. *"Our Kind of Movie": The Films of Andy Warhol*. Cambridge, Mass.: MIT Press, 2012.

Crowther, Bosley. "The Underground Overflow." *New York Times*, December 11, 1966.

Cruciani, Fabrizio. *Lo spazio del teatro*. Bari, Italy: Laterza, 1992.

———. *Teatro nel Novecento: Registi pedagoghi e comunità teatrali nel XX secolo*. Florence: Sansoni, 1985.

Cullen, Frank. *Vaudeville Old & New: An Encyclopedia of Variety Performers in America*. New York: Routledge, 2004.

Currid, Elizabeth. *The Warhol Economy: How Fashion, Art & Music Drive New York City*. Princeton, N.J.: Princeton University Press, 2007.

Curtis, Jackie. *Husband Number Six: Peter Groby*. In *Wild Orchids*, by Jackie Curtis. Corte Madera, Calif.: Accent Editions, 1983.

Dalla Costa, Mariarosa, and Giovanni Dalla Costa, eds. *Women, Development, and Labor of Reproduction*. Trenton, N.J.: Africa World, 1999.

de Duve, Thierry. "Andy Warhol; or, the Machine Perfected." *October* 48 (Spring 1989): 3–14.

Deleuze, Gilles, and Felix Guattari. *A Thousand Plateaus: Capitalism and Schizophrenia*. Translated by Brian Massumi. Minneapolis: University of Minnesota Press, 1987.

Dennett, Andrea Stulman. *Weird and Wonderful: The Dime Museum in America*. New York: New York University Press, 1997.

Deren, Maya. "Amateurs Versus Professionals." *Film Culture* 39 (Winter 1959): 45–46.

di Prima, Diane. *Recollection of My Life as a Woman: The New York Years: A Memoir*. New York: Viking Books, 2001.

Dolan, Jill. "Between Friends." In *A Companion to Lesbian, Gay, Bisexual, Transgender, and Queer Studies*, edited by George E. Haggerty and Molly McGarry, 325–40. Malden, Mass.: Blackwell, 2007.

———. "Building a Theatrical Vernacular: Responsibility, Community, Ambivalence, and Queer Theater." Introduction to *The Queerest Art: Essays on Lesbian and Gay Theatre*, edited by Alisa Solomon and Framji Minwalla, 1–8. New York: New York University Press, 2002.

———. *Sex Objects: Art and the Dialectic of Desire*. Minneapolis: University of Minnesota Press, 2006.

———. "Women's Theatre Program ATA: Creating a Feminist Forum." *Women and Performance* 1, no. 2 (1984): 5–13.

Dunkelberg, Kermit. "Grotowski and the North-American Theatre: Translation, Transmission, Dissemination". Ph.D. diss., Department of Performance Studies, New York University, 2008.

Dyer, Richard. *Heavenly Bodies: Film Stars and Society*. New York: St. Martin's, 1986.
———. *Stars*. London: British Film Istitute, 1979.
Eisenstein, Sergei. "Montage of Attractions." Translated by David Gerould. *The Drama Review* 18, no. 1 (March 1974):77–84.
Eliade, Mircea. *Rites and Symbols of Initiation*. New York: Harper and Row, 1965.
Elson, Diane, ed. *Value: The Representation of Labour in Capitalism*. London: CSE Books, 1979.
Erdman, Andrew L. *Blue Vaudeville: Sex, Moral and the Mass Marketing of Amusement 1895–1915*. Jefferson, N.C.: McFarland, 2003.
Eyen, Tom. *My Next Husband Will Be a Beauty*. New York: Samuel French, 2000.
———. *Ten Plays*. New York: Samuel French, 1977.
Farber, Manny. "Underground Films" (1957). In *Negative Space*. New York: Praeger, 1971.
Federici, Silvia. *Wages against Housework*. London: Power of Women Collective, 1975.
Ferlinghetti, Lawrence. *A Coney Island of the Mind: Poems*. New York: New Directions, 1958.
Ferrara, Eric. *The Bowery: A History of Grit, Graft and Grandeur*. Charleston, S.C.: History, 2011.
———. ed. *Lower East Side: Oral Histories*. Interviews by Nina Howes. Charleston, S.C.: History, 2012.
Fiedler, Leslie. *Freaks: Myths and Images of the Secret Self*. New York: Simon and Schuster, 1978.
Florida, Richard. *The Rise of the Creative Class: And How It's Transforming Work, Leisure, Community and Everyday Life*. New York: Basic Books, 2002.
Frei, George, and Neil Printz, eds. *The Andy Warhol Catalogue Raisonné: Paintings and Sculptures 1961–1963*, vol. I. New York: Phaidon, 2002.
Foucault, Michel. "Friendship as a Way of Life." In *Michel Foucault: Ethics, Subjectivity and Truth*, edited by Paul Rabinow, 135–40. New York: New, 1994.
———. *The History of Sexuality*, vol. 1, *An Introduction (La Volonté de savoir)*. New York: Random House, 1978.
———. *The History of Sexuality*, vol. 2: *The Uses of Pleasure*. London: Penguin, 1992.
Franck, Georg. *Őkonomie der Aufmerksamkeit: Ein Entwurf*. Munich: Hansen, 1998.
———. "Ökonomie der Aufmerksamkeit." *Merkur* 47, nos. 534/535 (September/October 1993): 748–61. Translated by Silvia Plaza as "The Economy of Attention." http://www.heise.de/tp/r4/artikel/5/5567/1.html.
Freeman, Elizabeth. "Packing History, Count(er)ing Generations." *New Literary History* 3 (2000): 724–44.
———. "Queer Belongings: Kinship Theory and Queer Theory." In *A Companion to Lesbian, Gay, Bisexual, and Transgender Studies*, edited by George E. Haggerty and Molly McGarry, 295–314. Oxford: Blackwell, 2007.
———. ed. *Queer Temporalities*, special double issue of *GLQ: A Journal of Lesbian Gay Studies* 13, no. 2/3 (Winter/Spring 2007).

———. "Time Binds, or Erotohistoriography." *Social Text* 84–85.3, nos. 3–4 (Fall-Winter 2005): 57–68.

———. *Time Binds: Queer Temporalities, Queer Histories*. Durham, N.C.: Duke University Press, 2010.

———. *The Wedding Complex: Forms of Belonging in Modern American Culture*. Durham, N.C.: Duke University Press. 2002.

Freud, Sigmund. "Three Essays on the Theory of Sexuality." In *The Standard Edition of the Complete Psychological Works*, edited by James Strachey. Vol. 7. London: Hogarth Press and the Institute for Psycho-Analysis, 1955.

Friend, Craig Thompson. "The Womanless Wedding: Masculinity, Cross Dressing and Gender Inversions in the Modern South." In *Southern Masculinity: Perspectives on Manhood in the South since Reconstruction*, edited by Craig T. Friend, 219–45. Athens: University of Georgia Press, 2009.

Frueh, Joanna. *Monster/Beauty: Building the Body of Love*. Berkeley: University of California Press, 2001.

Garland Thompson, Rosemary, ed. *Freakery: Cultural Spectacle of the Extraordinary Body*. New York: New York University Press, 1996.

Genauer, Emily. "Fair Mural Taken Off, Artist to Do Another." *New York Herald Tribune*, April 17, 1964.

Gilbert, James B. "Crusade Against Mass Culture." In *Cycle of Outrage: America's Reaction to the Juvenile Delinquency.* New York: Oxford University Press, 1986.

Grotowski, Jerzy. *Toward a Poor Theatre*. Translated by T. K. Wiewiorowski. New York: Simon and Schuster, 1968.

Grotowski, Jerzy, and Richard Schechner. "'Doctor Faustus' in Poland." *Tulane Drama Review* 8, no. 4 (Summer 1964): 120–33.

Groys, Boris. "The Loneliness of the Project." In *Going Public*, by Boris Groys. Berlin: Sternberg, 2010.

Gunning, Tom. "The Cinema of Attractions: Early Films, Its Spectator and the Avant-Garde." In *Early Cinema Space, Frame, Narrative*, edited by Thomas Elsaesser, 56–62. London: British Film Institute, 1990.

Gussow, Mel. "'Heaven Grand,' a Musical, Now Camping at La Mama." *Village Voice*, 1976.

Haenni, Sabine. *The Immigrant Scene: Ethnic Amusements in New York 1880–1920*. Minneapolis: University of Minnesota Press, 2008.

Halberstam, Judith. *In a Queer Time and Space: Transgender Bodies, Subcultural Lives*. New York: New York University Press, 2005.

Harding, James, and Cindy Rosenthal, eds. *Restaging the Sixties: Radical Theaters and Their Legacies*. Ann Arbor: University of Michigan Press, 2006.

Henderson, Mary C. *Theater in America: 200 Years of Plays, Players and Productions*. New York: Harry Abrams, 1986.

Hevey, David. *The Creatures That Time Forgot: Photography and Disability Imagery*. New York: Routledge, 1992.

Highberger, Craig. *Superstar in a Housedress: The Life and Legend of Jackie Curtis*. New York: Chamberlain, 2005.

Hoberman, J., ed. *Jack Smith and His Secret Flix*. New York: Museum of the Moving Image, 1997.

Hoberman, J., and Jonathan Rosenbaum. *Midnight Movies*. New York: Harper and Row, 1983.

Hodge, Alison, ed. *Twentieth-Century Actor Training*. London: Routledge, 2000.
James, David E. ed, *To Free the Cinema: Jonas Mekas and the New York Underground*. Princeton, N.J.: Princeton University Press, 1992.
Johnson, Dominic. *Glorious Catastrophe: Jack Smith, Performance and Visual Culture*. Manchester: *Manchester University Press, 2012.*
———. "The Wound Kept Open: Jack Smith, Queer Performance and Cultural Failure." *Women and Performance: A Journal of Feminist Theory* 17, no. 1 (March 2007): 3–18.
Joseph, Miranda. *Against the Romance of Community*. Minneapolis: University of Minnesota Press, 2002.
Kaplan, Donald. "Homosexuality and American Theatre: A Psychoanalytic Comment." *Tulane Drama Review* 9, no. 3 (1965): 25–55.
Kasson, John F. *Amusing the Million: Coney Island at the Turn of the Century*. New York: Hill and Wang, 1978.
Kaufman, David. *Ridiculous! The Theatrical Life and Time of Charles Ludlam*. New York: Applause, 2002.
Kelleher, Joe. *The Illuminated Theatre: Studies on the Suffering of Images*. London: Routledge, 2015.
———. "On Self-Remembering Theatres." Jonathan Burrows's website. 2008. http://www.jonathanburrows.info/#/text/?id=18&t=content.
King, Homay. "Girl Interrupted: The Queer Time of Warhol's Cinema." *Discourse* 28, no. 1 (2006): 98–120.
Koch, Stephen. *Stargazer: Andy Warhol's World and His Films*. New York: Praeger, 1973.
Koheler, Robert. "Review: 'Finishing Heaven.'" *Variety*, July 8, 2008. http://variety.com/2008/film/reviews/finishing-heaven-1200508478.
Kracauer, Siegfried. "Photography." In *The Mass Ornament: Weimar Essays*, edited by Thomas Y. Levin, 47–64. Cambridge, Mass.: Harvard University Press, 1995.
Kroll, Jack. "Ridiculous! 'Heaven Grand': Super Circus." *Newsweek*, November 3, 1969.
Kunst, Bojana. *Artist at Work: Proximity of Art and Capitalism*. Winchester, Eng., and Washington, U.S.: Zero Books, 2015.
Lazzarato, Maurizio. *Lavoro immateriale: Forme di vita e produzione di soggettività*. Milan: Ombre Corte, 1997.
Lefebvre, Henri. *The Production of Space* (1974). Oxford: Blackwell, 1991.
Leffingwell, Edward, Carole Kismaric, and Martin Heiferman, eds. *Flaming Creature: Jack Smith, His Amazing Life and Times*. New York: Institute for Contemporary Art, P.S 1, Serpent's Tail, 1997.
Lèvi-Strauss, Claude. *Les Structures élémentaires de la parentèle*. Paris: Presses Universitaires de France, 1949.
Little, Stuart B. *Off-Broadway: The Prophetic Theatre: A Documentary History from 1952 to the Present*. New York: Coward, McCann and Geoghian, 1972.
Maines, Rachel P. *The Technology of Orgasm: "Hysteria," the Vibrator and Women's Sexual Satisfaction*. Baltimore: Johns Hopkins University Press, 1999.
Malanga, Gerard. *Screen Test/A Diary*. New York: Kulchur, 1967.
Maringot, J. Gerard. "The Play-House of the Ridiculous." *Le Monde*, June 13, 1971.

Marranca, Bonnie, and Gautam Dasgupta, eds. *Theatre of the Ridiculous* (1979). Baltimore: Johns Hopkins University Press, 1998.

Marx, Karl. *Economic and Philosophical Manuscripts of 1844*. New York: Prometheus Books, 1988.

———. *Grundrisse*. Translated by Martin Nicolaus. New York: Vintage, 1973.

Matzke, Annemarie. *Arbeit am Theater: Eine Diskursgeschichte der Probe*. Bielefeld, Ger.: Transcript Verlag, 2012.

Mazars, Pierre. "Le Ridiculous Theatre." *Le Figaro*, June 15, 1971.

McNeil, Don. "NYU Campus Erupts, But No Berkeley Develops." *Village Voice*, December 15, 1966.

Mekas, Jonas. "*Flaming Creatures* and the Ecstatic Beauty of the New Cinema." *Village Voice*, March 2, 1963, republished in Jonas Mekas, *Movie Journal*. (New York: Collier Books, 1972), 82–83.

———. *Movie Journal: The Rise of the New American Cinema, 1959–1971*. New York: Macmillan, 1972.

Meyer-Herman, Eve, ed. *Andy Warhol: A Guide to 706 Items in 2 Hours and 56 Minutes*. Rotterdam: NAi Publishers, 2009.

Meyerhold, Vsevolod E. *Meyerhold on Theatre*. Translated by Edward Braun. London: Methuen Drama, 1991.

Miller, Henry. *Into the Nightlife*. Berkeley, Calif.: Henry Miller and Bezalel Schatz, 1947.

Morin, Edgar. *The Stars*. New York: Grove, 1960.

Moulier-Boutang, Yann. *Le Capitalism cognitif: La nouvelle grande transformation*. Paris: Editions Amsterdam, 2007.

Muñoz, José E. *Cruising Utopia: the Then and There of Queer Futurity*. New York: New York University Press, 2010.

———. *Disidentifications: Queers of Colour and the Performance of Politics*. Madison: University of Minnesota Press, 1999.

Nadel, Marlene. "NYU Attacked: 'Fraud,' Says Mrs Jacobs, 'Library Is Not a Library.' " *Village Voice*, June 23, 1966.

———. "NYU Shows Plans to Prove Library Is Really a Library." *Village Voice*, June 30, 1966.

Nakano, C. Y. "Heaven Grand in Amber Orbit: Punk Hit at La Mama." *Michael's Thing* 6, no. 39 (September 27, 1976).

Newton, Jeremiah, Francesca Passalacqua, eds. *My Face for the World to See: The Diaries, Letters and Drawings of Candy Darling*. San Francisco: Hardy Marks Publications, 1977.

Noguez, Dominique. *Une reinaissance du cinéma: Le cinéma "underground" américain*. Paris: Klincksieck. 1985.

Novick, Julius. "Theater." In *The Performing Arts and American Society*, edited by William McNeil Lowery, 96–129. Englewood Cliffs, N.J.: Prentice-Hall, 1978.

Palladini, Giulia. "The Amateur Hour: On Value, Personality and the Form of Appearance in the Economy of Attention." *South Atlantic Review* 75, no. 3 (2011): 59–77.

———. "Com-memorare Ellen Stewart, La Mama: Invenzione e custodia di una parentela." *Culture Teatrali* 21 (2012): 233–53.

———. "Ellen Stewart e La Mama: un'idea di teatro". M.A. diss., University of Bologna. 2005.

———. "Lo spazio del La Mama." In *La Mama dell'Avanguardia: Il teatro di Ellen Stewart, i rapporti con l'Italia*, edited by Moreno Cerquetelli, 11–69. Rome: Edizioni Interculturali. 2006.

———. "Mario Montez: An Archive of Femininity for the Past, and the Future," *Comunicazioni Sociali* 3 (2012): 136–51.

Pasolli, Roberto. "Off-Off e i nuovi autori degli anni '60." *Sipario* 33, no. 272 (December 1968): 22–28.

———. *Temple Slave*. New York: Masquerade Books. 1994.

Perebinossoff, Philippe R. "The Theater of Stylized Amateurism." *Journal of American Culture* 1, no. 1 (Spring 1978): 137–44.

Poggi, Jack. *Theatre in America: The Impact of the Economic Forces, 1870–1967*. New York: Cornell University Press, 1968.

Poland, Albert, and Bruce Mailman, eds. *The Off-Off Broadway Book: Plays, People, Theatre*. Indianapolis, Ind.: Bobbs-Merrill, 1972.

Propp, Vladimir. *Morphology of the Folktale*. Austin: University of Texas Press. 1968.

Pustianaz, Marco, Giulia Palladini, and Annalisa Sacchi, eds. *Affective Archive: A Catalogue*. Vercelli, Italy: Edizioni Mercurio, 2013.

Pustianaz, Marco and Palladini, Giulia eds. *Lexicon for an Affective Archive*. Bristol: Intellect, 2017.

Quietstone, Uhshur. "Heaven Grand in Amber Orbit." *Gay Power* 1, no. 4 (1969).

Rader, Dotson. "Twilight of the Tribe: The Wedding That Wasn't." *Village Voice*, July 31, 1969.

Regelson, Rosalyn. "Not a Boy, Not a Girl, Just Me." *New York Times*, November 2, 1969.

Richman, Vichi. "An Interview with Jackie Curtis Part I: 'Even Garbo Rearranged Her Jewels!'" *Gay Power*, May 1, 1972; "An Interview with Jackie Curtis Part II: I Started as a Baby!'" *Gay Power*, May 15, 1972.

Ridout, Nicholas. *Passionate Amateurs: Theatre, Communism and Love*. Ann Arbor: University of Michigan Press, 2013.

———. *Stage Fright, Animals, and Other Theatrical Problems*. Cambridge: Cambridge University Press, 2006.

Riviere, Joan. "Womanliness as Masquerade." *International Journal of Psychoanalysis* 10 (1929): 303–13.

Rolleston, James. "The Truth of Unemployment: Walter Benjamin Reads His Own Times." *South Atlantic Review* 61, no. 2 (Spring 1996): 27–49.

Rolnik, Suely. "The Geopolitics of Pimping," *European Institute for Progressive Cultural Policies (EIPCP)* (October 2006).

Rosenbaum, Jonathan. *WR, Sex and the Art of Radical Juxtaposition*, June 18, 2007. Criterion DVD collection booklet. https://www.criterion.com/.

Rosenthal, Cindy. "Ellen Stewart La Mama of Us All." *The Drama Review* 50, no. 2 (Summer 2006): 12–51.

Ross, Andrew. *No Respect: Intellectuals & Popular Culture*. New York: Routledge, 1989.

Roszak, Theodore. *The Making of a Counterculture: Reflections on the Technocratic Society and Its Youthful Opposition*. New York: Anchor Books, 1968.

Sante, Luc. *Low Life: Lures and Snares of Old New York*. New York: Vintage Books, 1991.

Sarris, Andrew. "The Sub-New York Sensibility." *Cahiers du Cinema* 10 (May 1967): 43–45.

Schäfer, Martin Jörg. *Die Gewalt der Muße: Wechselverhältnisse von Arbeit, Nichtarbeit, Ästhetik*. Berlin: Diaphanes, 2013.

Schechner, Richard. "Actuals" (1970). In *Performance Theory*. New York: Routledge, 1988.

———. *Between Theatre and Anthropology*. Philadelphia: University of Pennsylvania Press, 1985.

———. *Performative Circumstances from the Avant-Garde to Ramilla*. Calcutta: Seagull Books, 1983.

———. *Performance Studies: An Introduction*. New York: Routledge, 2002.

———. "Stanislavski at School." *Tulane Drama Review* 9, no. 2 (Fall–Winter 1964): 198–211.

———. "TDR Comment," *Tulane Drama Review* 7, no. 2 (1962): 8–9.

———. "Theatre Criticism." *Tulane Drama Review* 9, no. 3 (1965):13–24.

———. "Who's Afraid of Edward Albee?" *Tulane Drama Review* 7, no. 3 (1963): 7–10.

Schneider, Rebecca. *Performing Remains: Art and War in Times of Theatrical Reeenactment*. New York: Routledge, 2011.

S.D., Trav. *No Applause—Just Throw Money, or, The Book That Made Vaudeville Famous*. New York: Faber and Faber, 2005.

Seltzer, Marc. "Serial Killers," *differences: A Journal of Feminist Cultural Studies* 5, no. 1 (1993): 92–127.

Senelick, Laurence. *The Changing Room: Sex, Drag and Theatre*. London: Routledge, 2000.

Sewall-Ruskin, Yvonne, ed. *High on Rebellion: Inside the Underground at Max's Kansas City*. New York: Thunder's Mouth, 1998.

Shank, Theodore. *Beyond the Boundaries: American Alternative Theatre*. Ann Arbor: University of Michigan Press, 2002.

Siegel, Marc. "Doing It for Andy." *Art Journal* 62 (Spring 2003): 6–13.

———. "Gossip Ist Fabelhaft / Queere Gegenöffentlichkeiten und 'Fabulation.'" *Texte zur Kunste* 61 (March 2006):68–80.

———. ed. "Jack Smith: Beyond the Rented World," *Criticism: A Quarterly for Literature and the Arts* 56, no. 2 (2014).

———. "On Gossip." In *For More than One Tie*, ed. Tom Engels. http://olga0.oralsite.be/oralsite/pages/Marc_Siegel/.

Smith, Jack. *The Beautiful Book*. New York: Dead, 1962.

———. "The Perfect Appositeness of Maria Montez." *Film Culture* 27 (Winter 1962–63): 28–36.

Smith, Jack, and Sylvère Lotringer. "Uncle Fishook and the Sacred Baby Poo Poo of Art," *Semiotext(e)* 1, no. 2 (1978), reprinted in Smith, Jim, J. Hoberman, and Edward Leffingwell, eds. *Wait for Me at the Bottoms of the Pool: The Writings of Jack Smith*. New York: High Risk Books, 1997: 107–21.

Smith, Jim, J. Hoberman, and Edward Leffingwell, eds. *Wait for Me at the Bottoms of the Pool: The Writings of Jack Smith*. New York: High Risk Books, 1997.

Smith, Michael T. "Caffe Cino." http://michaeltownsendsmith.com/caffe-cino.

Smith, Michael T., and Nick Orzel, eds. *Eight Plays from Off Off-Broadway*. Indianapolis, Ind.: Bobbs-Merrill, 1966.
Snyder, Robert W. *The Voice of the City: Vaudeville and Popular Culture in New York*. New York: Oxford University Press, 1989.
Sontag, Susan. *Against Interpretation and Other Essays*. New York: Farrar, Strauss and Giroux, 1966.
Spivak, Gayatri. "Scattered Speculations on the Question of Value." In *In Other Worlds: Essays in Cultural Politics,* 212–42. New York: Methuen, 1987.
Stansell, Christine. *American Moderns: Bohemian New York and the Creation of a New Century*. New York: Metropolitan Books, 2000.
Stein, Gertrude. "Portraits and Repetition." In *Lectures in America*. Boston: Beacon, 1957.
Stewart, Ellen. "Ellen Stewart and La Mama." *The Drama Review* 24, no. 2 (June 1980): 11–22.
Stewart, Susan. *On Longing: Narratives of the Miniature, the Gigantic, the Souvenir, the Collection*. Durham, N.C.: Duke University Press, 1993.
Stone, Wendell C. *Caffe Cino: The Birthplace of Off-Off Broadway*. Carbondale, Ill.: Southern Illinois University Press, 2005.
Suárez, Juan. *Bike Boys, Drag Queens and Superstars: Avant-Garde, Mass Culture and Gay Identities in the 1960s Underground Cinema*. Bloomington: Indiana University Press, 1996.
Susoyev, Steve, and George Birmisa, eds. *Return to the Caffe Cino*. San Francisco: Moving Finger, 2007.
Tavel, Ronald. "The Life of Juanita Castro." Ronald Tavel's website. http://www.ronaldtavel.com/documents/the_life_of_juanita_castro.pdf.
———. "The Life of Lady Godiva." In *Theatre of the Ridiculous*, edited by Bonnie Marranca and Gautam Dasgupta, 13–50. Baltimore: Johns Hopkins University Press, 1979.
Taylor, Diana. *The Archive and the Repertoire: Performing Cultural Memory in the Americas*. Durham, N.C.: Duke University Press, 2003.
Tinkom, Matthew. *Working like a Homosexual: Camp, Capital, Cinema*. Durham, N.C.: Duke University Press, 2002.
Tish, D. "Wilson's Tale Told." *Other Scenes*, June 4, 1981.
Van Gennep, Arnold. *Les Rites de passage*. Paris: Gallimard, 1909.
Virno, Paolo. *A Grammar of the Multitude: For an Analysis of Contemporary Forms of Life*. New York: Semiotext(e), 2004.
Warhol, Andy. *The Philosophy of Andy Warhol (From A to B and Back Again)*. New York: Harvest Book, 1977.
Warhol, Andy, and Pat Hackett. *Popism: The Warhol '60s*. Chicago: Harcourt Brace Jovanovich, 1980.
Waring, Marylyn. *If Women Counted: A New Feminist Economics*. San Francisco: Harper and Row, 1988.
Watson, Steven. *Factory Made: Warhol and the Sixties*. New York: Pantheon Books, 2003.
Wertham, Frederic. *The Seduction of the Innocents*. New York: Reinhart, 1954.
Williams, Linda. "Of Kisses and Ellipses: The Long Adolescence of American Movies." *Critical Inquiry* 32, no. 2 (Winter 2006): 288–340.

Wolford, Lisa, and Richard Schechner. *The Grotowski Sourcebook*. New York: Routledge, 2001.
Wollen, Peter. "Andy Warhol: Renaissance Man." In *Who Is Andy Warhol?* edited by Peter Wollen and Collin MacCabe et al. Pittsburgh: British Film Institute, Andy Warhol Museum, 1997.
Woodlawn, Holly, and Jeff Copeland. *A Low Life in High Heels*. New York: St. Martins, 1991.
Yacowar, Maurice. *The Films of Paul Morrissey*. Cambridge: Cambridge University Press, 1993.
Zemon Davis, Natalie. *Society and Culture in Early Modern France*. Palo Alto, Calif.: Stanford University Press, 1975.

INDEX